TARRIS MARIE

Empress Creed

MEDIA

WWW.BLACKODYSSEY.NET

Published by
BLACK ODYSSEY MEDIA
www.blackodyssey.net
Email: info@blackodyssey.net

EMPRESS CREED. Copyright © 2025 by Tarris Marie

Library of Congress Control Number: 2024916879

First Trade Paperback Printing: February 2025
ISBN: 978-1-957950-66-2
ISBN: 978-1-957950-67-9 (e-book)

Cover Design by Ashlee Nassar of Designs With Sass

10 9 8 7 6 5 4 3 2 1

Manufactured in the United States of America

Distributed by Kensington Publishing Corp.

Dear Reader,

I want to thank you immensely for supporting Black Odyssey Media and our ongoing efforts to spotlight the diverse narratives of blossoming and seasoned storytellers. With every manuscript we acquire, we believe that it took talent, discipline, and remarkable courage to construct that story, flesh out those characters, and prepare it for the world. Debut or seasoned, our authors are the real heroes and heroines in *OUR* story. For them, we are eternally grateful.

Whether you are new to Tarris Marie or Black Odyssey Media, we hope that you are here to stay. Our goal is to make a lasting impact in the publishing landscape, one step at a time and one book at a time. We also welcome your feedback and kindly ask that you leave a review. For upcoming releases, announcements, submission guidelines, etc., please be sure to visit our website at www.blackodyssey.net or scan the QR code below. And remember, no matter where you are in your journey, the best of both worlds begins now!

Joyfully,

Shawanda Williams

Shawanda "N'Tyse" Williams
Founder & CEO, Black Odyssey Media

FROM THE SOUL OF THE AUTHOR

Before the aspiring Hollywood actress Pearle Monalise Brown became an art thief in the 1990s-based tale *Blaque Pearle*, Dulce Ella Monroe hailed as Empress, an ambitious queen-pin and fashion designer from Chicago's South Side during the Harlem Renaissance. Empress resurrected as a spin-off character from *Melodic Masterpiece*, who took flight in my imagination, and like all my anti-heroine protagonists, she began whispering her crime story in my ear.

I was raised by my grandparents, who'd been born and bred in the Midwest during the 1920s. I grew up listening to their music and watching the films that captivated them during their youth. Ella Fitzgerald, Sarah Vaughn, Louis Armstrong, and The Ink Spots were musical staples in our house and blasted through the speakers of my grandma's record player every day. The films *Stormy Weather*, *Imitation of Life*, and *Cabin in the Sky* were typical VHS "movie night" picks from my granddaddy. I was a nineties girl, rocking finger waves, a Sony Walkman, and Baby Phat, but the art, fashion, and glamour of the Harlem and Chicago Renaissance eras were engrained in my blood.

My granddaddy recognized early that I had been bitten by the artistic bug, and although we couldn't afford the dance classes I had begged him for, he bestowed a gem to me that I didn't recognize as priceless until over thirty years later. He placed in my hands what I consider the Holy Grail for my artistic journey. It was a book called *Brown Sugar*, written by Donald Bogle. *Brown Sugar* was filled with over one hundred photographs of African American women artists from the past and present, detailing over one hundred years of their influence and contributions to the world. Tears are falling as I write this because of what that did to my soul. That day, my granddaddy also shared with me the creed he lived by: *"If there's something you want to be good at in this world, Tarris, watch how the great ones did it before you, listen when someone is trying to teach you something, and read all you can about it."*

While writing *Empress Creed*, I thanked God for *our* stories, told by us and for us, that were preserved through our elders, historians, musicians, and artistic creators. I am grateful to my grandparents, who passed down their experiences to me. I was blessed to have grown up in a home filled with records, books, and films that encompassed the works of independent artists and filmmakers who inspired me. I read memoirs, watched documentaries, and immersed myself in the stories of others—all which I utilized to place my imagination in the 1930s to write this story.

Empress Creed is a women's crime love story set in the urban Midwest during the Great Depression, but the message I want to convey is that you are a royal descendant of God, born free and worthy to reign in this world no matter who you are or where you come from. Never forget it.

PROLOGUE
THIS IS AMERICA.
MY COUNTRY 'TIS OF THEE?

DULCE ELLA MONROE

October 1933 ~ Chicago, Illinois

I stepped out of Southway Hotel, and instantly, my toes went numb. The hostile wind cut through my dress and penetrated deep into my bones. It was Halloween, and Indian Summer had officially ended. While I had been engulfed in the romantic arms of Perry's midnight flames, Mother Nature had freed the hawk to spread its freezing temps around Chicago.

I glanced down at the bag tapping against my leg. Inside were Perry's records, souvenir platters from the best night of my life. The tunes from Duke Ellington and the "La Bohème" baritone suddenly resurrected the feelings I couldn't escape. Perry's tantalizing touch, especially the smooth roughness of his soft, callous hands, was forever imprinted in my mind. We had danced hours before, but the memory was as warm as chocolate chip cookies fresh from the oven. The thought emitted a sudden burst of heat that momentarily thawed my chill. I took a deep breath, still smothered in his fancy Parisian perfume and intoxicated by his love. But I had to snap out of it. Perry Savage was a king, looking to rule the love of a queen, and I was Empress. Unlike the love lesson Meek-Meek had tried to hammer into me, protection from a man was not my goal in life.

How could I relinquish my dream of running an empire before having tasted the throne's power?

The sun anxiously awaited its chance to brighten the deep blue sky, sending only a shred of the dimmest UV rays from below the horizon. Alone on the sidewalk, I only heard the clicking sound of my heels on the pavement. Chicago had never felt like a ghost town, so I sensed hidden preparators in the shadows. I picked up the pace and reached inside my pocketbook, craving a calming puff from my ciggy. Instead, I received the cool comfort of my hammer. I gripped the cold steel and kept moving.

At the corner, there was a boutique that always had dresses on display in the window fancier than the spiffy rags at Marshall Field & Company. I had never shopped at the boutique because the owner was known to dislike Negroes admiring her Parisian-inspired fashions. Besides, I designed everything I wore. Therefore, I would never step a pinky toe inside her shop…but the light bulbs were screaming from her sign hovering over the sidewalk. It was the only other thing that seemed alive on the street. The distance between me and the corner felt too distant, and everything was eerily still, like the Field Museum sculptures.

Where are the dames and gents of this bustling town?

To my left were lonely streetcar tracks, empty car machines, and a buggy with no horse. To my right, a barbershop, candy store, and food market. All were dark inside, with *"CLOSED"* signs and the window blinds shut.

I thought there were more lamp posts on this street.

Steamy haze snaked from the sewers, and I was relieved at the thought that something other than me and glimmers of light exuded energy on the block. Suddenly, a clack echoed behind the click of my heels. I refused to turn around and began to trot into a running walk. A steady rhythm of *clickity-clack, clickity-clack* got louder and faster until the clacking stopped. I kept clicking, though.

Immediately, a gun cocked from behind me, and a deep voice commanded, "Freeze, Empress. You know what this is. Turn around."

I lifted my hands. "What kind of fella pulls a pistol on a lady?"

He snatched my hammer from my hand, and I turned around. *Never trust a goon in an overcoat.* Those words repeated inside my head as I remembered Tommy's warning from the day before about the white man. He had a lifeless face, still as the movement on the street. His gold and pearl revolver was aimed directly at me.

"Funny how broads want to be ladies, but they act like goons," he said. "Like I had told you and your mob yesterday, man or woman, white or colored—they are all the same to me. A mark is a mark, you see."

"I see, but had you mentioned the jive about *me* being a mark yesterday, our encounter would have gone differently."

Still icy with his expression, he grunted. "About face."

I turned, and he urged me forward with the cold barrel pressed against my spine. After another aggressive nudge, we were on the move. I looked to my right and left; nothing else was alive until we stopped at a naked cherry blossom tree that waved with the wind.

"Take a left," he mumbled.

We turned down what looked like the longest alley in Chicago, stopping halfway at a dimly lit light pole. There was a loud *crack*, followed by glass shattering from close behind. I flinched. He had busted the bulb, and we were covered in darkness. I froze, not budging.

"Go," he demanded.

We moved forward and ended our journey at a dead end. He kept the barrel pressed between my shoulder blades until my breasts and cheek were smashed against a brick wall.

"Dead at a dead end," I uttered.

"Tell me where Countess stashes her lottery slips and dough."

"*Hell*, I don't know."

Clink.

I winced, losing all the breath from inside my body. I knew that sound. He had pulled the trigger. I turned around in terror.

"Hey, mister! Are you looney?" I yelled.

His gun was point-blank. My chest heaved, and beads of sweat surfaced from my pores. What had been dark in the alley was starting to come to light. I saw the whiteness of the man's skin, which seemed whiter and scarier than the day before. His lips were bluer like they'd been frostbitten overnight, and his eyes were hidden beneath the widest-brimmed hat I'd ever seen. He reached inside his pocket, removed a bullet, and placed it inside the golden chamber. Then he spun it like a merry-go-round.

"Two choices. Truth or die."

"What sick game are you playing?"

"Roulette, and the odds are still in your favor, Empress. I need the stash house location of Countess's dough and slips."

"You have the wrong dame."

Click.

"*God!*" I yelled.

It was the first time I had called the Lord's name. My stomach dropped to the concrete, and two solemn tears crept down my cheeks from behind my eyelids. One was for the love I'd lost, and the other for my present fear.

I stared down the golden barrel as his trigger finger awaited his next command. The rest of his hand was tightly wrapped around the glimmering-pearled butt of his revolver.

The roulette hitman hoisted another silver bullet into his other hand from his pocket and uttered my name barely above a whisper.

"Empress." Then, he asked the question that had been swirling inside my mind. "How do you wager the value of your life?"

I was a gambling dame, born as Dulce Ella Monroe, raised by a blues singer, prostitute, and pimp. Yet, I wanted to believe I was worthy enough to possess the sovereignty of an Empress. As a Negro American born three decades after Reconstruction, my odds of success were slim to none. I was bred on the South Side of Chicago with little faith in God's protection and entrusted luck with my destiny. I placed high stakes on the value of my life and depended on chance to solidify my future. I wagered my fate in the illusive embrace of Lady Luck instead of the loose lips of Uncle Sam and his rhetoric, *"All men are created equal."*

Long before the stock market crash of 1929 ignited the Great Depression, Negroes were suffering from suppression. I grew up crammed within the confines of Chicago's "Black Belt" as Negroes fled the southern fields of Jim Crow. On my block, day and night had switched positions for many of us because our parents had been employees of the red-light district. We had loathed the virtue the streets had to offer until we saw something that couldn't be unseen or felt that which couldn't be unfelt. Untainted, we played hopscotch, jacks, and kickball and used our imaginations—the same as the kids of the opposite hue from the opposite side of the tracks. Until our vices were resurrected from the scars of our generational curses, we were oblivious to the red-lined covenants, crime, and poverty that had kept us bound.

The world had shown us, *"All is not fair in love and war,"* *especially for Negroes.* So, I avoided the enslaving sun that had burned my ancestors' backs and took my chances in the criminal underground. I feared love, not believing it had power strong enough to conquer the soul of humanity.

Honoring the creed *"In cash we trust,"* I was like most gamblers, addicted to the thrill of winning and falling prey to the seductive jackpot bestowed to the most cunning. I worshipped Lady Luck and her uncertainty like admirers hailed Mona Lisa and her crooked smile. Still, if Lady Luck were a real dame, I'd whoop her ass for oppressing us after we built this country. But luck, like those of whites, had checkmate in the game of life, and I, like my fellow colored pawns, was unprotected by the Negro American plight.

CHAPTER 1
BABYBIRD

DULCE ELLA MONROE

May 1922 - Chicago, Illinois

Before love conquered my soul, love tamed my heart. Caged but free, I was a fearless wild child. The first time I felt true love was on an unseasonably hot morning in May when I was ten years old. Amidst a scuffle, my rage that had boiled over dissipated into drops of humidity, and my conscience, which had temporarily departed, was melting back into my body. I could feel the silky hairs from the previous night's hot comb press coiling into ringlets. My nose detected the sulfur hidden underneath the violet scent in Madame C.J. Walker's Hair Grower, my greasy scalp sizzling from the burning sun. I was hot as hell, and sweat beads ran river streams down the nape of my neck to the soles of my feet.

With my arms restrained, I was surrounded by a jeering crowd of kids while Leon lay on the ground, his lanky legs tightly curled into a ball. I swung my foot like I was playing kickball, and the tip of my Mary Jane rammed into his keister. As he yelped like a wounded pup, the kids screamed with more taunting laughter.

Out of nowhere, a woman with the loudest, sweetest voice shouted, "Set her free!"

"If we let her go, ma'am, she will kill him."

My friend, Beloved, was right. Leon would be dead if she and her half-twin sister, Treasure, hadn't double-teamed me.

Leon hopped up from the ground and windmilled his wild arms before two boys grabbed him. He had missed his last chance to redeem himself from the whipping I had just laid on him like the "Galveston Giant" boxer, Jack Johnson. Leon furrowed his nappy brows that had grown into a long bridge across his schnozzle.

"That's why you can't read, you lame-brained, *dumb Dora*," he spat while struggling to break free.

My arm, slick with sweat mixed with Vaseline, slid through Treasure's fingers. I charged forward, but Beloved threw herself around my legs.

"I'll show you dumb right across the other side of your kisser, blabbermouth punk," I spat back.

"Whoa!" a woman yelled over the cheers.

The crowd hushed and parted like the Red Sea. Stomping through the tide was a beautiful, motherly dame with rich, dark skin and an apple-shaped face. The chiffon from her blue dress flowed around her, making her look like an angel. She held a stack of papers in one hand and, in the other, a switch off the crab apple tree, freshly stripped of its ripe leaves.

She stopped directly in front of me. Her celestial presence covered me as a protective spirit that whispered, *Peace, be still.* Immediately, there was a melody in my heart, and it was the softest, clearest sound I'd ever heard. With only a smile, she put me at ease.

Beloved and Treasure released me, and I didn't move. The love in the woman's eyes remained, but the look on her face transitioned into Steven's character, Hyde, and told us all, *"Don't fuck with me"* as she shifted her gaze around.

"Break it up, or I will whip the black off your bottoms all the way to the schoolhouse door."

We took off running, and Beloved and Treasure waved. "Bye, Lil' Empress!"

I waved back, and when I turned to give the woman one last look, she had gone. Splitting off from the other kids, I shook a leg home.

I lived in a 3-bedroom bungalow with seven other people. Our red brick home was a flat, rectangular-shaped box with limestone accents, concrete steps, and a pint-sized porch no one cared to sit on. Our living room always smelled like salted pork and cigarettes. In the corner was a green couch with a plastic covering that glued to our skin during the heated months. Next to the sticky couch was Butta's soft brown chair and small table that housed *his* newspaper and *his* small radio. Everyone knew to never touch *his* shit.

Butta was boss, and we called him Daddy. He occupied the largest bedroom at the front of the hallway and maintained bathroom priority. If anyone, except me, was in the middle of a stream, they had to stop the flow to allow him to use the toilet. Butta was always a cool cat towards me, but he was a barking pup to everyone else. As I grew up, I learned Butta was a counterfeit hypnotist with limited mind control.

Two lively women, always dressed in fine silk dresses and fancy accessories, shared a room across from Butta. I rarely saw them since they didn't like being around children.

The smallest room at the end of the hallway was where Audrey "Meek-Meek" Monroe and I slept. We spent most of our time together snuggled in a twin bed. Meek-Meek was my mother and beautiful to me. Her chocolate skin was smooth as velvet, and her body was curvy and plush. She had the softest eyes whenever she awakened from a dream, but after a few blinks, they hardened back to stone.

Everyone, including me, called my mother Meek-Meek. She received her nickname from Butta because she rarely spoke and whispered whenever she did talk. All I'd known about Meek-Meek was that she was born down south, shipped to Chicago, and worked as a prostitute. She had refused to disclose anything else about her life.

Meek-Meek and I shared our small space with Miss Jonesy and her infant twins, Jim and Tim. Beloved was Miss Jonesy's daughter, but she lived on the next block with her biological daddy, his wife, and Treasure. Beloved and Treasure were born one day apart and looked almost identical. It was no secret they were half-sisters, but their mother had touted them around as twins. So, after eight continuous years of them dressing alike, everyone referred to them as such.

Beloved and Treasure were my only friends, and on dreary days, we would all play together. On sunny days, unless they were going to school, they were sentenced indoors, shielding their already brown-skinned pigment against what their mother deemed "a tarnished tan."

Before I entered our house, I heard Jim and Tim's piercing screams. Through the front-screened door, I saw Butta, sweaty and panic-faced, pacing the living room floor. He was flopping the babies in each arm like rag dolls. Butta was high-yellow, very tall, and always dressed sharp as a tack in bright colors and snazzy hats. His eyes were slanted like a cat, and he had a distinct gap between his teeth.

Relief swept across his face when I walked inside.

"*Thank God*," he said. "Take these. I don't do babies."

He placed them in my arms and plopped down on his chair. Then he lit a cigarette and exhaled the cloud while resting his ashy dogs on the coffee table. The smoke quickly filled the steamy living room like a sauna.

I wrapped Jim and Tim like a mummy, and they quieted once I placed them on the couch and opened all the windows.

"Where's the sitter?" I asked.

"She quit. Maybe you can take her place."

"Me? I'm just a kid."

"Age ain't nothin' but a number. *Never* turn down an opportunity to make scratch. You can remove any obstacle in your path with enough dough. Tell eggs in your way, *habla* moolah, and watch them attempt to break down the gates of heaven for you. Even the whitest cracker under the whitest sheet respects the color green."

"*What?*" I asked, looking confused.

"It's a piece of cake." He removed a shiny quarter from his pocket. "In this world, no dough means no go, *amigo.*"

I didn't know what he was talking about, but one quarter would afford me a piece of candy every day from the corner store for the next two weeks, so I was keen. I nodded as he placed the coin in the palm of my hand.

"Swell! Thanks, Daddy."

"Be savvy, Lil' Empress. Your time is worth every dime, so don't waste any minutes on broke niggas' jive."

Butta had given me the name Lil' Empress when I was a baby. He was a self-proclaimed descendant of an African king and deemed me the descendant of an empress since I had been the only female to possess any power over his heart.

He would tell me, "The only dame more powerful than a king is an empress, so remember to own that name when you run your game."

Butta reclined back in his seat and closed his eyes.

I walked over to him and asked, "Are you my daddy?"

"Hell no."

I was surprised and confused. "Then who is?"

"Beats me."

"Is Meek-Meek my mama?"

"Yeah."

"Are you Meek-Meek's daddy?"

"I'm her pimp daddy."

"What's a pimp?"

"Why are you asking so many questions? Who's been jive talking counterfeit in your ear?"

The brawl between Leon and me started because he had been spreading nasty rumors. He had said Meek-Meek was my sister and teaching me how to be a floozy and claimed Butta was my pimp. I didn't know what was true, but I did know I was nobody's floozy, and I was taught name-calling meant ass-whooping. So, I whooped his ass.

Butta burst into laughter. "You did Leon's ass right. From now on, call me Butta to avoid confusion." He put out his hand, and I gave him smooth five. "Tell your mama to answer your other questions."

I nodded.

Suddenly, there was an aggressive knock at the door. Butta quickly grabbed his gat from under his chair and peered out the window next to the screen door. His cigarette flapped between his lips as he opened the door.

"*Why* are you banging on my door this early in the morning, lady?"

"My name is Ethel, mister, but everyone calls me Mama Lee. I'm new to the neighborhood and looking for business."

"You're a little too refined to work for me, but come in."

Mama Lee walked inside, and it was the same woman who had broken up the fight between me and Leon earlier. She saw me and smiled, then handed Butta and me one of her papers. As I looked at it, I knew Leon had been right about one thing about me—I couldn't read. She pointed to the words after watching me struggle for a moment.

"This says *Mama Lee's No Baby Blues Nursery.* I watch children and charge fifty cents per day."

Butta handed her one dollar. "Lil' Empress, this dame understands marketing. I respect the hustle, and today is your lucky day, Mama Lee. I have two babies that need sitting."

She pointed at me. "What about the gal?"

"What about the gal?" he asked.

"Doesn't she go to school?"

"No."

"Why not?"

"Listen, dame, no mo' convo. You, Lil' Empress, and all your questions need to fade so I can get some shut-eye."

With that, he turned, walked into his bedroom, and slammed the door.

Mama Lee tucked the dollar bill inside her bosom and smiled.

"They call you Lil' Empress, but what's your real name, sugar?"

"Dulce Ella Monroe."

"*Wow!* That sounds like the name of a star. Where's your mama?"

"Work."

"Do you and your mama live here?"

"Yes, ma'am."

"Call me Mama Lee," she said while picking up Jim and Tim from the couch. "Do you know where the babies' things are?"

Mama Lee, who had moved in down the street, opened her front door. I immediately noticed unpacked boxes filled with albums and books scattered across her living room floor when we stepped inside. The scent of fresh lemon zest and sugar tingled my nose, and I smiled. Mama Lee opened the ice box and poured us two glasses of freshly squeezed lemonade from a pretty crystal pitcher.

"Are you a teacher?" I asked.

She took a long gulp. "I'm a singer who loves to read."

"Can you teach me to read?" I asked hesitantly.

"Sure, sugar."

Mama Lee grabbed a couple of children's books and took me to school in her living room. I was known for my sharp memory and zipped through the ABCs like lightning. She couldn't believe how quickly I was catching on. The more she fed my brain, the more I devoured.

When the twins got fussy, she turned on the record player. Bessie Smith began to sing about being "Down and Out" while Mama Lee hummed along. After quieting the babies' cries, she placed them on the couch and grabbed two boas from a box on the floor.

"Put that book down, sugar," she instructed.

Mama Lee placed the feathers around our necks and started singing while dancing. I followed her every move.

Then she took my hands and told me, "Understanding the beauty in art is just as important as the knowledge from a textbook. The best life lessons come from listening to music, especially the blues."

Later that day, Meek-Meek and Miss Jonesy arrived to pick me and the twins up from Mama Lee's house. After introductions,

Mama Lee begged Meek-Meek to enroll me in school, but Meek-Meek refused.

"I barely spend time with my Dulce because I work long hours. If she goes to school, I won't see her at all."

"Miss Monroe, I've only been around your daughter a few hours, and anybody can see this gal is a little genius. She could be the next Ida B. Wells."

"*Ida B. Wells?*" Meek-Meek got louder than usual. "With all due respect, *ma'am*, look at me and where Dulce comes from."

Mama Lee's body stiffened as she gave Meek-Meek the *"don't fuck with me"* face.

"It doesn't matter who or where this child comes from. It matters where she wants to go. Mrs. Ida B. Wells was born into slavery in Mississippi, and that didn't stop her. Dulce is gifted and deserves a chance to succeed without you or anybody else standing in her way."

Meek-Meek didn't respond. She scanned the room, and her glance locked on the stacked boxes of books.

"You're obviously educated, so what if I pay you fifty extra cents a day to teach her? And she loves children. She'll be a great helper."

Mama Lee loosened her tightened jaws and flashed me a comforting smile.

"What do you want to be when you grow up, sugar?" she asked me.

For as long as I could remember, I'd been fascinated by clothes. I had wanted to know why girls wore dresses and boys knickers. I loved seeing the dresses in Meek-Meek's magazines and had wanted to know why she would say she couldn't afford the same ritzy threads as the white women from Paris. That didn't seem fair.

Even as a young child, I knew I couldn't control how the world viewed the color of our skin, but I wanted the power to determine the hues and designs of the fabric we dressed over it.

"A fashion designer..." I paused before adding with a sudden burst of hope, "...in Paris."

"Sounds swell, sugar. Miss Dulce Ella Monroe, you will be the best fashion designer in Paris this world has ever seen."

December 1922 - Chicago, Illinois

It was a dark winter night, brightly lit by the cold moon. I was usually at Mama Lee's place every day, but days had gone by without me seeing her because she had been sickened with a red, swollen throat. Due to her needing another night to recuperate, her nursery was closed on this day, too.

Butta had converted our basement into a late-night juice joint called *Butta's Basement*. It was open every Sunday and Monday night, his slowest moneymaking days of the week. His joint offered fellow pimps, hoodlums, and any paying customers a place to gamble, drink hooch, and make whoopie.

That night, Meek-Meek and Jonesy were working in Butta's Basement, and I was alone in my bedroom with the window fully open. Dressed in my snowsuit and slippers, I sat on the sill, catching snowflakes on the tip of my tongue. I was mystified watching them drop out of the night like falling stars. It didn't take long for Mother Nature's snowfall to cover the scars of our neighborhood, and I loved watching it convert into a winter wonderland.

A new record was pumping music through the floorboards, louder than usual. Leaving my spot in the window, I headed for my seat on the top basement step.

When I opened the door, a smokey funk smacked me in the face. My senses had adapted to smoke clouds and the pungent scent of stale hooch and dirty sex, so I quietly took my usual place to observe all the forbidden activity. The basement was packed. In one corner of the room, a group of cats were playing craps. In the middle of the floor, couples smashed their bodies together like dogs in heat. There were card tables, stools, and two sofas scattered around the rest of the room. I scanned the wall and saw Meek-Meek wrapped inside the arms of a blimp with a nappy unibrow. Almost everyone was wearing a fur coat, making the basement look like a ghetto zoo.

I loved the new music, but my skin was sweating and sticking to the inside lining of my snowsuit. I was also suffocating, so I returned to my room, which was still freezing from having the window open. Leaving the door open, I mummified myself inside my blanket. No sooner than I closed my eyes, the bedroom door creaked and slammed shut. I kept my eyelids stuck together, hoping Meek-Meek or Jonesy would announce themselves, but when the door locked, I knew they weren't in the room. My body shook from the terrifying sound of clothes dropping to the floor. I slowly opened my eyes. The same blimp who had his arms wrapped around Meek-Meek was naked next to me.

I remember feeling sick to my stomach from his stench and terrified by the way he thrusted against my thighs, which were, thankfully, secured under the blanket. I didn't blink or move, hoping my stillness would turn me into a statue and make him want to leave.

Instead, he leaned over my face and whispered, "Hi."

His breath smelled like day-old dog doo-doo. He reached across me, lifted my body, and unrolled me from my cocoon. I was still dressed in my snowsuit, and he placed his lips against my neck. Then, he took his smelly fingers and removed my hair stuck to my face.

"You're a quiet kitten, just like your sexy mama."

He scooted closer, leaving no space between us, and unfastened the buttons of my snowsuit. I crossed my arms over my chest and turned on my side. He wormed, and his fingertips crept under my waistband. I rolled into a tight ball. Then, I bucked behind me like a horse, ramming the soles of my slippers between his legs. He cursed and, at the same time, released me. I took that moment of opportunity to escape. I ran to the windowsill and leaped out of the window. I crashed when I landed, but the blanket of snow was soft like a mattress. After standing to my feet, I took off down the street.

The sweat on my body was freezing as I banged on Mama Lee's door. She opened it with concern written on her face. She pulled me inside and stroked my face.

"What's wrong, sugar?"

I attempted to tell her but couldn't get my words out. I tried to cry, but the tears wouldn't fall. I got overwhelmed with fear and frustration. I was so confused I thought my brain was breaking. Losing control of my senses, I started shaking. Then, I closed my eyes, and her lips touched my forehead. When I opened my eyes, she was smiling, and that put me at ease.

She lifted my chin and refastened my buttons.

"With your head up, nothing will break you down."

I nodded, and she opened her closet. She removed her full-length fur coat and placed it over her body. She reached into the corner of the closet, pulled out an empty suitcase, and handed it to me. Then, she grabbed a wooden box from the top shelf. She opened it, and there was a pistol inside. She placed it in her right hand and gripped my fingers with her left.

Neither of us said anything as we tramped our slippers through the snow. We walked around to the back of my house to Butta's Basement. With Louis Armstrong's "Chimes Blues" blasting inside, she took the back of her pistol and banged on the door. Butta smiled when he saw us standing there.

"It's my favorite blue canary—Mama Lee. Are you here to perform?"

She smiled back and pointed her gun in his face. "No, Butta, I'm not here to sing."

"*Hell*, Mama Lee, put that away! You've lost your *damn* mind."

Mama Lee shoved him out of the way and led me to the middle of the dance floor. The music stopped.

She bent down in front of me and asked, "Which one, sugar?"

The stank-breath lurker was standing against the wall with Meek-Meek wrapped around him and a bottle of whiskey pressed against his lips. I pointed, and all eyes turned to him.

He rolled his eyes and took another sip of his drink. "She's lyin'."

Meek-Meek stepped to the side and blended into the wall.

Mama Lee released my hand and whispered in my ear, "Turn around and cover your ears, sugar."

I dropped the suitcase and did as I was told. I turned my back, and *pow!*

I quickly turned back around, and Mama Lee was standing over me. She handed me the suitcase and took my hand. The music started blasting again, and Butta yelled as we headed for the stairs.

"*Hell*, Mama Lee! Who's going to clean my damn floor?"

Mama Lee and I walked up the stairs and into my bedroom. She laid my suitcase on the bed and stuffed my clothes and favorite bedspread inside. Meek-Meek quietly entered the room as I was removing my wet slippers and putting on my snow boots.

With a pistol in one hand and my suitcase in the other, Mama Lee gave Meek-Meek her *"don't fuck with me"* face and walked past her.

I stopped before leaving for good. "Bye, Meek-Meek."

She didn't say a word. She simply backed up and became a figurine.

When Mama Lee and I made it back to her house, we changed out of our wet clothes, and she poured us a cup of hot lemon tea.

"Welcome home, sugar," she said, raising her cup in the air.

I smiled, and our cups kissed. "Thank you, Mama."

CHAPTER 2
WHATEVER I AM, YOU MADE ME

DULCE ELLA MONROE

June 1932 - Chicago, Illinois

"*P*ower?" Meek-Meek rolled her neck with her hands on her hips. "What power do I got?"

I had hoped she still had some spark left inside her, and when she showed she did, I rolled my neck with more attitude to ignite more of her fire.

"*You* have all the power."

Mama Lee raising me was the best thing that could've happened. I became the daughter she had always wanted, and she was the mother I had desperately needed. Meek-Meek and I had our unique relationship. As I aged, we had become more like sisters, which worked for us.

"Chile, please. All I have is pussy," she said.

"Pussy is power."

She got in my face and searched for signs of drunkenness. "Are you dizzy off giggle water?"

"Are you? Slavery is over, Meek-Meek. If *massas'* great-grandsons want to lay with a Negro woman, they can't go to their backyard anymore. They have to go to the red-light district and buy it."

Her voice lowered. "And there's no hope for a hoe."

"You're not a hoe. You're a prostitute, and prostitution has been a profitable profession since Genesis. And in every business transaction, there's supply and demand. You're the supplier, and your service is in demand. Butta is a useless middleman. He rapes your pocketbook like *massa* raped his slaves."

"What in the hell are you talking about—supply and middleman? You spend too much time with your nose in library books and not in the real world. Butta is a pimp and protects me. If it wasn't for him, I would have nothing."

"Butta would be broke without you."

"That's enough. What happened with that Sears and Roebuck job? If you really want to make clothes in Paris, Sears is a good place to start. I heard they're hiring high-yellow girls to work in the warehouse."

"We're in a depression, Meek-Meek. No one's hiring Negroes of any shade."

"Get you a hard-working husband to take care of you."

"I don't want a man to take care of me. I'm going to set up a meeting with Countess LeRoux and be her runner."

"A runner is men's work. Plus, I heard she uses her voodoo on folks. That's why Al Capone didn't mess with her. And they say she's not married because she likes a moll on her arm."

"Countess runs South Side better than Capone. Folks can't figure her out, so they make jazz up. Those same folks say Mama likes women, and her man is a lieutenant in the Army."

"You can do better than being Countess's runner. You're the smartest and prettiest dame on the South Side."

"Nothing is prettier than dollar bills, and the numbers lottery is fast, easy money. I'm going to stack my dough and open my boutique lickety-split. *You'll see.*"

"Fast money *ain't* easy money. *You'll see.* Here today, gone tomorrow, till you're broke."

"I'll never go broke."

She shook her head. "I don't understand you."

"Why? You made me, Meek-Meek."

"No, I didn't. You dance to your own jazz."

I grabbed her hands and swayed my hips. "Come, dance *with me* and leave this place."

She pulled away and stretched across her bed. "Girl, stop shucking and jiving. I'm tired and have to work Butta's Basement tonight."

"When I open my boutique, you *will not* work for Butta or anyone else. You'll see."

"Whatever you say, Lil' Empress."

Meek-Meek closed her eyes and immediately fell asleep. I sat next to her, watching the pulse of her breath. I placed the bedspread over her body, kissed her forehead, and for the first time, I saw a wide smile of serenity across her face.

June 1932 - Chicago, Illinois

The Depression, enflamed by the 1929 stock market crash, was wreaking havoc on the world like a diseased whore. She didn't care who she infected, but with no cure in sight, colored people had the worst of it. Having no jobs, money, or hope in America, upstanding citizens had turned into vultures. Starved during the famine, folks of all colors and walks of life were choosing a path of darkness and a life of crime. Most colored men were out of work, so more women took jobs. Women settled for working nightly shifts in dives and the streets. Others left their homes to take care of the needs of wealthy white folks.

Mama Lee had drastically dropped her nursery costs to adjust to the market. She took singing gigs, and I became her business partner. We were busier than ever, but our ends were barely met with our prices slashed and higher rent due. And I still had dreams of becoming a clothing designer while venturing down that dark employment path for Camille "Countess" Broudair LeRoux to make them come true.

Countess was a queen pin and an underground banker for Negroes who couldn't get loans from the banks. She was most notorious for running the largest numbers operation and illegal lottery in Chicago's "Black Metropolis." Every Negro, no matter how broke or wealthy, played the numbers lottery every day in our neighborhood. Countess had no age or amount restriction, so anyone could play and win. She would accept pennies from a child and dollars from a lawyer. And if you hit, payment would be delivered to your doorstep the same day. I knew a lady named Mae who hit and bought a new salon in Indiana.

I had tried to finesse my way into Countess's organization, but she was untouchable. I hadn't given up, but until I could arrange a meeting, I focused on learning how to sew to open my boutique. Drawing designs came naturally to me. I studied fashion design from books in the library but needed hands-on stitching lessons. Since I was too old and poor to fly to France to learn from the nuns in the same orphanage that had taught Coco Chanel, I reserved every sewing book from the library and started teaching myself.

It was a beautiful, sunny day, and every Negro in our neighborhood was outside. Mama was tending to her garden, and I was sketching on the front porch. I started bringing my first design to life using my cloth, needle, and thread. Beloved and Treasure had snuck up on me and started giggling as I struggled to get it right.

"Dulce, you look like a crazy old lady stitching in that rocking chair. What are you making?" Beloved asked.

I lifted my rectangle in the air, and they erupted into laughter.

"Hush," I said. "It's a pillowcase, and I'm just getting started."

Beloved had laughing tears in her eyes. "It's lopsided."

"How do you think Coco Chanel started?" I asked.

"Let me guess. She made pillowcases."

"I'm not sure, but I guarantee her first design was *not* couture," I responded.

Treasure walked towards me. "My mother signed me up for a summer sewing class at the South Wabash community center. She thought it would be good for me to learn, but I'd love to skip it. It starts in an hour. You can take my place if you'd like."

I screamed and embraced her. "You don't know how much that means. I'll make you a dress when I'm done."

Smiling, she said, "You can make me a baby nightgown instead. Philly and I are getting married." She placed two hands on her concealed baby belly.

I gave her an even bigger hug. "That's just swell, and congratulations! That just means I will make a pretty gown for your baby and a dress for you."

After my first day of sewing class, I was overwhelmed with gratitude to Lady Luck. Gathering the skirt pattern and fabric in my arms, I felt like my dream was coming true earlier than expected. It now seemed well within reach.

With a long walk home ahead of me, I started my way toward the back door to take a shortcut. The hallway smelled of elegance, and I followed the scent outside, where a shiny burgundy Cadillac with clean white tires was parked in the alley. In front of the car was a tall man dressed in a pinstriped suit, wing-tipped leather shoes, and a top hat. Next to him, Countess LeRoux. I couldn't believe she was standing a few feet away from me.

She was more striking than what I'd seen of her in passing. She had creamy peanut butter skin, plush pink lips, and crinkly fiery-colored hair. Her cheeks were covered with light-brown freckles, and she had rich emerald-colored eyes. She wore a green and black flapper dress and a matching hat accented with lace and feathers.

My lips quivered as I managed to say, "*Countess.*"

She glared directly into my eyes, then got in the backseat of her car. I ran after her, but her goon stopped me before I could reach her door. Her hand, covered with black lace, extended out of her window.

"Set her free," she commanded in a Creole French accent, and he quickly obeyed.

"Miss LeRoux, my name is Dulce Ella Monroe, and I want to work for you."

"How old are you?" she asked.

"Age ain't nothin' but a number. I'm smart, a hard worker, and a number wiz with the best memory of anybody you'll ever meet."

I stood there waiting for her to respond, but no words departed from her lips. I watched as her driver removed a huge box of sewing kits from the trunk and walked back inside the community center. Returning empty-handed, he got into the driver's seat, and the car proceeded down the alley. Defeat was burning a hole in my chest, but I refused to drop my head. I stood there, contemplating if I would chase Countess's Cadillac to beg her for a chance.

The car turned onto the street, and I shook a leg after it. Then, the car stopped in the middle of traffic, and the chauffeur stepped out of the driver's seat. He cracked a frowning smile before opening the backseat door. I ran even faster to catch up to them, and when I stopped in front of the driver, I was out of breath and had to deeply exhale to calm my dancing nerves.

"Thank you kindly, sir."

Countess lifted her head and turned slowly to me. She didn't smile, but a twinkle glimmered in the emerald of her eye. I beamed with excitement.

She faced forward. "Get in, gal."

I slid inside, and her driver shut the door. I couldn't stop smiling. I'd never been inside anything as ritzy, and I was seated next to the infamous Countess LeRoux.

In her soft, raspy voice, she asked, "Why do you want to work for me?"

"I admire you. You are a great businesswoman, and I want to learn all I can from you. You're feeding families and giving colored folks jobs and hope when the country is depressed."

"What is your goal in life?"

"I want to be a fashion designer."

She glanced down at my pattern book before letting her eyes travel from my shoes to my forehead. I smiled at first but became concerned when she rolled her eyes as if unimpressed.

"Tommy, stop at the Marshall Field & Company on State Street and get this young lady a sewing machine."

"Yes, Countess."

I wanted to throw my arms around her and say thank you, but I was speechless and afraid to touch her.

We drove to the heart of downtown, and since I had never left the South Side, the miniature skyline I saw from afar was suddenly larger than life. When the driver finally parked, we were surrounded by tall concrete mountains. The architecture, array of endless shops, and slew of white people captivated me. I was a visitor in foreign territory located only a few miles away.

The door opened, and the unexpected breeze broke my trance. Tommy placed a fancy Singer at my feet. I picked it up and felt like I was dreaming.

"Gee...swell...thank you so much." Countess cleared her throat, and I continued, "I am so grateful, Countess. I will pay you for it."

"You have a choice," she said. "I can take you home and wish you the best on your fashion dream. Or you can work for me, and I'll teach you everything I know."

I parted my lips, and she snapped her lace finger.

"Before you speak, I don't run a business school. I'm a real gangster involved in real gangster biz. Hoodlums like me get rich, go to the slammer, and die—hopefully, years after our enemies."

I never forgot Butta's advice to never turn down a money-making opportunity, and Countess LeRoux was the richest person I knew.

I placed my sewing machine on the floor and said confidently, "When can I start?"

She cracked a smile. "Alright, what do we call you?"

I smiled back. "Lil' Empress."

We cruised back to the South Side, but to a part I had never been before. We were driving down Grand Boulevard, and the houses looked like grey-stoned castles. Negro children, well-dressed like princes and princesses, were playing joyously outside of their homes. Parked like model cars on the street were fancy Lincolns and Cadillacs with shiny rims.

I was in awe and remembered a photograph from one of my library books. *This is the same street as Ida B. Wells.*

Our chariot stopped on 37th Street and parked in front of a tri-level, ivy-covered, limestone fortress with numerous arched grand windows. Tommy opened our car doors and escorted us through a large iron gate covered in gold. We passed through a small courtyard with a garden and wishing well. After he opened the front door, we entered the foyer. Hanging from the ceiling was a grand chandelier covered in crystals. The burgundy and gold tapestry were exquisitely designed, fit for royalty.

The circular staircase snaked to the top floor, and we ascended towards the top level. The steps creaked and our heels knocked, creating the sound of an ancestral rhythm that bounced off the walls. Every beat of our stride gave me goosebumps, and being in Countess's home confirmed I would do anything to be just like her.

We stepped inside her master suite adorned in shades of green and gold. A gold chandelier hung above her golden canopy bed, which was covered with the most pillows I'd ever seen. She motioned for me to sit on a fuchsia settee at the foot of her bed.

I sat down, and Countess walked inside her closet. When she came out, she was holding a purple silk dress that looked like something Billie Holiday had worn. I quickly undressed, and she slid the perfectly fit dress over my body. The V-shaped neckline revealed the pearl strand she placed around my neck. Turning me towards her, she tied the silk sash around my waist. Then, she reached inside her pocketbook and removed a tube of lipstick. I puckered my lips, and she covered them in ruby red. She took my hand, and we walked in front of a tall, glamorous mirror. She stood behind me and released my hair from the tightly tucked bun. The strands fell and nestled around my breasts. After placing a purple Chanel hat on my head, she smiled.

"Now you look like a fashion designer. People assess who you are by how you look, so always dress the part."

I nodded. "Yes, ma'am."

"From now on, call me Countess, and we'll call you Empress. Lil' sounds juvenile, and we need niggas to know you're a grown-ass woman who takes no shit."

Countess reached inside her pocketbook and removed a sheet of paper. She handed it to me, and when I looked down, I saw rows of three-digit combinations.

"Study those digits," she said.

I scanned them row by row until the paper had become a photograph in my mind. She quickly snatched the number-filled paper from my hand and placed a blank sheet and pen on my lap.

"Write down as many combinations as you can remember."

"In order?" I asked.

She didn't respond, so I closed my eyes and began writing. When I was done, I gave the paper back to her. Countess looked it over, walked to her closet, and returned with another one of her pocketbooks. She handed it to me. I looked inside, and it was filled with dollar bills. I waited for my first assignment.

"You really do have the best memory of anyone I've ever met," she said. "That dough is your first day's pay. You memorized twenty-one combinations in less than a minute, and I've got the perfect job for a wiz like you."

Earlier that morning, Meek-Meek had given me grief because I wanted to be one of Countess's runners. By nightfall, I had not only been placed in charge of all South Side's runners but also officially crowned Countess LeRoux's protégé.

CHAPTER 3
CHICAGO BOY

DULCE ELLA MONROE

October 1933 - Chicago, Illinois

I never thought Lady Luck would grant a dame like me a day of perfection, but on the eve of Halloween in 1933, I felt like the luckiest broad in the world. It was my birthday, and Midwestern October weather was always bipolar. Before the official start of a cold fall, Mother Nature's last smooch of warmth, called Indian Summer, would sweep across Chicago, and on the most memorable day of my life, I experienced its final embrace.

I had stayed up all night making children's costumes for the neighborhood fall fest, and Tommy, Countess, and I had just dropped them off at the South Wabash community center, along with bags of candy and food. We were cruising down South Side's South Parkway and stopped at a traffic light in front of a nameless corner store with pictures of musicians taped against the windows. Suddenly, something told me to get out.

I grabbed my clutch and tapped the back of the driver's seat. "Tommy, drop me off."

"In the middle of the street?" he asked.

"And why here?" Countess added.

"I want to buy some platters."

Tommy pulled over. "We'll go in together."

"No."

"Who's driving you home?" he asked.

"I know the way."

Countess studied me for a moment and grabbed her pocketbook. "Hell no. We're going to stick together. There's not enough coppers to keep up with all the hitters that's been swarming the streets."

"It's broad daylight," I replied. "Nobody's getting bumped off while the sun is up."

"Empress, stop being such a pill. It's your birthday. Come with us to see Duke at the Oriental Theatre tonight," she pleaded.

I sighed. I needed a break from the dives, juice joints, and, frankly, our mob. Rumors of Prohibition ending had bootleggers spooked because johns were cracking down on illegal gin mills and throwing more and more Negroes in the slammer. So, all the bootleggers were infiltrating the black lottery operations underground, looking for their revenue replacement for hooch. Countess's operation was protected by crooked coppers, but like she had said, they couldn't keep up with all the Chicago overcoats closing over bodies dropping dead around the city.

"I want to spend *my* birthday alone getting dizzy, drinking *my* gin, and listening to *my* platters in *my* house."

Countess pulled out a pretty glass vial filled with clear liquid. She removed the top and doused me with it.

"If you don't wear this, you'll be bored in an hour."

"What potion have you brewed?"

"A man magnet for your daylight rendezvous. Rose exudes love, and amber is an aphrodisiac."

I leaned forward. "How do I smell, Tommy?"

He took a whiff. "Like air."

"Empress, don't ask Tommy's ass. He's married. It worked for our ancestors, so it will work for you." She rubbed drops all over her body and more on mine. "I'm going to meet *my* man *tonight* at the Oriental Theatre."

I laughed and wiggled my door handle. "I will be smelling good in my house *alone*."

Suddenly, the door swung open. A white stranger in a black overcoat and large-brimmed hat stood on the sidewalk with his hand extended. His eyes were hidden under his brim's shadow. His lips were a bluish-pink like he needed oxygen. Hanging around his tanned neck were sweaty, stringy ringlets.

I didn't move. Neither did he.

Tommy appeared behind him. "She has a doorman."

The mystery man tipped his hat. "My apologies. It's a habit. My mother taught me always to open doors for ladies."

"What white mother teaches her white son to open doors for colored women?" I asked.

"It doesn't matter." Tommy stood firm. "The ladies in this ride have a doorman."

The man lifted his head, and his pupils were dark as midnight.

"Slavery ended over sixty-five years ago, ma'am. So, everybody is equal—man and woman, colored and white."

Countess, Tommy, and I burst into laughter.

"Mister, if you believe that, you're either not from America or you're jiving around," I told him. "Thank you for the gesture, but I'm alright."

His lips curled into a plastered smile. "Damn shame a man can't open a door for a dame without causing a fuss. You all have a wonderful day."

I hit Countess's arm. "Your damn man magnet is going to send me to the slammer."

She pulled out a small pistol and slid it into my pocketbook. "Keep your eyes open and be inside your cave before the streetlights come on."

"And *never* trust a goon in an overcoat," Tommy added while helping me out of the car.

Countess blew me a kiss as Tommy drove off and yelled out of the window, "The Duke tonight! Call us if you change your mind!"

When I stepped onto the sidewalk, the wind whipped purple, red, and orange leaves around me. I walked inside the store, and the classical music section consumed most of the square footage. Mama Lee had exposed me to all genres of music, and a rhapsody from Beethoven always calmed my nerves. As I perused the selections, I was suddenly drowning in a sweet teakwood scent. I turned around. A dark-chocolate-complexioned man was standing there looking debonair with perfect, full lips and a chiseled face.

His mouth dropped and extended into a huge grin when I looked into his eyes. He removed his hat and placed it against his heart.

"*Sweet Jesus!*"

"Do I know you, mister?" I asked.

He was dressed sharp as a tack in a crisp tan shirt and burgundy and brown plaid pants. He was accessorized with a gold watch, peanut butter-colored leather shoes with winged tips, and suspenders. He looked like a dream who had just stepped off a Harlem fashion runway.

When he didn't respond, I walked away. I knew he was following me because his sultry scent grew stronger instead of fainter. I stopped moving. He did, as well. He was so close to me that his breath hot pressed the kitchen hairs on my neck.

I turned, and Mr. Smell Good's eyes scanned my body until our gazes locked. There was an undeniable, instant attraction.

"Mister, why do you keep staring?"

"I'm sorry, Miss. I never lose my words."

"I'm talking about your eyes, not your lips."

"You look like a dame I know. You two could be sisters—twins, maybe. Are you related to any James?"

"No, I'm not. And I don't like people staring. It's bad manners."

"I apologize, doll."

"Stop apologizing and remove your eyes."

"I can't help it. You are the most gorgeous doll I've ever seen."

"You just said I look like a dame's twin. Now I'm the most gorgeous doll you've ever seen. Pick a line."

He smiled. "*If* you were this dame's twin, you'd be the prettier doll."

He was very charming, and I couldn't help but smile back.

"Thank you."

He offered his hand. "Can we please start over?"

We touched. His skin was soft, but his palms were rough with callouses when he grabbed my hand.

"My name is Perry Blair Savage," he continued. "I apologize again for staring. Your beauty had not only taken my words from my mouth, but I also stopped breathing. What's your name, doll?"

"Dulce."

He kissed my hand, and his lips and dark eyes sent tingles down my spine.

"Dulce is a beautiful name. What's your last name?"

"De Leche."

He laughed out loud. "*Bullshit, jive!* What kind of name is *De Leche?*"

"What kind of name is *Savage?* And you're not supposed to use bad language around a lady."

He bit his lip. "You are clearly a *fine* lady, but I won't hold my tongue for anybody. You could be Josephine Baker naked with bananas or President Roosevelt at the White House. I'm going to say how I feel."

"I respect that, Mr. Savage, but if you don't mind, I'm looking for a platter. Then I need to split."

"Maybe I can help you. I saw you checking out Beethoven. And please, call me Perry."

"Do you like classical music, *Perry*?"

"I love all music." He handed me a record with white people on the cover. "Let me buy you one of my favorites, 'La Bohème'."

"*Opera?*"

"Yes. Opera takes me to foreign places in my mind."

I was captivated by his mysteriousness. "Tell me the story of 'La Bohème'."

"It's a romantic tragedy about a seamstress and poet. The Italian baritone sings his heart out."

I was lost for words. My body started responding to him like it hadn't done for anyone else. My heartbeat sped up, and it felt like butterflies were twirling between my thighs. My mouth suddenly dried out, and I grew lightheaded like I had gulped a glass of giggle juice. I fought to keep my composure.

Then, he reached for my face and grazed my cheek with the soft side of his hand.

"Somebody just told me that staring was bad manners."

I cleared my throat. "I wasn't staring, Perry. I was listening attentively." I switched past him, and he quickly followed. "I'll take the opera album," I said while grabbing a Duke album by the register and handing it to him. "This one, too."

After he bought my platters, we stepped outside and lingered on the sidewalk.

My stomach roared. "I'm starved."

He looked relieved. "Me too. I know a good burger joint nearby."

"*Burger?*" I yelled. "Does it look like I eat at *burger joints?*"

He laughed. "Doll, everybody likes a good burger and milkshake. This place is delicious and a quick walk around the corner."

I yelled again. "*Walk?* You expect *me* to *walk?*"

He laced his fingers between mine and kissed my hand. "Your feet work, princess, and it's a pretty day. Will you walk with me, *please?*"

The Windy City tossed colorful leaves that tornadoed around us. Closing my eyes, I allowed him to pull me close to him. He placed his lips near my neck.

"Damn, doll, what perfume are you wearing? You smell exquisite—like a sweet rose and sugar cookie."

"It's a secret recipe whipped up by my Creole friend," I whispered in his ear. "It's supposed to put my dream man under a love spell."

He inhaled deeply, his warm breath tickling my cheek. "Are you trying to make me fall in love with you, Miss De Leche?"

"Maybe. Is it working?"

He smiled and replied, "Maybe."

I inhaled the stimulating scent of charming teakwood tattooed on his skin. "I didn't know they made men's perfume."

"It's one of a kind—from Paris, France."

"Did you know certain smells are aphrodisiacs?"

"Is that why I want to kiss you?" he asked.

I pulled away and started walking. "You want to kiss me because I put a spell on you."

"I think you're right." He took my hand and twirled me around. "Wrong direction, Miss De Leche."

We held hands on the way to the burger diner and took our seats in a booth. We ate and conversed with our bodies smashed together. Perry was an off-duty soldier born in Georgia but living with his brothers in Harlem. They had all traveled to Chicago together.

Perry fascinated me, and having no time for companionship, I had never felt that way about a man. He was honest, smart, well-rounded, and intelligent with street sensibility. I saw myself with him until he shared his desire to be a family man.

"Do you want a lot of children?" I asked.

"I love kids, so I want a bunch of Savages running around. What about you?"

"The innocence of children brings me so much joy. I've watched over other folk's babies all my life, but I don't want any of my own."

"I believe the right man could change your mind."

I laughed. "You don't know me. How soon do you want to start a family?"

"As soon as God delivers the right doll into my life."

"How would you know?"

He placed my palm over his heart, and our pulses thumped into one rhythm.

"I would feel her capture my soul with one touch of her hand."

We stared into each other's eyes, and fear instantly snatched my hand away.

"In the Army, do they call you Captain?"

"That's right."

"Did fighting in combat fuck you up?"

He smiled and moved centimeters from my lips. "Naw, doll, I'm the one who fucks motherfuckers up."

I laughed and choked on my milkshake. "You're the bees-knees. I don't think I've ever giggled this much without drinking gin or whiskey."

He touched my chin and turned my face back towards him. "If a man doesn't make you laugh, he's incapable of pleasing you."

"Today is my birthday, Perry."

"Happy birthday, doll. How old are you?"

"Grown."

"I would *love* to take you to see Duke at the Oriental Theatre to celebrate tonight. Would you go with me?"

"I would rather hear Duke and that opera platter in your hotel room, Captain Savage. Do you want to split?"

We leaned into each other. Perry closed his eyes and gave me the clowest, sexiest kiss I'd ever had. I parted my lips, and our tongues danced flirtatiously inside each other's mouths. We kissed more intensely until he slowly released my bottom lip with his teeth.

He opened his eyes. "I'll do whatever you want me to, Miss De Leche."

I snatched another kiss from his lips and pulled his hand. "Let's fade, Daddy."

Perry was staying at the ritzy Southway Hotel. The Southway was Negro owned and popular because it was featured in the Negro Motorist Green Book. It was where many musicians, famous entertainers, and notable, wealthy Negroes stayed when they visited Chicago. I had never been inside the tall red brick building, but when my shoes sank into the plush burgundy oriental rug in the lobby, I knew it was the berries like folks had been saying.

Perry took my hand and led me past the baby grand piano and gold tapestry. We kept walking until we arrived at the last room at the end of the long hallway decorated with paintings by Archibald John Motley, Jr. Perry opened the door to a large suite with a private bathroom and a fancy bed almost as big as the room. Everything was perfectly in place as if no one had been there.

"What kind of soldier boy wears exclusive French fragrances and stays in swanky hotel suites?"

"First, Miss De Leche, I'm a soldier, but nothing about me is boy," he said while pouring me a glass of whiskey from a pretty crystal bottle. "And second, I'm a man who goes without until I get what I want."

I stepped closer to him. "And what is it that you want?"

"I'll tell you after you tell me what you want for your birthday."

"Right now, I want a cigarette."

He smiled and opened the window. Then, while standing over me, he removed a cigarette from a pack of Lucky Strikes. I reached inside my pocketbook and pulled out my new gold and diamond cigarette holder. His eyes locked on my pistol. I closed the flap, and he pulled a fancy gold and diamond lighter from his pocket. His lighter and my cigarette holder were the perfect set. We smiled, and he lit our cigarettes. Right away, we began bumping gums and smoking like we had known each other for years. He poured us another glass of hooch from his fancy bottle and played my Duke Ellington on his record player.

I was much bolder and more comfortable in his presence than any man before him. My bank was usually closed to strangers, especially to an out-of-towner in his hotel room, but Perry had a gal spellbound. I sashayed onto his lap, and he wrapped his bear arms around me. My fingertips brushed his jawline, and I untucked a gold necklace that was secured tightly around his neck.

"Is this your wedding ring?"

"If I was married, Miss De Leche, no way would I be here with you. It was my father's ring that had belonged to my grandfather. When my daddy died, I was a teenager, and he left me his ring and in charge of our family."

"Sounds like a huge weight to carry."

"No, doll. Protecting my family is my honor."

"What are you protecting them from?"

"The world."

"You don't sound like you're from the Bible Belt."

Perry removed the hair from my face. "I've lost my accent from city living, but I'll never forget the claws of Jim Crow. What do you do for a living, doll?"

"I should be asking you the same thing."

"I told you already. I'm a soldier."

I was mystified and equally suspicious.

"What do you think I do?" I asked.

"You don't want to give me your real name, and you're very selective with how you respond to me."

I pressed my lips against his ear. "Dulce is my real name." He took my face and placed it inside his hands, then stared into my eyes and began reading me like a mystery novel.

"You're overly cautious, well-educated, and street savvy. You're accustomed to nice things, but you've experienced hard times. You're a gangster's daughter, which is why I believe you like children, but because of the danger of your lifestyle, you can't see yourself as a mother."

The way he gazed, smelled, and smiled made me want to confide my everything, but I chickened out instead.

"What type of soldier knows about the lifestyle of a gangster?"

He continued searching for my truth. "Am I right?"

"My father died in a car accident before I was born. My mother is a whore, and I've never stepped one foot inside a classroom."

He took a sip of his drink and exhaled a cloud of cigarette smoke. "Then somebody else well-educated raised you."

"I'm a fashion designer, Perry."

He put out his cigarette. "No fooling?"

"No fooling."

"What threads do you design?"

"Everything, including children's costumes."

"That explains a lot."

His finger waltzed over the top of my hand as he stared into my eyes. My body screamed, and I squeezed my thighs together.

"Did you make the dress you're wearing, doll?"

"Yes. Do you like it?"

"It's breathtaking. I love everything about it." He removed my cigarette from my fingers. Then he put it out and grabbed my hands. "Dance with me, doll."

"I'd love to." I stood up and placed my hands around his neck. "You are the finest soldier with the ritziest rags I've ever met."

He locked my wrists above my head, and his fingers rained down the skin on my arms.

"And you'll never meet another like me."

Duke Ellington's "Creole Love Call"—one of my favorite songs—was blasting through the record player. He spun me around, and his chest felt like a strong wall against my back. I danced like a snake; he followed my rhythm. His charm and sexy moves sent me into a lustful frenzy.

Taking my hands, he locked my wrists behind his head. I welcomed his hands to caress my entire body. He ran his lips from my shoulder to my neck. I moaned, and his manhood knocked against the hardness between my thighs. He gasped, spun me around, and examined my throat like a surgeon searching for my Adam's apple.

I laughed and raised my dress above my knees.

"I'm all doll, baby. You were feeling my hammer," I said while removing my pearl-colored Colt 1903 and garter belt from my thigh.

"Thank God." He gulped a shot of whiskey. "What the hell does a fashion designer need with *two* heaters?"

I sat on the bench at the foot of the bed. "I have to protect myself from the unruly savages of the world."

He crawled between my legs and brushed his lips against mine. "I'm a savage, but nothing about me is unruly."

"Tell me, what kind of savage are you, Captain?"

One of his hands gripped my thigh; the other softly stroked the nape of my neck. His tongue slowly danced to my ear.

"With your permission, I would love to show you."

I wrapped my tongue around his finger and placed it between my thighs. He closed his eyes and licked the brown sugar from his fingertips. Then, he took his time fondling my lips with his kiss.

While unbuttoning his shirt, I asked, "How do I taste, baby?"

He pulled my dress above my head, smiled, and dropped it to the floor.

"Like the sweetest *de leche* I've ever had."

His sloppy kisses traveled from my breasts to below my waist. He slowly removed my hosiery and got undressed. We were naked, but he stopped his touching to stare at me. I was in unchartered territory and getting antsy.

"Hurry up, Captain, before I change my mind."

"Hush, doll, and let me love you. I'm trying to figure out what door I want to open first."

"Love? I don't know what that feels like."

"I can show you, but you have to open more than your legs to me."

"You'd be my first."

He gently picked me up, placed my body across the bed, and climbed on top of me. As I held him in my arms, I knew there was no place I'd rather be. We grabbed each other's faces and uttered no words, but our souls confessed devotion through silent intimacy.

Balled up inside by the new emotions, I closed my eyes.

"Look at me, Dulce," he whispered.

I opened my eyes, and after he loved me down with one look, he pressed his lips against each lid. Next, my mouth was taken over by the fullness of his lips. As he ran his fingers through my hair, my scalp tingled with desire, and when I arched my back, he slid his arm around my waist. His kisses swept across my clavicle and moved below my stomach.

"I love the way you taste," he whispered.

Untamed drops dripped from inside me, and I twisted the sheets around my hands. He licked harder and faster until I trembled inside and out. Soulful tears poured down my face.

Perry pecked my fluttering eyelids. "Are you okay, doll?"

My face was soaked with sweat and tears as I asked, "What just happened to me?"

He smiled. "Did I please you?"

"Everything you do to me feels *so damn* good."

"I'm just getting started."

He removed the hair stuck to the dew droplets on my face. I closed my eyes, and he placed my arms around his neck. He pushed, but the gate to my hips was tightly sealed. He worked his tongue and fingers between my legs, strumming me like a wet guitar.

"Are you ready for me?" he asked.

"*Yes.*"

"I'm talking to your body, doll, not you."

After another long French kiss, he worked his way back to my face. He rocked forward and broke through my heart's barrier. We both yelled.

He looked alarmed. "Did I hurt you?"

I sank my teeth into my bottom lip. "Yes, but keep going."

He stopped and kissed my chin. "No. Only what pleases you pleases me, so tell me what to do."

"Go slow."

He nodded. With a tender kiss, his lips never left me, and I relinquished my body into his gentle sway. I welcomed him with drowning desire, locking my arms and legs around him.

He smooched his lips against my forehead. "I promise, doll, I've never felt this way about anyone."

Holding his face in my hands, I told him, "Me either, Captain."

Suddenly, the veins on his neck protruded like webs, and he sank his nails into my lower back. My teeth held his bottom lip hostage, and we thrust with so much passion until our bodies melted into one. Our breaths slowed to one rhythm as we embraced each other. Before getting up, he kissed me. Seconds later, I heard him running bathwater into the tub. He returned with a wet cloth, and when he lifted the sheets, he yelled like he'd seen a ghost.

With his eyes fixated underneath the sheet, I snapped, "What did I tell you about staring?"

"I lost my words again."

"I told you, Captain, you were my first."

He didn't respond. I snatched the sheet from his hand and wrapped myself up. Sensing I was slightly embarrassed, he lay beside me and began to unravel me.

"Dulce, I'm sorry. I didn't realize you'd never…" He kissed me. "Will you let me love you?"

I nodded, and he picked me up. After placing me inside the tub, he bathed and massaged my entire body.

"How are you, doll?"

I smiled. "I would be better if you were in here with me."

"You don't have to tell me twice."

He lifted my hair from my back and slid behind me. I turned around, and he smiled.

"Everything about you is so damn perfect, Miss De Leche."

"I'm far from perfect, Captain."

"You're perfect for me, and for your belated birthday, I'm going to plan the perfect day as a present for you."

I slowly kissed him and stared into his eyes. "My birthday isn't over yet, and you've already given me the perfect present for this perfect day."

It was before dawn, and I awoke naked inside Perry's arms. He was breathing deeply, and I sat up to watch him dream. His face and body were carved into perfection. I was in awe and happy that Lady Luck allowed me to experience his love.

My mind drifted to a beautiful place; Perry and I were together. I got balled up by the thought again, and my heart started swirling with many foreign emotions. Terrified by the feelings, I grabbed a pen and piece of paper from his desk and began writing.

October 31, 1933

Dearest Captain Perry Blair Savage,
I want to thank you for the best day of my life. I will never forget you. I've learned nothing this good lasts forever, so I want to remember what perfection feels like. I truly wish you the best.

Love always,
Miss Dulce De Leche

CHAPTER 4
RUSSIAN ROULETTE

DULCE ELLA MONROE

October 1933 - Chicago, Illinois

*H*ow *did I wager the value of my life?*

I'd figured life was a gamble, and I'd just experienced perfection, so I didn't know. But I had chosen to forfeit the game of love with Perry and had to confront my twisted fate in a game of Russian Roulette. I wanted to dry the teardrops that had drizzled down my face, but there was no escape. I was face-to-face with the barrel of a white hitman's golden revolver, and inconspicuous bullets occupied two out of the six chambers.

His haunting, expressionless face remained rigid. Using his boney fingers, he placed another silver bullet in the chamber. I closed my eyes and heard the terrifying spinning sound. Sweat cried down my body, leaving trails of cold streams stuck to my skin.

"Keep your hands up, and no more yells. Where does Countess keep her stash?"

I opened my eyes. "Who is Countess?"

I held my breath and...*click.*

Tears of torture dashed down my face, but I was no rat. I had no doubt. *I was going to die.*

Another bullet and chamber spin, and my legs gave way. I crouched like a tiger and quickly stuck my hands between my thighs. The tips of my fingers stroked my garter belt and glided along the steel of my pistol. My palm, dripping with perspiration, was on the grip. Before my fingers wrapped around the metal, he pulled my wrist above my head. I stomped like a spoiled child in frustration.

"Hands up and stay up." He continued, "You're losing favor, Empress. Are you ready to end the game?"

This hitman wasn't fucking around, so he knew as well as I did that the game would only end with me in a casket—one way or another. The slightest leak inside any organization would cause it to tank. Loose lips sank ships, and I swore a silent oath of death before I'd let that happen to Countess.

"Who is Empress?" I asked.

Click.

I grabbed my stomach and hollered. *"Goddamnit."*

"Stay up and shut up." He added another bullet. "Talk."

I closed my lips and shook my head.

He spun the chamber and sang in a monotone, *"Round it goes. Where it stops…"*

Click.

My heart leaped against my chest. I had thought that was the end, so I struggled to remain standing.

"You're one lucky broad," he said.

While trying to catch my breath, I huffed, "And you're one looney goon motherfucker."

He added the sixth bullet and kept his rod pointed at me. "You don't value your life at all."

He showed no signs of mercy. I was drained but refused to cower. I had heard that one's life flashed before their eyes before dying, but that didn't happen to me. All I saw was a white man dressed in all black with a pretty gold and pearl revolver about to end my life.

I took my last breath and lifted my head to stare death in his face.

"Just get it over with," I said, then inhaled and waited.

His trigger finger inched backward. I twitched, but this time, no sound departed from my lips. Also, no *bang, pop,* or *pow* resounded from the hitman's hammer. He looked confused, and I was shocked. His jaw tightened, and again, his finger pressed against the trigger. I ducked, and nothing. His gaze shifted to the chamber.

I quickly gripped his shoulders and rammed my knee between his legs. He growled through his teeth, and I took off. I couldn't see ahead of me, but I flailed my arms like a wild woman.

"Help!" I yelled.

Out of nowhere, a high-pitched sound like a note sung by a soprano pierced through my eardrums. There was a thunderous roar like a lion from behind me, and a ghostly complexioned woman dressed in all white stepped out from the shadows like an angel.

Am I dead?

Curious if I was a phantom between realms, I did something a sprinter should never do. I whipped my head around. I saw darkness and quickly faced forward. When I did, I had no choice but to brace myself. I took a deep breath and crashed face-first into the lamp post before me. My body ricocheted onto the concrete. Pain radiated from the back of my skull to my limbs, and everything went black.

CHAPTER 5
CIRCUS

DULCE ELLA MONROE

As I had awakened from every nightmare, I woke up with my conscience stuck between fact and fiction. I took a deep breath, and the scent of a butcher's delivery truck smacked me in the face. Immediately, I gagged and opened my eyes. Everything was blurry, and an excruciating pain thumped against the back of my head. I grimaced and tightly shut my eyes. My heart was pounding through my chest. I took another deep breath; the foul scent was more intense. I gagged again, but this time, I puked. I reopened my eyes, and while deciphering my whereabouts, a wet towel swiped across my face.

"Who's there?" I asked.

I tried to lift myself, but I was taped down.

A southern, raspy voice, mixed with a foreign English accent, whispered, "Stay calm, Empress. I promise everything's okay."

"*Calm?!*" I screamed as I struggled with my makeshift cuffs.

I turned to the right and was confronted by a long, black feline with blue and yellow eyes.

"*Ahhh!*" I yelled.

It was a tiger. Its mouth opened wide enough to swallow my head, giving me a clear view of its huge gums and razor-sharp teeth, and I was suddenly drowning in its trashy breath from its

50

yawning. I fixed my mouth to scream again. Before I let out a peep, it extended its long, pink tongue, and the tip touched my chin. It quickly created a thickly layered path of saliva to my forehead, and then, my delayed yell soared to high hell.

"Enchantress, get down," the low-pitched voice commanded.

The tiger looked up, and when I turned to my left, I hollered again. The striking woman I had seen in the alley was standing over me. Her skin was snow white. She had pale pink lips shaped like ripe melons, and her grey eyes were as bright as her skin. Her all-white hair was conked in deep waves like Josephine Baker. A curl shaped like an upside-down question mark was pasted against her forehead. She smiled.

Wanting it to be yesterday, I panted, "Tell me I'm dreaming."

"You aren't."

"Am I dead?"

"No, you are not."

The tiger moved its paws from the table and walked slowly to the woman's side. It purred and snuggled against her thigh.

"Empress, my name is Juno." She held up a pair of scissors. "I'm going to free you, but please don't make any sudden movements."

She cut the tape from around my wrists and ankles. I was horrified but obeyed her.

"I'm sorry," she continued. "I imagine being taped down with a tiger in your face is far from the cat's pajamas, but quick movements make Enchantress jumpy."

I lay still as the spinning room came to life, like for Dorothy in *The Wizard of Oz*.

I clicked my heels and began chanting, "There's no place like home."

She offered me a tall glass of water and two aspirin before helping me to sit up.

"I promise you're safe."

I threw back the aspirin right away. "Where am I, and how do you know me?"

"You're in Oz, and the Wicked Witch is dead." She giggled in self-amusement. "Just jivin'. You're in my basement, and everybody knows you and Countess are the toughest broads on the South Side."

Her basement was decorated as a glamorous Hollywood film set. She took my hand and helped me to an ivory sofa with plush furry pillows. Her feline followed us and stretched out on a long black pillow at our feet.

"Shouldn't that tiger be in a zoo or locked up in a cage?" I asked.

"Enchantress is professionally trained and does not need a leash. My pussy won't hurt a soul unless I tell her to."

I cracked a smile. "Well, thank you and your pussy for saving my life, but really, spill the biz."

Juno was from a small town in Georgia. Since she could remember, everyone had told her that she was like her mother—a canary blessed with the voice of an angel. Juno was a Negro born without melanin, and as a child, she sang with her mother for coins in southern dives. The enslaving sun had kept Juno indoors to avoid burns to her delicate, vulnerable skin while her mother worked in the tobacco fields. Her mother was saving money to move them North, hoping for a better life with cooler, cloudier days.

A ringmaster named Showman Shockley had gotten word of a colored girl with milky skin and a melodic voice, and he came knocking at their door. He had told her mother he wanted Juno to perform in his circus show and would send Juno's weekly wages directly to her. She told him that she would agree if allowed to accompany her daughter. He refused her request, and she refused his offer. Shockley tipped his top hat and left.

The next day, at sunset, Juno was running through the tall stalks in the fields, searching for her mother. Shockley stepped into her pathway. He placed a shiny coin in her hand and told her that her mother was waiting inside his car with more. When Juno tried to flee, Shockley captured her and threatened to harm her mother if she told anyone. That day, Juno was thrown into *The Shockingly Shockley Circus & Company* and forced into an act called "The Tiger Enchantress."

Enchantress was a tiger cub when young Juno was placed inside her cage. For ten years, they toured overseas as roommates, and Juno trained Enchantress to do tricks using the notes from her singing voice. To keep Juno isolated, Shockley sentenced her to Enchantress's cage and had told mystified crowds and his performers that Enchantress was once a white tiger from Africa and that Juno had turned it into a Negro tiger. He had convinced them that Juno had been blessed with the voice of an angel and cursed with the hands of a devil. Afraid Juno could turn white people into Negroes, everyone stayed clear of her touch.

It wasn't until ten years later, when the circus left Europe and arrived in Chicago, that Juno's mother would be able to track her down. When she did, her mother hired an NAACP attorney, and they were reunited and awarded one of the biggest settlements ever awarded to a Negro.

I couldn't believe what I'd heard. "Whatever happened to that looney, lunatic motherfucker Shockley?"

Juno opened a China cabinet, grabbed a showman top hat, and placed Mr. Roulette's large-brimmed hat on my head.

"After I freed Enchantress, the same thing that happened to the looney, lunatic motherfucker with the golden revolver happened to Shockley."

"I owe you my life."

"You owe me nothing," Juno replied, picking up a stack of fresh clothes from the coffee table. "Stay, eat, and freshen up."

"How long have I been out?" I asked.

"A few hours."

"I will be back to see you, but right now, I really need to split," I told her.

Juno pulled up at Countess's house, and I ran to the front door. When I entered, I was instantly comforted by the warmth of the furnace and familiar surroundings.

"Hello!" I shouted.

Tommy walked into the foyer and pinched his nose. *"Damn,* you *stank."*

Countess got halfway down the steps and gagged. She covered her face with a handkerchief and pointed at me.

"You made whoopie *at the zoo."*

"Are you drunk?" I answered.

"A barn," she insisted.

"Stop jivin'. Mandatory meeting."

Countess ran down the remaining steps and into the kitchen.

I heard her puking before she stopped long enough to yell, "My nose never lies! You smell like a sweet man, sweaty sex, and a jungle."

Tommy fanned the air. "No, Empress smells like plain ole' *dookie."*

CHAPTER 6
PHANTOM OF THE OPERA

DULCE ELLA MONROE

October 1933 - Chicago, Illinois

I had survived a nightmare, but the Halloween horror of 1933 was far from over. After I brought Countess and Tommy up to speed on what had happened to me, she insisted I stay at her house. Tommy drove me home, only to gather my things for the night, and brought me back to her pad.

I swallowed two more aspirin and shook off the day, pulling myself together to attend one of the most anticipated events of the year.

The only shindig Countess attended without fail since she'd arrived to Chicago as a teen was The Masked Ball. This soirée was held every Halloween and hosted by Noam, a ritzy Jewish millionaire banker. No one had ever seen him without his legendary mask, but he was drop-dead gorgeous even with half his face covered.

At the start of every ball, Noam would come out in grand fashion, greet everyone with a wave, and vanish. At the night's end, he would step onto his balcony before an explosive firework show, lift his hands, and bid us adieu. He would disappear once more, and the grand show would light up the sky. No one would see him again until the following year's ball.

It was my second year attending, but for the first time, I designed our ball gowns and Tommy's suit. I had created Countess a silk and lace emerald ball gown with a golden mask. My gown was designed in purple satin, with the cinched waist bodice covered with black lace, pearls, and amethyst. As a last-minute accessory, I added the hitter's humongous brimmed hat to my ensemble, embellished with ostrich feathers to accompany my mask.

After finally getting myself keen enough to be presentable, I headed downstairs. Countess and Tommy were waiting for me in the foyer.

When I reached them, Countess looked concerned. "Are you feeling better?"

"No, but I'll live."

Tommy looked sharp as a tack in the navy tux and mask.

"What's with the looney's hat?" he asked.

"I'm hoping whoever hired trigger fingers will be at the party, and the hat will get their attention."

"Did you find out anything from the streets?" Countess asked Tommy.

"He's the Roulette Hitter and has been shaking down all the lottery businesses, including the white ones from across the tracks. Whoever hired him is looking to get dough quick."

Countess placed her lace gloves on her hands and smiled. "Whoever hired him is a dead man."

Every year, Noam would create a unique theme and decorate grander than the previous year. The diverse attendees included politicians, artists, rich gangsters, and sixty winners of a public lottery. All invitations were hand-delivered by a masked woman. This year's theme was "Smoke and Mirrors," and I couldn't wait to see the grandeur Noam had in store.

Noam's home was designed in the style of a medieval castle. Made of Midwestern limestone, his fortress was perched on a hill miles from Chi-town's downtown and surrounded by water. He made his domain accessible only from a wooden bridge he kept blocked except for specific times before and after the ball. The front door opened at 9:06 p.m., and he kept the drawbridge open another six minutes before closing it for the night.

We were stopped before we reached the bridge. Masked men collected our invitations and mandated that we wear our masks until we were completely off the premises. One of the men then placed a card in our faces.

"Your car will be waiting for you at the number on this card. That same number is used to identify your table for the fireworks show," he said.

We looked at it as he extended his hand. Then, he tore it up and escorted us to a fancy horse-drawn carriage. We got inside, and our breaths quickly fogged the interior mirrors until our faces were no longer visible. We trotted onto the wooden bridge, over the water, and arrived at the entrance.

Women of all shapes, creeds, and colors were dressed in the most extravagant gowns. Every hairstyle imaginable—from buns, conked waves, and long curls—was used to crown their heads. The men, just as versatile, were styled in classic tuxedos and custom zoot suits. On that one night, if you were invited inside Noam's home, who you were and where you came from didn't matter.

It was 9:06 p.m., and the entrance door creaked. Smoke wormed through the crack until the door swung open. Countess, Tommy, and I stepped inside and onto the floor tiled with cracked mirrors. The same was true for the walls, so no matter where we looked, we viewed our reflections in fragments.

Pale women dressed in sheer, crystal-covered gowns and wearing white pompadour wigs began playing Bach's "Cello Suite No. 1 in G Major." Waitresses in the same attire handed us sweet wine in crystal goblets.

"What do you think Noam wants us to get from this?" Countess whispered.

"I believe Noam is a profound thinker behind that mask," I said.

Tommy gulped his drink. "Or he's a plain ole looney goon motherfucker."

The room was crowded with people, and the music stopped. Dressed in a 19th-century tuxedo, Noam stepped through red curtains at the top of the cascading staircase and onto the balcony. Before he spoke, his eyes shifted my way. Our eyes locked, and I swore I saw life escape him.

Noam looked away, lifted his hands, and said, "Welcome." Then, he departed.

Women covered in sheer leotards flipped from the balcony, holding onto nothing but two red ribbons. Synchronized, they began to twirl like ballerinas. The crowd gasped in amazement as the graceful acrobats pirouetted midair. Noam peeked at me from behind the curtain and ducked away.

Having also noticed Noam's glance, Tommy whispered, "Noam is sweet on Empress."

We headed to the appetizer table, and I grabbed a small plate of assorted hors d'oeuvres.

"I believe Noam is sweet on this hat."

"But he's rolling in dough," Countess whispered.

"I think he had feelings for the Roulette Hitter."

Tommy coughed like he was choking. "Noam's a looney goon *pansy*?"

I hit his arm and took a bite of cake. "If Noam knows who tried to kill me, how do we get to him?"

Suddenly, a bell rang. Men and women dressed as ghosts and jesters lined up with stacks of papers in their hands. We walked over and received maps that led us to the fireworks show. The blueprint consisted of mazes and different exits to the courtyard.

All the lights went out, and the crowd yelped. A woman began singing opera, and like magic, candles lit harmoniously around the room. As smoke surrounded us, the crowd scrambled to find their way out.

"Luckily, I'm an Abercrombie at navigation," Tommy said while studying the map.

My headache returned and pounded against my skull. I exhaled and leaned my head back. To my surprise, hanging above our heads were huge arrows.

I pointed. "Look."

We quickly followed the path and arrived at the courtyard first. Noam was posted on the balcony. Scattered across the grounds were white tables with red rose centerpieces. We found our table located several feet behind a fireworks cannon. We sat down, and when I looked to the balcony, Noam had gone.

Once everyone had entered and were seated, Noam returned, lifted his hands, and said, "Adieu."

The first explosion spread into a pumpkin across the sky. Everyone cheered.

"I have to use the john," I said, standing up.

Countess frowned. "Can't it wait? This show is my favorite part of the night."

"I'll go alone."

Tommy stood up and helped Countess out of her seat. "Hell no. We stay together."

We headed for the commodes, and...*boom!* We turned to see our table ignited on fire. There was another explosion, and Tommy pulled us to the ground.

"Looks like the cannon backfired. Are y'all okay?" he asked.

There was a shrill followed by screams, and Countess, Tommy, and I took off running towards the house. We were out of breath when we made it inside.

"I smell cigarette smoke," Countess said, stopping in her tracks.

Tommy headed towards the front entrance. "Let's split and get the hell out of this spooky house before everybody else."

Countess pulled out her gun and sprinted in the opposite direction. We chased after her. She stopped at the entrance of a long hallway behind the staircase. There was a massive door at the dead end, and we raced towards it.

Before we made it to the exit, someone yelled, "Stop!"

We turned, and Noam was standing there. He flicked a cigarette butt onto the mirror-tiled floor.

"I was hoping I would catch you."

"So did we." Tommy yanked his blade from his ankle. "We know that you know the Roulette Hitter."

Noam turned red and opened his jacket. "Please, I am not armed. Just tell me where you got that hat."

"What's it to you?" I asked.

"It belongs to my brother. He never misses my parties, and he never takes off his lucky hat."

I pulled the jammed golden revolver from my garter belt and raised it in the air. "Your brother tried to kill me with this today. Do you know why?"

"My father had used that gun to play Russian Roulette with us as children until his tragic end. My brother is sick in the head because of it. Please tell me where he is so I can get him help, and I'll tell you everything."

I placed the hammer on the ground. "That is tragic. If you tell me who hired him, I'll give you your daddy's gun *and* tell you where your brother is."

Staring angrily into my eyes, he replied, "I hired him."

I kicked the gun across the floor. "A tiger ate your looney brother."

He quickly picked up the revolver and pointed it in my direction. Suddenly, there was a strident ruckus and loud sound of rumbling gallops. I gasped, and Noam turned. Two screaming stampedes came charging our way from both sides of the staircase. Tommy, Countess, and I did an about-face and bolted for the backdoor. A gun fired. We turned back around, and Noam's body dropped to the floor. Blood pooled around him. The front of the masked herd halted with quickness. The rear tripped and toppled, and their bodies quickly stacked to the ceiling. Tommy, Countess, and I looked into the faces of the hollering pyramid and then turned helplessly to each other. We took one step backwards, shrugged, and jetted out the backdoor.

For the second time, I felt like Dorothy from *The Wizard of Oz* and uttered, "There's no place like home." I was grateful when we finally pulled up to my house.

"Are you sure I can't convince you to stay with me tonight?" Countess asked.

"I'm sure."

I closed my eyes and had started drifting off, when the car door opened. The frosty wind whipped me back to life.

"The coast is clear in your pad," Tommy said.

He helped me out of the car and across the slick pavement. A snowflake fell onto my nose as we made our way to the front door. I looked up, and the snow began to pour like rain.

Once inside, I shut the door and started the furnace. Then, I lit a ciggy and took a long, hot bath. After bathing, I dried off and stepped into my gown, slippers, and fur coat before going to the kitchen to make myself a hot toddy. Then, with the mug cradled in my hands, I went to my bedroom, lit a candle, and opened the window to watch Mother Nature lay a thick blanket over my neighborhood. The streets were calm outside, but I fought to quiet my mind.

CHAPTER 7
SUSPENDED

DULCE ELLA MONROE

November 1933 - Chicago, Illinois

After the ungodly hours of Halloween, a blizzard struck. Overnight, the Windy City was buried under heaps of snow. By the afternoon, temps dipped below zero and froze the city to tons of ice bricks. The radio's newscasters warned Chicagoans to stay inside after reports of frostbitten fingers and toes, numerous car collisions, and frivolous injuries from loonies ice skating over Lake Michigan.

I had trouble sleeping but hadn't left the bed. To busy my mind, I spent the restless hours of the night sewing children's hats, mittens, and scarves to donate to the South Wabash Community Center. Then, my phone rang. When I answered, it was Countess.

"Pack a bag," she commanded.

"For what?"

"We're going to Louisiana."

"Have you looked outside?" I asked.

"A blizzard ain't nothin' but a pile of snow. Be ready in an hour."

I had looked forward to spending the next few days snowed inside, listening to my platters, sewing, and getting dizzy with gin and giggle water. But Countess was not only my friend; she was also my boss. So, whenever she said let's go, I obliged by responding, "Let's go."

She hung up, and I called Meek-Meek. As I'd promised, I had retired her from working for Butta. However, the last time I saw her, she looked worse than ever. Her bobbed-styled wig had become a permanent accessory on top of her head, but the youngest of hairdos did little to eradicate the years' hardness that had aged her decades.

Butta answered. "Butta's Basement."

"Let me talk to Meek-Meek," I insisted.

"I'm not the hoe operator."

"How is she doing?"

"Empress, this is not *your* hoe-spital. So, stop sending your stool canary, Mama Lee, over *here* to spy and sing the songs of my biz over to you."

"Do you want me to stop sending Mama over *there* with your dough?"

I felt his grin through the phone, and he lightened up. "Now you know *hablo moolah*."

"Then stop busting my chops and put Meek-Meek on the phone."

He mumbled under his breath, and seconds later, Meek-Meek whispered, "Merry Christmas, Lil' Empress."

It was the first day of November, but I replied, "Merry Christmas, Meek-Meek. Why have you stopped eating?"

"I've been catching up on years of sleep."

"Please let me move you into an apartment."

"I'd rather stay here with Jonesy."

"I wanted to let you know I'm going to Louisiana for a few ticks. So, if you need anything, call Mama."

She raised her voice. "You're going with a man?!"

"No."

For years, Meek-Meek had voiced her concern that Countess had cast a spell on me and we were lovers involved in a Boston marriage.

She sighed, and I continued, "Tell me what you want from Santa, and I'll make sure you get it before I leave for my trip."

She yawned, *"Peace,"* and hung up.

Countess wanted to fly to Louisiana by airplane, but we'd heard on the radio that all flights had been canceled. So, Tommy, Countess, and I shook a leg from the South Wabash Center—where I dropped off my donations—to the west bank of the Chicago River to Union Station. While stuck in traffic, Tommy tossed the day's newspaper at Countess and me. It landed between us in the backseat.

The headline read:

Noam Levi Zila, known for his ritzy yet riveting
Halloween soirées, left his guests injured from countless freakish
accidents and horrified after his suicide spectacle.
The masked millionaire died penniless.

Tommy whipped his head around. "Like I said, Noam was a plain ole' looney goon motherfucker."

During the entire ride in the car, Countess kept saying she heard a voice inside her head urging her to hurry home. She'd gotten so hysterical that I was worried she had gone looney, too. She finally calmed down when Tommy pulled up to the train station. While the car was still in motion, she opened her door.

"Wait a damn minute! I need to park," Tommy snapped.

She gave him Mama's *"don't fuck with me"* look. Tommy halted and left the Cadillac on the streetcar track. He grabbed our bags, and we took off running. We entered the massive waiting area of the building. It was filled with hundreds of people walking, and they stared as Tommy and I chased the tail end of Countess's fur coat. The interior was reminiscent of an ornate cathedral with an extremely high barrel-shaped glass ceiling.

We dashed up the stairs, pushed through the crowd, and didn't stop until we arrived at the ticket counter. By the time we made it to the agent, we were out of breath. Tommy placed our luggage at our feet, waved goodbye, and faded.

Countess flung her pocketbook on the counter. "Two tickets for the next train to Le Marais Isle, Louisiana."

"There are no more colored seats," the ticket lady said, her red lipstick smeared across her teeth.

Countess rolled her eyes. "Negroes can sit where they want in Chicago."

"That train is going through Jim Crow country, so Negroes sit in the colored section only."

Countess slapped a fan of twenty-dollar bills across the counter. "We'll take a private room in the *green* section."

"I've never done that for a Negro, but that room will cost you four hundred dollars...*each*."

Countess reached inside her pocketbook and slammed another sixteen fifty-dollar bills on the countertop. The woman didn't budge.

The train whistle blew, and the conductor screamed, "Last call to Tennessee, Mississippi, and Louisiana!"

Countess clenched her teeth. *"Tickets."*

The lady fumbled and slowly counted the bills of eight hundred dollars aloud. She then printed each ticket and held them in her hand. When she started slowly stuffing each bill of the extra dough between her breasts bulging from her brassiere, Countess belly-flopped across the counter and snatched the tickets from her hand. The lady froze, and I pulled Countess down as a copper blew his whistle while heading swiftly in our direction.

I took off running with our bags, and Countess followed. The officer blew his whistle again, and the high-pitched sound was louder than before. The train chugged. Countess had passed me and jumped onto the steps. She reached out her hand, and I tossed one of the bags. It landed at her feet.

"Forget the bags, genius," she yelled, extending her fingers. "Give me your hand."

The train gained momentum, and my right hand connected with her fingertips. Our fingers wrapped around each other, but it was hard to get a grip because our hands were dripping with sweat. Startled, I slipped from her grasp after another ear-piercing whistle blew near the nape of my neck.

Countess was gone, but I kept running. The copper was breathing heavily from behind, and his stomps were at my heels. One by one, train cars sped past me.

"*Gotcha,*" a man said.

After a tug at my coat and a pull at my wrist, I closed my eyes.

Completely winded and trembling, I took a deep breath. My vision was blurred from the sweat spilling into my eyes. The perspiration on my skin had become glued to the interior of my fur coat, and it was too heavy to remove. I blinked. I thought I was dreaming. Standing before me was a Negro soldier big as John Henry. He didn't smile or frown. I looked to my left and right, and long wooden benches were crammed with colored folks of all ages who were dressed for church. They also neither smiled nor frowned. Cluttered around their feet were suitcases, bags, and satchels. Their heads were faced forward, but I was side-eyed through their pupils.

My suitcase handle was wedged inside my fist, and I straightened my body upright despite the turbulent sway of the train. The man hoisted me up and reached across me to carry my luggage.

"No, sir, you've done more than enough for me," I said with a smile. Then I placed my bag down and reached inside my pocketbook to remove a handful of bills.

He pushed my hand away and whispered in my ear, "Keep your dough, miss. The look on that cracker copper's face, when I pulled you onboard, is all the payment I need."

A little girl near the aisle snickered, and her mother gripped her hand. I slid the bills into his jacket pocket anyway and another into the little girl's mother's hand. She nodded, and I trudged forward.

Suddenly, a man yelled, "Tickets!"

The hairs stood at attention on the nape of my neck. I sighed, wishing for nothing more than to be home with my platters, sewing machine, and whiskey. A white man was collecting train tickets from the white section of the car. Standing there empty-handed, I thought I would turn and make a dash for it. I searched behind me, but I was in the very last car.

"Swell," I grumbled.

I had already made a comic scene fit for Hollywood, but I realized my performance wasn't over. I kept walking toward the section adjoining the white and colored cars.

"*Tickets!*" he yelled again as we faced each other in the rocky breezeway.

Faint, my brain screamed. *Fall out like a white damsel in distress, but get ready for the impact from hitting the floor 'cause no white man is gonna catch your colored toots.*

I took a deep whiff and braced myself for the dingy wooden panels under my feet. Suddenly, a foul stench drifted into my nostrils from underneath a door to my left. It was the "colored" commode. I could've tried my faint routine, but instead, I quickly opened and shut the toilet door behind me. I knew the ticket man saw me enter, but to my relief, he didn't knock or wait. I exhaled as he walked by, yelling for more tickets.

"*Pardon!*" a woman whispered from behind me in an alarmed French accent.

"*Pardon moi, madame! Shhh!*" I said, hushing her as I reached back inside my pocketbook. "*S'il te plaît, Francs.*"

"*Francs!*" She shrieked with laughter. "*But habla moolah!*"

I swiveled, and Countess was standing behind me with her handkerchief tightly secured around her face. She looked like a glamorous bank robber. We embraced and burst into a quiet giggle.

Before I could utter another sound, she whispered, "Your French is not bad, my friend. Thank God you're here. That ticket fellow looks like he would give a colored gal grief for having a 'suite' ticket, so I thought I'd be safer here until he passed by."

When he went to the last row of the Negro car, Countess and I espionaged our way to our suite, posing as colored French women. We exhaled when we got inside, but then there was an aggressive knock on the door. I opened it cautiously and saw a white butler holding a serving tray of tea and cake.

"May I come inside?" he asked.

Amazed at his politeness, I stepped aside, and he placed the items on a small table next to two red couches facing each other near the cabin's window.

"I'll take your coats," he insisted.

He removed the weight from our shoulders and hung them inside the closet.

"Would you like me to unpack your things?" he asked.

"*No,*" I said, mimicking Countess's Creole accent.

Countess handed him our tickets, but he didn't bother to look at them.

"If you need anything, I'll be down the hall."

"*Merci*," I said.

He bowed. "My pleasure."

He quickly left the room, closing the door behind him.

"Did that white man bow to me?" I exhaled and plopped down.

Countess's mood had returned to melancholy. She sat down and looked somberly out the window.

"My dogs are barking." I kicked off my shoes. "Do you mind if I close the curtain on my side?"

She got up and converted the couch into a bed. Then she closed both curtains. I stretched out and closed my eyes. The train's soft sway and rhythmic chug-a-lug rocked me like a baby. Sleep was a luxury I hadn't afforded in months, so I curled into a ball and drifted to dreamland.

November 1933 - Le Marais Isle, Louisiana

We had left freezing winter and, in three days, entered tropical summer. Countess didn't eat or speak the entire trip. Her eyes had been fixated on images only she had seen. Worry lines had deepened into red streaks across her face, and I was hoping she'd find whatever she needed to find at our destination.

We stepped onto the empty platform. From the unkempt look of the exterior, Le Marais's station was abandoned. Wearing our fur coats, we looked like two grizzlies in the tropics. Countess walked like she was in a state of confusion. When she opened the station doors leading to the town's entrance, I felt we were transported to the 1800s.

As we walked through the backdoor, I was worried we were going to be snatched and sold into slavery under the gazebo. The shops and buildings showed no signs of life. Countess's mouth dropped, and her worry lines deepened into creases.

"When was the last time you were here?" I asked while removing my coat and flinging it over my shoulder.

"Four months ago."

We walked and searched for anything living. We turned the corner at the end of town, and two horses connected to a buggy were parked in front of a long wooden building. A large "Carriage Station" sign was freshly painted across the top. Countess ran, and I struggled to keep up. I had never been so hot in my life; the humidity had me drained and drenched.

We burst through the door of the building like two ditzy dames. An old fellow with a dark, wrinkled face and young body greeted us with a Southern gentleman's charm. He was sophisticatedly dressed in a three-piece suit and top hat.

"You two are the prettiest ladies I've seen in a long time." He placed spectacles over his eyes and stepped in front of Countess. "You're LeRoux's girl."

She pulled out a twenty-dollar bill. "Can you take me to them?"

He fumbled with his words. "I can't…well…I can…but…."

She pointed at the five-dollar fare sign. "I gave you four times the fare."

"Yes, ma'am. I…I can show you better than I can tell you."

Sebastien, our carriage driver, folded our coats inside sacks, carried our luggage to the red buggy, and covered the open windows with a large white net. Once he helped us inside, we took off, rocking and bumping over the uneven road in silence.

"Don't you have a car, mister?" I asked as my fanny slipped on the wooden seat.

"No, ma'am. Everybody travels on foot, bike, horse, and buggy. This town has old wooden bridges that can't support the weight of automobiles."

Our journey away from town started on a muddy two-lane road. On each side of us were giant sugar cane stalks. No one was coming or going. We trotted through an open field that stretched for miles. After crossing over a wooden bridge, we stopped so Sebastien could quickly switch his top hat for one brimmed with a cascading net that covered his body.

The large shadow of a hawk hovered over us as we continued on, and we followed it into a dark forest of tall trees growing from the swamp water. Long vines and Spanish moss smacked against the buggy as we trotted along. Black moths, dragonflies, and monster-sized bugs were flying around us and sticking to our nets. The songs of the swamp were filled with insects hissing, leaves rustling, and birds chirping.

"I'm spooked," I said.

Perplexed ever since we arrived, Countess asked, "Where is everybody?"

Sebastien kept silent as we passed a sign that read "Welcome to Le Marais Isle." Soon, the horses stopped at the edge of a wooden bridge that dove into a body of water that stretched further than the eyes could see. Countess gasped, then let out a scream so horrifying that I thought she was possessed.

Sebastien opened the carriage door. Countess didn't move as tears streamed down her face. I wanted to comfort her, but I didn't know what had her so troubled. She removed a crucifix from around her neck and dropped her head.

Sebastien offered his hand. "Let me help you out, Miss LeRoux."

Trembling, she stepped out. "This can't be true."

"What are those green bushels floating on top of the water?" I asked, exiting behind her.

Sebastien bowed his head. "Those are treetops."

Countess fell to her knees. "*Mon Dieu.*"

With my brain finally processing what I was witnessing, I grabbed her hand and kneeled beside her. Le Marais Isle was entombed underwater.

"*What happened?*" she shrieked.

"Late on the eve of Halloween, we heard a loud *boom, boom, boom*," Sebastien explained. "By the time we figured out what had happened, Le Marais was underwater."

"*Who would do that?*"

"The State's been looking for a way to expand the southern port to the Mississippi, and I guess those crackers said Le Marais was in the way."

My heart twisted into knots. "Why hadn't we heard of this in the papers? And what's being done about it?"

"The same thing that's been done for the other Negro towns desecrated to the ground."

"Did anyone make it out?" I asked.

"Not one soul. I stick around to drive folks here to pay respect to their kin."

"*When will this country stop killing us?*" Countess sobbed.

With the sun setting, Sebastien said, "I need to take you ladies back before the bugs eat us alive. Please join my family for supper. You can stay with us for the night."

Countess stood up and wiped her face. "We ain't scared of bugs." The saddened look on her face disappeared, and she spritzed us all with a citrus-smelling bottle she snatched from her pocketbook. "Also, you can leave our things, Sebastien. We are staying here."

"*Where?*" he and I asked shockingly.

"We thank you for bringing us, but we need our bags, please." She handed him another twenty dollars. "Come back for us…"

She paused and closed her eyes. "…when the sun and moon face each other at dawn."

Countess's mumbo jumbo had me convinced she'd lost her mind, and I didn't know how to respond. I had seen her face of conviction before, so I knew no one would be able to change her mind.

"Miss LeRoux, your people have become lost souls. Folks who stay here at night don't come back."

"Our bags, please, and thank you," she told him, then turned to me and said, "Let's go."

I nodded. "Let's go."

CHAPTER 8
I'M ON MY WAY

DULCE ELLA MONROE

November 1933 - Le Marais Isle, Louisiana

I loved nightfall, but there was a haunting difference between the city's "heat of the night" and the country's "dead of the night." I feared the latter. Countess and I were standing so close to the water's edge that I could hear the fish quivering in their scales. The screaming waves created a vicious presence that had me feeling like death was upon us, but Countess's gaze was fixated beyond the horizon. We hadn't spoken since Sebastien had departed.

Earth's light switched off, and our dark atmosphere got darker. I searched for the moon and stars, but Mother Nature had covered us with a blanket of fog. I lit the lantern, and suddenly, a winged shadow hovered over us. I looked up, but nothing was there.

I grabbed Countess's hand. "What was that?"

"That ain't shit but an owl."

I reached inside my purse and lit a cigarette. "The country stinks."

"That's fresh air, city girl."

I took a puff. "Countess, what are we doing here?"

"Waiting."

"For what?"

"My daddy."

I was convinced Countess had lost her mind. Knowing everyone dealt with loss differently, I stayed by her side and hoped we would be lucky enough to make it through the night.

"Feels like we're waiting to die," I mumbled.

Mosquitoes as large as fireflies hovered over our heads, buzzing like hornets. Picking up Sebastien's net, I stretched it over us like a cage.

"I know bites from these mosquitoes swell to the size of an orange."

Countess chuckled. "Those ain't shit but crane flies. They don't even bite."

A black swarm of bugs nipped at our net. When I lifted the lantern to see more clearly, I hollered.

"*Flying cockroaches?!?*"

"Those ain't shit but water bugs. Turn off your lamp, and they'll leave us be."

"Do you have anything for itching?" I asked.

She looked down to search her pocketbook, and I hollered again.

"*Countess! A baby alligator is crawling on your shoulder!*"

She sprayed me with peppermint oil before grabbing its tail. She placed the creature on my neck and cracked a smile.

"This ain't shit but a lizard."

Its cold, slimy body crawled up my face and onto my cheek.

"Stop jiving and get this *thing* off me."

She extended her hand. It scampered up her arm, and she played with it like a toy.

"We used to throw these on each other when we were kids," she told me, smiling.

"I prefer Chicago, where we kill bugs and rodents with swatters and traps."

I lifted the net and tossed the cigarette butt into the water. As we sat quietly, water splashed on our faces.

I laughed. "Let me guess. That ain't shit but a jumping fish."

She pressed her pointer finger against her lips and blew out the lantern's flame. Then, she tightly gripped my wrist and eased backward. From the strength of her hold, I could tell there was something more dangerous than a fish in the water.

I grabbed hold of her hand, and after a few more steps, she screamed, *"Run, Empress!"*

We took off, and she slipped. I reached and pulled her up. That's when an alligator leaped from the waves. It swung its tail and soared like a dolphin. I yelled, nearly breaking my vocal cords, and the gator landed perfectly where we had been sitting. We took off again as it humped towards us. I turned my head, and the alligator was scurrying like a roach, nipping at our heels.

"That sucker is fast," I yelled, and we picked up the pace.

Countess stopped and huffed. "The coast is finally clear."

"That was scary," I said, placing my hands on my knees to catch my breath.

But then, something told me to turn around. When I did, I saw the alligator a few feet away, snapping its jaws. I took one step back and pulled Countess's arm.

"It's right behind us," I whispered.

She yanked away. "Please, Empress. An alligator ain't shit when it's tired."

I sprinted towards the trees. "Camille Broudair LeRoux, I'm burnt toast."

"Come back! Where are you going?" she yelled from behind.

"Chicago!"

She caught up to me and tugged my arm. Suddenly, there was a buzzing sound ascending from the water. Countess and I turned to the sea, and a glowing light was coming our way. She dropped my arm and sprinted towards it.

"Daddy."

I didn't care who it was. They had a boat, and I was willing to be anywhere but where we were.

We made it to the dock, and standing inside a motorboat was a handsome man dressed in a light blue suit. He had cayenne pepper and salt-streaked hair down his back, a beautiful smile, and a deep Creole accent.

"Hey, baby girl. Give me some sugar and keep the boat steady while I grab your things."

"Dulce and I will toss them to you," she smiled excitedly. "I knew you were coming."

Confused, I asked, *"How?!"*

After he had all the bags, he helped her inside and grabbed her face. He kissed each cheek and threw his arms around her.

"I'm glad your heart is still connected to me." He stuck out his hand to assist me inside. "Dulce, I've heard much about you."

"Nice to meet you, Mr. LeRoux. I'm glad you're alright, but *how?!"*

The wind and water licked our faces as the boat jetted over the waves. A gentleness smothered the screams of the sea, and the sounds of the ocean were more like a ballad. Since the fog had cleared, the stars reflected as diamonds floating over the tides. Countess stood beside her father, and the breeze sent their strands soaring like flames. I was a spectator in the backseat, about to witness one of the greatest miracles I would ever see.

We arrived at a V-shaped peninsula; the bushes seemed to part like gates. We pushed through a maze of trees that had grown upwards from the water. At the path's peak, we passed through two freshly bloomed magnolias trees. A short pathway of palm trees led us into a dark cavern lit by torches. Cascading with ecstasy from the cave's center was a waterfall. We sailed around a large wooden pirate ship with *Nouveau Jour* faintly painted on the bow. Once we came to a stop, he roped his boat to a pole that read *Welcome to LeRoux Palm Isle.*

CHAPTER 9
FEELING GOOD

DULCE ELLA MONROE

November 1933 - LeRoux Palm Isle, Louisiana

The year before Le Marais Isle had gone underwater, Countess's mother had seen it happen. Mr. LeRoux was mayor, and Mrs. LeRoux was known for having God's gift of prophecy. So, when she told him what she had seen in a dream that night, he sold their estate and bought a cheap, tiny island located on the heel of Louisiana's boot. After he purchased the land, he and his brothers surveyed it. At that time, it was covered by trees, wildlife, and *Nouveau Jour*, a shipwrecked transatlantic slave ship.

Mr. LeRoux's brother was an architect and began designing a new town on the island. They solicited a trusted group of men and secretly built it using materials they had said were for Le Marais.

One year later, on the eve of Halloween, the newly appointed mayor from a white neighboring town and a group of state officials came to Le Marais Isle to discuss the southern port expansion. When Mr. LeRoux introduced them to Mrs. LeRoux, she fainted. While she was blacked out, she said God revealed to her their devious plan to blow up the levee that night.

As soon as the men left, Mr. LeRoux called a mandatory town hall meeting and told his people everything Mrs. LeRoux had seen. He also told them she had seen everyone make it out alive, but only if no one told a soul until she'd given the word. Moving on faith, each person quickly packed two bags and boarded *Nouveau Jour* like Noah's Ark. An hour later, the levee was blown up, and Le Marais went underwater.

After Mr. LeRoux finished telling the miraculous story, Countess and I followed him to the top of the cavern and stepped outside. Brightly ablaze before us was a bonfire. Dancing joyously around the flames were men, women, and children with chocolate skin of various shades. Rainbow-colored umbrellas were twirling, different patterns of skirts and men's jackets were blowing, and all styles of boots and shoes were shuffling. On a small stage were two men—one playing the accordion and the other creating music with his metal vest. The songs were sung in French, but the beat was so electrifying that I didn't notice the language barrier.

Waiting at the door was Mrs. LeRoux, unmistakably because she was a sophisticatedly aged version of Countess. She raised her red umbrella over her head and smiled.

"Bonjour, mes amours," she said, greeting us.

Countess ran into her arms, and they lovingly embraced. After our introductions, her mother grabbed our hands, and we jitterbugged our way to long tables filled with dishes of gumbo, turtle soup, crawfish etouffee, grilled alligator, and beignets.

Unplugged from America's Depression, I was able to commune with Negroes exhibiting no signs of pain, fear, or oppression. The band sped up the music's rhythm, and my body responded without thinking. Then, one of the most gorgeous men I'd ever laid eyes on grabbed my hand. He had the perfect face,

and his head was crowned with thick black hair. His bushy brows
and long lashes brought out the brightness in his eyes. In his other
hand, he held a tan cowboy hat.

He bowed and asked in his Cajun accent, "Can I have this
dance, miss?"

"Can you keep up with a city girl, country boy?"

He spun me around and smiled with a foreign enchantment.
"I'd like to try, *mon chéri.*"

We stepped twice to the left and twice to the right, and he
spun me around again. With his chest pressed against my back,
he tightened his grip around my waist. I swayed my hips, and he
joined.

Sexily, he wrapped my arms around his neck and whispered,
"How am I doing, city girl?"

I was melting in his arms. "Just swell."

He spun me around and led my body into a dip. "That's 'cause
I ain't from the country, baby. I'm from the swamp."

I closed my eyes, and Perry swooped into my daydream. He
pressed his bare chest against my body and whispered, "Hey, Miss
De Leche."

I gasped. Perry's image faded, and the beautiful swamp man
was standing before me.

"*Qu'est-ce qui ne va pas, mon chéri?*"

"*What?*"

He stroked my face. "What's wrong, my darling?"

"My...my legs are tired."

"We can split. Do you drink whiskey?" he asked.

"Can an alligator fly out of the water?"

We laughed as he scooped up a jacket from a chair and
grabbed one of the torches from the party. Then we walked hand
in hand towards the cavern, descending a dark path next to the
cave along the way.

"I don't want to go into the wilderness, mister. I've seen enough wild animals and bugs tonight."

He smooched the palm of my hand. "Please, call me Dumas."

I smiled. "My name's Dulce."

"Miss Dulce, you're in good hands. Trust me, I'm taking a beautiful lady to a beautiful place."

We stopped at the opening of a tunnel and walked inside. It led us behind the cascading waterfall I'd seen earlier.

"Dumas, this is the prettiest thing I've ever seen."

He leaned in. "Are you...sweet like the translation of your name?"

Removing two cigarettes and a lighter from my pocketbook, I replied, "I'm more of a vicious vixen covered with sugar."

He turned my chin, and we locked eyes. "Can I have a taste?" he asked.

I placed my hand on the nape of his neck and gave him a slow, sensual kiss. He was a great kisser, but he didn't give me goosebumps.

Our lips departed, and with a big grin, he removed a flask from his jacket pocket before we sat down.

I placed a cigarette in my mouth. "It's so damn clean up here, maybe we shouldn't smoke."

He lit a fire to our cigarettes and exhaled. "I do it all the time."

We each took a swig of whiskey. I removed my embroidered handkerchief from my pocketbook and dapped the sweat dripping down his forehead.

He touched my wrist and examined it. "That's exquisite. Where did you get it?"

"I made it."

"DM are my initials, too," he said.

"What's your last name?"

"Monroe."

"No fooling?"

He laughed. "No fooling, *mon chéri.*"

"What if we're related?"

"My parents are Negro and Creole from France," he explained. "What about yours?"

"Negros from Africa."

He touched my face. "That means if you marry me, you won't need to change your name."

We kissed, and again, I liked it, but my heart didn't flip flop.

I couldn't help but notice *Nouveau Jour.* Seeing it and knowing what it was used for was aching me deeply. I closed my eyes, and tears cascaded from my soul.

"Do you feel the spirit?" Dumas asked, and I nodded.

He wiped my tears and held me in his arms.

"The ship's interior was left as Mayor LeRoux found it," he explained. "He wanted us to see the chains bolted to the stained floor. Small enclosures were throughout the ship, with metal cuffs hanging from the ceiling. Beneath us was a crawl space with hundreds more chains lined up on the floor. The pain and blood etched into the wood were like ancient hieroglyphics stabbing into our bones. The night we heard the explosion, all anyone could do was cry. Ever since that moment, we've been celebrating God's glory in gratitude for our freedom and lives."

November 1933 - LeRoux Palm Isle, Louisiana

I woke up feeling heavenly. The scent of sweet peppermint and lemongrass romanced my nostrils. My muscles were relaxed inside a warm cloud of sheets. I yawned, sat up, and looked over at Dumas, stretched out on a chair.

"It's still night, *mon chéri,*" he said, rising from under a blanket.

"I don't remember anything we did after you told me your story."

He walked over and kissed my forehead. "That's because you fell asleep in my arms. Camille brought your bags and changed your clothes. Are you hungry?"

"Just coffee, if you have any. And thank you for trusting me with your experience. I know how sacred that was."

He brought over a cup and sat next to me. He didn't have to say a word; I felt his feelings through his eyes. I touched the soft skin on his cheek, and he planted the sweetest kiss on my lips. He was a fine gentleman. I only wished I was a different type of woman who felt the same way.

I kissed him back. "Thank you for everything."

Getting on his knee, he kissed my hand. "Stay with me, Dulce, and be my wife."

"Dumas, I can't," I replied, even though his words had melted my heart.

"Why not? I would dedicate my life to loving you and taking care of our family."

"I don't want that kind of love."

"Every human deserves to be loved, Dulce."

"I want to go where I please, when I please, how I please, and with whoever I please without asking for permission."

He placed his hand against my face. "*Mon chéri*, who hurt you?"

"Dumas, you are going to make a keen dame *very* happy."

"I want that dame to be you. You came into my life like an angel."

I snickered. "I'm more like Medusa, baby."

He ran his finger across my lips, and we kissed again.

"I'm not scared of Medusa. She was a beautiful dame before the pain of her past turned her into a monster. I believe the right kind of love could've changed her back."

The love in his eyes pulled at my heart. He caressed my face in his hands, but a thunderous knock interrupted the moment. He looked disappointed as he went to open the door. It was Countess, standing there with a smile on her face.

"Hello, Dumas and Dulce. I hate to interrupt, but Dulce, let's go."

I nodded. "Let's go."

After a hot bath and dressing in fresh clothes, I felt like a new dame. I walked into the living room where Dumas was sitting in a kingly-sized chair. Next to an oil lamp, he was reading Langston Hughes' *The Weary Blue*.

"I love that book," I said. "His poetry touches a part of me I can't describe."

He stood up and walked over to me. "Are you sure you can't stay with me, Miss Monroe? I believe I can heal that wound in your heart."

"I believe that's true. But it's the bugs and alligators that are driving me away, not you."

He grabbed my bags, and we took the scenic route to the LeRoux house. Torches lit the streets, guiding us past the majestic palm trees and countryside houses. LeRoux Palm Isle was a fantasy island in the center of the swamp.

We stopped in front of a baby blue and white two-story house surrounded by an outdoor balcony and tall columns. Dumas walked me to the door. As he held my hands, we started kissing. The sky was turning lighter, and the moon wasn't moving.

I reached inside my pocketbook and placed the handkerchief with our initials in his hand.

"I have to go, Mr. Monroe, but I promise I'll never forget you."

"They say you never forget your first love." He pressed the cloth against his lips. "And you're forever in my heart, Miss Monroe. *Au revoir, mon chéri.*"

When I walked inside the house, Countess sniffed around me and said, "They didn't make whoopie, but Dulce is sweet on Dumas."

Mrs. LeRoux was shuffling around in the kitchen lit by oil lamps. "Dumas is sweet on Dulce," she laughed, "but Dulce likes a different kind of jelly on her roll."

I couldn't deny the shrill that came from inside of my core. "Is Mr. Jelly from my past or future?"

"And what about me, Mama? Where's my Mr. Jelly?" Countess asked.

"I'm not telling either one of you anything. Knowing can change your path."

Their family mystified me. "Mr. LeRoux, how did you tell Camille you were coming?"

"I don't want to spook you, Dulce," he replied.

"The only thing that spooks me in Louisiana is the swamp at nightfall," I said with all seriousness.

"Well, I've been told I can reach people through their thoughts, but it's not consistent, and I can only reach those closest to my heart."

Smoke from two pots on a firewood stove sent sweet aromas around the room. Countess walked over and took a whiff.

"Tea tree, lemon, eucalyptus, cinnamon." She sniffed again. "Rosemary and something unfamiliar. What ailment are you curing?"

Mrs. LeRoux poured us each a small shot glass of the elixir.

"Drink. There will be a flu and scarlet fever outbreak that will wreak havoc in the country." She then poured a spoonful from a small bottle into my mouth. "You will need extra protection, Dulce."

"What about me?" Countess asked.

"You're fine."

There was a knock at the door. Thinking it was possibly Dumas, I followed Countess to answer. Instead, there was a pretty, powdered-sugar-skinned young lady with thick, black wavy hair, emerald eyes identical to Countess's, and pink pouty lips. She had one hand on her hip; the other held a suitcase.

"Camille, I'm coming with you," she demanded.

Countess snapped, "*Non, vous ne l'êtes pas.*"

"*S'il te plaît?* I want to go to the city. I'm going *folle.*"

"Stop it. You are not going crazy," Countess said, then kissed her cheek before turning to me. "Dulce, meet my little cousin Orin. Please tell her Chicago is hell."

"She's right, Orin. This place is much better."

"Stop treating me like a child," she whispered. "Let me work for you, *Countess.*"

Countess pushed her out of the door. "Don't say that name out loud."

"Why? You should know better than anybody that Auntie is well aware that you and *Empress* are gangsters."

"Go home, Orin. I promise I'll send for you to visit when Mama says it's safe. *Je vous aime.*"

Countess kissed her again, but before Orin departed with disappointment, she whipped around and told her, "You're gonna need me."

Her statement perplexed me.

"Orin sees the future?" I asked when Orin vanished into the shadows.

"She knows the past."

It was dawn, and the moon was still facing the sun over the horizon. Before we left LeRoux Palm Isle, Mrs. LeRoux gave us all specific instructions. Mr. LeRoux took us back to the mainland, and as instructed, Sebastien was waiting next to his buggy. When he saw us arrive by motorboat, he removed his hat and fell to his knees.

After we told Sebastien everything that had happened to the people of Le Marais, he was instructed to spread the word. The story made its way through neighboring Negro towns, and colored engineers and architects volunteered to design and build a bridge connecting LeRoux Palm Isle to the mainland. Sebastien created a new transportation company to take families and friends back and forth across the water by boat and carriage.

Countess and I had shaken a leg back to Chicago. Once back home, Countess contacted Juno to get the name of the ambitious attorney she had used for her case, and he expedited deserved justice for the citizens of Le Marais. He and a team from the NAACP worked with the government to provide immediate electricity, gas, and resources to LeRoux Palm Isle.

Sadly, though, the attempted massacre never made major headlines, and the case against the mayor, state officials, and everyone else involved never made it to court. As retold by white folks, the near tragedy of Le Marais was reconstructed as a mythical Negro folklore. White folks had convinced non-spectators that the town's downfall was the result of God's "natural disaster" instead of the "dirty deeds" of the devil.

CHAPTER 10
BLUES FOR MAMA

DULCE ELLA MONROE

October 1934 - Chicago, Illinois

Like the memorable year of 1933, Indian Summer departed on the night of my birthday, and Mother Nature released the hawk, freezing hell over the Windy City. And on that icy Halloween in 1934, I buried Meek-Meek.

High rollers and strollers from the midnight streets and red-light district used the untimely occasion to put on a fashion show. Our sins, camouflaged by expensive animal skin, spoke for us. All the sexy, cunning felines like Countess and Juno wore fox. The quiet humpers like Jonesy wore sheep. For the elegant, like Mama Lee, Russian sable. The gangsters and predatorial pimps had wrapped themselves in wolf.

Butta was shivering next to me, knocking his knees together like maracas.

"I'm going to miss Meek-Meek. She was loyal." His teeth chattered loudly. "Damn, this new Alaskan sable ain't worth a dime. I'm still cold."

"That's because you're wearing skunk, not sable," I whispered.

"Empress, no fooling?"

"No fooling, Butta. Your coat is made of *skunk* fur."

Pastor Elliot raised his hands in the air. Meek-Meek had loved Pastor Elliot's Easter sermons, even though Resurrection Day was the only day she would go to church. Respected members of his congregation had made a fuss about the sinful stains we'd leave over the saints in the church, so Meek-Meek's service was banned from being held inside Elliot's church. But once I slid extra dough into Pastor Elliot's love offering, he agreed to perform Meek-Meek's eulogy outside the sanctuary.

"We are all sinners in need of a Savior," he bellowed.

"Yes, Lord! Hallelujah!" the choir of gangsters, molls, pimps, and whores shouted.

Pastor shouted back, "Audrey Meek-Meek Monroe is gone too soon!"

Amens echoed through the wind.

I agreed with him. I knew Meek-Meek had an untapped life inside her, but she hadn't set it free. My heart ached as he spoke, and tears slowly dripped from my eyes. Always on time, Mama used her warm handkerchief to ensure they wouldn't become icicles.

Jonesy had found Meek-Meek comatose next to an empty bottle of sleeping pills. And that morning, Meek-Meek and I had just talked about how our lives were about to change. I had hoped our transformation would happen together, but she chose an eternal life in dreamland—the only place I'd seen her face rest peacefully.

After the service, Butta tried to maintain a cool stroll next to his stable as he wobbled towards me and tipped his hat. "Countess, Juno, Mama Lee."

Enchantress growled at him.

"Cool it, kitty," he growled back. "I ain't scared of you." When she crouched down, he smiled. "There ain't no pussy I can't control."

I shook my head. "Butta, stop jiving around before Meek-Meek haunts you."

"I ain't scared of no damn ghost." He handed me a sealed envelope. "Meek-Meek left this for you," he said, then turned and dipped off with a frozen limp.

Countess, Mama, Juno, Enchantress, and I slid into an all-white limo and rode in silence.

Tommy, who was driving, took his eyes off the road long enough to turn around and ask, "Is everybody going to the repass?"

"Take me home."

Mama protested. "Dulce, sugar, this is not the time to be alone."

"I want to read Meek-Meek's last words," I told her. "I'll come by the house later."

She squeezed my hand. "Okay, sugar. We'll be there waiting."

My life had drastically changed in the last year, and I needed time alone to recalibrate. I had watched Meek-Meek wither, and when I'd thought she was ready for a new beginning, she ended her life.

Mama's longtime boyfriend, Ready, had come home from the Army, and I'd been spending more time at her house than ever, stitching and increasing my responsibilities at her nursery. Until then, I had been Countess's second lieutenant since she'd taken me under her wing, but I was demoted because I lost focus on her operation. No, I hadn't forgotten that my aspiration was to become an international fashion designer. I just got myself stuck in a quick-sanded funk.

Through my record player, Lucille Bogan sang "Drinking Blues." I poured a glass of hooch, lit a Lucky Strike, and slid onto the gold settee in my bedroom. After a deep exhale, I opened the letter Meek-Meek had written me.

October 29, 1934

Dear Lil' Empress,

Don't sing the blues for me, 'cause I'm no good. I'm tired of existing and ready for whatever the afterlife has in store for me. Thank you for always pushing me to be better. I was never deserving of your love, and once I confess why, I pray you forgive me.

I ain't your real mama. I stole you from a family at Provident Hospital. I was visiting a friend who'd just retired from the street life. She told me one look from her new baby had turned the darkness in her hardened life into bright sunshine. Her new glow gave me hope.

After I left her room, I prayed for that same happiness from a child. Then, I overheard a doctor say a Negro woman from Gary, Indiana, was doing bad. She'd just had emergency surgery and was unconscious and alone. The woman had been expecting one child, but the doctor told the nurse he had delivered two babies. He thought his patient wasn't going to live to see them. I thought that was a sign from God. I thought God wanted me to save one of those babies because I'd just prayed and asked for one.

You were wrapped in a white blanket like an angel. I chose you because you were the most content baby I'd ever seen. I grabbed you from the hallway and hid in the broom closet. You stayed quiet, and I had convinced myself you were mine while you lay asleep in my arms.

Then, your daddy showed up, tall and stately like W.E.B. Dubois. He was dressed in a navy blue factory uniform, so I assumed he worked at the steel mill. When he got there, your mama miraculously woke up.

The nurse came out searching for you, and when she couldn't find you, she called another nurse to help her look. They

*were frantic, and your daddy came out to see if everything
was okay. The nurse smiled and handed him your twin. I
overheard the nurses in the hallway swear to keep your
disappearance hidden.*

*When I left that hospital, it was the happiest day of my life.
I know it was a horrible thing to do. I was selfish, but I
wanted to feel real love from someone. I quickly realized I
was already too damaged and broken to feel loved. I'm so
sorry I took that perfect life away from you.*

*Lil' Empress, you've always been smart and talented. I'll rest
in peace and dream you'll have a family like the one I stole
you from. Please take my advice. Quit hustling, and use your
brains and good looks to get you a man who loves hard. You
deserve a happy ending.*

Love, Meek-Meek

My hands were trembling, and I got dizzy. Every emotion
imaginable raced around my body. Questions were screaming inside
my head, but no one was there to answer them. Through my falling
tears, I reread the letter repeatedly, and the words chipped away at my
heart like an ice pick. Before it shattered, there was a knock at the door.
I cleaned my face. "Who is it?"

"It's me, *mon amour.*"

In the doorway was Matthieu LeBlanc, a fine vanilla-
skinned French man I had met at the same record store where I'd
encountered Perry. Matthieu was tall and slender-built, with jet-
black wavy hair, thick eyebrows, and the sexiest French accent. He
had impeccable style and always wore new designer shoes.

Matthieu was devotedly in love with me. When I had asked if
he'd really marry a Negro dame, he'd said he didn't see color. Each
month for the past three months, he had dropped on his knee and

opened a velvet box with a huge diamond, and all three times, I declined his marriage proposal. He'd brought up Josephine Baker and how we would be accepted in Paris as husband and wife, but I didn't love him like that. Yes, I liked him, but he deserved true love. We got along as the perfect couple, but regardless of his color, I couldn't see myself married.

Matty—my nickname for him—was a wealthy investor who moved from Paris to Chicago last year. We loved jazz, blues, classical, and opera music. Matty shared my fashion addiction, art taste, and most anything, so we would spend hours together talking.

"Hello, Dulce." He kissed me with his soft pink lips and handed me a bouquet of flowers. "So sorry for your loss."

"Thanks, Matty, baby."

I brought him a cup of tea, and he looked into my eyes. "Dulce, darling, I'm moving back to Paris. I miss my home."

Knowing what he'd say next, I waited for him to ask me. I would say yes, but only as friends. I was ready to get the hell out of Chicago.

Then, he said, "And Dulce, darling, I'm not asking you to come with me since you've made it clear I'm not the man for you."

He had asked me countless times to go to Paris with him, and when I was finally ready to say yes, he didn't ask. I laughed out loud.

He smiled. "What's so funny?"

I shook my head and lit a cigarette. "Nothing, Matty. When are you moving?"

"As soon as I can get rid of this horrible investment property I bought in Indiana."

"Why did you buy something there?"

"When I first moved to Chicago, I heard Gary, Indiana, was booming with immigrants looking for steel industrial jobs. The property has been vacant all year, and I can't give it away."

I felt the universe shift.

"Matty, I'll buy it from you. How much are you selling it for?"

He smiled and wrote down the address. "We can go tomorrow so you can take a look."

I shook my head. "I don't need to see it. I'll take it. How much?"

He took my hand and spoke with his loving eyes. "Happy belated birthday. *Pour toi, mon amour*, one dollar."

"A checker?"

"*Oui.*"

"I need to hear you say it."

He smiled again. "I'm offering you, *mon amor*, Dulce Ella Monroe, my darling, the Indiana property for one checker."

"*Oui*, Matty!" I screamed. "I'll take it."

November 1934 - Chicago, Illinois

Two days later, Matty and I walked into First Chicago Bank with his accountant. I paid him one dollar bill for his property and, as a bonus, one quarter for his brand-new 1934 Mercedes Benz Trossi Roadster.

Outside the bank, we embraced, and I handed him a box. He smiled while opening it. Inside were a royal blue tie, handkerchief, and scarf I designed for him. He handed me his address in Paris and heated my body, iced from the windy hawk, with a steamy kiss.

"Dulce, if you ever want to visit me in Paris, I'll send for you. And think about moving, please. I truly believe the Parisians would love you and your designs."

"Thank you, Matty, for everything. I'll write you every week."

After another warm kiss, he walked to his limo. His wavy curls blew in the wind, and he flashed his gorgeous grin one last time. My French vanilla beau would make some lucky broad very happy, but she wasn't me.

His chauffeur, Charles, tipped his hat, and they drove away.

November 1934 - Gary, Indiana

On Interstate 94, it took fifty minutes to get from South Side Chicago to Gary, Indiana. I exited Broadway and was surrounded by green fields covered with snow.

I left Hell, Illinois, for Nowhere, Indiana, I thought to myself.

I drove over rocky railroad tracks and looked around. Throwing snowballs in the middle of the street was a group of Negro children dressed like cute Eskimos.

"Car!" they yelled.

They scrambled alongside my car with sweet faces and waved. I kept driving, and like magic, crowds of nicely dressed colored folks appeared on both sides of Broadway, strutting in and out of various shops. I passed a large food market, barbershop, hair salon, and several clothing boutiques. Streetcars passed by on rails, coming and going on each side of the road. I continued down the street until I stopped in front of a red brick, three-story building tightly nestled between a fancy theater and a large church. There were only a few windows and not a single sign hanging outside. I looked down at the address Matty had given me and then up at the building again.

Exiting my car, I stood with my hands on my hips. "I'll be goddamn."

I opened the door to go inside and almost had to cover my ears from its loud screeching. Dust mites swarmed in the air, and I inhaled cold, musky air. My steps echoed as my heels tapped on the smooth wooden floor. My breath was icy from the chill when I exhaled in awe. Above my head was a gold chandelier and the balcony of the staircase.

I screamed and danced around my empire. For one dollar, I was standing in the middle of a new hotel lobby.

CHAPTER 11
B*TCH BETTER HAVE MY MONEY

DULCE "EMPRESS" MONROE

May 1938 - Gary, Indiana

Lady Luck was back in my life, and until Memorial Day weekend, 1938, I'd been on a four-year winning streak. Gary, Indiana, had turned out to be my "Little Chicago," and because it felt like an extension of Chicago's South Side, the city's rhythm was easy for me to master. I'd built a chocolate empire in my new home away from home, which had thrived despite the woes of the Depression. Since moving there, I'd been on cruise control, not realizing turbulence was waiting to rock my world.

I was headed to The Palace, the hotel I purchased from Matty. It welcomed colored folks traveling through the Midwest and offered them a comfortable yet luxurious place to stay. If only for one night, I wanted Negroes to feel like royalty in my hotel. The Palace was also the mask for my underground gambling—"numbers"—enterprise. Seduced by the sexiness of power, I ignored Meek-Meek's advice about the fleeting effects of fast money, and the idea of owning a fashion boutique became a distant thought.

America was rebounding from the calamity of the Depression, but Negroes still had it bad. Gary surged in population like the rest of the industrial cities in America, and employment for whites, including European immigrants, was picking up steam. Negro Americans, on the other hand, were holding their breath in the fumes. Colored sharecroppers in Jim Crow's south didn't receive a penny of Uncle Sam's New Deal, so many of them had gotten displaced and migrated north. The promise that federal debt relief would be guaranteed to all farmland owners didn't apply to anyone with a hint of color because Uncle Sam had left Jim Crow in charge of funneling state funds. Didn't Congress know that giving racist states the power to divide a financial pie between Blacks and whites was like leaving Lucifer in charge of sending souls to heaven?

No relief for the Negro farmers had forced them to abandon their crops. White farmers, protected by their New Deal, raped Negroes of their land with governmental backing. So, colored southerners relocated to cities like Gary, looking for work, but found they'd better get behind American whites, European immigrants, and northern Negroes before they would be considered.

And like Countess's mama envisioned, sicknesses hit the country. Because it was common for seven people to share one household in Negro neighborhoods, when one person got sick, everyone got sick. So, every Negro in America had gotten some illness amidst the Depression.

Scarlet fever and influenza had spread rapidly, and with hospitals overflooded, Negroes were forced to stay indoors, cover their faces, and place "sickness" warning signs on their doors, hoping to see their ailments through. Luckily, Mrs. LeRoux knew I would need extra protection and had given me a dose of her elixir.

So, in a desperate need for Negroes to spread out and find refuge, Gary became Chicago's little sister and was given the nickname Little Chicago. Identical to The Windy City, factory employment competition was high, and jobs were scarce. Steel mills started rehiring white folks, and slowly, trickles of colored folks were back to working the menial jobs whites had left behind. Thankfully, I'd been trained by Countess, and my business was one of the only in the city hiring Negroes.

Ready, Mama's longtime boyfriend, was my driver and the lieutenant of my organization. Always dressed as a distinguished gentleman, his attire consisted of a three-piece suit, top hat, and cane. He and Mama had met when she was touring on the road, and he was an off-duty Army officer. They became an item when they were young but, for whatever reason, had decided not to marry. He'd been honorably discharged from his duty because of his diseased kidney and had been a permanent civilian for the past five years.

We pulled underneath the twinkling lights of The Palace's sign. The hotel had twenty rooms, ten of which had private bathrooms. The rates started at one dollar per night or five dollars per week.

Chicago's South Side hotels frequently sold out. The Palace, located only forty miles away, provided quality service, comparable accommodations, and lower prices. It was also marketed in the Negro Motorists Green Book, which informed colored people that they had an unsegregated place to rest their heads while traveling. With Gary located within a few hours of Cleveland, St. Louis, and Louisville, I couldn't have asked for a better business model.

The Palace also extended extra services that couldn't be printed on advertisements. Beloved, my childhood friend who was also a madame, leased five hotel rooms indefinitely for her ladies' services, and I received twenty percent of her nightly earnings.

Mama ran her home nursery and managed entertainment in the hotel speakeasy in the basement. Since Prohibition had ended, a full-service bar and small stage were made available to the hotel guests on the weekends. Also in the basement was our stash house. Treasure, my other childhood friend and Beloved's sister, helped manage the hotel's financials and underground operations. Her husband, Philly, worked as the stash house manager.

My empire netted $30,000 annually, making The Palace the most prosperous Negro-owned business in Gary. We had police protection for four years, and until the city appointed the new mayor, Dan Dunstan, we'd been untouched.

Mayor Dunstan was white and stood slightly over five feet. He had stringy brown hair with strands snatched over the bald spot on top of his head. As a reputable boxer, stylish dresser, and athletic build, he gained instant popularity with his gift of gab. He had charmed the city with his jovial "play-hard, work-harder" rhetoric, but they quickly learned he played much harder than he worked.

After Dunstan was sworn in, he pulled into city hall with a brand-new, all-white Rolls Royce Phantom and driver. In a short time, he'd purchased a plot of land to build a new mansion, bought another fancy car, and updated his wardrobe to high-end designer labels while Gary's progress had stalled. With Dunstan being known to make shady deals under the table, our city was now under the rule of one of the most crooked mayors in the country. But he would have to kill me before I'd bow down at his feet.

Ready got out of the driver's seat and opened my door.

He gave me his arm. "Empress?"

I smiled and nodded. "Ready."

He and I walked inside the Victorian-style lobby, which was filled with guests in town for Memorial Day weekend. Mama worked at the front desk during peak days and always greeted everyone with a smile. We walked over, and she gave us a cautious grin.

"Good morning, Empress and Ready. Mr. Conan is here to see you."

Eddie Conan, known as Irishman, and one of his goons were standing stoically against the back wall. Irishman was tall with thin legs like stilts, a round beer belly, blonde hair and mustache, and greenish blue eyes. He was the leader of Gary's Irish mob. Like me, he'd been a young apprentice under one of Chicago's head mobsters and had relocated across the Indiana state line to start his own business.

His numbers and gambling operation mirrored mine but was on the opposite side of the tracks. With the thousands of European immigrants who had moved to Gary for job opportunities, his business was also thriving. We'd both capitalized on our niche markets, but our paths had never crossed before that day. He had stayed on his side of the tracks, and I'd done the same.

Ready whispered in my ear, "What does that cracker, Irishman, want?"

"Money for that cracker, Dunstan; I'd bet my last penny," I whispered back.

We walked towards them, and Irishman stepped forward.

"Good morning, Miss Monroe. Can I have a few minutes of your time?"

"Follow me," I told him.

We walked down the short hallway. My office was a small room with a dark wooden table and a custom purple and gold chair. Irishman sat in the brown leather seat across from me. His goon and Ready stood on opposite sides of the closed door.

"What can I do for you?" I asked.

"Miss Monroe…"

Ready interrupted. "Her name is Empress."

"Empress," he clarified, "I'm here on behalf of Mayor Dunstan. He said he'd spoken with you about his new business tax, and I'm here to collect."

"Did that new forty-percent rate apply to your business?" I asked.

"That's not your business."

"And my business isn't your business, but here you are. Tell Dunstan I'm not giving him *a penny* above what I gave Mayor Clay, which was more than reasonable."

"Unfortunately, Empress, Dunstan made your business my business. So, you know how it goes if you refuse to pay up."

Ready opened the door. "You know how it goes if you threaten someone in their own house."

Irishman stood up to leave, but before walking out, he turned to me. "I advise you to get ready, toots."

Ready placed his cane across the doorway, blocking their exit. "I stay Ready, *toots*."

Ready removed his blockade, and they left peacefully. As we followed them into the lobby, I balled my fist.

"Get Philly and Treasure. Mandatory meeting."

We conducted meetings in the basement stash room, which had no windows and was dimly lit by two lamps. We maintained security in the basement twenty-four hours to protect the safe and lottery slips. The walls and floors were dark, and the limited ventilation created a musty smell of mildew and old cigarettes.

"How in the hell do we battle the city mayor and Irish mob at the same time?" Philly asked after I relayed the conversation Ready and I had with Irishman.

"We strategize," I answered. "Good news is, we're smart and nimble."

"Agreeing to his terms would break us," Treasure chimed in.

"That's right. That greedy cracker wants two hundred and fifty dollars per week, roughly half of our profits. That will only be the beginning until he kicks our black fannies onto the street."

Ready nodded. "Now that he's using the Irishman for muscle, we need more soldiers, and I know who to get."

Philly cleared his throat. "Dustan also put the squeeze on the coppers, so they're no longer allies. Two officers keep post outside of Bobby's barbershop and harass our runners for information. Luckily, the hidden pockets you stitched inside their trousers keep the slips concealed, but we need a new place for folks to place orders."

"We don't want to confuse our customers," I said. "Philly, put a doorway between Bobby's barbershop and Mae's hair salon. Mae's customers have been complaining about going into a barbershop to place their bets. We'll also use Mae to take orders."

"Are you sure you want to hire a dame bookie?" Ready asked.

"Yes, old man. Welcome to the 1930s. And I want dame runners. We need the coppers off our tail, and they won't expect it. Treasure, stop by Mae's and get her onboard."

We adjourned with the perfect start of a perfect plan, but I should've known perfection was the devil's illusion.

After the meeting, I headed outside for fresh air. On my way to the front door, I heard a deep, unfamiliar voice.

He grabbed my wrist. "Dulce Ella Monroe."

"I don't know you, mister," I said, snatching my hand away.

From behind, Ready smacked the man's arm with his cane. "Keep your hands to yourself, nigga."

The mystery man put both hands in the air. "Hey, I'm sorry. Dulce and I are from the same neighborhood. I'm Leon Krosser."

I examined his face, and under the smooth, dark skin and well-groomed beard and mustache, I saw the boy with the long, nappy brow I'd beaten up when we were kids. Still tall but stocky, he flashed a perfect smile, and I smiled back.

"Yes, I do remember you," I recalled.

Ready looked suspiciously while Leon and I embraced. It had been a long time since I'd felt the intimacy of a man's touch, so his body lit my flame instantly.

"You're quite a looker. All grown up, Lil' Empress."

"You're plenty rugged yourself, Leon."

I touched Ready's hand when he reached between us. "Cool it," I told him.

Ready backed away, keeping his eyes locked on Leon. Mama walked over and took Ready's hand. He grumbled, and they walked away.

Leon and I went over and sat on a sofa in the lobby and laughed about old times. He'd left South Side shortly after our childish encounter because his father had died.

"I'm sorry to hear that. I know it was hard to lose your father as a child. What brings you to Gary?" I inquired.

"I'm on my way to Cleveland to visit a family member," he replied, then stroked my face and asked, "What do you say, pretty lady? Let's fade?"

I nodded, and he grabbed my hand. We headed towards the lobby door. When he reached for the knob, Ready popped his wrist with his cane.

"She has a driver," he said.

"Cool it," I ordered again.

"Alright," Ready continued, "I'll trail you."

"*Ready*, take the rest of the day off and spend it with Mama."

He frowned as Leon led me to his red Cadillac. Ready was still on our heels and stopped at the curb.

"That old man is something else," Leon whispered while opening my car door.

I waved my hand out of the window. "Go find your woman, Ready."

He was still standing there when Leon took off.

I placed a fresh ciggy inside my cigarette holder, and Leon immediately pulled out his lighter. He put a flame to it, and I took a puff.

"Thank you, daddy."

"Do you want to take a trip down memory lane and stroll through our old neighborhood?" he asked.

He had already driven in the opposite direction, but I didn't care.

"Hell no. I don't go to South Side unless I have to."

"Swell. I wasn't going to take you there anyway."

He sped past Gary's factories and steel mills, which served as the city's backdrop. The clouds from the tall smokestacks turned the blue sky grey. Then, Leon's perfect smile disappeared, and his face and jaws stiffened hard as a brick.

I sighed and blew smoke in his face. "Where are you taking me, nigga?"

"I'm a punk, remember?"

"I didn't forget, blabbermouth."

He took a sharp right into a warehouse parking lot. The car screeched as its weight shifted onto two tires. My body slammed against the door, and my cigarette fell out of my hand.

"You're the blabbermouth," he spat with tears mounting in his eyes. "My daddy died because of you."

I struggled to regain my balance. "What in the hell are you talking about?"

"You had him murdered in Butta's Basement."

I closely examined Leon's face and suddenly recognized his resemblance to the stank-breath, unibrow blimp who had lurked into my room when I was a little girl.

"You've got it all wrong. I was a child, and your daddy was a grimy pedophile."

He slammed the brakes, and my forehead smacked into the dashboard.

"You're a *liar*. And Dunstan wants his money today *or else*."

My vision was blurry. "You better take me back to my hotel *or else*."

We glared at each other, and I punched him in the kisser.

Grabbing a fistful of my hair, he yanked me towards him and said through gritted teeth, "You're not tough."

I took my hand and searched my lap for my fallen cigarette.

"What kind of man puts his hands on a lady?" I asked.

He tugged harder at my scalp and pressed his lips against my ear. "You're no lady. You're a goon and always have been, so I'm handling you like a goon, goon."

I stretched my fingers to the limit, and finally, the tip of my pointer finger made contact with my cigarette holder. I latched onto it and quickly smashed the lit end into Leon's eye. He yelped and released his grasp. I reached for the door handle. My fingers wrapped around it, but before I could open it, he snatched my hair again. My neck popped, and my head whipped onto his lap. His burnt eye had swollen shut, and he wrapped his arm around my neck.

"Not so fast," he said while I struggled for air and pulled at his forearm. "Instead of taking an eye for an eye, I'm gonna slash your foul kisser."

I fought to break free, but he tightened his hold. My breath was escaping my lungs as he revealed the blade of his pocketknife. He pressed the shank behind my ear and slowly began to draw a line under my jawbone. Screaming, I slid my fingertips inside my garter belt and wrapped my fingers around the grip. With my pistol finally locked in my grasp, I aimed behind me and quickly fired. Instantly, a surge of oxygen laced with gunpowder entered my chest. I looked up and screamed again, and Leon slumped over me. Trapped beneath his weight, I slid my back against the driver's side door and used my legs to thrust him towards the passenger seat. Covered with blood and yelling, I fought for composure. My hands were unsteady as I gripped the wet steering wheel.

Placing the car in drive, I hadn't noticed a long, white Rolls Royce sitting idle a few feet away. The driver and I exchanged shocked glances before he quickly reversed. When it swerved around, I caught Mayor Dunstan's weaselly face.

Lost in a vengeful trance, I safely rolled into The Palace's back entrance. Pistol drawn, Philly walked cautiously towards Leon's car. When he saw it was me, he sprinted inside, and within seconds, he returned with Ready and Mama. Ready opened my door and was holding a bucket and sack when I looked up. After bandaging my neck, Mama wiped the blood from my face and quickly undressed me. She placed my clothes in the sack and covered my body with her coat and hat. Philly pulled behind us with my car and helped me get inside. Ready sped off in Leon's car with Mama and I trailing closely behind. When we got to Broadway, we turned left, and Ready turned right.

The next morning, I woke up and heaved. I leaned over, and Ready was there holding a trash can. He handed me a wet cloth as I hurled.

"Killing isn't ever easy, even if it's done in self-defense," he said.

I rolled over and spent the entire day in bed. The distorted image of Leon's face was haunting me. I'd seen death at the hands of another, but it was the first time I had pulled the trigger. And because of my chosen path, I was self-assured it wouldn't be the last.

I rose before the sun the following day. Unsure of the time, I stepped onto the balcony. The sky was a dark shade of purple, and the only glimmer of light was from the fireflies surrounding me. A warm breeze licked my lips as I blasted the record "La Bohème."

Ready walked up next to me. "Are you okay, Empress?"

"Not really, but I'll live."

"I already told Mama I'm taking Dunstan out. I don't have long to live with this bad kidney, so killing him would be an honor."

"No, Ready. I'm hiring a full-time bodyguard and the extra soldiers you suggested."

"I'm the only bodyguard you need. I knew that nigga was no good, and I won't allow a slip like that to happen ever again."

I grabbed his hand. "I know, Ready, and you'll always be my lieutenant. But I want you to spend more time with Mama. Killing Dunstan in retaliation will start an instant war, and we aren't prepared for battle…yet."

"*Battle?* My small brigade killed hundreds of German soldiers in World War I, so getting rid of a measly mayor and one flake of the Irish mob ain't shit."

"I respect you and everything you've done in your lifetime, but I need you to listen to me. Do it for Mama. She always puts the needs of everybody ahead of herself, and she deserves to be loved by you for as long as she can."

He grumbled and muttered, "Fine, but I need to approve this bodyguard nigga first."

"Of course. I've already arranged a meeting with Countess. She has a guy she says she trusts with her life."

Ready and I pulled up to Countess's house. I hadn't seen her in a tick because she'd just been released from the slammer.

Tommy answered the door. When we walked inside, Enchantress purred against my leg.

"Empress, Countess is mad as hell at you," Tommy warned as he closed the door.

Before I could respond, Countess was charging down the steps, dressed glamorously in cabaret high heels and wearing a handkerchief around her face like a bandit.

"I should kick your ass for having Juno deliver this stinky cat off at *my* pad, Empress. This is not a zoo."

"It won't be here long. I need Enchantress's instinct to sniff this nigga for evil before we hire him."

"My nose doesn't lie either. Trust me, my guy Snipes Creed is solid….and he's a plenty-rugged *fine* gent."

"*We* don't give a damn how he looks," Ready snapped.

I smirked. "Speak for yourself, old man."

CHAPTER 12
CHICAGO FREESTYLE

PERRY "SNIPES CREED" SAVAGE

June 1938 - Harlem, New York

I thought my life was as good as it was going to get. Five years ago, I had forgone my naive soldier fantasy as a devoted family man and formed a longtime affair with Harlem, my city of refuge. I had planned to never leave. Harlem had become the perfect moll for a gangster like me and had provided a sweet haven from the Georgian claws of Jim Crow, where I'd spent my enslaving childhood in the America that Uncle Sam had deemed the land of the "free."

The southern scars from the cotton boll had etched blisters under the skin of my hands and would never let me forget where and how far I'd come. While working the cotton fields, my five brothers and I had always heard stories of Harlem and how it would be the city of our dreams. So, after my parents died, we packed up and arrived as teenagers, enlisting in the United States Army. Upon arrival, it was even more glorious than we had imagined. One brogan onto 125th Street off the Harlem Railroad, we knew our tattooed wounds from the south would be the only souvenir we'd keep from our rural hometown.

There were six of us, and after we completed our service, we were honorably discharged and started our unwelcome journey back into civilian life. There was no work or respect for Negro servicemen in America, especially during the Depression. After scaping our dough together to rent a one-bedroom pad with no running water or private toilet, my brothers and I had chosen to build our own enterprise, ignoring the shackled laws of Uncle Sam for coloreds. My eldest brother, Major, quickly finessed and hustled his way into the underground streets and founded our Savage legacy—an illegal gambling business. My brothers and I vowed to protect it and each other from the womb to the tomb.

I'd always been a loner and sworn protector of the family. So, they weren't surprised when I told them I was ready to start my side hustle but would remain a statued fixture in our family legacy.

I started a side gig as the man who niggas—white or Negro— hired when they needed someone to do the jobs they couldn't do. My hands got filthy on most jobs, so when I wasn't working, I would take a couple of days off to drink, listen to platters, and confess my evil deeds to God. Then, I would write down my transgressions before I shook a leg to the next gig, where I'd get dirty all over again.

I had gotten the name Snipes from being an expert marksman in the Army. The name Creed was given to me because I didn't accept any contracts that would require me to harm a woman or child. I was most notoriously hired for my espionage capabilities to plant and extract evidence on patsy jobs. And with an increasing number of gangsters battling for the same territory, I had been booked solid and busy.

But I had no biz lined up for the first time in a long time. I didn't like idle time and had quickly grown tired of shucking and jiving with my brothers, so I had planned to spend the evening with a hot dame I would spend cold nights with. However, while on my way out the door, I received two calls within one hour, and both jobs were within one-hour driving distance from each other. So, I canceled my date, packed a bag, and shook a leg twelve hours to fulfill both contracts in the Midwest.

June 1938 - Chicago, Illinois

The Windy City was one of my favorite towns to visit, especially in June because of all the blooming trees that lined South Side's streets. I always stayed at Southway Hotel and never left the city without spending time in a record store where I'd met a gorgeous doll who had infiltrated and exfiltrated my life like a spy.

She had given me the privilege to access her loving innocence, and I had given her my heart in totality. But in the end, she left me with a *"Dear Perry, fuck you"* letter, and every time I visited Chicago, I'd prayed I would bump into her so she could return the love she stole from me.

June 1938 - Gary, Indiana

After a couple of hours of shut-eye in the hotel, I drove to Gary, Indiana. I had never been there before, but from all the white faces I was seeing, I knew I wasn't on the Negroes' side of town.

I waited at the gas station for the instructions for my first gig. Not wanting any attention, I kept my head down and my ass planted inside the car. Irishman, a mobster I'd done a couple of jobs for, walked over and knocked on the window. Then, he opened the passenger door and placed a leather briefcase on the floor. After he walked off, I reached over and opened it. Inside was one thousand dollars for a patsy job, twice the dough I charged for planting evidence.

I crossed back over the railroad tracks, going in the opposite direction on Broadway in Gary, Indiana. Big green fields were on my left and right. Driving through the hills reminded me of the country, and I had ill memories. After my car rocked over another set of tracks, I finally saw colored folks walking on the streets lined with Negro shops and dives.

According to Irishman's instructions, I turned left at a dark brown church and right on Washington Avenue. I confirmed the address and pulled into an empty alley behind the skinny three-story brick building. I slid through the open window and felt like I was inside a cellar as I passed the water heater, black furnace, and boxes stacked with records and books. With my hand on my pistol, I crept up two flights of steps that yelped like a cat in pain. I opened the door on the top floor, which led me directly to the kitchen. I inhaled fresh lemon and roses. A bouquet of fresh flowers was in a crystal vase against the yellow-painted wall. On the right was a swanky library surrounded by Negro artwork.

This nigga loves to read, I thought.

Across the hall was a sewing room with two sewing machines, reminiscent of a smancy French boutique. Fashion magazines and drawings were on a table, and a pair of knickers and a pageboy hat hung on the wall.

The décor throughout the house was very feminine and smelled like a garden from all the fresh bouquets in each room. As I perused, I kept thinking this man's dame had exquisite taste. I was intrigued by who they were, which was a gigantic violation of my profession. But the harder I tried to deny my curiosity, the more I was dying inside. I began to search for a glimpse of their lives in photographs, but there were only colored paintings on the walls from artists.

I slowly opened the creaking door to the bedroom, which was more lavish than any other room. I peeked inside the closet, and oddly, there were no men's clothes—only elegant, expensive-looking dresses. Right away, an intoxicating scent of sugar cookies and roses sexed my nostrils and sent me soaring to Miss De Leche. Images of her smile, body, and face flashed before me like a film. I tried to shake her off, but I couldn't escape whatever spell she had placed me under.

I walked to the dresser, and there was a huge wooden jewelry box filled with expensive jewelry. Next to it was a golden and crystal cigarette holder that matched my lighter

Could it be her? I asked myself.

My heart rate was pulsing out of control. I'd never gotten distracted at a gig, but I couldn't help it. I went back to the living room. A record player was next to a rack of records on a long table. For kicks, I went through the records in search of "La Bohème," but it wasn't there.

I laughed at myself for getting worked up. I searched the house for a man's presence, and there was none. There was children's clothing in the sewing room, but no toys or signs of a child living in this home. The mark for this patsy job was a dame who lived alone. So, it was obvious that Irishman had dishonored my creed by hiring me to incriminate a woman. No one had ever crossed me. Therefore, I had to devise a plan to make him pay for the disrespect. It needed to be done without including my brothers or starting a one-man war with the Irish mob.

I did another sweep to remove any trace of my presence. On my way out of the bedroom, I noticed a small record player on the nightstand. I tried to talk myself out of looking inside, but the essence of the house had Miss De Leche written all over it. My hands were sweating inside my gloves as I slowly lifted the top. Under the spinner was "La Bohème".

Seeing that record took my breath away, and I sat down at the foot of her bed. There was no turning back. I needed to see her again, and in order to do that, I needed to know her real name. I walked straight to the kitchen and began searching inside the kitchen drawers. I came across a stack of letters from Matthieu LeBlanc from Paris, France, addressed to Dulce Ella Monroe. My mind started racing, but I had been inside her house too long. I ensured I put everything back inside her drawers in its original place and crawled out the basement window.

Once outside, I jumped into my car and sped off to Chicago to get the details of my second gig. I had to stay focused. I needed the distraction, and Countess LeRoux was one of my favorite clients and people.

June 1938 - Chicago, Illinois

I arrived at Countess's doorstep, and Tommy greeted me at the door. We chatted as he escorted me to the sitting room. Countess was the only client I'd ever had a personal relationship with; she was my eldest brother's dame. They were sweet on each other, but with them running separate operations in two major cities, they were unwilling to relocate. For a long time, they had kept their long-distance love hidden, but Major and Countess were easing their way into the limelight in Harlem.

Countess was sitting on the sofa and drinking tea. She smiled and rose out of her seat.

"Snipes, you're early as usual."

I walked over, and we embraced. "When Countess says let's go, I say let's go. What's shaking?"

"A job, but it's not for me, and it's much more involved than what you're used to. But I believe your services and their pay will be mutually beneficial."

I didn't like surprises, especially the way Countess sprung her biz on me. But my brother had told me that he trusted her with his life, so I trusted her with mine.

Still irritated, I asked, "Who is he, how long is the job, and how involved is it?"

She shifted her eyes behind me. "*She* is my trusted friend, and I'll let her give you the details."

As I turned around, Countess said, "Snipes Creed, meet my good friend and fellow queen pin, Empress."

It was like time had stopped. Empress was Miss Dulce De Leche, and she was more gorgeous than I remembered. She was so sexy dressed in all black that I couldn't help but smile.

Her eyes traveled from my eyes down to my feet.

"Ritzy rags and shoes you're wearing," she said.

I bit my lip to hide my cheesy grin. "Thank you, and your dress is breathtaking."

Countess walked next to us and cleared her throat. "Do you two know each other?"

Dulce gave me her hand. "I've never met a *Mr. Creed*. Nice to meet you."

I kissed the delicacy of her skin, and her sweet scent melted onto my lips.

"The pleasure is all mine, *Empress*."

I had so much to say and wanted to be angry, but her longing eyes wouldn't let me. She had missed me, and I believed I had confessed I missed her more without uttering any words.

I felt a large animal rub against my legs. I thought it was a huge dog, but when I looked down, it was a black tiger. I staggered backward and almost fell over. My heart leaped out of my chest.

"What in the *hell*?"

Dulce laughed. "Meet Enchantress, Mr. Creed. She works in my organization, and this pussy can detect unruly savages who wish me harm."

Enchantress purred against my leg, and I smiled. "Looks like that pussy knows there's nothing unruly about me."

Dulce bit her lip and stepped forward. "When can you start, Mr. Creed?"

I stepped closer. "I'm available whenever you need me, Empress."

She smiled. "You're hired."

From the hallway, a male voice shouted, "No the hell he ain't!"

I turned to the doorway, and an older man dressed like he was going to the opera was walking towards us. He created space between us with his cane.

"I don't know you, nigga. So, you need to interview."

Dulce moved respectfully out of his way. I had no clue what the job entailed, but there was no way I wasn't getting hired to be near her.

I extended my hand to the man. "I'm Snipes Creed, sir. Let me know what service you need, and I'll work up a proposal by morning. We can discuss it whenever you're available."

He gave a firm handshake. "I'm Ready, Empress's lieutenant."

Ready looked familiar, and I studied his face. Then, I recalled seeing him in old photographs from comrades.

"Are you *the* Ready Clark from the World War I Harlem Hellfighters?"

"I am."

I saluted with respect. "Sir, you are a legend. I served 1930-34."

"At ease." He studied me, and his stiff stance softened. "Come by The Palace Hotel in Gary, Indiana, at 08:00 hours tomorrow morning. Empress owns the place, and we need security detail and a bodyguard for her."

"Yes, sir. I would like to come by the hotel this evening to scope the place. I'll book a room if that's okay."

Dulce strutted in front of me. "When you stop by the front desk, I'll make sure you get the largest suite with the private bathroom, and it's on the house."

I bowed. "It was a pleasure, Empress and Ready. I'll come by in a couple of hours." I turned and hugged Countess. "Thanks for referring me."

Dulce and her tiger followed me to the door where Tommy was waiting. I stepped outside, and immediately, sweat exploded from my pores. I was being pulled between two jobs, and the doll who had stolen my heart was the culprit in the middle.

CHAPTER 13
LOVE ON THE BRAIN

DULCE "EMPRESS" MONROE

June 1938 - Gary, Indiana

As Ready drove us back to The Palace, he broke my trance with a loud snap of his fingers. "*Empress*, when are you going to tell me how you know that goon Snipes Creed?"

"I don't know a Mr. Creed."

"Then he'd *better* control his googly eyes if he wants the job."

I knew Perry's eyes weren't just googling. They told me how much he had missed me, and my eyes confessed the same in return. Every ounce of me had missed every ounce of him, and he was a delightful sight for my sore eyes.

The odds that we would reconnect the way we had only meant one thing—Perry Blair Savage was unequivocally meant to be with Dulce Ella Monroe. But the soldier I had met five years ago had become Snipes Creed, and Empress didn't know a Mr. Creed. So, as far as I was concerned, he and I had just been formally introduced.

Later that night, Mama, Beloved, and I were sitting at a table near the stage at Mama's Blues, the speakeasy joint in The Palace's basement. Alberta Hunter, a blues singer Mama had toured with, stood center stage. She began serenading us with "Two Cigarettes in the Dark," and couples got up to dance.

The club was packed, and glitzy broads and gents dressed in glittery gowns, spiffy rags, and zoot suits were gliding across the floor in a Negro's rendition of the tango. The window fans, operating at top speed, struggled to erase the haze of the humidity in the atmosphere. The flames on the candles twinkled like small cosmos, setting the perfect mood for dirty dancing. The smell of fresh flowers mixed with cigarettes and whiskey was an aphrodisiac to me, and my body swayed like the ocean.

Beloved smacked my arm. "*Who* is that fine fellow?"

Mama smiled. "*He's* sugar's man."

Perry walked down the stairs like he owned the room. He stopped and conversed with Ready and Philly. He looked directly into my eyes and tipped his hat with a smile. I shivered as tingles raced from my thighs to the tips of my toes.

As I remembered, he looked like he'd stepped off a fashion runway in Harlem. He looked the same but was more reserved and had aged like fine wine.

"Mr. Creed is *not* my man. He's interviewing for a job."

Mama squeezed my hand. "Sugar…"

Before she finished speaking, Beloved shrieked, "He definitely knows *you*. Look at how he's looking at you."

He strolled over in his three-piece suit and stood in front of me. "Good evening, ladies." He tipped his hat. "Mama Lee, Empress, and…"

"My name is Beloved."

"Nice to meet you, Beloved. I'm Snipes Creed." He extended his hand to me. "Empress, would you dance with me?"

Beloved pushed me towards him. I gripped his fingers, and he led me through the crowd. He stopped at an open space in the middle of the floor and spun me around. Then, he placed one hand on my waist and took my hand into his.

He moved my palm against the back of his neck. "Purple is definitely your color, Empress."

His fingertips ran down my arm and ignited flames that hardened my breasts against his chest.

"Purple is my favorite color."

"I remember," he whispered. "And you're still the most gorgeous doll I've ever seen."

"*Me?*"

"Yes, *you.*" His lips got closer to my ear. "You still smell *so damn good.* Was Countess LeRoux the Creole friend who whipped up that spellbinding perfume?"

"Come again?"

He spun me around again and placed his warm lips against my ear. "You heard me."

His hands interlocked with mine, and he held me tightly in his arms. Our bodies swayed like a river, and with each movement, I was drowning. My back rested against his chest, and my head fell on his shoulder. I closed my eyes as his arms secured me against him.

His lips grazed the back of my ear. "What happened to your neck, doll?"

"What?" I asked in a daze.

He repositioned my curls and gently loosened the scarf I had wrapped around my neck.

"You have a fresh scar. How did you get it?"

"I was attacked."

He quickly spun me around to face him.

"*What?*" His body stiffened, and anger replaced the softness in his eyes. "Did Irishman send him?"

We stopped dancing, and I inquired, "How do you know about Irishman?"

"I'm going to be the man guarding your body, so it's my job to know all the lowlifes in town."

I gushed with anticipation, and we returned to our sensual dance.

"I'm most certain our city mayor, Dunstan, was behind it, but I killed the man he had sent."

"Now I understand why you had a .22 strapped to your thigh."

I didn't respond, and he led my body into another sexy sway.

"*You* were the actual gangster and not the daughter of one."

"Excuse me?" I asked.

He stopped dancing and held my face in his hands. "When are you going to stop running from me?"

I got ready to throw myself around him and confess how much I'd missed and needed him in my life. My lips parted, and he waited with anxiety written over his face. Suddenly, he pulled me to the ground and covered me with his body. He took out a pistol and fired one shot. Simultaneously, another gun had gone off from across the room. Everyone screamed, and then the room filled with deadly silence.

I sniffed fresh gunpowder and looked up. Smoke was snaking from Perry's barrel. Ready was across the room, and the tip of his cane was smoking like a shotgun. Two colored goons were bloodied on the ground next to their pistols.

"Not today, motherfuckers." Ready snubbed the dead bodies with his cane and then pointed at Perry. "Snipes, you're hired."

Perry helped me up and motioned for Mama and Beloved to crawl over to us while everyone else scampered around us in a panic. He led us to the backroom, and Philly was waiting at the door.

"Empress, are you still strapped with that .22?" Perry asked.

"Always."

I released the detective special from my garter belt. Mama and Beloved stared at us. Perry handed the pistol in his hand to Mama, and he removed a pocket pistol from his ankle strap, giving it to Beloved.

"If a stranger comes in here, shoot with no hesitation. Mama Lee, stay by the back door. Empress, near the front, and Beloved, stay in the middle. Hold tight. I'll be back in a tick. Don't open the back door for *anybody*."

He was leaving empty-handed, and I grabbed his wrist. "Wait. Don't you need a weapon?"

He winked and pulled two large handguns from under his vest.

"They don't call me Snipes for nothing," he said, then knocked on the door and spoke through the crack. "Philly, I'm checking the back alley and outside perimeter while I sweep the place. The ladies are strapped and in position."

"Cool, Snipes. Alberta Hunter's security has already gotten her out of here."

When Perry ran out of the back door, I deeply exhaled. Beloved and Mama cleared their throats.

Beloved grinned. "Snipes Creed is *definitely* your man."

Mama stood at the door with her pistol. "He's no stranger either, sugar."

"*Mama*," I pleaded, "I do not know a Mr. Creed."

Her eyes narrowed with suspicion, but she didn't say anything.

Beloved whipped her hips around like she was churning butter. "From what I saw on that dance floor, y'all know each other *very well*."

Mama began to sing Bessie Smith's "Need a Little Sugar in My Bowl" while Beloved pretended to make whoopie to the table. Mama rolled her shoulders with each beat as she belted, *"I need a little sugar in my bowl...a hot dog between my rolls."*

We erupted into laughter.

Philly knocked on the door. "You dames are having too much fun."

After thirty minutes, Perry came inside and quickly escorted me, Mama, and Beloved to my car in the back alley. Ready was in the driver's seat, and once Perry secured the exit, we sped off. I turned, and our eyes met. He tipped his hat with a sexy grin.

Mama whispered more of Bessie Smith's tune. *"Mmm...a little sugar in my bowl."*

We crackled like hyenas, and Ready swerved. "Y'all scared the shit out of me. What's got you broads all dinghy?"

Mama touched his neck and hummed. "Nothing, papa."

June 1938 - Gary, Indiana

Early the next morning, Perry requested a meeting. Ready and I walked through the busy lobby and entered the speakeasy in the basement. The place was spotless and smelled like fresh laundry.

"Ready, this place looks better than it did before."

"Snipes told me to hang back with your mama and eat my sandwich while he took care of everything."

He released a smile I'd never seen from him, and I smiled, too.

"Ready, are you impressed with Mr. Creed?"

"I admit, youngblood takes care of business with a silkiness I think is smooth."

Philly opened the stash house door, and I stopped at the doorway. Perry was standing before me, and at the table behind him were four strange men. Two of them greeted Ready with a love much thicker than blood, and the other two looked my way but didn't move. They were all dressed sharp as a tack in nicely tailored suits.

"Empress, can I meet with you outside for a quick tick?" Perry asked.

I followed him to one of the tables by the stage. He pulled out my seat.

"Good morning."

I sat down and crossed my arms. "Good morning."

"I don't like surprises, so I know I should've given you a heads-up about the visitors before the meeting."

"Yes, you should've, but I understand. You stayed up all night and cleaned up the place, and it looks mighty keen, Mr. Creed."

"All the men in the room arrived before dawn from Harlem, and I wanted you to meet them before you saw them working. Bear, the big one, is your full-time bodyguard. Next to him is Geese, and he's going to be a part-time lookout. The other two are Harlem legends, Tony and Red, who fought by Ready's side. All of us are loyal, skillfully trained for combat, and willing to die for you."

"I hired you, not some Bear, to be my bodyguard."

"The only way I can guard your body is if I protect your entire empire."

I was instantly covered with goosebumps. "Next time, check with me before you bring new people into my organization."

He stood up and offered his hand. "Understood, but my objective is to keep your mind and body at ease. So, I need you to trust my judgement when it comes to doing my job."

He spoke with a gentle firmness that gave yet demanded respect. He was waiting for an answer, and I nodded.

"Understood, Mr. Creed."

We walked inside, and he got straight to business.

"The men who attempted to shoot up the place last night were members of Leon Krosser's gang from St. Louis. They had gone rogue, but luckily, their new leader is a loyal comrade of mine and assures there won't be any more issues. Any questions?" He turned his focus to me. "Empress, you are welcome to hang, but I was going to lay out the specifics of my security plan to ensure you are not compromised again."

I got up to leave. "Catch me up later. I trust you, Mr. Creed."

Over the following week, Perry and I exchanged long, unbroken glances, but neither of us had brought up the memorable night from our past. Every morning, he would tip his hat with a sexy smile. I'd brush against him in the hallway, and he'd secretly graze the skin of my hand. Our pre and post-team meetings had become intimate sessions where we would joke and talk for hours.

One afternoon, Butta unexpectedly strolled through the lobby door unannounced with a new gold cane and green top hat. He had a new stable dressed in fitted, candy-colored flapper dresses. They didn't get within fifteen feet of me before Bear stopped them.

"He's okay, Bear," I said, then greeted Butta with a smooth five. "You walked in here looking like a leprechaun at the end of a rainbow. Where's Joncay and the old crew?"

"They're expired and retired. So, out with that crew and in with the new."

"What brings you to The Palace?" I asked.

"I need a few minutes with you and Ready."

Ready was just about to take a break to eat one of Mama's special sandwiches. He had a sandwich at least three times a day and got grumpy whenever he was interrupted from eating.

Butta, Bear, Ready, and I headed toward the basement while Butta's female crew waited in the lobby for him to return.

When we reached the basement door, Butta sneered at Bear, "Just the three of us— Empress, Ready, and me. No one else."

Bear growled, and I touched his arm. "Cool it, Bear. I've known Butta all my life."

"Yeah, cool it," Butta fired. "'Cause I don't trust no *new* niggas."

"You cool it, too, Butta," I said. "He's doing his job."

We walked through the door, and Bear slammed it shut. At a corner table, Butta spilled the bee's knees with disdain on his face.

"Empress, after one of my girls was done humping one of Irishman's goons, she overheard him on the phone, and he said, 'That Harlem nigga better hurry up and take Empress out, or Irishman is going to take him out.'"

My heart jumped out of my body. *"What?"*

"That's right. One of your new niggas is a stool pigeon, and I bet it's that nigga Snipes Creed."

Ready tossed him a wad of dough. "Thanks, Butta."

He stuffed the cash into his sock, making his ankle look swollen. "Anytime. I'll see myself out."

He left, and Bear jogged down the steps.

"Get Snipes, and shut the door behind you," I snapped.

Ready cocked his cane. "I can't believe that slick nigga had *me* fooled."

"No, Ready, I'm going to kill him."

Perry came down the steps. The door shut, and his smile faded when he saw Ready and me armed and waiting.

Immediately, he lifted his hands in the air. "I'm going to remove my weapons."

Ready pointed his cane in his direction. "Hurry up, new nigga."

Perry stared into my eyes and unbuttoned his jacket. He pulled two guns from his holster vest, two from his waist, a small pistol from his left calf, and a knife from his right ankle strap.

I placed my .22 against his temple. "Spill it."

After he explained every detail of the predicament he'd gotten himself into, Ready aimed his shotgun at Perry's chest.

"Empress, let me shoot him, *please.*"

I didn't budge. "You had a week to come clean, but you've been sneaking and sniffing like a rat."

Ready stepped closer to him. "That's right. I ain't convinced."

"You said you trusted me to do my job, and I'm going to handle Irishman. I'm no rat, Dulce, and you know it. I've been in your face waiting for you to face me."

"What is he talking about?" Ready asked.

"You're Snipes Creed, Perry, and I don't know you or the new niggas you brought into my organization."

"I'm Perry Blair Savage, the same man you met five years ago. Bear and Geese are my brothers, who were a part of my family's gambling organization led by my other brothers—Major, Slide, and Styles—in Harlem. You know everything else about me."

Ready looked at me. "Is he really Perry Savage?"

I nodded and lowered my weapon. Ready sat down.

Perry took my gun and pointed it at his heart. "The day you left me, you broke my heart. I drove around the South Side looking for a Negro doll with long hair named Dulce de Leche. Niggas laughed in my face."

Ready snickered as he bit into his sandwich.

Perry continued, "I stopped by the record store every time I visited Chicago, praying I'd run into you, and look at how our paths crossed. It's fate. I didn't pursue you like my heart wanted this week because of the look in your eyes."

"What look?"

"Fear."

I laughed out loud. "I'm not scared of *you* or *anybody*, not even the devil."

He placed my gun on the table. "You fear *love*, doll. I bet you're scared to let God love you, and there's no purer form of love than agape."

I turned away, and he gently nudged my chin so that I faced him.

"Dulce, you slipped away from me the first time, but God brought me into your life to show you what real love feels like. And as I said five years ago, I can show you if you let me."

"There are people in my life who I love."

"That's love of the heart. I'm talking about love from the soul. I feel it whenever we're close or apart. I'm in love with you, Dulce, and I would *never* hurt you. I'd die for you." He stroked my face. "I believe you love me, too, but you're scared of how right it feels. Please, let me be your man and love you the way you deserve. All I need is one shot to prove we are made for each other."

Frozen like ice, I whispered, "I need you to leave."

I held my breath and watched the fight in his eyes retract. After concealing all his weapons, he walked out the door without saying another word. I deeply exhaled and placed my gun inside my garter belt.

After a loud crunch, Ready smacked with onion hanging from his mouth. "Damn, Empress, are you really going to let youngblood leave? I've never seen a man humble himself for love like that—he meant every word of that shit."

Still trying to catch my breath, I huffed. "Eat your sandwich, old man. Nobody asked you."

Bear took me home, and I went straight upstairs to run a hot bath and light a cigarette. "La Bohème" played through my record player like it had every night since I'd gotten it. As Perry had mentioned, the baritone sang his heart out.

Was Perry right? I thought. *Do I fear the righteousness of his love?*

I quickly got out of the tub, dried off, dressed, and grabbed my coat. Then, I ran downstairs to Bear.

"Take me back to The Palace."

Before I knew it, I was face-to-face with Perry's door. I lifted my fist to knock, and it slowly opened. His arms reached out the doorway and wrapped around my waist, pulling me inside before closing the door. The entire room was candlelit with dancing flames as he stood bare-chested before me. He placed a single red rose against my lips. I put my hands behind his neck and inhaled the sweet fragrance. Then, he placed the rose in my hair and brushed my cheeks with his fingertips.

"How did you know I was coming?" I asked.

"I prayed to God."

He placed his forefinger under my chin and gently lifted my head towards his face. I closed my eyes and received endearing kisses on my chin and forehead. I untied my black jacket, revealing the purple lingerie underneath. He went to hang my jacket on the coat rack, and when he returned, he weaved his fingers between mine.

"You are so beautiful."

I placed his hands around my waist and flowed my fingertips along his muscular shoulders. All the desire I had stored for him dripped from inside me. Our lips reunited, and he slowly removed each of my garments with care.

"Dulce, I love you with all my heart. I was your first, and I will be your last."

I removed his pants and kissed him with passion. "That means you're my only."

He took my face in his hands and asked, "Are you telling me everything is how I left it five years ago?"

"Perry, I went to that same record store over the years hoping to bump into you, too, because I fell in love with you that night. So, I'm forever yours."

He dropped to his knees. The lusty stream of love poured from between my thighs to his lips. One stroke of his tongue, and I grabbed the back of his head. He French kissed me harder and deeper until I was weak. Standing up, he wrapped my legs around his waist and entered inside me. Before I yelled, he swallowed my pain with an intense kiss. With my back pressed against the door, he moved slowly and placed my arms above my head.

"Are you ready to let me love you, Dulce?"

"Yes, Perry," I moaned. "Show me what real love feels like."

He gripped my body and carried me to the couch, laying me down. My back arched as he rocked his hips like a boat on a river, reaching a spot that caused me to tremble uncontrollably. He groaned with every shiver until soulful streams of pleasure exploded from my body. He yelled and joined me in ecstasy. After our bodies relaxed, he gently kissed away the tears that had fallen from my eyes.

"Why do you cry when I make love to you?"

"It's hard to put into words."

"Tell me something, because I feel like I'm hurting you."

I touched his face and closed my eyes. "It feels like every millimeter from my scalp to my pinky toe is stimulated until I transcend into a perfect place between Earth and heaven." I opened my eyes and continued, "The feeling is from a pleasure within, not pain."

He smiled. "No fooling?"

I rolled on top of him. "No fooling, Captain. Now, teach me how to love you back."

He pulled my face to his. "Just use your body to express how you feel inside."

I pressed my heart against his chest and kissed him with all the love in me.

After a night of endless passion, the sunlight woke me up. I opened my eyes, and everything in the room was perfectly arranged. When I lifted the sheets, I was surrounded by rose petals. Next to my pillow was a letter.

Dearest Dulce,

Miss de Leche, I'm in love with the taste.
Sugar flows sweet, chocolate river from her waist.
Decadent, gangster, love cries from her soul.
Candy-coated agape…roll, Jordan, roll.
Tears with a smile, fresh rain and sunshine.
And I love you…Forever yours, my forever mine.

Perry

I had fallen back asleep and was awakened by Perry's lips. A gush of heat ran from my head to my toes. The mouth-watering scent of savory fried bacon, sweet cinnamon pancakes, and creamy grits traveled into my nostrils. I opened my eyes, and Perry's love was waiting.

"Good morning, doll. Are you hungry?"

I snatched a kiss from his lips. "Good morning, Perry. I can't believe you write poetry."

"I write how I feel, and sometimes my emotions rhyme."

"You've given me more to love about you."

He smiled and placed a spoonful of grits on my lips. "Mama Lee told me you like sugar on your grits."

I took a bite. "*Mmm*, melts in my mouth. Want a bite?"

He shook his head. "No, thank you. Sounds disgusting. Where I'm from, we put salt, pepper, and cheese on grits."

I placed the spoon down. "Perry, I need to talk to you."

"Me too. You go first."

"No, I'll eat while you talk."

"You're my woman, Dulce, and I'm too grown to hide that."

"Don't you think that will blur the lines for the employees?"

"The boundaries have already been set. You control the nucleus of the organization, and I control the perimeter."

"What about our enemies?"

"The enemy line falls under the jurisdiction of the perimeter, so I'll worry about that. And let's keep Palace business between Empress and Mr. Creed. Behind closed doors, Perry Savage will focus on Dulce De Leche." We kissed. Then, he looked into my eyes and asked, "Now, what did you want to talk to me about?"

Fear held me back. "Another time."

CHAPTER 14
FOUR WOMEN

DULCE "EMPRESS" MONROE

June 1938 - Gary, Indiana

I didn't think it was possible, but for one day, America worshipped a Negro god, hailed by the name Joe Louis. The Nazis had planned world domination and used Max Schmeling, their German heavyweight boxing champion, as their first missile launch on America. But, like most white folks, they underestimated a Negro's capabilities. Little did they know Joe Louis had the God-given power to conquer the world.

For the biggest event in American history, The Palace invited anyone wanting to witness the action to Mama's Blues, free of charge. We placed posters on every corner in the city, and like the rest of the world, I couldn't wait to hear Joe Louis whoop Max Schmeling's ass.

As I passed Perry in the lobby, he smiled and tipped his hat. "Good morning, Empress."

With a wink, I smiled back. "Good morning, Mr. Creed."

With everyone busy that day, Bear and I proceeded into the basement so I could conduct a meeting. As we headed to the meeting room, Ready led a crew in preparation for the fight. Bear knocked on the door of the stash room, and Philly let us in.

Perched on the table, Mama sang Ethel Waters' "Stormy Weather." Like always, Beloved was dancing while Treasure quietly worked on finances. Perry knocked before escorting Martha and Linda—my newest runners—inside. They were disguised as beauty stylists and holding hair product bags full of betting slips and money. Perry tipped his hat and left in a hurry.

"How is Mae doing?" I asked them.

"Giddy! Broads are feeling extra lucky and lined up around the corner, waiting to place their bets and get styled for tonight," Martha replied.

Treasure immediately started counting the dough. "That means Henry is going to sell out of *Gary Tribunes* at the corner store. Folks will be scampering around for papers, hungry to get today's handle."

The handle was the combination we used to determine our lottery winners. It was always the last three digits from the official racetrack bettors printed daily in the city's newspaper.

Perry returned, his expression as hard as stone. "Martha and Linda, I'll take you to Geese, and he'll follow you back to the shop."

"Take a load off, Snipes. You're always so serious," Linda said as he escorted them out.

Philly knocked three times and opened the door. "There's a white-looking broad who says she's Countess's cousin. She says you were expecting her."

"Yes, Philly. Let her in."

Countess's cousin, Orin, had been itching to move to the Midwest for years, and luckily, Countess had sent her my way.

After introducing Orin to the group, I asked, "Are you sure you want to step into the dark side?"

"What's darker than LeRoux Palm Isle with no electricity and running water? The state hasn't sent any relief to restore the island since the storm months ago. They're letting it decay so they can force the colored folks out, build it back up, and resell the land to rich white folks."

I shook my head in disgust. "They won't let us keep anything of value. Well, are you sure you want to work for mc and not Countess?"

"I'm sure. I don't want her sniffing me like a hound every day. I've had enough of my family using our hoodoo on me."

"You look white," Treasure said.

"It doesn't matter how I look. I'm Colored—my grandmother was a slave like everybody else's in this room."

"What do you like to do?" Beloved asked.

"I like money, hooch, and good sex."

Beloved laughed. "Who doesn't? I treat all my girls like royalty. A white-looking dame with brown sugar between her thighs would make you, me, and Empress rich."

Mama hit Beloved's arm. "What's wrong with you, chile?"

"That's the berries, Mama Lee!"

"I already have a position for Orin."

"You want me to be a spy," Orin confirmed.

"It's not the berries, but are you up to it?"

"Who is he?"

"Shane Killian, the nephew of an Irish mobster named Irishman. Shane is good-looking and athletic, and he just graduated from Indiana University. He writes for the college newspaper and has written an article that rebels against racist crackers. I want you to get close and find out whatever you can."

"And he likes colored women?"

"I'll pay you fifty dollars a week to make him like whatever you tell him to. But if you ever sense anything fishy, call the hotel straight away, and we'll get you out…by any means necessary. I made a promise to Countess to keep you safe, and I won't break it." She pointed to her temple and smiled. "Lucky for us, my good sense can see folks' bad sense. Call you in a week."

Negroes stuffed into our joint like sardines, and the time had finally come. Live from Yankee Stadium, the announcer presented Joe Louis vs. Max Schmeling. We cheered as if watching the fight in person in New York City.

"Joe Louis is going to kill that German!" Ready yelled.

Bear yelled back, "Hell yeah! Joe gave up women to focus on training."

"No fooling?" Ready asked.

Bear nodded. "No fooling. That white boy is dead."

Ready sat like a grouch as everyone got dizzy off giggle juice around him. He stood up like he'd had enough. "Damnit, I need my sandwich, and I left it in the kitchen."

Mama grabbed his hand. "Papa, you should wait. The fight is about to start. Joe said he's going to knock Schmeling out in the first round." Ready quickly grabbed his cane, and I walked with him to the base of the steps.

"I'll be back in a tick," he said.

Perry ran down the steps and slipped his arms around my waist. "Everything is secured, Empress."

"Mr. Creed, can you please relax…*with me?*"

"Once the fight is over, Captain Savage will do whatever Miss De Leche tells him to."

He pecked my lips and disappeared up the stairs.

The fight started, and it felt like America stopped moving. The bustling room went silent as soon as the fight bell rang.

The announcer began talking. "Louis gives Max two hard lefts to his face, a right to his head, two lefts to his jaw. Out of the clench, Louis gives two shots to the body, a left hook, a right hook, a left to the head. Schmeling hits the ground out cold. Eight... nine...ten! Max Schmeling is defeated by knockout! Joe Louis is the new heavyweight champion of the world!"

The room exploded as we heard loud cheers and exploding fireworks from the streets outside. We screamed, shouted, and hugged each other like we'd been freed from discrimination. That moment was one of the best feelings of my life. The only thing missing was Perry.

Ready ran back to the table with salami hanging from his mouth. "Tell me I didn't really miss it!"

Mama stroked the disappointment from his face. "The fight in over, Papa."

He looked around the room and slammed his sandwich on the table. Out of nowhere, Perry was on the stage with a microphone. He winked at me and then stared seriously at the audience.

"Joe Louis kicked Schmeling's ass, folks. So, it's time to shake a leg through the side door and celebrate anywhere but here."

He stepped offstage and herded the crowd outside like a shepherd does his sheep.

Beloved pulled up a chair and sat next to me. "Empress, Snipes really loves you. How did you get him?"

I removed Countess's glass vial from my pocketbook. "Countess put this on me minutes before we met. She used it when she met his brother, too."

Hesitantly, she asked, "Is it voodoo?"

"Countess said our ancestors used it as a man magnet."

She snatched the vial and doused her neck and arms with it. "In Jesus's name, bring my dream man to me."

No sooner had I replaced the vial inside my clutch than two attractive men walked over.

"Hello, lovelies," one of them said.

Beloved batted her eyelashes. *"Well, hello, fellas."*

The other man slurred his words. "We want to buy pussy."

She smacked her lips. "My girls are booked for the night."

"How much for you and your friend?" the other asked, reaching for my face.

I pushed his hand away. *"Scram."*

Out of nowhere, Bear grabbed both of their collars and dragged them away from our table. The taller one broke loose and started punching Bear in the back. Bear, as well as the scampering crowd, seemed unaffected. He wrapped his boulder-sized arms around the head and neck of the other one. Within seconds, Bear had choked him out cold. Then Bear turned around and knocked the taller one with a Joe Louis knock-out punch. After quickly dragging them out of the side door, Bear rushed back to our table.

"Empress, sorry I took so long. Are you ladies alright?"

Beloved smiled flirtatiously. "I am now, big daddy. Is he alive?"

"He's just sleeping."

"Did you learn that in the Army?"

"Snipes taught me how to fight." He kissed her hand and smiled. "Damn, you smell good. Do you have plans for tonight?"

"Looks like I'm hanging with you, daddy." When he stepped behind us, she whispered to me, "Thank you."

Every time after we made love, Perry would leave me with his sweet, loving words. I would pinch myself at times to make sure I wasn't dreaming.

Dearest Dulce,

The effortless grace, Aphrodite's face.
Cinched waist, sweetest taste.
I embrace, my favorite place.
No replace, permanent space.
No mistake, no debate.
Never erase, spiritual lace.
My love estate, till Heaven's gate.
I'll await. Perpetuate.
My soulmate. It's God's fate.

Perry

As I reread this love note a second time, there was a soft knock at the door. I leaped out of the bed and fixed my hair. Then, I swung the door open with my eyes closed.

"Morning, Forever Mine."

It was Mama, her face covered with solemnness. "Morning, sugar."

I covered myself with my robe. "What's shaking, Mama?"

"Juno wants you to call her."

"Is she okay?"

"She will be when joy cometh in the morning."

"What's wrong?" I asked.

She touched my hand. "I'll let her tell you."

There was a soft knock on the door. "Who is it?" I asked.

Perry smiled through the tiny crack I held in the doorway. "It's me, doll."

I swung it open. "I'm forever yours, my forever mine."

He wrapped his arms around me. "My forever till the end of time."

Mama cleared her throat. "The love sure is strong in this room. I'll leave you two alone."

"Don't leave, Mama Lee. I was checking on Dulce," Perry told her.

"It's alright. I need to do some gardening before it gets too hot."

Before she left, I threw my arms around her. "I love you, Mama."

Mama held my face in her hands and sweetly kissed my forehead. "I love you with all my heart, sugar."

Perry opened the door for her, and she grabbed his hand.

"My Sugar has always loved me, Perry, and I know that. But that's the first time she's said it out loud. No matter what happens, remember you're the one who brought that love out of her."

After closing the door, he turned to me and stroked my face. "Are you alright, Miss De Leche?"

"What does everybody know that I don't?"

He handed me the phone. "I'll let Juno tell you."

"How can I connect your call?" the operator asked. "Direct or collect?"

"Direct."

Juno answered, hysterically sobbing through the phone. *"Empress."*

"What's wrong?"

"It's Enchantress," she cried. "She didn't wake up this morning."

"Juno, *I'm so sorry.*"

"I knew this day would come, but I wasn't prepared for the pain. It really hurts. I can barely breathe."

"Enchantress was a valuable part of our organization, and we're going to give her a proper homegoing. Snipes will make all the arrangements if that's alright with you."

"I would love that."

We hung up, and Perry was waiting with his arms folded.

"What did you just sign me up for, doll?"

"I need you to get the fellas and pick up Enchantress from Juno's. Then, I need you to get with Guy and Allen Funeral Home and arrange a homegoing service with a full program. Oh, and get a golden casket. That was Enchantress's favorite color."

Perry stared at me and burst into laughter. "No fooling?"

"No fooling."

"Dulce Ella Monroe, we cannot place a circus tiger in a coffin and bury it in a human cemetery."

"Says who, Perry Blair Savage?"

"Everybody knows pets get buried in a backyard or pet cemetery, if they're lucky."

"I want Enchantress embalmed with a vet and properly buried. Juno has been through so much, and she deserves this. Plus, this duty is outside the perimeter, which falls under *your* jurisdiction."

He placed his forehead on my shoulder and grunted. "Please don't make me do this, dollface."

I slid my arms around his neck. "If it weren't for Enchantress, your *dollface* wouldn't be standing here, daddy."

He picked me up, and I locked my legs around his waist. He held me against him.

"If *my doll*, who knew she already had me wrapped around her finger, would've stayed inside my arms that night instead of sneaking off like a thief, she wouldn't've needed a circus tiger for protection 'cause she already had a soldier."

I pressed my lips against his. "At ease, Captain. Looks like you have your doll wrapped around you forever. So, what are you going to do about that?"

"I can show you better than I can tell you."

Perry didn't waste a day putting my plan into action. It was a hot, sticky night, but the sky had been covered with diamond-like stars. Ready drove Countess, Mama Lee, Beloved, Juno, Juno's mama, and me from Chicago to Gary inside a long, white limousine. The entire ride, Juno sobbed as she told us circus stories.

We finally arrived at Guy and Allen Funeral Home, where Perry, Bear, Geese, and Tommy were standing around a hearse. Ready parked, and the men helped us out of the limo. As Juno had requested, everyone was dressed in white, and Perry handed us each a tall white candle and calla lily. Bear and Tommy lifted the golden casket, and we followed them up a hill along a trail of apple blossom petals that had fallen at our feet. We arrived at a tall tulip tree and stopped. At the base of the trunk was an open grave and a golden-plated headstone with Enchantress etched across it.

As we were lining up, Juno fainted. Geese caught her in his arms, and she quickly woke up.

"I've got you, Juno," he said. "Hold my hand."

Mama stood before us and closed her eyes like she was waiting for God to tell her what to say. When she finally looked at us, her words for the eulogy flowed from her lips like a waterfall.

"Heavenly Father, you use everything and everyone as vessels. Enchantress was no different. When Juno was taken from her mother, she was placed in a cage with a strange tiger. It was you, Lord, who protected young Juno like Daniel in the lion's den. You transformed Enchantress from a wild predator to a tamed protector and used that same tiger to keep Juno safe from danger and loneliness.

"For years, Juno had been enslaved, well after slavery had been abolished. Most folks, including each one of us standing before you, would have broken, died, or gone insane. But you instilled Juno with bravery beyond human understanding. She used your gift of song to train a tiger, and together, they have blessed folks all over the world with the angelic talent you blessed Juno with.

"Enchantress used her natural instincts to save Juno and possibly other children from the evil ringmaster. The way in which it was done is for you to judge, but everyone here has sinned against you. We ask for your forgiveness and grace. We are all imperfect, but please use us as vessels in the way you used Enchantress so that we can protect and help each other and others to get closer to you. *Amen.*"

CHAPTER 15
FOREVER MINE

DULCE "EMPRESS" MONROE

July 1938 - Gary, Indiana

For forty days and nights, Perry's love rained down on me. Unlike the flood of devastation, his standout affection was more like misty rays—light and steady. I had no idea it was the calm before the storm. With no Dunstan drama to intercept, we had frolicked inside our own world with naked emotions until my betrayal caused him to take cover.

I woke up that morning wrapped in Perry's sheets. Next to a bowl of fresh fruit and a glass of orange juice, he left me a red rose and a note.

> *Dearest Dulce,*
>
> *My doll, Miss de Leche, is so sweet,*
> *Wrapped in strawberry licorice down to her feet.*
> *Saccharin honey drips from both her lips,*
> *Melts in my mouth like sugar on her grits.*
> *The dip and sway of her hips drive me insane.*
> *Can't wait for that sexy dame to take my last name.*

Forever mine, I'll love you till the end of time.

Perry

After a long soak in the tub, I started my day later than usual. Mayor Dunstan and Irishman had been quiet—another warning that a tornado was brewing. Life with Perry had been imperfect harmony, and I wasn't ready for the wind to change.

Once dressed, I headed downstairs to where Perry stood at the front lobby door. He winked and tipped his hat as I approached.

"Good morning, Empress."

I grazed against his body. "Good morning, Mr. Creed."

Bear was at my heels and ran to the car to open the back door. "Mama Lee's?"

"Yes, please."

Even with all the windows down, the summer heat was unbearable. We traveled to Mama Lee and Ready's cozy home on Washington Street, one block from my house. Her yellow bungalow was almost identical to the house where I had spent most of my young years. She maintained a beautiful flower garden in the front, with fruits, vegetables, and spices in the back. The heat was beaming, and I looked forward to sipping on the fresh lemonade Mama always had waiting for me. Bear dropped me off like he'd always done whenever Ready was there to keep watch, and I deeply inhaled the fresh gardenias as I made my way inside.

As I opened the door, I called out, "Hello."

No one answered, and I strolled through the living room. Ma Rainey was loudly singing the blues through the kitchen record player. Mama was waiting for me in the backyard with two lemonades. She rocked on her white wooden rocking chair. I sat next to her, and she handed me a glass. Her cold silence spoke more intensely than the words she was screaming from inside, so I took a sip and listened.

"Mama, can you fix me another sandwich and leave it in the icebox?" Ready called from the kitchen.

She glared at me and walked inside. I understood and followed her, but she shut the door in my face. So, I turned back around. I stood on the porch and deeply inhaled the scent of her fresh seasonings from the garden. A fiery breeze cut through my dress. Then, I felt the heat from a manly chest.

"Forever mine, you are so *damn* fine," Perry whispered against my neck.

Immediately, sweat poured down my body as I stiffened from his touch.

"What's wrong, doll?" He turned me around and revealed the concern in his eyes. "What has you shaken up?"

My composure was gone, and my voice trembled as I stuttered, "I-I didn't expect to see you."

He smiled. "It was slow today, so I came by to check out Ready's pad. Plus, I heard you were here."

My lips quivered. *"P-Perry."*

He stroked the hair stuck to the dewy guilt gliding down my face.

"Dulce, you're shaking. Talk to me."

From behind us, we heard, *"Mommy!"*

Unable to bear seeing Perry hurt, I looked down at the smile that always made my love boil. I bent down, and my son almost knocked me over with a strong hug and sweet kiss. I picked him up.

"Hey, sweetie. You are a delight for my sore eyes. How I've missed you!"

"I've missed you, too!" Excited to see a new face, he wiggled free and beamed at Perry. "Hello, Mister. My name is Pierre."

Perry deeply exhaled and kneeled to shake his hand.

"Wow, Pierre. That name sounds *French*." For the first time, Perry gave me a vicious look. "My name is Mr. Creed. Nice to meet you."

They shook hands, and Perry pretended his wrist was broken. "That's a mighty handshake."

"My mommy said I have hands like my daddy."

"Your daddy must be a boxer."

"He's in the Army. Do you want to see a photograph of him?"

Perry sniped at me with rapid fire from his stare down. "*Please, Pierre, I would love to.*"

Tears streamed down my face, and I was frozen. When Pierre ran inside the house, I parted my quivering lips.

"Perry, let me explain."

"*No.*"

Pierre ran back to Perry with his drawing pad. They sat on the rocking chair, and my hand pressed against my heart.

Pierre pointed to the first page. "That's me in the middle."

"Wow, you're an artist," Perry said. "What's in your mommy's hand?"

"Her sewing machine. She's a fashion designer and travels all around the world."

Shame engulfed me as Perry shot me with another glare. "Does *she?*" he asked with surprise. "What's your daddy holding in his hand?"

"An Army rifle."

Perry leaned in closer to the pad. "What are those letters on you and your daddy's shirt?"

"Our initials."

I walked over to them and said, "Pierre, please give Mr. Creed and me a minute."

Perry commanded my silence with his eyes, and I backed up.

"What's your middle and last name, Pierre?" he asked.

"Blair Savage."

A tear fell down Perry's face. "How old are you?"

My son lifted five proud fingers in the air. "In two weeks."

Perry's face was wet with emotion as he placed his hands on Pierre's shoulders. "Do you know your daddy's name?"

I tried to interject, and Pierre saluted with pride.

"Captain Perry Blair Savage, soldier at war."

Perry grabbed his chest, and I felt his soul break. His face was soaked with tears, but he didn't speak.

"Mister, why are you and my mommy crying?" Pierre asked.

Perry cleared his throat. "Pierre, our eyes are sweating. At our age, intense humidity can make your eyeballs overheat."

Pierre laughed. "Old people have a lot of problems."

Just then, Mama rushed outside and extended her hand to Pierre. "Come help me make everybody sandwiches, sweetie."

Pierre waved as they walked back inside. Perry buried his face in his hands, and when I tried to console him, he swatted me away.

"Perry, I'm *so* sorry," I pleaded. "I didn't want you to find out like this."

He lifted his head, exposing his red eyes and drenched face. I reached for him again, and he dodged me like the plague. He wiped his face and stood up.

While punching with frustration at the wind, he yelled, *"God,"* until his voice cracked. Then, he turned his back to me, whispered, *"I can't,"* and walked away.

CHAPTER 16
TIGRESS AND TWEED

DULCE "EMPRESS" MONROE

July 1938 - Gary, Indiana

Without Perry's smile and sexy tip of his hat, my heart was wrenching in agony. Yes, I deserved his iciness and the withdrawal of his affection, but I was hoping for the chance to reverse the curse I had cast upon our love. Lost in helplessness, I decided to drown my somber wakefulness in whiskey and cigarette smoke, but the deeper I sank and the cloudier the tobacco, the clearer my truth—I was a no-good, lowdown scoundrel for what I'd done.

I had lost the pre- and post-treasured moments between us gifted by Father Time, and the hours without an intimate exchange crept by me, feeling like years and driving me insane. Perry had given me the poetic justice of his silence, withholding all communication. Dying inside, I decided I would do anything to win him back.

There was a soft knock on my office door, and I stuffed my nearly empty gin bottle inside my desk drawer. I put out my cig and fanned away the smoke from my face. Hoping it was Perry, I quickly touched up my lipstick.

"Come in."

Bear spoke through the door. "Empress, Snipes just called us for an emergency meeting downstairs."

Bear and I headed to the stash room that Perry had converted into a war room, which he'd stocked with enough guns and weapons for battle. I was hoping to get a private recap to plead with him. Instead, I walked into the room filled with him, Ready, Geese, Tony, and Red awaiting my arrival.

Perry pulled out my seat. "Empress, Mayor Dunstan requested a meeting to discuss new terms."

"Last time we met, he wanted over forty percent, and I refused. Only if he's willing to go lower am I open to negotiate."

"He's been quietly searching for a new dirty chief willing to do all his dirty work, and now that he's found him, he owns the entire squad of coppers and Irish mob. So, I doubt he goes lower than what he previously offered you."

"Then Dunstan can kiss my ass."

Perry turned his attention to the men at the table. "*Smooth*. Fellas, let's get ready for war."

Ready tapped his cane on the floor. "*Smooth*, 'cause I was born *Ready*."

"Snipes, I have loyal soldiers if you need them," Tony chimed in.

Perry nodded. "Call those cats. I've already made calls, too."

"*Whoa!*" I shouted.

Yes, Dunstan made my skin crawl, but I needed to avoid bloodshed if I could.

"Everybody cool it. Mr. Creed, when and where does he want to meet?" I asked.

"Tomorrow before sunrise. City Hall."

I stood up. "Fine. Set it up. Gentlemen, contact your trusted soldiers, but no trigger-pulling till Snipes gives the word."

I cracked a smile at Perry and waited for the tip of his hat, which I didn't get.

Early the next morning, Bear was waiting in the driver's seat of my Mercedes in the back alley. I walked down the stairs. Standing at the bottom step, Perry was dressed in a tan, brown, and purple plaid jacket, with a pair of shiny gators on his feet and a brown-brimmed hat on his head. I had tailor-made his rags, and the way it gripped the muscles on his body, I began to ache even harder for him.

He looked up, and I finally saw a peek of hope from his remaining love for me in his eyes.

"Good morning, Empress. I secured all the locks and windows. I have extra security at The Palace in case Dunstan tries anything while we're gone."

I knew he wouldn't be able to resist me in my purple satin dress that I had purposely shortened above the knees. My threads screamed, *Perry, take me back, and Dunstan, kiss my ass.* As I sashayed down the steps, I saw him grip the banister and sink his top teeth deeply into his plush bottom lip.

I stopped directly in front of him to straighten his already straight tie.

"Good morning." I swept my lips over the spot below his earlobe and gently whispered, "You know purple is my favorite color, *Mr. Creed.*"

He didn't move until I moved. When I did, he led me out the door and to the back seat of my car. Perry did one last security check around the house before getting in the front seat. Ready's and Tony's Cadillacs followed us as we cruised through the empty, dark streets to City Hall.

Gary's City Hall was the largest building in town, with several columns across the front and accented with a large copper dome roof. With no skyscrapers in Gary, the city's backdrop was tall factory buildings topped with long chimneys puffing smoke. I stepped out of the car, and the air thick with smog reeked of the mill's ashes. As our gang strolled past the line of police squad cars parked in front of the limestone-colored building, I was unafraid.

Mayor Dunstan was waiting at the door beside Irishman and the newly appointed police chief, Egbart Wraith. Chief Wraith was a burly man with a round face, sandy brown hair, and a thick mustache.

Mayor Dunstan flashed a devilish grin. "I need to tell my secretary to call the *Gary Tribune* to witness history. I'm the first mayor to allow Negroes into City Hall. You all should feel honored."

"We're here for business, not a fake photoshoot to straighten your crooked image," Perry fired back.

Dunstan looked surprised at Perry's candidness. "I don't like you."

"I can live with that."

Irishman tapped Dunstan's shoulder and whispered in his ear.

Dunstan smiled slyly. "Empress, please, come in and welcome."

We followed him down a shiny white and gold marble floor to the first set of double doors on our right. I sat at a rectangular wooden table in a brightly lit meeting room with individual portraits of U.S. Presidents and previous Gary mayors on the wall. A large United States flag was next to the blue with golden torch State flag.

Dunstan sat across from me. Behind him was Irishman, Chief Wraith, and two goons. All my knights were behind me except Geese. Geese stood guard outside the conference room door next to one of Wraith's police officers.

Getting right to biz, Dunstan said, "Miss Monroe, I want us to work together as silent partners."

I narrowed my eyes. "My name is Empress, and I can't be partners with a man who tried to kill me."

"I admit we got off to a rocky start, but I want to make it right."

"What do you want?" I asked.

"Three hundred dollars per week."

"That's more than your last request."

"Inflation costs, Empress. I have more Negroes coming to my city every day, which brings more money to *your* pocket."

"We are in a depression, so the only thing inflating is the unemployment rate. I paid Mayor Clay one hundred dollars, which included copper protection. I'm willing to go to one hundred and fifty dollars, which is a thirty percent increase. That is more than reasonable considering the financial state of Negroes in America."

He laughed. "You have to pay to play in *my* city. Three hundred dollars per week is my final offer, and that price gives you immunity from the police and mob."

"Dunstan, I pay plenty, including the increased quarterly county taxes you levied on the colored businesses on my side of the tracks."

"Empress, please. You have a nice gambling and prostitution operation." He smiled. "I don't mind contacting the FBI, and Irishman tells me they'll also find evidence of murder and drug trafficking linked to you stashed somewhere in your home."

Perry interjected. "I *heard* that same evidence was stashed inside an imitation White House—newly built by a crooked city council administrator—on Pennsylvania in Glen Park. I also heard there was possible proof of conspiracy somewhere here in City Hall."

Perry had told me that he had planted the evidence Irishman was going to use against me inside the walls of Dunstan's new mayor's mansion being built. He and I smirked. Irishman and Dunstan's faces turned fiery red. Suddenly, clicking sounds of cocked pistol hammers filled the room.

Chief Wraith pointed his pistol at Perry. "Mayor Dunstan, I'm tired of this tigress cunt and her jive nigger."

Perry had one pistol pointed at Irishman and the other at Wraith. "Apologize to Empress, or we will make history for being the first Negroes to shoot up City Hall."

Dunstan turned to his people. "Fellas, please, put down your weapons so Empress and I can conduct business."

Dunstan's men reluctantly dropped their weapons, but Ready, Tony, Red, Bear, and Geese kept their guns drawn.

"Our guns drop after Empress's apology," Perry commanded.

Dunstan grunted between his teeth. "I apologize on behalf of Chief Wraith."

Chief Wraith looked appalled. "Mayor..."

Dunstan lifted his hand and asked me, "Can we continue?"

I could see Perry was still upset, but I nodded.

"Cool the heaters, *gentlemen*," Perry ordered our gang.

The tension in the room was as thick as a layered wedding cake.

Dunstan continued his rhetoric. "Empress, white Americans have also suffered great loss from the Depression. Our city's unemployment rate is aligned with the country at over twenty-five percent."

"Please don't attempt to compare our struggles. The Negroes unemployment rate was over fifty percent, and while whites are going back to work, we're still waiting on the unemployed sidelines."

"The sooner I can get my white workers back in the factories, the sooner Negroes can file in, and the better off the entire city will be."

"You don't give a hoot about this city," I continued. "You're stealing from the taxpayers to fund your Glen Park mansion and Rolls Royce. Now you want to steal from me and the other Negro businesses to refill the cookie jar you can't keep your greedy hands out of."

"*You're* a hypocrite, Empress. You Negroes are not picking cotton or in chains anymore. You're actually taking jobs away from the White folks that freed you. And you, Empress, steal from *your* people to buy fancy threads and a Mercedes Benz."

"Don't forget about their tailored suits, designer shoes, *and* Cadillacs," Wraith added.

I stood up. "Mayor Dunstan, you are a conniving thief, and I'm done with this conversation."

"If you walk out of that door without agreeing to my three-hundred-dollars-a-week offer, war is inevitable."

"Good thing Empress is surrounded by soldiers who understand the rules of engagement," Perry said, standing next to me while the rest of our men stood closely behind us.

From the Harlem Hellfighter's motto, Ready bellowed, *"Don't tread on me!"*

The others responded with the line, *"Goddamn, let's go!"*

Perry offered his arm, and we walked out the door. City Hall had opened for business, and all the white people gawked at us while parting like the Red Sea as we strolled out of the front door.

The sun stung us at the door. Perry walked me to the car and slid next to me. We hit Broadway and were followed by Irishman, Chief Wraith, and two police cars. When we turned right on 15th Avenue, they kept driving down Broadway.

"Perry, where are we going? I want to go to The Palace."

He didn't say anything until Bear parked in front of my house. Then, he got out and stood at the door.

"Lay low today while I rally the troops," Perry told me. "We'll discuss strategy tomorrow morning."

I huffed but didn't protest. After I got out of the car, Perry, Bear, and Geese followed me inside the house. They searched every crevice, and Perry handed me one of his pistols.

"Sleep tight with this by your bedside."

"I don't need any damn guns, Perry, and you know that."

He didn't respond as he turned and left.

After listening to records, designing Bear another suit, and soaking in the tub, I sat on the balcony with my countless cigarettes. Lost in thought about my uncertain future, I knew I only wanted to live each day with Perry by my side.

Could he be done loving me? I wondered.

I stepped onto the balcony to watch the sun drop and moon rise while listening to "La Bohème." Mother Nature delivered a kiss of wind, and I allowed the night breeze to play beneath my nightgown.

Unsatisfied with ghostly affection, I screamed to the ground level, "Bear, take me to The Palace!"

He yelled back, "Snipes ordered. He wants you here."

After Bear locked up the house, he drove in the silent night to The Palace. From the car's window, I watched as the night creatures of the underground awakened from the shadows on Washington Street and visited the busy brothels and nightclubs that had appeared abandoned during the day.

Bear escorted me to the door once we pulled up in front of the hotel. Two young men were playing craps on the sidewalk.

"*Scram*," I shouted. "Don't play that jive in front of my place of business."

Startled, they jumped up. "Empress, we are very sorry. It won't happen again."

I looked closer and realized they were Jonesy's twins. I couldn't believe the babies I had looked after were all grown up.

"Jim and Tim?" I asked.

"Yes, ma'am."

"What are you doing here?"

"We told Mama Lee we needed a job, and Mr. Creed hired us as lookouts."

"How's Jonesy?" I asked.

"She's a saint in the church."

"That's keen." I gave them each money from my clutch. "Give Jonesy one hundred dollars and split the rest. Keep watch, and no more craps in front of my hotel."

"Swell! Yes, ma'am." They smiled and dispersed.

I walked to the third level, and Bear departed. Standing there, I banged on Perry's door.

"Who is it?" he barked.

When I didn't answer, he slowly cracked the door open.

"Our business recap is tomorrow morning, Empress."

"Perry, I don't care about business right now. *We* need to talk."

He attempted to close the door in my face, but I pressed my weight against his barricade. I was no match for his strength, and to my dismay, he shut it.

I kept knocking. "Let me in. *Please* stop shutting me out."

The door slowly cracked open, and he stood against it shirtless in red satin night trousers. He was so fine and plenty rugged that it took a minute for me to catch my breath. I was tongue-tied, searching for my words, and he looked annoyed. He went to close the door again, and I stood in the doorway.

"Wait. Can I come inside, please?"

His eyes were filled with hurtful emotion, and he didn't budge.

"*Please?*" I asked again.

He pulled me inside and shut the door.

"I don't know what you want from me, Dulce. I tried loving you, and it wasn't good enough. I'm not the man for you."

I reached for his face, but he avoided my touch.

"Perry, that's not true. You're the only man for me. I love you, and I love how you love me."

His eyes were red like he had been crying.

"*Bullshit.* Even if Pierre wasn't mine, do you know how honored I would have been..." His voice cracked, and he gained his composure. "I would have been honored that you loved me enough to share your son with me. But instead, you hid the greatest gift you could've given me, *my son,* from *me.* The way you hurt me nearly killed me, and I cannot forgive your betrayal."

"I was going to tell you. I've been telling Pierre ever since he came out my womb about how much I love you, and he wants to be like you—"

"*Stop lying.* You don't think I'm good enough for you. You walked out of my life ashamed, and you're ashamed of me now. You're selling our son fantasies. You have him thinking I'm traveling the world at war, and I'm right down the street."

"Perry, please. I'm not ashamed of you. I'm madly in love with you. I was waiting for the right time to tell you."

"*Right time?* We've been together every day for months. When do you see him? Why isn't he with you?"

"It's complicated."

"No, it's simple. You run from everything and everybody. Pierre thinks you're an international fashion designer. What will you tell him when he finds out his mother is Empress, a criminal queen pin who did not travel the world but lived a few blocks away?" His words stabbed me like sharp needles. "You cannot hide from this, and I will *not* let Ready and Mama Lee raise *my* son. I thought God brought me into your life to protect you, but I see He wants me to protect our son...possibly from you."

"Goddammit, Perry, that's enough," I snapped. "You've spewed enough venom for a lifetime. Dunstan has wanted me dead since he got elected, and after the stunt and guns you pulled today and the evidence you planted, you are more of a deadly target than a harmless protector, Mr. Snipes Creed. I hide Pierre from the world. I even hid him from Meek-Meek to protect *him* from *my shit*, and now that you're back in my life, we have *our shit* to shield him from. What do you think Dunstan will do when he finds out Empress and Snipes Creed have a son together?" He was quiet, and I continued, "What's the plan to protect our innocent son while we go to war? How many lives have you taken from around the country? How many people would use Pierre to retaliate against us?"

I waited for a response, but he didn't answer.

"So, yes, it's *very* complicated, and our son lives with Mama Lee, his real protector. Do you know how much vileness I saw growing up in a whorehouse? Mama Lee saved my innocence, and *she* is saving Pierre's. So, don't you *ever* question what type of mother I am."

He looked pained. "I understand why you hid him from the world, Dulce, but why *me*? I'm his father, and I love you and him with every breath in me."

"I know, and I'm sorry you found out about our son the way you did—I'm no good for keeping Pierre away from you for as long as I did. I got so lost in your love, and I let time get away from me. I was selfish, but I'm so happy you know now because *Pierre* needs you in his life."

He didn't resist when I wrapped my arms around his neck.

"You love me so good; you give me life. *I* need you, Perry. You're my oxygen." He allowed me to kiss the juicy melons on his face, and I didn't let up. "I know I drive you crazy, daddy, and I'm done running. I'm not the woman you thought I was. You fell in love with a thug hiding behind an angelic face. I'm complicated and not easy to love. But you've taught me so much. Please don't stop me from loving you back when I'm just getting started."

My love continued to infiltrate his emotional force field.

"Perry, I'm so in love with every part of you. I need you. Without my oxygen, I can't breathe."

He placed my face inside his hands and stared into my soul. "Listen to me. I won't survive another one of your heartbreaks, so promise me access to Pierre and *all* of you. If that's not possible, love me enough to let me go."

"You have us and me forever. I promise I won't fuck us up again. Please keep loving me."

He kissed me with so much power that I went limp inside his arms.

"You don't have to tell me twice," he said and placed me on the edge of the bed.

With his teeth, he removed my pantyhose.

"I'll never stop loving you, doll." After several tongue kisses from my lips to between the wetness of my thighs, he whispered, "Did you miss me? You love me, don't you?"

My head fell back, and I moaned. "Yes, Perry. I've missed you so much."

"I'm talking to your body, doll."

He laid on the floor and pulled me on his face. His tongue moved like a tidal wave. Swiftly, he lifted me to the bed and wrapped my legs around his neck. With passionate force, he disrupted my water flows with his hardened anticipation. The turbulence caused a tsunami inside me. We both yelled, and tears rained from within.

"Dulce, you are the mother of my son, and I will keep our legacy safe at all costs. I love you with every fiber of my being. *Trust that.*"

"You will feel the love I have for you from my soul, Perry, with no fear. And I will kill a motherfucker twice if he comes for you or our son. *Trust that.*"

He kissed all over my face. "You drive me crazy, woman."

"I'm a crazy dame—crazy in love with you, daddy."

Dearest Dulce,

I'm your oxygen; we create life and breath
Me with no you, a sentence of living death
Pheromones attract, spellbound from the start
Distant hearts broken, but we never part
Forever mine, forever yours, eternal revere
Blindfolded trust, our faith doesn't fear
True love we've conquered, our souls freed
To one pulse, one spirit, Empress Creed

Perry

CHAPTER 17
ROLL JORDAN ROLL

DULCE "EMPRESS" MONROE

August 1938 - Gary, Indiana

I didn't understand the depth of what Charles Dickens meant when he wrote, "It was the best of times, it was the worst of times," in the book *A Tale of Two Cities* until I had soared to the highest of highs and sank to the lowest of lows within minutes. For the first time, I had experienced floating on an angelic cloud toward heaven, but an hour later, the pain of the devil's pitchfork stabbed me back to the earthly playground.

Mama Lee and I were putting the finishing touches on Pierre's birthday cake when she started singing the old Negro hymn "Roll Jordan Roll." I usually never interrupted her whenever she was lost in her magical melodies, especially when her eyes were closed, but after her last slow drawl on the word *"roll,"* I had to stop her.

"Mama, why on Earth are you singing that depressing spiritual when we are getting ready to celebrate my baby's birthday?"

"What's depressing about crossing the holy water to heaven?"

"Where was the holy in the water when the slave ships were on the Transatlantic?"

"Sugar, your faith is most tested when you are in troubled waters. Many of our ancestors made it to freedom using the water of rivers. You must believe God is with you if you want to get to the other side."

I wasn't sure what I believed, but I didn't want to hear one of her sermons.

"Can we please sing 'Happy Birthday' and leave the hymns in church?"

"I sing whatever, wherever, however, and *whenever* the spirit tells me to, especially when I'm in *my* house." She grabbed the lemonade pitcher and smiled. "Now, sugar, let's go sing 'Happy Birthday' to my sweetie, Pierre."

Pierre blew out five dancing flames on his lemon crème cake topped with strawberries. Laughter and love crocheted Perry, Pierre, Ready, Mama Lee, and I together like a beautiful blanket. Perry and I had seen Pierre every day since we reunited, and everything about the day was perfect.

After cake and lemonade, Mama Lee, Ready, and Perry went inside. Perry returned alone, holding a gift wrapped in shiny red paper.

He handed it to Pierre. "Happy birthday, Pierre."

Pierre lit up. "Gee, thank you, Mr. Creed."

Perry got on his knee and handed him a piece of paper. "But before you open your present, I want to read something I wrote to you:

Dearest Pierre,

You're my Savage heir, and I'm your daddy.

Love always, Captain Perry Blair

Pierre looked up at me with innocent eyes of confusion. Perry and I had discussed at length how and when we would share this moment together with our son, but nothing could've prepared us for what was to come.

"Pierre, sweetie, Mr. Creed is actually your daddy—the soldier I've been telling you about…Perry Savage."

"So, Mr. Creed is your code name while you're on missions?"

Perry nodded. "Yes, and I just finished my last one away from you."

"What took you so long to come home?"

My heart broke, and I started to answer, but Perry reached for my hand. Gently, he squeezed my fingers, easing my overwhelming guilt.

"I'm sorry it took so long, but I promise I will never leave you or your mommy ever again for as long as I live."

Pierre threw his arms around Perry's neck. "I knew you would come back for us. Mommy, will you stop traveling, too?"

I tried to wipe my tears, but there were too many to catch.

"I'm home for good, and I also promise never to leave you again."

I placed my arms around them, and the bands of our love transferred between us.

"Since we're together as a family, shouldn't Mommy have our last name?"

Perry wiped sweaty tears from his face and stood up. "Yes, she should. Go get Mama Lee and Papa Ready."

Pierre ran into the house and returned with Mama Lee and Ready behind him. They all sat down on the rocking chair.

My heart was jumping out of my chest as I whispered to Perry, "What are you doing?"

He pressed his finger against my lips. "Be quiet, and let me love you."

Perry called for Pierre. Pierre stood next to him, and Perry cleared his throat.

"Pierre, when a man loves a woman and wants her to have his last name, he has to marry her. To do that, you need to ask, and prayerfully, she says yes."

Perry got on his knee, and Pierre followed. Again, my tears cascaded. I was speechless.

Mama Lee gasped.

"You are silky smooth, youngblood," Ready cheered from behind us.

Perry grabbed my hand. "Dulce Ella Monroe, from the moment I laid eyes on you, I knew from the depths of my soul you were the one for me."

Pierre grabbed my other hand. "Me too."

Perry smiled and said, "Pierre, reach inside Daddy's pocket and open the box for me."

Pierre did as he was instructed. Inside was a golden ring covered with diamonds that shimmered from the sun's rays.

Before I knew it, I shouted, *"Yes!"*

Perry kissed my hand. "I didn't ask you anything yet."

"Yeah, Mommy. We didn't ask you anything."

Perry reached over, picked up the ring, and placed it on the tip of my finger.

"Will you do me the honor of being my wife and allow me to love you—Forever Yours, Forever Mine—beyond the end of time?"

Pierre smiled. "Will you marry me, too?"

I grabbed their faces and kissed their lips. *"Yes, and yes!* I love you so much, Perry and Pierre. This is the best day of my life."

Perry slid the ring on my finger. Then, he picked us up and spun us around.

Mama Lee started serenading us to the clouds with "I've Been Saving Myself for You" by Ella Fitzgerald. As I stood enchanted in love, the wind huffed and shoved me with a sucker blow. I stumbled off balance, but Perry held me up.

"I've got you, doll. You're falling over like you're dizzy off giggle water."

"I'm super dizzy, drunk from your love, Captain."

Perry kissed my ear. "Wait until I put my loving on you tonight."

Pierre ripped his gift open while Perry and I gazed into each other's eyes.

"Daddy, will you play baseball with me?" he asked, grabbing Perry's leg.

Ready yawned. "It's a perfect time for a nap."

"Come on, old man," Perry said, tossing Ready the ball. "You said you're better than Moses Fleet Walker."

Ready caught it and threw back a strong pitch. "Some other time, youngblood. Have fun with your son."

Mama Lee and I were admiring my ring and rocking in her chair.

"Mama Lee, do you have any Coca-Cola?" I asked.

"I'm all out. Let's go to Henry's and get a few."

Grabbing my pocketbook, I yelled from the porch, "Perry, we're going to Henry's to get Coca-Colas!"

He looked concerned. *"Where?"*

"The corner store."

He sprinted towards me. "I'll go, doll."

I touched his chest. "Spend alone time with Pierre. Henry's a few blocks up the street. We'll be back in a few ticks."

He looked at me and then at Pierre, who was happily waving while holding his new mitt. Perry discreetly removed a gun from his ankle holster.

"Take this."

"Perry, stop giving me all your pistols," I told him, gently shoving his hand.

He grabbed my face. "I've got plenty more guns, but only one of you."

While looking lovingly in his eyes, I kissed his lips. "At ease for once, Captain. And you know I never leave without my .22."

"You drive me crazy, doll," he said, kissing me back.

Pierre ran over to us, and Perry scooped him up.

"Give Mommy extra sugar before she leaves."

After several more kisses from them, Mama Lee and I left and got inside Ready's Cadillac.

"That man really *loves* you, sugar," Mama Lee said while driving. "I'm so happy for you."

I screamed, "I'm getting married, Mama! Can you believe it? I've already designed our dresses in my head. I'll wear white with purple accessories, and you, blue, of course."

We laughed, and Mama Lee touched my hand. Then, her smile disappeared as she got serious.

"It's time for Pierre to move in with you and go to school."

"But, Mama—"

"Sugar, he's a little genius just like you. I'll look after him from time to time, but he needs to start school in the fall *and* live with you and his daddy. Do you understand?"

Tears began raining down my cheeks. "Mama, I can't raise him without you. I'm in boiling water right now, and I need you to save him from me like you saved me from Meek-Meek."

She wiped my face. "Dulce, sugar, God does the saving. He used us as each other's vessels. I had the real blues when you came into my life. I was singing to babies and questioning my purpose. When you became my helper, I was able to sing for a real audience again, and that brought me back to life. I had the opportunity to sing with Duke and the Count at The Palace when I thought my career was over, and I just witnessed the most beautiful proposal I've ever seen. You're nothing like Meek-Meek; you never will be. Remember what I said about troubled waters. God's testing you, so promise me that you will have faith strong enough to get to the other side and will not raise Pierre in fear."

My spirit wasn't ready for the challenge, but I uttered, "I promise."

She parked in front of Henry's, and we strongly embraced for what felt like the last time.

Henry's Place was a bright green and yellow general store on the corner of 23rd Avenue and Washington Street. The building was small on the outside, but inside, you could find whatever you needed. Mr. Henry, the owner, took pride in his stocked shelves and friendly service. He was a kind Jamaican gentleman with a strong Caribbean accent who would always greet everyone in his native tongue and island smile. His head and face were kept clean-shaven. His everyday attire was black pants, a white knee-length jacket, and a black bow tie.

He walked straight and tall, like he was born a king, as he approached us.

"Wah gwan, Miss Empress and Mama Lee."

Mama Lee smiled. "Hey, Mr. Henry. We need six Coca-Colas, please."

"No problem. How's Mr. Ready?"

"He's resting his old bones."

"Age is merely a number," Henry said.

Mama Lee laughed. "Whoever made up that saying was young. Old people know age means getting old."

I reached inside my pocketbook and handed Mr. Henry thirty cents, and he grabbed my hand.

"*Ooowee*, Miss Empress. Look at that big diamond. You know, *every* single man in Gary wanted to snatch you off the market. Who's the lucky man?"

I smiled. "Snipes Creed."

"The ritzy, stylish cat from Harlem? He always looks serious, like he's watching the world turn." Henry nodded. "Yeah, he looks bold enough to ask for your hand."

"That's my man."

Mama Lee and I said our goodbyes, and as we were heading back to the car, a handsome young teenager holding a fancy camera walked up to us. He was tall and slim with a bright smile and round face. His camera was black with a chrome top and half the size of all the other cameras I'd seen. He also had a nice leather case strapped across his shoulder.

"Miss Empress and Mama Lee, can I take your photograph?"

"Where did you get this camera?" I asked. "I've never seen one like it."

He smiled with pride. "My daddy bought it in New York City. It's a Kodak 35."

Realizing Mama and I had no photos together, I held onto her tightly.

"Take two photo pictures so you can give me one," I told him.

"Yes, ma'am, Miss Empress."

With two snaps followed by rewinding sounds, he captured the aftermath of the happiest moment in my life. Mama Lee's floral scent was on my neck from our tight embrace, and I inhaled the sweetness of her love.

I reached inside my pocketbook and handed him a dollar bill. "This should cover the cost to buy new film."

"Gee, swell. Thanks, Miss Empress," he said, stuffing the money in his pocket. "Mama Lee, my mama loves your voice. Can I have your autograph?"

She screamed with excitement. "Yes, Lord! My first autograph. Sugar, I'm officially famous." She reached inside her pocketbook and grabbed a pen and a small piece of paper. "What's her name, baby?"

"Her name is Dolores Smith, and she *loves* jazz and the blues."

Mama Lee signed *Dolores Smith, Mama Lee loves the blues, too,* on the paper and handed it to him. "She sounds like my kind of woman."

"I want to be a singer when I grow up, too," he said.

"What's your name, baby?"

"William Smith."

"You need a stage name. Let me hear you sing."

He had a baby face but manly singing voice. He bellowed from his heart.

"Roll, Jordan, roll…"

Mama Lee hummed with her eyes closed while he sang. After he finished, we clapped, and Mama Lee opened her eyes.

"Yes, my Lord. I feel like shouting. How old are you?"

"Thirteen."

"Would you believe I was singing that song about an hour ago? You've got a soul connected to our ancestors, baby, so keep that spirit alive. Let's give you the stage name Willie Kinsman."

I touched his shoulder. "And Willie Kinsman, if you want to make extra dough, we can use some help running errands. Come see me at The Palace early next Saturday if it's okay with your folks. I bet Mama would let you practice on the microphone in the basement."

"Swell, Miss Empress. That would be swell. This is one of the best days of my life."

We all laughed, and I said, "Mine too."

The wind began to shove us around. Our dresses and Willie's camera bag started flying like flags. We sang and danced against the breeze. My hair whipped across my face, and when I uncovered my eyes, Mayor Dunstan's long, white Rolls Royce Phantom slithered towards us. It stopped, and he got out.

Willie Kinsman waved frantically. "Mayor Dunstan is in our neighborhood!"

Looking terrified of Willie's camera, Dunstan covered his face and tipped back inside. From the dark shadow, a black police squad car lurked into the empty lot behind the store.

Nervousness took over my spirit, and uneasiness filled the pit of my stomach. Chief Wraith and another cop got out, and the Phantom sped off.

I placed my body in front of Willie Kinsman and shooed him away in a desperate tone.

"Willie, go on. Run home now."

He whipped from behind me and lifted his camera to his eye. "I want a photograph of the new police chief."

After the first click, followed by the rewinding sound, a look of displaced fury consumed Wraith's face. My heart throbbed with fear as Chief Wraith charged swiftly towards us.

"Give me that damn camera, boy," he barked with aggression.

Unwilling to part with his treasure, Willie Kinsman held it closely to his heart and asked, "*Why, officer?* I didn't do *nothing.*"

Wraith reached for his camera, but a wild gust of wind threw Wraith off balance. He reached for Willie again, but this time, Willie dodged his hand, and Wraith tripped over his own feet.

The devil rose in Wraith's face as he spat, "You just pushed me."

I also witnessed years of resentment boiling over from inside his core through those mean eyes, and I raised my hands in protest.

"Chief Wraith, no crimes have been committed. You know he didn't push you. You tripped over your own feet. So, accost the wind and take me instead."

Out of nowhere, my forearms were snatched behind me—a sharp pain shot through my back and arms. I felt the cold handcuffs snap around my wrists. Flames shot through my joints as the other officer squeezed the cuffs tighter.

"You're under arrest for attempted assault on a law officer," he accused.

"Miss Empress didn't do nothing, officer, and neither did I," Willie Kinsman said while firing two more shots with his Kodak.

With Willie focused on rewinding the dial on the camera, Wraith raised his black billy club above his head.

"*No!*" I shouted.

Before the club struck, Mama Lee stopped Chief Wraith's blow by grabbing his arm.

"I can't let you do that, officer. He's just a boy."

Gripping his billy club, Wraith wrapped his burly arm around Mama Lee's neck and yelled, "*You* are under arrest for assault on an officer."

Seeing her struggling for air, I told him, "Wraith, you've arrested us, so let her go and take us to the station."

He didn't let up. "I'll take you when I'm good and damn ready."

I screamed so loudly my voice cracked. "*Somebody help! He's choking Mama Lee, and she can't breathe.*"

Henry and two female customers ran out of Henry's back door. Immediate terror swept across their faces, and Chief Wraith tightened his grip.

"Mr. Henry, we didn't do nothing," Willie Kinsman cried. "He's squeezing Mama Lee's neck, and she can't breathe." He shook his head and took another picture.

Chief Wraith clenched his jaws so tightly that the veins protruded from his face like worms.

Henry walked slowly towards us. "Officers, I know them. They are nice women. Please, let Miss Lee go. Chief Wraith, she can't breathe."

Mama Lee started to cry. It was the second time I'd seen her weep, and I didn't want it to be her last.

"I have faith. You're going to be alright. Did you hear me, God?" I screamed to heaven. "I have faith."

She rested her hands gently on Wraith's arms and began humming "Roll, Jordan, Roll."

I closed my eyes and started to pray for a savior. When I opened my eyes, a crowd had formed in the parking lot.

"*Let her go! She can't breathe!*" someone yelled, and they began to chant repeatedly.

The officer who was holding me fired a shot in the air.

"Everybody shut your trap holes and stay back!" he shouted. "Or I will shoot!"

The chants lowered to pleading whispers. My face was drenched with emotional tears and sweat.

As calmly as I could, I said, "Chief Wraith, *please*. It's me you want, so lock me up and let her go."

Henry stood in front of the officer's pistol. "Let Miss Lee go and kill me instead."

Wraith didn't let up. "Tell her to stop resisting."

"She's not resisting," I cried. "She's humming, and she can't breathe."

"She's fucking breathing if she's singing," he hollered.

Mama Lee went silent and completely still. Chief Wraith squeezed the final tears from her eyes until she went limp in his arms. I turned manic and began kicking and screaming like I was insane. The officer picked me up and slammed me onto the backseat of the squad car face-first. They threw my Mama, locked in handcuffs, on top of me.

I wiggled my way up and kissed her damp forehead. Unable to bear the lifelessness in her eyes, I looked out the window, and through my tears, I saw Perry sprint into the parking lot. Ready and Willie Kinsmen were close behind. They were too late. My faith in a savior had gone; the devil had choked the celestial out of my guardian angel, and God made me watch.

CHAPTER 18
I SLOW-DANCED WITH THE DEVIL

LEROY "READY" CLARK

August 1938 - Gary, Indiana

Mama Lee would say, "God possesses all power." I would argue, "A vengeful enemy is the forfeit of its opponent, so never underestimate the devil's power." I had known the strength of the enemy's grip, and it had a hold on me so tight it felt like death was my only option to be set free.

My vice was liquor, and like Adam, the serpent had convinced me I could become like God if I had consumed the forbidden fruit. To feel invincible, I had drunk whiskey every day, all day. While leading my platoon on the battlefield with my potion, I had the strength of Samson and the will of David, and I wanted that feeling to never end. But like any venom, too much consumption kills, and my kidney was nearly dead. I had tried to hide my illness, but my addiction had taken control of me, and I had become too weak to walk on my own two feet.

After being honorably discharged, I had come home to Mama with only months left to live. Like an angel, she began healing me with the herbs, fruits, and vegetables from her garden. It wasn't until I had taken a bite of one of her special sandwiches that we realized her sandwiches reversed my urge to drink. Five years later, I was still alive. And like I had once carried liquor bottles wherever I went, during sobriety, I always kept one of her sandwiches within arm's length.

Mama Lee had died, and I wasn't there to save her like she had rescued me. With my angel gone, the devil slid into her place, knowing that without the celestial instructions of her voice reaching the command of my ears, I was a dead man walking.

I was in my car, staring at a bottle of whiskey. I needed to hear Mama tell me to put it down. I needed her to snatch it out of my hand. And so, I waited. The longer I sat, the more my mouth dripped and desired a taste. I tried to lick the longing from my lips, but the devil whispered, *If you want to hear her voice again, take a sip.*

I popped the top, and the fumes traveled up my nose. Instantly, I thought of my comrades and the strength I had once possessed. I closed my eyes, remembering when I didn't need a cane to walk and the things I'd done that saved the country. I wanted to feel Godly again.

I leaned in closer to the tip of the bottle and deeply inhaled. A drop of liquor touched my nose and trickled onto my lip. I swiped it with my tongue, and a tingling sensation boiled inside me. I waited for Mama Lee, but all I heard was the devil whisper again. I placed my lips over the opening and wiggled my tongue inside.

I tilted my head back, and the liquid traveled down my throat. My veins set aflame. I went numb, and it felt so good. My car, the last place my love had been, was filled with her flowery perfume. I placed my face against the seat and breathed her in. All I wanted to do was see her again, but the only way I could do that was in my dreams.

With no rhythmic pattern, I slept, drank, awakened, and drank again. I had lost touch with time and reality. I only remembered night was dark and day was light. Days passed, and I was still waiting to hear Mama Lee's voice. The devil and I had spent more time together. The way I was so easily seduced by its temptations, I was convinced the devil was a dame.

Having drunk myself into delirium, I heard the devil tell me, *Ready, add a pill to your whiskey, and you will not only hear your angel, but you will also see her.*

I summoned a drug dealer from the shadows. He wasn't hard to find and sold me four pills. I parked my car and chased one down with my moonshine. Instantly, the burning yearning to make love grew inside me. Every nerve in my body was aroused; the way the sky's color faded from navy to purple made me want to fuck the wind. The steering wheel brushed against my hand, and immediately, I stiffened hard as a brick.

The devil had moved from my shoulder to my lap and whispered, *Go to a place where you can please a woman, and then your angel will speak to you again.*

I knew Mama Lee was in heaven, but the lust of Lucifer entranced me. I pulled up to a brothel on Washington Street known for the finest colored women in the Midwest. I guzzled down more of my hooch and popped another pill in my mouth.

As I slowly opened my door, a blue 1932 Chevrolet Confederate blasted past me like a rocket. The force of wind slammed my door shut, and I was held hostage inside. I knew the owner of that car. My lusting desires were replaced by ravaging rage. Sweat dripped from every pore in my body as I gripped my cane and cocked it like a shotgun.

Out of the Chevrolet stomped a tall, white man with a round face, sandy brown hair, and a thick mustache. He tried to disguise himself under a tan hat and overcoat, but I was certain it was Chief Wraith.

The devil slithered around me. *Ready, it's time for revenge.*

I quickly opened the door. The devil and I were one, and we tangoed up to Wraith.

"Chief Wraith," I called to him.

He lifted his head, and our eyes connected. "What do you want?" he asked.

"Your life," I growled.

He reached for his pistol, but I sent him where we both belonged with one blast to his chest. His blood rolled down the pavement like a river.

Wraith was dead, and I was relieved, but the devil still hadn't let go of me. We slow-danced back to my car, and once back inside, I zipped down Broadway. I turned right at Route 12 and sped towards Lake Michigan on Lake Street. I made it to Miller Beach and parked in the perfect spot overlooking the lake. With my sweet poison and venomous pills in both hands, I downed it all. Then, I stumbled out of my car and slumped onto the sand.

Miller Beach was where I had promised Mama Lee we would go one day. Our home was less than fifteen minutes away, but I hadn't taken her. I had planned to ask for her hand to make her the honest woman she deserved to be, but I hadn't done it. I loved Mama Lee more than anything in the world, but I let time escape us before I got the chance to show her how much.

The poison had taken over the blood in my veins, and all my senses climaxed. I took off my shoes to allow the sand to suck my toes. I deeply inhaled fresh water, and the scent massaged my nostrils. I could hear the calming breath of the seagulls sleeping peacefully on the mountainous dunes. The sky was dark blue and covered with pink and purple clouds. The sweet melody of the crashing waves and resting seagulls was like the perfect lullaby.

I hadn't realized the devil was dirty dancing on my lap. I didn't respond, and she disappeared.

I deeply exhaled and rested on the sand. *"Finally."*

I began to hear nature's prelude from the roaring sound of the lake's tides. Then, a warm, manly hand touched my shoulder.

"Alright, old man," he said, "I let you have your time alone, but after that mess you left for me on Washington, you've got to lay low at Tony's and Red's for a while."

"Youngblood, I knew you would be the one to find me, but I thought I would be dead."

Perry stood next to me, wearing all black and with his top hat pulled low over his eyes.

"I've been keeping my eyes on you. We're going to get you cleaned up. It's time to go, *now.*"

He grabbed my arm, and I pulled away. I handed him the black velvet box I was holding.

"Reach inside my pocket and grab the letter. It has my last wishes. Now go so I can repent and go to heaven before it's too late."

"*What?* No, Ready, Mama Lee wouldn't want this. Dulce just got out of the slammer, and she and Pierre won't be able to take losing you, too. We all need you to come home."

I snapped, "Youngblood, have you ever danced with the devil?"

"No, sir."

"I have. Without my angel here to intercede, the devil holds onto me, and it's like I live in hell on Earth. You have the woman of your dreams, so *please* let me be with mine."

Suddenly, he threw his arms around me and cried, "I'm going to miss you."

"Me too. Tell Dulce I love her." We embraced as true comrades, men, and friends. "Alright, sweaty eyes, leave me in peace. And do not write me a love poem when I'm gone."

"I'll do it while you're here." He got on his knee and grabbed my hand. "Roses are red, Ready wears blue..."

I cried with laughing tears, and my body became heavy.

"Perry, let me settle things with the Lord so I can see my angel in heaven."

Perry stepped out of sight, and I closed my eyes, praying until my body melted onto the sand. Then, I opened my eyes and watched the sky turn pink, covered with lilac clouds. A small hole opened in the clouds for the sun to shine through. The seagulls woke up, soared through the sky, and sang like they were set free. The sun gracefully rose from the horizon.

For the first time, I saw glory. A peaceful embrace that could only be heaven-sent wrapped around me, and my spirit surrendered. The roll of the tides created a sweet melody.

I closed my eyes, and finally, I heard my angel sing, *Roll, Jordan, roll.*

CHAPTER 19
LADY SINGS BLUES

DULCE "EMPRESS" MONROE

August 1938 - Gary, Indiana

My heart had two empty spaces, and my pulse was no longer steady. Overwhelmed by the grief from two emotional goodbyes in one day, my everything ached. One of Ready's final wishes was, *DO NOT bury me. Cremate me at Guy and Allen, and toss my ass in the lake with the seagulls.* I was unable to fight the painful sorrow, and in moments of being down and out, Mama Lee had taught me to surrender my soul to God and rest my spirit in the blues.

After listening to Juno sing Mamie Smith's "You Can't Keep a Good Man Down" at Lake Michigan's shoreline at Miller Beach, Pierre, Willie Kinsmen, Juno, Countess, Beloved, Philly, Bear, Red, Tony, and Geese waited as Perry and I stepped into the water. The waves were ice picks stabbing at my feet. The tongue of the waves licked around my calves, and I froze. All day, my tears had fallen without permission, and the salt had stained my cheeks as chalky debris from eroded river streams. I felt like an ice sculpture. Then, the wind sent a steamy breeze over me, and my body's temperature became nearly perfect.

Perry and I walked deeper into the song of the waves and waited. Before our eyes, the sun dipped beneath the horizon, and we gave Ready our final silent farewells. Perry walked further out and set Ready's ashes free.

Once in the car, Pierre quickly fell asleep on Perry's lap before Bear pulled off. I had never been to Miller Beach. Unlike the peninsula of Louisiana, Lake Michigan was soothing.

I admired the moon's fullness as we drove down Lake Shore Drive. It was so bright that night felt like day. Hundreds of seagulls flocked off the sand and perched on the tides. Hypnotized by all the beauty, my drained eyes drifted into dreamland.

Later that night, I awakened, sandwiched between the two fellas in my life. They had me drenched in sweat. Pierre was snuggled closely to my bosom like a baby kangaroo. The top of his head was pushed against my throat. Perry's body was hugged against my back like a bear. His long arm was extended across me, and he wiggled closer and pulled Pierre tighter into my chest. They were asleep on my hair, and I had no space to move.

I squirmed to get more space, but Perry wrapped his leg around my calf when I shifted my body. Pierre hooked his right arm around my head after he slapped my face. I loved them dearly, but lying between both of their snores was perpetuating my insomnia.

I had not experienced peace since I watched a devil kill an angel. There was no torture more horrifying than that, and I was stumped. *Why would God allow that to happen?*

While riding with Mama Lee's corpse on my lap, I had nothing but time to replay the event in my head. Then, I had been tossed into the slammer, where every minute felt like an hour. The images in my mind were suffocating, and if I saw her face in my mind for too long, I stopped breathing. And so, I had started experiencing moments when it felt like I was choking to death.

Although I had planned Mama Lee's homegoing as a celebration, I didn't like it. I despised funerals and didn't understand why people thought it was comforting to say everything was beautiful when you just watched a loved one get buried underground. Where was the beauty in that?

But I had known Mama Lee like I knew how many moles I had on my body, and she wouldn't want anyone crying over her. She would want singing, dancing, and music playing, and I did that in her honor.

Word of how she had departed had already spread like fire. So, with hundreds of supporters wanting to pay their respects, her funeral was more like a sold-out concert. I knew she was singing and dancing in heaven with a smile on her face.

I had requested that anyone who loved her show up wearing her favorite color, which was her favorite style of music—blues. Musicians, friends, fans, and previous kids she had helped raise took their blue representation seriously by not only dressing in blue attire but carrying blue flags, umbrellas, and instruments. I designed her the most beautiful blue gown adorned with pearls, crystals, and sapphires. It was the dress I dreamt she would wear to my wedding. I had placed a light blue orchid pendant that sparkled with sapphires in her hair.

As Ready requested, Perry slid the sapphire ring Ready had planned to marry Mama Lee with onto her left ring finger. After her committal, trumpets blasted in a smooth shrill of affection, followed by the hum of the bass guitar. A snare pumped life into our hearts with the timed rhythm of his drum.

Willie Kinsmen and Juno sang a beautiful duet, harmonizing their bluesy rendition of "Roll Jordan Roll." Then, we spent the rest of the afternoon dancing to Mama Lee's favorite songs, performed by her favorite artists.

There were countless people Mama Lee had touched, but no one knew anything about her family or where she had grown up. As she'd done in my life, she had appeared like magic after a gust of wind, dressed as an angel in blue. Whenever I asked about her life before music, she would say, "I was born from the blues."

I didn't understand. *Why did God need Mama Lee in heaven when so many Negroes needed a savior like her on Earth?*

Perry got up and turned on the electrical fan. "Are you okay, doll?"

Before I could respond, he'd fallen back asleep. He threw his arm and leg across my body, Pierre's hand smacked my face, and I lay there praying for shut-eye.

The aroma of warm maple syrup, buttermilk pancakes, and sizzling fried ham permeated the room, and I thought I was dreaming. The quiet buzz of the fan rose, and the perfect breeze tickled the hairs on my skin. I opened my eyes and was able to stretch across the entire length of the bed. I rolled around a couple of times just because I could. The bedroom window was open, and the sunshine peered inside. I sat up and smiled, not noticing Perry and Pierre were in the doorway.

"Damn, you're so beautiful, doll," Perry said.

Pierre echoed, "Just damn beautiful, doll."

"Pierre, get Mommy some sugar from the kitchen."

Pierre ran out the room, and Perry slid a breakfast tray in front of me.

He grabbed my chin and loved on my lips. "Good morning."

I smiled and kissed him back. "Hey, good looking. I had no idea you could cook."

Pierre ran inside with the sugar and sprinted back out.

Perry placed the spoon inside the sugar jar and sprinkled a little over the grits. "My mama taught all of us how to cook. Since I'd been staying at The Palace, I never had a chance." He slipped a spoonful into my mouth. "How are you feeling?"

"Mama used to tell me joy cometh in the morning, so I feel better."

He gave me a sample of the pancakes, and they were delicious. "Dunstan will be quiet for a tick," he told me. "The press is in his ass for what happened to Mama Lee and the homicide of the chief. Also, I planted evidence of his racketeering and ties to the mob, so the feds are crawling into every crevice in the city. We need to keep our heads down and hands clean until they leave."

"I hope they lock him up. Call a meeting so we can get everyone on board."

"Everything is already done. Philly hid the stash. Treasure removed all gambling traces from the figures. Beloved is hotel manager, and her girls are officially hotel staff."

I moved onto his lap. "I can't believe I have a man who can think for me when I don't feel like thinking."

"What do you think about us getting married this weekend? I want to set a good example for Pierre since we're all living under the same roof now. While things are quiet, we could get away for our honeymoon. But let me know if it's too soon."

I wrapped my arms around him. "Perry, I would love to, and I know Mama and Ready would want that."

"Swell. Afterwards, I'll take you to Harlem to meet my brothers."

I picked up my spoon and shoved my sugar grits in his mouth. "Perfect. After that, we can fly to Paris for our honeymoon."

He frowned like he was eating chitterlings. "*Hell no, doll.* I'm not sharing you with that French nigga."

"I told you Matthieu is a good friend, and he's married."

Perry grabbed his tan hat and kissed my lips. *"Hell no.* I'm going to The Palace. I'll let Bear know I'm leaving so he'll keep an eye out."

Pierre jumped in the bed. Perry gave him a kiss and smooth five.

"You'll be asleep when I get home, Pierre, so I'll steal your kisses while you're asleep."

"I'll leave my kisses on the pillow so you don't have to steal them."

I got up and walked him to the door. "I'll let Matthieu know we're coming."

With a sexy tip of the hat, he protested, *"Hell no to Paris, doll,"* and walked out of the door.

CHAPTER 20
SWEET AND PUNGENT

DULCE "EMPRESS" MONROE

August 1938 - Gary, Indiana

It was late, and the sultry sounds of jazz migrated into my ears while the sweet aroma of fresh flowers tiptoed up my nose. The cool satin from a rose petal outlined my lips, and I opened my eyes. The dimly lit room was illuminated by three tall candles inside a golden candelabra.

Perry was seated next to me in nothing but a white towel, his glistening muscles carved into perfection. Drops of water were violating his skin.

He kissed my hand. "Will you dance with me, doll?"

We got up, and I placed my hands around his neck. He pulled my body close to his. His skin's moisture was like glue, and my silk gown didn't want to let go. His fingers went on a voyage across my shoulders and behind my neck. My head rolled with the slow tempo, followed by my hips. Perfectly in sync, Perry's body led mine into a smooth rhythmic melody. Holding tightly to the small of my back, he carefully dipped me into a backbend and removed my gown. My fingers traveled down the lined muscular trail beneath his towel and dropped the barricade.

He spun me around and lifted my hair, allowing my neck to embrace the lock of his lips. His tongue moved like soundwaves over my shoulder. Then, he slowly dipped his fingers between my thighs, catching each drip of my honey.

"*Mmm*," he whispered. "Miss De Leche, you're packed with sugar so sweet that I'm addicted, baby. Your dessert is my treat."

From behind, he wrapped my leg around his waist and used my fingers to strum between my legs like a cello. Then, he took my hand and licked every drop from my fingertips as he entered me. Enraptured, I moved the way his body directed me.

With his sweet moans in my ear, I repeatedly whispered his name. Our bodies conducted harmonious compositions that made our hips roll in response. Unable to withstand the peaked pleasure, I shook uncontrollably and slid onto the bed.

His tongue traveled down my spine and between my cheeks. He consumed every inch of my body until I was totally weak. He flipped me on my back, and when we plunged into the essence of each other's core, he caught my orgasmic yell with a loving kiss. His tongue entered my mouth, and his fingers laced between mine.

"*Damn*, your sweet scream is like candy to my ear—your voice melodic, nectar, crystal clear."

He sped up, and cries escaped my eyes and body. We pushed and pulled, and I contracted and released him with the might of my muscles until we transcended above the worries of the world. I never thought I would be the dame to end up with a man who gave me pleasure without pain, but I was thankful Lady Luck sought fit to make me one of the lucky ones.

The next day, Pierre swung open the door, banging it against the wall.

"Good morning, Mommy and Daddy!"

My body was wedged against Perry's chest, and we both were dazed under the covers.

Perry awakened sleepily. "Good morning, son. Close the door and give Mommy and Daddy a couple more minutes to wake up." The door shut, and Perry's hands crept down my back. I threw his pajamas at him and slipped into a gown and robe.

He pulled me towards him. "How are you holding up?"

"The thought of marrying you helps take the pain away."

"I'll make sure it stays that way."

I slid onto his lap and wrapped my arms around his neck. "Are you ready to make an honest woman out of me?"

"I was ready five years ago," he replied, softly nibbling at my ear.

"How many times are you going to throw that in my face?"

Pierre busted through the door and jumped on Perry's back. He spun him around and tickled him next to me. In that moment, I experienced true serendipity and was grateful for Perry's resurgence into my life as my emperor—gallant with the heart of a knight.

The sun was resting behind downtown Chicago's skyline to our west. The lake's breeze wet our faces with kisses. To celebrate Perry and my union, Bear, Geese, Red, Tony, Willie Kinsmen, Countess, Juno, and Beloved joined us. We were back at Miller Beach, where Ready asked to sleep eternally near the sound of Mama's voice.

Young Willie Kinsman was there to capture our moment with his fancy camera. Perry got Pastor Carpenter, a young preacher from Gary's African Methodist Episcopal Church, to conduct our ceremony. Everyone was smiling and dressed sharp as tacks in their Sunday best.

Even though Miller Beach was less than five miles from downtown Gary, it felt like it was in a different part of the country.

The feel was fresher. The air was crisper, like it had been purified with frankincense.

I designed a lace champagne wedding gown and the perfect sunhat that hung over my eye. I'd gotten inspired by the latest Chanel gown I'd seen in *Harper's Bazaar* magazine, which raved about the new look of tighter fitted gowns with exposed shoulders. I accessorized my look with my favorite color and bright red lipstick.

To my right was Perry, who stood picturesque in the grey pinstriped tuxedo I had made him. He was dapper, sporting Ready's top hat and cane. To my left was Pierre, dressed like his miniature clone.

I had questioned my faith. However, as I stood before Pastor Carpenter, next to my two favorite fellas in the world, I felt like I was floating on God's hands, held steady in His palms. After a few minutes of vow exchange, Willie Kinsman and Juno provided a soulful duet of the song "Smoke Gets in Your Eyes."

Perry leaned in and locked his lips with mine, and our bond was forever cemented. All I heard were cheers and several clicks of Young Willie's Kodak.

Perry lifted my chin. "You are officially Mrs. Dulce 'Empress Creed' Savage."

"I love the sound of that."

"Look!" Pierre yelled.

We turned, and out of nowhere, a family of five brown and white deer appeared across the street. They were grazing at the bottom of the green hills at Marquette Park. None of us had ever seen anything like that in the city. We were staring at them, and they were staring back.

Willie Kinsman snapped a picture and walked towards the street. "I need to get closer."

Pierre ran after him. "I want to go, too."

He stopped and turned for our approval. Perry fanned them away.

"Go," he told them. "Quickly and hurry back."

Tommy tipped his hat. "Countess and I are headed back to Chicago."

"Can you stay for a tick? We're having ice cream at the parlor."

Countess gave us a big hug. "I wish, but I have a flight to catch. Let's go, Juno."

They walked to the car, but Juno stayed behind.

"Y'all go ahead," Juno called out to them. "I'm helping Geese with getting his restaurant ready for the grand opening."

Geese gave Perry a wide grin and smooth five. "Congratulations, big brother. You know Bear and I will keep things steady while you're gone. Give our brothers my love. Welcome to the Savage family, Empress."

Geese opened Juno's car door. He and Tommy drove their cars away.

"Do you think Geese and Juno are sweet on each other?" I asked.

He shrugged.

Perry and I watched Pierre and Willie Kinsmen chase deer through the woods. Bear and Beloved had a love connection and were snuggled up on the hood of his car. Red and Tony were smoking cigarettes and recounting old war memories they shared with Ready.

I looked into the sky and heard Mama Lee utter her love inside my heart. *I'm proud of you, sugar,* she said. I was in a state of serenity, and my soul was in the sweetest place.

I clenched hold of Perry, and he placed my face in his hands. "You're the most beautiful bride I've ever seen, and I'm the luckiest man in the world." He kissed my lips with intensity. "I knew I would turn you into a Savage when I first laid eyes on you."

"I can't wait to see what happens when two Savages come together for the first time in matrimony."

Perry picked me up, and we twirled as I wrapped my arms around his neck.

"I can show you better than I can tell you," he teased.

My heart was already overflowing. Perry's kisses poured more love into me, and I felt like I would explode.

Suddenly, a cool breeze blew over us, and Perry stiffened like a corpse. His loving eyes transformed into the look of a wild man, and two beads of sweat ran down his forehead. Curious at what he'd witnessed, I tried to turn my head, but he held onto my face. In my peripheral, Beloved scurried past us like she had seen a ghost. Then, the clicking sounds of cocked revolvers entered my ears. For the first time, I watched fear creep into Perry's eyes. A sudden chill penetrated through my veins.

"Doll," he whispered, "grab the keys from my right pocket, pick up the boys, and take them for ice cream at Joe's Parlor. Move quickly, and don't turn around."

A tear fell down my face; his thumb caught it.

"Wait for me to carry you across the threshold."

Before I could speak, he placed his finger on my lips. Trembling, I grabbed the car keys and took one last look into Perry's eyes, but his focus was beyond me.

As I walked quickly through the sand, I heard a man say, "This is a whites-only beach, which means no niggers allowed."

Instantly, my feet and heart stopped, and I reached for my .22 inside my trusty garter belt. Then, joyous laughter projected from across the street. Pierre and Willie Kinsman were running vicariously and taking pictures of deer in the fields. My body was suddenly planted in the driver's seat. I don't remember how I got there, but Beloved was frozen next to me.

I peeled off and stopped in the middle of the street.

Rolling down the window, I called out, "Boys, let's go!"

"Aww, do we have to?" Pierre pleaded.

I smiled through my fear. "Yes, sweetie. We're going to get ice cream."

Cheering, he and Willie ran towards us and jumped into the backseat. Innocence intact, the kids were laughing and ecstatic that they had seen a family of deer. I looked over at Beloved, whose face screamed the sentiments of my thoughts.

Will our sons, enriched with melanin, have futures brighter than the blackness of their dark-skinned forefathers?

"Is somebody following us?" I whispered to Beloved.

She shook her head, and our anxious hands locked together.

After one final glance at Miller Beach, the essence had dramatically changed. The tall sand dunes with Coca-Cola bottle curves looked like heaps of dirt. The song produced by the seagulls sounded like the gawk of crows. The allure of the dancing waves became as still as the Dead Sea. The sweet, crisp fragrance of the air transformed into pungent fumes of spoiled perch.

My fear turned into hate. I hated the men I wasn't allowed to see. They were thieves who'd stolen the sacred from my blissful moment. They proved that amidst the most beautiful place, no pretty can hide the true ugly of the world.

As promised, I took the boys for sundaes at Ice Cream Joe's parlor on Broadway. The sky was dark, and there were no stars in the sky. Inside, the parlor was bright white and smelled like fresh lemon zest. Then, the sweet smell of sugared milk hit our noses. Expecting a parlor full, Joe led us to the large booth decorated with dozens of red roses Perry had dropped off earlier that day. From Joe's face, I could sense he knew something had gone wrong.

Joe gently placed his hand on my shoulder. Then, he smiled and set a bowl of vanilla, chocolate, and strawberry-flavored ice cream scoops in front of me with fresh strawberries, whipped cream, caramel, and chocolate cookie crumbles on top.

"Your man, Snipes, created this new sundae called Empress Creed. Trust me, everything always feels better after a bite of ice cream."

Fighting back tears, I swallowed a spoonful. All the flavors merged and trickled down my throat. My hate dissipated, and by the end of my sundae, I was rejuvenated with unspoken strength.

Before I dropped off Willie Kinsman, he smiled and looked at his camera. "Mrs. Empress, thank you for the ice cream. I had a swell time and can't wait to get these pictures developed."

Minutes later, we pulled up to the front of our house on Washington Street.

"*Daddy!*" Pierre jumped out before I fully parked the car.

I couldn't wait to get inside Perry's arms and walked quickly towards him.

Pierre ran next to Beloved and yelled, "Mommy, I'm staying with Miss Beloved and Uncle Bear tonight." Then he ran into my arms, gave me a kiss, and jumped onto Bear's back.

I ran into Perry's arms, and as promised, he lifted me and carried me over the threshold. Once he put me down, I grabbed his hands and pulled him into the bathroom, where I ran the hot water to fill the tub. Then, I unbuttoned and removed all his clothes. I was grateful to see no physical bruises, but in his eyes, I saw scarred emotions that ran deeper than any physical pain. His fists were balled tightly, and his jaws clenched shut.

In his ear, I whispered, "Perry, don't think about anything or anyone but me loving you."

After he lowered himself into the tub, my fingers started a massage at the top of his head where his crown belonged. I rubbed and removed as much stress and pain as I could with the stroke of my hands and the touch of my lips from his head to his toes.

When he tensed up to speak, I placed my finger on his lips. "Relax, and let me love you."

He kissed my finger.

I left for a moment and returned with the ice cream Joe had given me. Perry's head was rested against the tub's edge, and his eyes were closed. I placed a spoonful in his mouth. For the first time since he'd been back, he smiled.

"Perry, I promise to never stop loving you."

He squeezed me in his arms. We were two Savages freed from the bounds of the world—alone together uninterrupted, possessed with unlimited passion. We made love unconditionally, without limits. Frustrations, fears, and burdens lifted that night as we merged into one body, one soul, and one heart.

CHAPTER 21
ECHOES OF HARLEM

DULCE "EMPRESS" SAVAGE

August 1938 - Harlem, New York

The demanding cars honking, continuous shouting, and repeated slamming on the car's brakes kept me from getting a wink of peaceful shut-eye.

Perry didn't want to spend our first night as the Savages in Indiana after whatever happened on the beach between him and the racist whites took place. So, after we consummated, he carried me and our luggage to the car, and we headed for the likes of The Statue of Liberty. He jammed his foot against the floorboard for what felt like the hundredth time, and our car jerked before stopping. I braced and caught myself from crashing into the dashboard.

"Hey! Watch where you're going, why don't you?!" I yelled.

Perry laughed out loud. "You already sound like a New Yorker! Welcome to Harlem, doll."

Growing up on the South Side of Chicago, I was no stranger to crowds and hustle. But when we crossed onto Harlem's 125th Street, it was shockingly different. The energy was fuller and more electric. There were more shops snuggled onto one block than I'd seen on the entire South Side of State Street. In Harlem, the sidewalks and streets were exploding with vibrant color. The buildings were majestic concrete mountains with beaming signs brighter than the sun. The countless street cars zoomed by without a care in the world.

We drove past The Apollo Theater, which shouted Count Basie & Band's name with fire-red letters plastered across the grand marquis. On 142nd Street, carts lined the streets from different vendors selling fresh food and produce. I saw the greenest lettuce, large football-shaped potatoes, and the longest catfish I'd ever laid eyes on.

People of all ages, colored with luxurious hues of brown, covered every inch of the concrete. Gals and gents were dressed sharp as tacks in exclusive threads ritzy enough to grace any fashion runway. Flapper girls flocked together—with long legs, high heels, flashy hats, fancy dresses, and pearls draping from their necks—appeared ready to perform onstage with the great Katherine Dunham.

A crowd surrounded a group of older gents gathered in a shouting checkers tournament that had stopped traffic on the side of the road. Little girls dressed in fluffy dresses and boys in suspendered knickers played together in delight. The sun's rays welcomed me with open arms, and I reveled in the embrace.

The wind huffed through the window, and Perry touched my thigh. "Are you ready to meet my crazy brothers?"

"Of course."

With a loving touch to my face, he smiled. "I love you, doll."

I kissed his hand. "I love you back, good-looking."

We stopped in front of a brownstone covered with ivies. Eyebrow-shaped window frames surrounded a tall, arched doorway, and every window was open. Congregated on the stoop, in front of a gigantic red door, was a handsome group of chocolate-

colored men who looked like glass figurines. Perry and I got out
and followed the tune of musical tapping feet and rhythmic hand
claps. Two men somersaulted like acrobats onto the street, and the
group of men roared and cheered them on.

I giggled. "Perry, are they always like this?"

He nodded and pointed them out. "Yes. My brothers, Slide
and Styles, have been having dance-offs since we were kids."

Styles and Slide's feet were serenading the crowd like
classical piano keys intermitted with jazzy improvisations. They
both looked to be muscularly fit and well over six feet tall. Styles
was dressed in a tan vest and pants, a cream shirt, a brown plaid tie,
and peanut butter shoes. When he danced, he lifted his pants and
showed off his red plaid socks.

Slide wore a white shirt with an undone striped tie hanging
off his neck, brown suspenders, tan pants, and tan and white wing-
tipped shoes. Slides' hair was curly and parted on the right side,
and he shimmied with every glided step.

Both men had smooth dark skin, dark eyebrows, and curled
lashes like they were wearing mascara. Standing on each end of
the stoop were two stoic-looking guards with stoned faces. One
looked stocky, like a sumo wrestler with a ponytail. The other guy
was thin with huge hands and feet. They were holding machine
guns like pocketbooks.

Styles and Slide finished dancing, and their audience quickly
dispersed. Perry's brothers ran over and hugged him, nearly
knocking him over.

"*Snipes!*" they yelled in unison, both dripping in sweat.

He looked shocked at their affection. "Why are y'all acting
like you didn't know we were coming?"

A light brown-skinned man with black wavy hair, thick
eyebrows, and deep dimples smiled. It was Major, Perry's oldest
brother, sporting a light blue shirt, grey plaid pants, and a grey

vest. He had been standing in the doorway and walked down the steps to greet Perry.

"'Cause they didn't know," Major told him. "I wanted them to be surprised." He kissed my hand. "You are lovely, Empress. Welcome to the family, sister-in-law."

"Thank you. Nice to meet everyone."

Styles pushed Perry. "What? You got hitched?"

Perry wrapped his arms around my waist. "I didn't want to wait. Plus, my son was ready for his mama to have our last name. Everyone, Dulce Empress Creed Savage."

Slide walked over. "You two are like a Negro fairytale. Let's see a picture of my nephew."

Styles gave me a hug. "Empress, you have my brother lovestruck. We remember how he told us about this beautiful dame with long hair from Chicago named Dulce De Leche, who kept him from meeting us at the Duke concert five years ago. We made fun of his ass for years when he said you disappeared. We thought maybe he had gotten dizzy off hooch and made you up."

They burst into loud laughter.

I put my arms around Perry's neck. "I'm real. Lady Luck brought us together and made sure we found our way back to each other. We're locked in for life now."

Perry proudly pulled Pierre's picture from his wallet. "That's right, doll. Meet your nephew, my heir."

They all stared at the photograph in awe.

Styles smiled. "Golly, he looks like you."

Major snatched the photo and nodded with approval. "Yes, he's *definitely* a Savage. Let's get out this heat—it's frying us like bacon."

We walked into a cherry wooden foyer that extended down a long hallway. The carved wooden posts and banisters on the staircase looked like Egyptian art. The white sculptured ceiling was accented with a twinkling chandelier. I was hypnotized by the rainbows that twirled like ballerinas from the dangling crystal beads.

Down the wooden staircase walked Countess. She was decked out in a green and white polka dot sleeveless top with a scarf tied into a big bow around her neck, a green fit-and-flare calf-length skirt, and tan heels. The front of her red hair was pinned back and fluffed down her shoulders.

"Hey again, you two. I was just coming outside to greet you."

We hugged, and I said, "I should've known this was the flight you had to catch."

Major kissed her like they were the only two in the room. "My strawberry can't stay away from home too long."

"I do love to be dipped in your chocolate, good-looking."

He wrapped his arms around her waist. "Marry me, and let me cover you permanently."

"I'll marry you when you move to Chicago."

"Dammit, woman, you are so goddamn stubborn. You know I'm not moving."

She folded her arms. "Neither am I."

His smile quickly faded. "Chicago is as racist as Jim Crow South. I have my family enterprise here."

"Major, daddy, let's not fight in front of company." She wrapped her arms around his neck. *"Please."* Then, she whispered something in his ear, and a grin broke down his iced face.

"I think you put a voodoo root on me."

She switched up the stairs. "We'll catch up at dinner, Empress. And Major, for the record, Harlem is just as racist as Chicago."

"Camille, you better get to the room before I get worked up again."

She winked. "I like it when you're worked up."

He shook his head. "Goddamn, that dame drives me crazy."

Perry gave him a smooth five. "I know *exactly* what you mean, big brother."

Our soles clacked up the wooden staircase to the third floor. Major opened two tall cherry oak doors, and we walked into the master suite with white carved plaster walls and ceilings. I stared at the white marble fireplace. There was a large dressing room and closet. We passed the sitting room and library on our way to the bathroom at the end of the hallway.

I marveled at all the spectacular details. "Wow, Major, this is the ritz."

Perry gave him a smooth five. "Thanks, brother. Looks amazing."

Major placed down my bags. "I wanted the newlyweds to enjoy the master. Tonight, we are going to the Cotton Club. Styles and Slide's dance performance premier is tonight."

Excitement filled my body about what dress I would wear.

"I can't wait! I've read books about the Cotton Club and have always wanted to go."

Perry smiled proudly. "Wow! I can't believe our brothers actually booked a professional gig. I've been watching them fool around for so long that I took their talent for granted."

"I'll see you downstairs in two hours. Empress, I would appreciate anything you can say to get Camille to move to Harlem."

"Major, I will say that I've *never* seen Countess so carefree."

He looked hopeful. "Camille has me out of character, so I know she's the one. I'm ready to build my legacy and have a bunch of red-headed sons."

"*Major!*" Countess called from across the house. "I'm waiting, big daddy."

Perry hugged Major. "Sounds like you're not the only one out of character, big brother."

Major smiled. "That's 'cause she's in love with a Savage."

They burst into laughter.

"See you two newlyweds in three hours," he said.

I stopped him. "Don't you mean two hours?"

Countess yelled at the top of her lungs. *"Major!"*

With a look of a lion's hunger in his eyes, he lifted three fingers in the air and split.

Perry threw me over his shoulder and ran down the hallway.

"At ease, Captain Savage!" I screamed.

"Your wish is my command, my Empress."

He tossed me on the bed, pulled off my shoes, and threw them across the room. Then, he got down on all fours, looked at me with tiger eyes, and started removing my pantyhose.

"Put that wild beast back in his cage. I want to tour the suite."

"Before your tour, your captain needs you to about-face on his lap."

After a long kiss, I took off my dress and did as he commanded.

"You don't have to tell me twice."

I was suffocating and couldn't breathe. Sweat seeped out of my body and created a puddle beneath me. My heart pounded inside my chest like a hammer, as if it wanted to break free. I shot up, lightheaded and dizzy like I'd been on a merry-go-round.

No matter how hard I tried to gain control of my body, only small puffs of wind would enter and exit my lungs. My hands started shaking until my body tremored like an earthquake. Unable to speak, I cried uncontrollably. I felt like I was choking. Immediately, Perry grabbed my face with a pained look of concern showing in his eyes.

"Dulce, what's wrong? Do you need a doctor, doll?"

I shook my head and pointed my shaking finger towards my pocketbook.

He sprinted across the room and scrambled inside. "Do you have medicine you need to take?"

Still gasping, I told him, "*Cigarettes.*"

"What?" He put on his pants. "*Hell no.* You need a medic."

"No!" I cried out. After every word, I sipped for air. "I need cigarettes to calm my attack. I *can't* breathe."

Seeing that I was still trembling, Perry wrapped his arms around me like a warm blanket. He placed my head against his chest and gently stroked my hair.

With his lips against my forehead, he said quietly, "I'll be your cigarette, doll. Hold onto me and breathe."

I wept into his chest as my breathing calmed.

"Dulce, how often do you have these attacks?"

"Every day since Mama died."

He wiped my face and soothed me with kisses.

"Every day since Chief Wraith killed Mama, I've lost control of my breathing," I continued. My air started to escape me again. "Perry, everyone I love dies…Meek-Meek, Mama, and Ready." I became terrified and panicked. "Oh no! I'm cursed. You and Pierre must get away from me, or you'll die, too."

Perry held me tighter. "No, doll, that's not true. Don't ever think or say that again. You are a gift from God. You're the best thing that has happened to us."

"*Why* did God make me watch her die like that?" Flashbacks of Mama Lee losing air triggered me to hyperventilate again. "Perry, I *need* my cigarettes, *please.*"

He kissed my forehead and wrapped my arms around his waist. "You need oxygen when you can't breathe, and I'm right here, doll. Hold on to me and inhale."

With my ear against his smooth, bare chest, I felt the pulse of his calming heartbeat like a steady drum. His fingers softly ran through my hair as his biceps locked around me. I nestled inside his muscular cocoon, and all the tension in my body eased.

"Perry, squeeze me tighter and never let go."

"I promise to never let you go."

We synchronized our air as one, and complete tranquility swept over me. My life was in his hands. Perry, my emperor, knightly protector, and poetic lover, had officially become my healer.

Major and Perry admired Countess and me as we clacked down the steps.

Major whistled. "*Golly*, little brother, we have the hottest dames in Harlem."

Perry stood like a dream, dressed in a cream three-piece suit, baby blue silk tie, and tan leather oxfords. On his head was a cream and soft-blue brimmed hat. Major wore a black tuxedo jacket with matching pants and a black and white polka dot tie. His hair lay down in waves with a razor-sharp side part.

"That's a fact, Jack," Perry bragged as he jumped up the steps and offered his hand to me. "You look gorgeous, Mrs. Savage."

His touch made the hairs on my body stand at attention.

"Thank you, and you look debonair, Captain Savage."

He pressed his lips beneath my earlobe. "How are you feeling, doll?"

"Swell. All I needed was my oxygen."

As we walked to the door, Countess remained glued to the steps. She tapped her foot until Major turned around.

He looked puzzled at her obvious dismay. "Camille LeRoux, let's go, Strawberry."

She crossed her arms over her chest. "I'm waiting for you to jump your ass up the stairs for me."

"*What?*"

She didn't budge. "You heard me. Come get me."

"Say you love me, and I'll meet you halfway."

She rolled her eyes, and he walked towards the door like he was leaving.

"Fine," she blurted. "I love you."

He quickly trotted up the steps and placed his lips against hers. "I love you, Creole Queen, but next time you want me to do something for you, just ask, and I'll make it happen. Do not command me like your dunce of a servant. Smooth?"

She slowly nodded. *"Oui."*

He lifted her chin. "Now, tell me you love me like you mean it."

She slowly kissed his lips. *"Je t'aime, mon amour."*

Major's two guards opened the front door, and we headed to his all-black Cadillac.

"Let's fade to the Jim Crow Cotton Picker Club, family!"

"Where?" I asked.

"The Cotton Club *was* in Harlem, but white folks didn't allow Negroes to step inside except to shuck and jive for their entertainment. It was not until after the Harlem riot that they let us inside the Times Square location. If it weren't for my brothers, I would never step one foot inside."

As we rolled into New York City's theater district, the buildings grew taller, the lights shined brighter, and the noises got louder. The city's pot was melting with a variety of spices, from the exotic cars driving on the streets to the various races swarming the sidewalk. We drove past foreign machines, couture fashions, and nationalities I had never seen before. New York City seemed decades ahead of the rest of America—I felt like a movie star on a Hollywood set, featured in a film about being transported into the future.

Our car stopped in front of the infamous marquis that shouted *Cotton Club*. On the top floor at Seventh and Broadway, we stepped inside. Duke Ellington and his orchestra played up-tempo jazz, adding to the electric energy. I always loved hearing Duke's live performances at Mama's Blues. But this stage was extremely extravagant, surrounded by tables of Negro and white people who were chatting, dancing, and eating carefree. We sat at a table one level above the stage, and the Cotton Club's $1.50 dinner menu was placed in front of us. My stomach barked, reminding me I hadn't eaten anything in two days.

The waiter came over. "Madame Queenie invited you all to sit with her."

Madame Queenie was the infamous numbers queen from Harlem who'd battled white mobster Dutch Shultz for years. She was exquisitely dressed in a golden, shimmery gown, emerald-colored hat, and gloves. Around her neck was a pearl choker.

We walked to her front table, which was positioned stage right. We were so close to the stage that I could detect the lemon cleaner in the bleach engrained into the wood.

Major kissed her hand. "Madame Queenie and Bumpy, thanks for having us."

In a sultry, French Caribbean accent, she said, "Major and Snipes, it's always a pleasure. *Bonjour*, Countess."

"*Content de te voir, Madame Queenie.*"

Perry pulled out my seat. "Madame Queenie and Bumpy, this is my wife, Empress."

Queenie and I shook hands. "Empress from Gary, Indiana. Nice to meet you. I love Countess's dresses you design for her. You must make me one," she said.

I couldn't believe she knew who I was. "The pleasure is truly mine, Madame Queenie. You are a living legend, and I would love to design your gown. You always look *magnifique*."

"Does everybody like steak?" Bumpy asked, and everyone nodded.

Bumpy had a serious demeanor, even when he smiled. He was Madame Queenie's right-hand man, dressed in a black pin-striped suit and red tie.

Raising his hand to summon the waiter, Bumpy placed our order.

"Bring us all filet mignon, French fried potatoes, and lobster salad. Also, two bottles of champagne for the table and a glass of lemonade for everybody."

The men began smoking cigars and talking amongst each other.

"Empress, what is it like living in Gary?" Madame Queenie asked.

"It's a grain of sand compared to South Side where I grew up. Because it's small and there is little to no competition, the colored businesses stick together. But it's like living in any American city as a Negro—we make sure we stay on our side of the tracks."

Queenie shook her head. "That's the truth. Shame what they did to that blues singer."

"How'd you hear about that?" I asked.

"It was in today's *Chicago Defender*."

The *Chicago Defender* was a nationally distributed, Negro-owned publication that kept us informed about our news headlines from around the country.

My hands trembled, and my breaths shortened. My throat immediately dried out, but my mouth was watering.

"Are you alright?" Countess asked.

As I fumbled inside my pocketbook in search of a cigarette, Countess stuck a lit Lucky Strike between my lips. Once I inhaled and exhaled the smoke, my shakes subsided.

"You knew her?" Madame Queenie asked.

I nodded. "She raised me, and I was *there* when it happened."

"*Heavens.* What happened to her killer?"

"He's rotting in hell, hopefully."

"Good riddance," she replied, then whispered, "If you are ever in a street war with whites from across the tracks, you need a white ally. It took me years and the loss of dozens of *good* men to learn that lesson. Find a white man younger and more ambitious than whoever is against you. Put them against each other like they do us all the time."

She reached across the table and grabbed both Countess and my hand. In silence, we locked our jeweled hands together.

"Y'all blessing the food without us?" Bumpy asked.

Queenie winked at us. "We're talking women's business."

Perry came beside me and offered his hand. "Would you dance with me, doll?"

Duke Ellington's "Creole Love Call" beckoned us to the dance floor.

Grabbing his hand, I stood up. "Of course."

"Do you remember this song?" he asked while escorting me to the center of the floor.

"I had thought, *Damn,* I'm in love with this fine-ass soldier."

He smiled. "I thought, *Damn,* I'm going to marry this gorgeous dame."

In a jazzy waltz, we twirled, and the orchestra hypnotized us into a trance. As one callused hand gripped mine, the other held the small of my back. Nothing or no one existed to me in that moment. His body commanded, and I followed wherever he led. His body spoke with each movement, and I quickly responded. He dipped me backwards, and his firm grip sent heated chills up and down my spine. I surrendered as he pulled my face in front of his. His lips were so full of lusciousness that I wanted to suck them off his face.

"I love you, Captain Savage."

"I love you back, Mrs. Savage."

The music stopped, and we descended back to the Cotton Club.

When we returned to the table, the aroma of cigarette smoke, wood, and savory food filled my nose. Shortly after we sat down, our meals arrived. The orchestra started its magical melodies, and red and blue lights flickered. Backstage echoes of tapping feet seduced our ears, and everyone roared and clapped.

From the shadows danced a man with one pegged leg. Amazed at his talent, everyone cheered. Then, Styles and Slide tapped an acrobatic routine alongside two tall dancers with silver feathered dresses that sparkled like diamonds. Perry and Major yelled like they were watching a boxing match. The entire show captivated me till the very end.

After the finale, we headed back to our cars.

Madame Queenie waved. "*Au revoir,* ladies and gentlemen."

Bumpy shut her door, and after her car drove off, Bumpy's car pulled behind ours. Major and Countess entered the Cadillac from the street. Perry opened my door and showered me with sugared kisses.

"Goddamn! Save it for the bedroom, Snipes!" Major jived.

Before Perry responded, his eyes turned wild. His attention turned to a man creeping behind us with midnight skin and dressed in all black—overcoat, pants, shoes, and a large, brimmed hat. I had eerie flashbacks. Tommy's warning repeated inside my head: *Never trust a goon in an overcoat.*

The veins stuck out of Perry's neck like spiderwebs. I reached between my thighs for my .22, but he pushed me inside the car and slammed the door before I could assist.

The man pulled out a blade and lunged at Bumpy. In two steps, Perry had the hitter's wrist and was behind him. There was a loud crack like a turkey's wishbone snapping on Thanksgiving. Perry's left arm quickly wrapped around the man's neck into a death grip. Major jumped out of the car and grabbed the knife that had fallen to the ground. Perry secured the anaconda hold around the hitter's throat. The man's legs shook, wiggled, and went limp in seconds.

Bumpy's men hopped out of their car and threw him into the trunk before anyone else noticed. Major eased the unsuccessful hitman's knife into Bumpy's hand.

Perry straightened his hat. "His arm is broken, so he should stay put for a few ticks."

Bumpy shook Perry's hand with a look of gratitude. "Snipes, I owe you a solid. Tell me how you put the nigga to sleep so quickly without killing him."

He pointed to a small area on his neck. "Cut off his blood supply to his brain."

Major grabbed Perry's arm. "Let's scram. We don't want coppers sniffing around us."

Bumpy agreed. "See you around, fellas."

Major gave Perry a smooth five when they got inside the car. "*Holy shit!* My little brother just saved the Godfather of Harlem!"

My thumb swiped the one bead of sweat escaping down Perry's temple. I stroked his hand as his chest heaved in and out like an accordion. While Major went on to tell stories about how Perry had always been the epitome of their family's monarch, I thanked the high heaven that he became mine.

CHAPTER 22
OOH LA

PERRY BLAIR SAVAGE

August 1938 - Paris, France

I had said *hell no* to spending my honeymoon in France, and I meant it. But somehow, Dulce worked me over with her magic, and I was walking behind her, shlepping our luggage through Paris's Le Bourget Airport. She was gracefully gliding around like she wore skates. Her hair swayed and bounced against her back, and a smile had been tattooed across her face since the plane landed.

I'd never seen her so carefree, but I understood why. Unlike America, there were no "Whites Only" or "Colored" signs posted around the airport. White people smiled at us like old friends. One lady even complimented Dulce's dress. But I couldn't enjoy the atmosphere as much as she did because I was weakened from air sickness and could barely maneuver through the terminal.

Outside, a colored band was playing jazz. It reminded me of Harlem, but a member was playing the violin, making it sound foreign like we were indeed in a different country.

I gagged and took a deep breath. "What day and time is it, doll?"

"Tuesday. Four o'clock p.m."

"What time is it in New York?"

"Ten o'clock in the morning." She smiled and did a twirl. "Perry, do you feel the different energy?"

After another twist to the band's tunes, she dropped all the coins from her pocketbook into their bucket. She was unaware of the spectators who couldn't take their eyes off her, especially me. Since we'd married, her skin shined brighter, her body felt softer, and her scent permeated stronger than ever.

"The way your body moves in that dress, I'm feeling more than energy."

Her eyes narrowed like a tigress. "Just wait until tonight, *Monsieur* Savage. This music reminds me of Louisiana. Dance with me."

I was too sick but didn't want to spoil her happiness. "I'd rather watch, doll."

Distracted by her essence, I hadn't noticed a tall, white man dressed in a tailored black suit step in our vicinity. His nose was long and skinny like his body. He tugged at my bag, and I went into attack mode.

"Touch my bag again, and I'll strike you so fast folks will think you had a heart attack."

"Perry!" Dulce yelled.

I knew my words could get me thrown in the slammer, but I didn't care.

The man backed up. "My apologies if I startled you, Mr. Savage. Hello, Mrs. Savage.'"

"Charles, you know you call me Dulce, and my husband's name is Perry."

He bowed and extended his hand. "Nice to meet you, Mr. Savage. I'm Charles, and I work for Matthieu. I can take your bags, sir."

I was speechless as he took our suitcases from my hands.

Sir? I thought. *What kind of Negro is Matthieu?*

We followed Charles to a royal blue Mercedes Benz, and my body gave out. Too tired to talk, I closed my eyes. After two hours of sleep in four days, a twelve-hour drive to Harlem, and a horrible multiple-day flight, my body felt like it had been rung dry from a mop. I sank into the leather seat.

"Perry, are you okay, daddy?"

My head melted on Dulce's lap, and my arms wrapped around her waist.

"I just need to close my eyes, doll."

All it took was one kiss and stroke from her fingertips, and I blew out like a candle.

Flames as tall as trees surrounded me. The thick black smoke formed clouds above my head, choking my throat like a python. The heat cooked my skin, and the sizzling rattled louder and louder until it took all the sound from my ears. I couldn't stomach the smell of burnt barbecue from the cooking of my flesh. Salted tears poured from my eyes, and it stung as I fought to keep my lids open.

Through the fire, I saw Dulce. She struggled to reach me. She called my name, but I couldn't reach her grasp. The fire grew higher and hotter. Pierre was on her hip, and a group of men covered from head to toe in white sheets marched towards them.

I held my breath, took a few steps backwards, and sprinted into the fiery donut between us. Before being engulfed by flames, I saw disappointment in Dulce's eyes, I failed.

"*Ahhh!*" I screamed in agony.

"*Perry!*" Dulce yelled in response.

I opened my eyes, and she was over me. A cool calmness swept over me as she wiped my forehead with a handkerchief. Her dress was balled inside my fist, and I released the grip I had on her hips.

"What are you battling in your mind, daddy?" she asked while massaging the muscles in my hands.

I grabbed her hand. "How do you always smell like sugar cookies and rose petals?"

She smiled. "You missed some of the most beautiful scenery."

"No, I have the most gorgeous scenery in the world in front of me."

I grabbed her face, and her lips reignited the candle that burned inside me.

"I love you, Mrs. Savage."

"I love you back, Captain."

Charles, waiting patiently at Dulce's window, opened the door. We stood in front of a pink and red brick cottage with white trim and a wooden roof. Waiting for us with a smile was an attractive, tall woman with smooth skin the color of tea without cream or sugar. Her big, round eyes seemed to take up most of her petite face. She was young, but her eyes possessed wisdom like she'd been in the world for decades. Her hair, ears, and fingers sparkled from huge diamonds. Kinky twisted curls swayed at her shoulders, held down with two diamond clips on the crown of her head. Her fitted pink dress accentuated her shapely body. She gleamed with wide red lips.

"Dulce, I'm so happy to finally meet you," she said in a heavy French accent. "Matthieu talks about you all the time. He adores you."

She pressed her lips on both Dulce's cheeks and wiped off her lip prints.

"Belle, likewise. This is my husband, Perry Savage. Perry, meet Belle LeBlanc, Matty's…I mean, Matthieu's wife."

Belle immediately kissed my face, and I was taken off guard. Her lips were unwelcome, but I tried to respond coolly.

"Nice to meet you," I muttered.

Belle grabbed Dulce's hand, and I followed them past the white bench on the front porch into the red wooden door. The large rectangular windows invited the sunshine into the cozy house.

A colored butler and white maid stood at attention before us. *"Bon jour, Madam Le Blanc. Bon jour, Monsieur y Madame Savage."*

Already impressed, I needed to meet the Negro who had a white driver and maid. I had never seen a white cleaning lady in my life. Freshly salted smoked ham, newly baked buttermilk biscuits, and seasoned turnip greens seduced my senses.

"Belle, where is Matthieu?" Dulce asked.

"He had an important meeting that ran over. He's on his way home. You can freshen up and meet us for tea at the main house whenever you are ready."

"Main house?" Dulce and I asked simultaneously.

"Yes. Our home is across the courtyard. You are in our guesthouse. Charles will drive you wherever you want to go during the day. Desmond is your butler and excellent chef, and Sophie will keep everything tidy for you. Desmond and Sophie will leave at six o'clock every day. You can arrange drive times with Charles."

She kissed us on the cheeks and left. Desmond carried our things, and we followed him to our bedroom.

"How many bedrooms are in this house?" Dulce asked.

In a deep French accent, he answered, "Three bedroom and bathroom suites. I prepared you dinner. I'll unpack your things while you eat. I heard *Monsieur* LeBlanc pull up when you were talking outside."

My nose hadn't failed me. Covering a silver tray was ham, greens, potatoes, and biscuits. Desmond shared that his mother was from Alabama and had taught him how to cook. For dessert, he prepared a moist chocolate cake. I scarfed the food like it was my last meal.

"You know I don't like surprises, doll. Do you need to tell me anything about *Matty*?" I asked while we ate dessert.

She went on and on about how Matthieu had an innocent crush on her years ago. I didn't doubt her feelings for me, but I hated I hadn't known how he felt about her in their past sooner. Matthieu already made me uncomfortable with his wealth, white servants, and adoration for my wife, and I was ready to leave.

"Perry, Matthieu has a beautiful wife, and I have the best husband in the world. Take your bath while I tour the house," she said, then kissed me and switched out the door.

As I got ready, there was a knock.

"Come in, doll."

"It's me, *Monsieur.*" Sophie, the white maid, came in with towels and turned on the tub water. "Do you like your temperature hot or warm?"

I couldn't believe a white lady was running my bath water. "*Hot?*"

She tossed in a fistful of rose petals, smiled, and walked out.

After a clean shave, a fresh bath, and new clothes, I felt like a new man. There was another knock on the door. When I opened it, Dulce was standing there in a yellow silk dress with a lavender sash that snuggled against all her curves. Her hair hung down her back under her lavender sunhat. She smiled through her plush, red lips and glowed like honey.

"*Damn,*" we both let out at the same time, then laughed.

I pulled her body close to me and smelled her rose-scented neck. "Matthieu may have to wait."

"First, let's have quick tea with Matthieu and Belle, good-looking. Then, I want to come back here to play hide and go seek."

As she took my hand, I followed her like a lost puppy who had found their owner.

We walked past a large vegetable garden filled with tomatoes, greens, and herbs and crossed the courtyard. Through the circular driveway was the front of a castle-like mansion. Dulce walked in front of me. I watched as her hips swayed side to side like an arrow on a compass, and her hair blew in the wind like kite ribbons.

She pulled me to her. "What did I tell you about staring at me, Captain Savage?"

"I can't help it, doll. You're so damn hot and gorgeous."

Before we knocked at the door, a young, well-dressed white man opened it and leaped across the threshold.

"Dulce!" He pulled her by her waist and kissed her smack-dab on her lips.

Every muscle in my body tensed into a rage, and before I swung for his face, Dulce gripped my hand. I was shocked—she'd accepted another man's kiss and stopped me from reacting. I didn't care if he was white, yellow, or green.

"What in the hell is going on here?" I asked as they both smiled into each other's eyes.

The white man puckered up, and I thought he was going to speak. Instead, he leaned in towards my face. I dodged his kiss that landed on the air. Dulce pulled me back, and I looked over at her like she had lost her mind.

He bowed. "Perry, my apologies for the French greeting. I forget that it can make Americans uncomfortable. So nice to meet you." Then, he extended his hand for a shake.

Dulce stroked my arm as I shook it with all my might.

"Perry, this is Matthieu LeBlanc."

Matthieu reached for her, and she let me go, grabbing both his hands. He twirled her around, and they danced around me in a waltz.

"Dulce, darling," he said, "when did you design that dress? It fits you perfectly. Tell me, what color is it?"

She twirled in his arms and sang, "Lemon zest and lavender bloom, Matty baby."

My mouth dropped. The way they were swirling around each other, I thought I was hallucinating or at a ballet.

Again, I asked, *"What in the hell is going on here?"*

They ignored me, lost in their private daze.

"You're so delightful, Dulce darling. How I missed you! Perry, aren't the colors of her designs divine?" He straightened the knot on his tie with a look of pride. "Dulce, did you see the tie and scarf you made for me?"

Belle came from behind them and chimed in, "He wears that set every week."

Matthieu hadn't stopped grinning and turned all his attention to me. "Perry, you know I tried to get Dulce to move here with me. Paris would *love* her designs."

I looked at Dulce, and she looked away. I was flabbergasted. "No fooling?"

He laughed with so much joy that I thought he was drunk.

"Yes, my friend. No fooling. I was once in love with your wife before my Queen Belle captured all of me. I'm *so* happy you are here. Please, follow me inside."

I studied Matthieu LeBlanc as he led us graciously inside his house. I wanted to hate him, but unlike racists, my heart wouldn't allow me to hate what I didn't understand yet. All this time, I thought Matthieu was a rich Negro.

Once inside, he and Dulce talked in the foyer as old friends, and I listened as they discussed the places they had visited in Chicago, the music and movies they had listened to and watched— and they were all colored. He and his wife hadn't stopped loving and hugging on each other since we'd gotten inside. It was difficult for me to process it all.

They led Dulce and me through the foyer. To the east was a sitting room with a large fireplace that covered the entire wall. On the walls were paintings with wild patterns and designs, different paintings of Negroes and whites. I never would've imagined a white man to have Negro sculptures featured in his home, but Matthieu did, and his album collection was like mine—filled with Bessie Smith, Duke Ellington, Count Basie, Josephine Baker, Bach, and Mozart.

We sat down in a parlor, and a black maid poured tea into our cups.

Matthieu smiled happily. "Vivian, this is *Monsieur* and *Madame* Perry and Dulce Savage from America. Dulce became a good friend of mine when I lived in Chicago."

Vivian greeted us with her French accent and wise eyes. "*Bonjour, Monsieur and Madame.*"

Dulce smiled back. "*Bonjour.* Call us Perry and Dulce, *s'il te plaît.*"

I hadn't spoken yet because I kept tripping over my thoughts. Every time I thought I understood the path Matthieu was taking us on, I would get ready to comment. But something in the conversation would switch, and I'd get lost.

"What were we talking about?" Matthieu asked before sipping his tea.

I cleared my throat and finally spoke. "Outside, you were telling me how you tried to get Dulce to move to Paris with you."

"Yes, Perry." He smiled widely. "I asked her to marry me *three* times, but she kept denying me."

My mind was again taken off course. When my eyes met Dulce's, she shifted in her seat.

"No fooling?" I asked again.

Matthieu pulled Belle onto his lap and kissed her neck.

"No fooling, my friend. Obviously, God had other plans. He designed Dulce for you." He kissed Belle's lips and stroked her face. "And he created Belle, my Parisian queen, for me."

She wrapped her arms around his neck. *"Je t'aime, Matthieu."*

They began necking as if we had left the room. I glanced at Dulce, and she smiled uncomfortably. She knew how I felt about being taken off guard by surprises, and she knew if she didn't get me out of there, I was going to lose my mind.

"Matthieu and Belle," she said, "thank you for your hospitality. Perry and I love our cottage. I am very tired with the time change and long flight."

Matthieu stood up and extended his hand to me. "Of course, Dulce. I'm so happy to see you. Perry, I'm going to smoke cigars and drink scotch with a few of my neighbors. If you want to come by after you walk Dulce over, you are welcome to join us. We drink and play checkers for an hour or two."

I squeezed his hand tightly. "Thank you for the invite."

They walked us to the door, and Dulce and I trudged back into the guesthouse in silence. As soon as we got inside, I slammed the door.

"Dulce, you set me up. Why didn't you tell me the nigga Matthieu was white?"

"Nigga? Perry, you're talking crazy."

Our voices echoed through the empty home.

"You don't have to be colored to be a nigga."

"Perry, Matthieu is not a nigga. He's genuinely one of the nicest people I know." She placed her arms around my chest. "And I told you about Matthieu and his fondness of me. That's ancient history. Let's play hide and go seek. I've missed your body."

"You never told me he was white *and* that he proposed to you *three* fucking times."

"Perry, who cares about what color the man is and the past? He is married and loves his wife, and I'm madly in love with you."

My entire body tensed up again. "I care. How do you think I felt listening to a white man talk about whisking you off with him to Paris? The way he kissed you on the lips, I don't know who he's in love with."

She massaged my shoulders. "Perry, please stop. There's nothing to be worked up about. The kissing is part of his culture, and I've never liked him in that way."

"Are there any other proposals from men I need to know about?"

She looked away, then at the floor. "There was a man named Dumas Monroe who mentioned wanting us to get hitched, but he's happily married with five kids by now."

"Monroe?!" My heart dropped. "You've been married before me?"

"Perry, please, no. You know I was born with the name Monroe. I've *never* wanted anybody but you. So, can we please make love? You look *so* rugged and fine in that suit, daddy."

She knew exactly where and how to touch me, but I was too upset to be seduced.

"No, I need to talk to Matthieu now, and you and I are leaving when I'm done."

I left Dulce pouting to confront Matthieu Le Blanc man-to-man. When his doorman let me inside the mansion, I stormed into his cigar parlor, which was occupied by a group of men. Matthieu jumped up from his corner chair to introduce me to them. I was warmly greeted by an Italian bank president and Negro classical music composer. A European painter and African attorney played checkers on a gigantic yellow and black checkerboard.

I'd been taught Africans lived in huts, so to meet an African man who was political, wealthy, and highly educated took me beyond surprise. But the most intriguing man he introduced me to was Alexandre Dupont, whom Matthieu called "My Eyes."

Matthieu had been born with an eye disease that prevented him from seeing color. He also said anything he looked directly at vanished before his eyes. Things and people before him dwelled in his blind spot unless he shifted his gaze into his peripheral, where everything was clear but colorless.

Matthieu demonstrated. "When I put my hand this far from my face, it disappears into my blind spot."

No spectacles nor his riches could fix his sight because there was no cure for his eye disease. He'd been unable to see color all his life with progressive sight loss, making him partially blind.

As a child, he had befriended Alexandre Dupont. Alexandre was colored and spoke fluent Spanish and French. His parents owned a profitable vineyard that had been in the Dupont family for over a century. I never knew Negroes who owned land during the years of enslavement, so the thought was nearly unreachable for me to comprehend.

When Matthieu and Alexandre played as kids, Alexandre described things for Matthieu that his eyes couldn't decipher. Matthieu bragged about how brilliant Alexandre, now a statistician and mathematical genius, had been all their lives.

They were business partners. Matthieu decided what companies' stock he wanted them to invest in. Alexandre analyzed charts and figures and moved their money around to make them more money. They were rich—born wealthy, but with proper investments, they had more dough than they had ever imagined.

To wrap my brain around what they explained, I asked, "So, you are gambling men?"

"No, sir," Alexandre answered in his mixed foreign accent. "There's science to the math."

They had become richer from the Great Depression, while everybody I'd known headed to the underground streets because they had lost everything.

After a few gulps of scotch and puffs of tasty cigars, I grabbed all the dough I had on me.

"My Eyes, get me the best price on stock for steel, guns, and ammunition."

He opened a notebook and wrote down my order in a binder on a table in front of him. He then returned a piece of paper to me, which I stuffed in my jacket pocket.

Wanting to understand how Matthieu saw the world through his eyes, I listened intently as he tried to articulate it as best as he could. He saw beauty in patterns and textures. Sound and music touched him more deeply than the average person. He was drawn to different materials and aromas. Things were blurry far away but made more sense when directly in his face. I asked if he knew why he preferred Negro women, music, and art.

"God made me so that I cannot see color, so I don't see race in art," he answered. "Belle is not colored or Negro. She's my wife—more beautiful than a work of art. I love how Belle's lips take over my mouth. Her spongy hair and versatility enthrall me. The roundness of her hips and body excites every part of my being. Her voice and scent soothe me. Every part of her from the inside out is designed perfectly for me."

My mouth dropped again. "No fooling?"

He touched my shoulder. "No fooling, my friend."

"I feel the same way about Dulce."

"Because love," he said, "like music and art, is colorless."

Alexandre Dupont refilled our scotch glasses. "Let us toast to love."

Matthieu was unlike any man I knew. He was the richest, kindest, and happiest person I had ever met. He surrounded himself with good people, like the men in his parlor, and I admired that.

What would the world be like if God made us all color-blind?

Renewed in my thoughts and sentiments for Matthieu and the world, I walked into the guest cottage. French jazz blasted through the house. Dulce had left the bedroom door open for me. She sat on a couch against the window, wearing nothing but red high heels and lipstick.

My everything was aroused. *"Goddamn."*

She looked at me with hungry eyes and then dropped an empty bottle of champagne on the floor. "You found me."

Immediately, my clothes hit the floor like Superman from the comic books. I crawled between her legs. Her fingers locked around my neck as I kissed the lips on her face. My lips and tongue traveled down her body.

> *"When I thought perfection couldn't get any better*
> *Empress, my muse, my masterpiece draped bare in leather*
> *Shoes—red kissed on her lips and feet*
> *Curls caressing her breasts, lust leaking from her peach*
> *Fruit garden, body palace, I explore every room*
> *Until she releases that bridge, open, fresh bloom*
> *Nectar sweet, pleasured pleas, I can hardly hear*
> *My tongue speaks Ooh Laa when her thighs hug my ears*
> *'Cause I'm her junkie, sugar addict, I'll never stop*
> *Treasured kisses, no levee, I want every drop*
> *And I'm a Savage roaming free, released from my cage*
> *Let loose in heavenly habitat, between her legs, my stage*
> *Where my words, like my love, free flow, twenty-four*
> *Her heart, my soul's haven, entangled, Je t'aime, mon amour."*

Her body responded to every word as each syllable poured from my soul. Sexily, she turned around, and we formed the number sixty-nine. We made love in every position until we were out of breath. She cried ecstasy tears and rested her body over me like a warm satin sheet. My fingers combed through her kinky silk threads as her cheek rested against my heart.

"Perry, how do you put words together?"

"My words come from the love in my heart, which comes to me without thinking."

"Where do you think your love for me comes from?"

"God."

"What about Lady Luck?"

"Luck is for gamblers."

"What's wrong with that if you're always lucky?"

"No one is lucky all the time. So, you'll spend most of your life unfulfilled, waiting for something superficial that may never come." I kissed her forehead. "God's love is consistent and forever. When you acknowledge that, you'll be free."

"No Negro is free."

"God is testing your faith, doll. Believing in the unknown can be scary, but you must believe in Him to get to the other side."

"Mama said that the day she was murdered."

She dropped her head, and I lifted her chin.

"Don't you believe Mama Lee was sent to you as God's angel?"

She paused for a long moment and stared into my eyes. "I do, and in this moment, I realize so were you. I will protect that and our love forever, Perry."

That night, Dulce and I surrendered completely to each other. Every kiss, touch, and movement was the perfect creation, and I vowed with my life never to let anything separate us from our love.

CHAPTER 23
PARIS, PARIS, PARIS

DULCE ELLA-MONROE SAVAGE

August 1938 - Paris, France

After a light, rejuvenating breakfast the following morning, Perry and I shook a leg to get ready to conquer a full day in Paris. Charles was reading a newspaper in the car when we slid into the backseat.

"Bonjour," he greeted with a smile, then closed a privacy divider between him and us that shut like window shutters.

We headed to *L'Arc de Triomphe*, one of the most notable monuments in France. It is known as a Parisian symbol of victory and detailed beauty. If Paris were a dancer, it would be the prima ballerina. The lines and curves of the architecture exuded love and precision. I marveled at *Champs*-Èlysèes, the infamous street in Paris that I had only seen photographs of.

All the buildings were artistically constructed like costumes with detailed grandeur, which added to the city's captivating essence. Colorful shops and cafes accessorized the city's ensemble, making Paris the most elegant place I'd ever seen. At every turn and corner, I felt the positive energy released by the Parisian fashionistas and dapper gents on the roads. Perfectly groomed gardens and maple trees swayed gracefully on each side of the streets as they welcomed us with open arms.

I was so giddy. "Perry, isn't *L'Arc de Triomphe* on *Champs-Èlysèes* beautiful?"

"It's pretty, especially with you in it," he replied, looking out the window.

"Can you believe we're in Paris?"

Charles parked and opened the partition. "We're here," he said.

I wrapped the purple cape I had designed around me. "Time to see Paris, *Monsieur Savage*."

When the door swung open, Perry was waiting to grab my hand. He was dressed in a grey plaid three-piece suit with a navy, sky blue, and grey striped tie. He matched his grey and navy hat with grey wing-tipped shoes.

He winked. "*Madame De Leche*."

"*Merci*."

We stared at the tall, magnificent Eiffel Tower. Of all the stately monuments I'd seen, I had never witnessed a building as commanding. People swarmed around us, not showing a care that we were colored. I was starting to feel God's steadfast love for me, but I was convinced only in Paris—wrapped in Perry's arms—could I truly be free.

"Perry?"

He was on guard like a watchman but gave me his full attention. "Yes, doll."

"I want us to raise Pierre in France."

"Come again?"

"There's too much hate for Negroes in America. Being here makes me feel lighter—like the shackles are broken. And look at the fashion. We can leave the underground for good and start a new legacy. I could open a store and sell my designs. Then, I can put my fashions in the department stores. Paris respects colored soldiers for what they did in World War I, and you can be a writer. What do you think?"

He spun me around. "I write only for you and God."

"But you can write for a newspaper, or I bet you could write books. Writers are good at putting words together, and you're the best. *Please, daddy?* I want us to feel love from the country where we reside, and we won't ever feel a lick of affection in America. Pierre doesn't deserve the hate white people have for him because he's colored."

"I'm not saying no, but that's going to take planning. The French respect class and dough—*Parisian Nègres.* If we move here broke, we will be considered no-class, *Nègre niggers*, which would be much worse for our legacy."

I put my hands on my hips. "And what exactly is a *Nègre nigger*, Perry?"

His finger covered my lips. "We'll talk when we get home." Seeing my disappointment, he lifted my dropped chin and said, "I want to focus on our honeymooning while we're here."

A tall, thin white woman wearing a blue bonnet approached us and squeaked, "*Madame.*"

Instantly, she started speaking in French, and we shrugged. She ran away and returned quickly with a younger woman.

"Good afternoon," she said. "My mother and I want to know where you purchased your lovely cape."

My heart warmed. "This is a Dulce *Paris* creation. I designed it."

"The material is gorgeous. Where do you sell your designs?"

"My husband and I were just discussing our relocation plan from America. I'll have a shop here very soon."

She handed me a piece of paper with her name and phone number. "Please call me when you open. We will be your first customers and bring others your way."

As they walked away, I asked Perry, "Now, was that Lady Luck or God?"

The higher we rose on the Eiffel Tower, the lower Perry shrank with his eyes closed.

I grabbed his hand. "Perry, what's wrong?"

"Doll, do you feel that?" He grabbed the railing in a shocked look of fear. "Oh my God. We have to go."

His breathing grew fast and unsteady. His dark chocolate face was losing color.

"Oh, God."

He let go of the railing and threw his arms around my waist like a lost child.

"Okay, Perry, we'll go."

At the next stop, we got off the lift and took it on its way back down. When we touched the ground, he bolted to the trashcan. I followed and handed him a handkerchief when he was done heaving.

"Do you feel better?" I asked.

"We made it to safety, doll. The Eiffel Tower is rocky. Paris needs new engineers."

I giggled. "I think you're afraid of heights."

"That's ridiculous. The tower leans like the one in Italy."

"And you thought the plane was crashing the entire flight."

"Listen to me, doll, your Captain isn't scared of a damn thing. I just saved our lives."

"Whatever you say, good-looking." I wrapped my arms around him. "Tell me, why are you trembling?"

"It's chilly out here."

I wiped the sweat that dripped down his face. "Okay, daddy, let's split from the French leaning tower before it crushes us."

Charles drove us to Montmartre, the Parisian haven for Negro artists and entertainers. Colored ladies dressed in polka dots, stripes, florals, and prints covered the streets with neat, keen styles adorned with hats, pins, and flowers. Their jewelry and shoes screamed *I'm fabulous* as loudly as their dresses. The colored men were dressed dapper in plaid, stripes, and bold colors, with their matching hats cocked with confidence.

Artists were scattered, seated at small tables and on benches with their canvases, soaking in the inspiration. Jazz blasted from cabarets as our car crept by. My window was lowered, and the wet, cool air licked my face. I inhaled deeply and was seduced by the charming, musky scent. Love at first sight, I committed adultery against America, making sweet whoopie with the sexy Harlem City of Lights.

When we got out of the car, New Orleans-style jazz serenaded Perry and me into a lively cabaret, Le Grand Duc. We jitterbugged through the door and did the Charleston straight to the dancefloor. The drummer who kicked the high beat was Eugene Bullard, the owner. He had moved to Paris after he served for the U.S. Army in France after World War I.

After Eugene left the stage, he and Perry met and traded comrade stories over cigars, and I inhaled the intoxicating *noir* scent of my new mistress, Montmartre. Montmartre was perfection, blending the spirits of my two favorite cities—Paris and Harlem. I closed my eyes and visualized my shop next to the 52, rue Pigalle. Dulce *Paris,* the illuminated sign in my daydream, felt so real that the heat from the light bulbs cinched my skin.

Perry walked to the table with a bottle of champagne. "Doll, I just found out Langston Hughes used to work here."

"I'm ready to live here, Perry, *now.*"

"I know, doll."

I was hopeful but could see in Perry's eyes that he didn't feel the same way. I dreaded America would be my forever home.

CHAPTER 24
BACKLASH BLUES

DULCE "EMPRESS CREED" SAVAGE

November 1938 - Gary, Indiana

It had been months since Mama Lee's murder, and it still felt like it happened yesterday. The feds had left Gary and Mayor Dunstan unscathed from prosecution, and all had been quiet until it wasn't.

I was seated uncomfortably in Mae's Beauty Shop. The sizzling sound of hot grease and the distinct scent of searing hair kept me gagging. With my white, floor-length mink off, my body was icy cold like an igloo, and with it on, I was burning in an inferno. So, I settled to wear it halfway-off, halfway-on. Before the businesses opened, Perry stopped at Bobby's Barbershop for a haircut while I was getting my hair pressed and curled.

Mae pulled the hot comb from my root to the end, and I winced as a burning drop of grease dripped onto my scalp.

"Empress, are you alright?" she asked.

All my senses were intensified, and I gagged for what felt like the hundredth time.

"Can I have a glass of water, please?"

"Pressed out, your hair is down to your waist."

"I usually just keep it rolled up."

"You must have Indian in your family. How do you feel now?"

I swallowed a hint of bitter vomit with my sip of water. "I'll live."

Mae handed me the *Gary Tribune*. On the cover, Mayor Dunstan proudly stood beside his newly appointed police chief, Blakely Wraith. He was the younger brother of the late Chief Egbart Wraith, and Dunstan was holding a ceremony at noon to welcome him to the city. Wraith had come from Natchez, Mississippi, and we'd already gotten word that he was a son of a bitch.

The headline shouted across the front cover for everyone to see: *It's a New Day.*

Mayor Dunstan had been quoted as saying, "With the growth in Negro population, Indiana has seen an increase in crime and a decrease in our jobs, which is troubling for our Lake County citizens. But it's a new day. Chief Blakely Wraith will restore our order, and I will restore our jobs."

"So, *we* are the cause of all the riots in our neighborhoods and job loss?" Mae asked with disgust.

I shook my head. "White folks want to blame somebody for the Depression's damage. Accusing Negroes of taking jobs and making them feel unsafe is giving racists more ammunition to wreak havoc on us."

Perry stormed in, sporting his long, black fur coat, black leather gloves, and gray and black brim hat. "Empress, did you read what Dunstan said in the paper?"

"I saw it."

He walked over and lifted my head. "What's shaking? Are you feeling alright?"

"Can you take me to see Countess before the snowstorm hits? She has an elixir for me."

"Of course." He smiled and touched my curls. "Mae, you have my wife's hair looking like a billion bucks. Have any coppers been snooping over here? They've been harassing Bobby more than usual."

"I think they are getting hip to folks placing bets over here. They come around and stare in my window but haven't made any moves."

"Have Martha and Linda call the hotel before they leave here with the dough and slips. They need an armed escort, and I will see that they have one."

No longer able to withstand the scorching smell, my stomach churned, and I ran to the trash can.

Perry wiped my sweaty brow with his handkerchief. "Let's go to Countess right now."

He placed my mink around my shoulders. We stepped outside, and the hawk wind soothed me.

Perry's warm lips touched my forehead. "At least you don't have a fever."

"I feel swell. I needed to get away from that shop. Now I'm hungry."

November 1938 - Robbins, Illinois

The grassy fields on each side of the expressway were covered in pure white. There was no sun or clouds, only a grey sky. As Perry talked in the background, all I could think about was sinking my mouth into a hot slab of barbeque ribs. After thirty minutes, we pulled up to a small brick building with a line of Negroes wrapped around the corner of Claire Road. Out front was a short wooden sign: *Porky's*. Clouds from the grill escaped the front door, and the smokey aroma foreplayed with my tastebuds.

Porky's was Geese's barbeque joint and the second location he had opened in Robbins, Illinois, after outgrowing the first. He grilled the best ribs with the savoriest sauce in the Midwest. Geese was the youngest, quietest, and most business-savvy of Perry's brothers, which was why Perry made him a part-time lookout—so he could focus on his entrepreneurship. In addition to being an excellent cook, he fought and served food in the same Harlem brigade in the Army with his brothers.

We parked next to a long, bright blue Lincoln in the nearly full lot. Snow flurries scattered around us like powder as Perry opened my car door and helped me out.

"Empress and Snipes!" a familiar male voice called from the Lincoln.

Perry looked over. "What's shaking, Butta?"

"Nothing but these cold bones, youngblood. You and Empress slide in the back. I was going to pay you two a visit."

Perry opened Butta's back car door, and we climbed in next to each other.

"What's the berries?" I asked Butta.

"I'm working, watching over my new business venture." He paused to take a bite of rib tips. "Geese put his whole foot in this food. These are the best damn ribs I've ever had."

"What new business?" Perry asked.

"Your brother and I have a silent partnership. On cold days like this, johns give my girls, who stay posted out front of Porky's, the signal to meet them in the back. Then, the girls take the order like waitresses inside to Geese. When the food is ready, they deliver the customer pork *and* pussy. Everybody wins."

"How are the girls winning?" I asked.

"Don't get high and mighty, Empress. Nobody leaves the car, and most of these johns are lonely and old. Therefore, my girls are making easy scratch. So, like I said, everybody wins."

Like aspirin, Perry could only take Butta in small doses and was starting to look annoyed.

"What did you want to tell us, Butta?"

"That new Gary sheriff, Wraith, is putting together a racist group like the KKK and appointing new deputies, giving whites from across your tracks guns and power to put Negroes six feet under."

"How do you know this?" Perry asked.

"Those white boys have to be dumb or don't give a damn. First, they drive up to my girls and ask, 'Have you ever been with a nigger?' Of course, my girls lie and say, 'No, daddy, I've only been with white men all my life.' Then, those crackers let them inside and talk amongst each other like my girls are deaf. My girls say they even conduct meetings while they're all humping."

Perry tossed Butta a wad of money. "Thanks for the smooth solid. Be sure to keep me updated anytime you hear something."

He stuck the wad into his sock. "Anytime, youngblood."

I gave him a smooth five. "Thanks, Butta."

As soon as we got out, Mother Nature sneezed a strong gust of wind and coughed buckets of snowflakes over us. I looked over, and no one moved from their place in line outside of the restaurant.

"It looks like the storm has hit us early, doll. We'll have to get to Chicago when it clears. Wait in the car."

Perry left and returned with containers of ribs and potato salad. "Guess who was behind the counter?"

"Who?"

"Juno. I think they're sweet on each other."

I shook my head and snatched my box. "She would've told me."

"Geese said his ribs are like Countess's elixir. Would you believe he's selling folks plain bread dipped in his barbeque sauce for twenty-five cents?"

The lunch line grew like a snake as more snow dropped from the sky. The smell of the smoky sauce humped my nostrils, and saliva dripped from my mouth. I removed my mink and threw it in the backseat. Then, I ripped the top off the container.

Perry laughed. "Are you hungry?"

Like a junkie on smack, the spices satisfied the craving from within, and I couldn't stop eating.

We skipped the slippery expressway and took the street way home. Perry drove cautiously since we were surrounded by snow and caught in a white-out. During the drive, I finished an entire container of ribs and a tub of potato salad.

Perry touched my thigh. "How are you, doll?"

I smiled. "Just swell!"

The car finally crawled towards Broadway. Outside Gary City Hall, crowds of white folks scattered the streets to watch Chief Wraith's swearing-in ceremony. In their hands were signs that read: *Restore Our Order, Restore Our Jobs, It's a New Day.*

As we drove slowly, folks threw snowballs at our car and chanted repeatedly, *"Give us back our order. Give us back our jobs."*

"Perry, these crackers have lost their minds."

"Don't worry, doll. I'll run these white niggas over before they think about hurting you."

He plowed through the chaos of chants and name-calling until we reached Pierre's school. Excited to play in their fresh winter wonderland, Pierre and his classmates didn't budge as they created angels and snowmen, clueless of the angry mobs that had gathered minutes up the road.

We picked Pierre up and drove into our quiet neighborhood, tranquil with bleached-out trees, grass, and houses. As I watched him create more innocent fantasies in the snow, my spirit ached for the future of humanity. That one cover story from Mayor Dunstan in the *Gary Tribune* exasperated divisiveness that changed our world forever.

CHAPTER 25
CITY BURNS

DULCE "EMPRESS CREED" SAVAGE

November 1938 - Gary, Indiana

The next day, as we drove down Broadway Avenue, Perry and I got worked up again from all the newly posted signs and posters lining our neighborhood. The words boldly touted, *Give Us Back Our Order, Give Us Back Our Jobs*. White folks had never crossed over the tracks, but according to their signs, they wanted us and everyone else to know *It Was a New Day*. Perry's jaws clenched as he tightly gripped the steering wheel.

I gently stroked his cheek. "At ease, Captain."

He kissed my hand and changed his disposition to a wide grin.

"Who's ready to sled?" he turned and yelled to the backseat.

Pierre and Willie Kinsmen raised their hands and yelled back, *"Me!"*

Perry parked at the top of the snowy hills on Broadway. The area was covered with colored families bundled up like Alaskan natives. Their smiles displayed they were having the most joyous time of their lives.

Perry grabbed a red and a blue sled from the trunk and opened my door. "How are you feeling, doll?"

"I'm swell, good-looking."

Pierre jumped onto my lap and kissed my cheek. "Can you help us design a suit for our snowman later, doll?"

I kissed him back. "Of course, good-looking! You know Mommy would love that."

We looked across the tracks, and a white family of four mirrored us. The duplicity caused us all to freeze in our tracks. We glanced each other's way and exchanged expressionless sentiments before piercing each other with contentment. Then, they joined the slew of white families amongst them, booming with resounding bliss while sledding and building winter wonderlands. Pierre and I joined hands with Perry and Willie Kinsmen and did the same.

After a heavy dump of snow, those hills were Colorado mountains to us. For hours, excitement and family fun were seen and felt from our separate sides of the city. Our experiences were so alike that if our skin were colorless, we would've been identical—screaming wildly, wearing the same clothes, and sliding on the same sleds while exuding the same radiant energy. But our differences—engrained as American fiber—remained segregated and visible, imprinted as vividly as the color of worldly newspaper headlines, clearly in black and white. So, instead of acknowledging our similarities as human beings, we pretended a wall was dividing us, ignoring the mirror that reflected the equality of our universal pursuits: true love and happiness.

Willie raised both hands in the air before he went down the hill. "Look, Mrs. Empress!"

Pierre sat in front of Perry and raised his hands in the air, too. "Look, Mommy! No hands, doll!"

I waved, and my heart was full. I had everything I needed and never imagined.

All the families lined up for a sled race.

Perry held Pierre's hand and their sled as he waited to go back down the hill. "Count us off, doll."

I raised my hands and hollered, *"Ready! Set! Go!"*

The sleds took off, and the expression of freed bliss was on every face. In the middle of euphoria, a white Phantom cast a black shadow over all the purity.

"What does this cracker want?" I muttered under my breath.

"I was wondering the same damn thing."

I turned to find Perry holding Willie and Pierre's hands while standing next to me. The other fathers and their families were on the other side of me. The hill was covered with empty sleds.

"How did you get here so fast?"

"As long as I'm alive, doll, I'll never be more than two steps away from you."

Mayor Dunstan tipped out in a black overcoat, brimmed hat, and shiny leather shoes. By his side was a *Gary Tribune* reporter. Dustan's shoes sank into a pile of snow, and he shook it off.

"Who wants a shiny coin?" he asked with a smile.

When no one responded, he sloshed over and bent down in front of Pierre. Perry stepped forward.

"What about you?" Mayor Dunstan said, waving his gold coin in Pierre's face. "I bet you want a coin."

"No, thank you," Pierre politely responded.

Dunstan then turned to a little girl. "What about you, sweetheart? Do you want a shiny coin?"

"No, thank you."

"Girls and boys, do we know this man?" Perry asked like a captain in his army.

"No, sir!" they yelled back.

"What do we do if strangers get too close?"

They shouted, "Run quick or kick them in the dick, sir!"

"As you can see, Dunstan, our kids don't take from strangers. So, you can take your fake *coin* to the other side of the tracks."

"Because you'd rather waste *your* coins on fancy fur coats and boots." Mayor Dunstan smirked. "And you need to teach these kids the Bible, not vulgarity."

"Nothing is more vulgar than a strange man enticing kids with fake coins. The only man I knew to do that kidnapped a girl and caged her with a tiger in the circus." He looked down at the mayor's feet. "And it looks like you could use some fur-lined boots for those frostbitten toes. Girls and boys, what are the books of the Bible?"

They began reciting, starting with the Old to New Testament.

"Now, tell the mayor the presidents of the United States," Perry commanded.

They started with President George Washington and ended with Franklin D. Roosevelt.

"Boys and girls, what is the first line of the Gettysburg Address?" Perry asked next.

They shouted with pride, "Four score and seven years ago our fathers brought forth on this continent, a new nation, conceived in Liberty, and dedicated to the proposition that all men are created equal, *sir*."

"Do you believe in Lincoln's creed, Mayor Dunstan?"

Dunstan huffed between his teeth. "Lincoln knew, like everybody else knows, that God created black and white, which are color opposites. And opposites will never be equal."

Perry looked at the *Tribune* reporter. "We instill in our colored children equality passed down from our American president, while our city's mayor believes in *opposites*."

Dunstan's face turned red as a tomato, but he smiled. "That's not what I said." He shivered and sloshed back to his car. Before entering, he turned and yelled, "Don't forget *I* created more jobs for the Negroes in this city than any other mayor in American history."

"Aren't those the Negros' jobs *you* want to take back?" Perry asked.

Dunstan slammed the door and glared in our direction for a while. Perry didn't move a muscle. The mayor drove off, and everyone went back to sledding.

After the sleigh rides, Perry asked if all the families could drive down Broadway and remove the racist posters. We collected them as a caravan and when we were finished, we parked across the street from Gary's City Hall.

As Police Chief Wraith was opening Mayor Dunstan's Phantom door, we got out of our cars, and each man tossed a sign inside a steel garbage can across the street. Perry was last. He held up the poster, "*Give Us Back Our Order. Give Us Back Our Jobs. It's a Now Day,*" so everyone could see. Then, he took out a match, set the poster on fire, and dropped the flame into the drum. We watched the fire turn into smoke. The smoke turned to ashes. After a strong thrust of wind, Mother Nature wept raindrops over the city.

The rain cleared when we pulled up to our house, but it had turned to nightfall. We walked into the house, and there was a loud yell.

"*Surprise!*"

The lights clicked on, and Perry didn't move.

"What's the occasion?" he asked, confused.

Major, Slide, and Styles stepped from behind the kitchen counter.

Major smiled. "Man, I know we did not drive over twelve hours in the snow *and* hide in this dark house for two more hours to find out you forgot your own damn birthday."

Perry placed his hands over his face. "*Damn.*"

He wiped tears from his eyes when all his brothers embraced him. "Are your eyes sweating again, Daddy?" Pierre asked.

While I took Perry's coat, Pierre ran to the bedroom and handed him a sketch. "Happy Birthday, Daddy. I wrote you a poem: *Daddy's strong, never wrong. Loves me and our doll all day long.*"

"That is beautiful, Pierre. I'm going to hang it up right now."

I wrapped my arms around him. "Relax. Happy birthday, good-looking."

He picked me up and spun me around as I hung up the picture. "This is the best birthday of my life!"

Major placed several bottles of whisky on the counter. "The party is just getting started."

Beloved turned Count Basie's "One O'clock Jump" loudly on the record player. Geese pulled several pans of food from the oven and his infamous homemade sauce from the fridge. Juno served everyone his Porky's barbequed ribs, pork shoulder, and spicy sage sausage. He prepared hot water cornbread, baked macaroni and cheese, and fresh potato salad for the sides.

Styles and Slide placed their tap shoes on and danced around the kitchen like The Nicholas Brothers. Willie Kinsmen and Pierre followed them around, copying their every move. The entire room was swinging and jumping. Cigarette smoke circulated the room with the laughter. Perry was totally relaxed and carefree for the first time I'd seen since meeting him.

Everyone was dizzy from all the hooch. It was one in the morning, and no one wanted the night to end. Perry had carried Pierre and Willie Kinsmen to bed hours ago. Despite having been up twenty-four hours, Major, Slide, and Styles planned to split to Harlem to sleep in their own beds.

In the last ferocious game of Spades before hitting the road, Perry and Major were partners and teamed up against Geese and Juno.

Geese stuck a card to his forehead and stood up. "Hurry up and play the damn card, Perry. It's past you and your old brother's bedtime."

"Gangsters don't sleep, youngblood," Perry replied, throwing down an ace.

Geese peeled the card from his forehead. "Nighty night, senior citizens! Better nap before you drive to Harlem, Major! Y'all are set!"

Before Geese slapped it on the table to display a dramatic victory, Major threw all his cards in the air. "Forfeit, cheating-ass Geeser!"

Geese swiped Major's face with the big joker he was holding. "That's Boston, and you know it! I'll beat your old ass right now for calling me a cheater."

"I've been waiting for a rumble, *Geese the Cheat.*"

Geese swung his fist, hitting Major in the kisser. His head bobbled on his neck, and Major retaliated unsuccessfully with a missed punch. Geese dodged and punched Major again as he danced around him like Joe Louis.

"Perry, you better teach your old-ass brother how to squabble."

Bear, Slide, and Styles laughed as Perry stumbled over to them. *"Break it up, Savages."*

Major pushed them out of the way. "Everybody move so Geese can take this ass whooping."

They cleared the path. Major charged at Geese, swung, and slid past him onto the table. The cards scattered onto the floor, and Major closed his eyes and started snoring.

Countess walked over to him and touched his face. "Oh Lord, he's asleep."

Juno placed a lemon pound cake on the table next to Major. "A lady named Mrs. Mary Lee brought this over for you, Perry."

"Bless her. I love her cake."

For another hour, we drank, ate cake, and listened to music.

Major stretched as he rose with a refreshed look on his face. "What did I miss?"

Styles took a bite of the cake. "You missed Geese beat your ass."

"Geese the Cheat?" Major replied, fixing his hair and grabbing a piece of cake. "He sucker-punched me."

"Did you say rematch?" Geese said, standing up.

Major laughed. "Alright, baby brother, I give. But you and your woman *were* talking across the board."

"Call Snowflake a cheater, Major, and *I* will pound your face into the floor."

"*Snowflake?*" everyone echoed.

Geese spun her around, and they kissed. "That's right. Now everybody knows I'm sweet on Juno, *and* I can whoop Major's ass."

"That's right, Cat Daddy," she said.

Major poured champagne into glasses. "Amen to that! Welcome to the family, *Snowflake.*"

As we lifted our glasses and clinked them against each other, a gun fired from outside.

"*Perry Snipes!*" someone yelled.

One finger snap, and the house went pitch black and silent. Perry and Major dove to the floor with their guns drawn. Everyone had unholstered their weapons and was scattered around the house.

The backdoor rattled like thunder from someone banging.

Perry swooped his rifle from under the couch, ran over, and placed the barrel through the back window.

"It's me, Snipes," a familiar voice called.

"*Red,* who's in front of my house?" Perry asked.

"That new chief and Irishman. Two coppers are on each side of the block. Irishman's two goons have Chicago Typewriters. Tony is keeping watch from the alley. We'll keep the back secured."

Perry's eyes turned demon-dark, and veins raised from his face like keloids. He pulled a shotgun from under the kitchen counter.

"I can't believe those *niggers* brought machine guns to my house."

Major walked behind him. "Let's show them how Savages really squabble."

I grabbed two rifles and the pistols from the top kitchen shelf.

Perry snapped his fingers. "Doll, you and the ladies take the boys to the attic and hold tight."

We booked it to their room. The boys were groggy, and we wrapped them in blankets. They didn't notice the danger around them. We led them upstairs for what they thought was a *Peter Pan* night adventure. They snuggled beside each other and drifted off to sleep.

"Countess and I are going on the balcony," I whispered to Beloved and Juno.

Beloved grabbed my arm. "But Snipes said—"

"I'm his wife," I said, cutting her off, "and I won't stay here while he's outnumbered."

Countess and I ran and lay on our stomachs on the balcony floor. Growing extremely nauseous, I dripped with trails of sweat. A thump began to pound against the back of my skull.

Countess touched my forehead. "Empress, you are clearly sick. Go back upstairs. I'll hold it down."

"Stop fretting over me, Camille."

Chief Wraith raised his hand in the air and fired a shot. "Perry Snipes, outside! Or we're coming in!"

Perry quickly opened the door, and he and his brothers lined the porch.

"Another move, and we're at war," Perry commanded.

"Are you Perry Snipes?" Wraith asked.

"Who wants to know?"

"I'm the law. He's facing vandalizing and arson felonies, but the mayor will erase the charges if he comes with me to resolve past due taxes."

Major stepped forward. "All of us are Perry Snipes."

"Do you speak for all the *jiggs?*"

"We're one blood with one voice, *whiggs*," Major responded.

"Drop your weapons or else."

Perry stepped forward. "Tell Dunstan if he wants to discuss business, he needs to set up a meeting during regular business hours."

Chief Wraith looked at Irishman and burst out laughing. "How in the hell did my brother allow these jiggs to think they have any power?"

The Phantom drove down the street and stopped. Irishman, his men, and the police stepped to the window. After a few ticks, they started to disperse.

Wraith walked over to Perry and spit at his feet. "You lucked out this time, but it's a new day, jigg."

November 1938 - Gary, Indiana

It was sunrise, and no one had slept.

"I wonder what last night was about?" I asked while pouring everybody's coffee.

"I sense they are planning an attack," Major said. "And we need to be here for the rumble."

Perry returned inside from watch duty on the porch. "Major, you need to get some shut-eye so you can head back to tend to family business in Harlem."

"You are family business."

Countess yawned. "And I have extra soldiers. Chicago has quieted since Capone moved his operation to Miami."

There was a loud thud at the door, and everyone rose to attention.

Perry rushed to the window and called back, "Cool your hammers. It's the newspaper boy."

The *Gary Tribune's* headline read: *Mayor Dunstan Calls Our Great President, Honest Abe, a Liar.* The bad press had already hit the radio airwaves, and Bear turned on the news.

Perry pointed at the paper's cover story. "This must be why he stopped last night from happening."

"I don't trust that no good mayor." Major ordered his other brothers, "We stay."

He and Perry began discussing possible war plans. I knew Dunstan was a politician and would not come after us while his city was under scrutiny and governmental fire. I raised my hand to speak but became overheated and short of breath.

"What's shaking, doll?"

I ran outside to the cold air, hoping to get some relief. Beams of sunlight laserd directly into my eyes. I squinted as tears fell down my face. I could hear Perry calling from behind me, but my ears were burning from the sound of the train's whistle from up the block. Somebody's baby started crying, and I covered my ears. I took another deep whiff. A strong surge of Perry's night sweat, whiskey, cigarettes, cake frosting, and morning breath hit my nose and punched my stomach. I gagged. Perry draped my fur over me, and I threw it on the ground.

The clouds started to spin like cotton candy, and it felt like all the blood had rushed out of me. I fainted, but Perry caught me before I hit the ground. The family circled around me.

Perry lifted my head. "Doll, you're scaring me. Is it another attack?"

At that moment, I knew what it was, but I was too weak to respond. Instead, I touched his lips and closed my eyes.

CHAPTER 26
FORWARD

PERRY "SNIPES CREED" SAVAGE

May 1939 - Gary, Indiana

I paced like a soldier in the band. The color of my fingers was gone. My heart raced faster than the Olympic track star, Jesse Owens. Dulce, the strongest woman I'd ever known, was hollering in pain, and I felt helpless.

"Perry, stop staring and get your ass over here," she said.

"I'm sorry, doll. What do you need?"

"I can't breathe."

"Hold on to me. I'm your oxygen."

She yelled and squeezed my hand until my fingers popped. Using my other hand, I wiped the sweat dripping down her face.

"Mr. Savage, it's time. Do you want to see?" the doctor asked.

I left Dulce's side and stood behind the doctor. Between her legs, I witnessed a miracle right before me. I placed my hands over my mouth, and God held time so I could reflect and see how blessed I was.

"Perry!" Tears rained down Dulce's face, and she reached for me. *"I can't fucking do this!"*

"You're doing it, doll. Push one more time for our baby girl."

"Are we having a girl?"

"I think so. All I can see is a head full of hair."

I stopped breathing, praying my air would reach Dulce to relieve her. Within seconds, our baby girl coughed and was placed on Dulce's bosom. Instantly, love overflowed and poured into every thread of my body. I had witnessed God's most beautiful creation—life.

Dulce was lost in love as our baby girl suckled on her breast. Mesmerized, I got in the bed next to them. Our baby girl, full of sweetened love, drifted off to sleep. Pierre ran into the room and climbed between us. Willie Kinsman took several pictures, capturing the most sacred day of my life.

"Mr. Creed, I can't wait to get these developed," he said.

"Wait, Willie," Dulce whispered. "Get one of baby girl with her daddy."

"I can hold her?" I stuttered. "I've never held a baby before."

"It's not rocket science," she replied with a chuckle.

Dulce's dewy face was renewed with serenity, and my loving respect for her had grown into the outer realms of human understanding.

Once we realized Dulce was carrying our child, she changed into a different kind of woman. She ate healthier, took daily walks, and exercised, preparing her body and our baby for delivery day. Mama Lee had helped her with Pierre, and Dulce had done those same things. Our son was the smartest, healthiest kid I'd ever met. So, I put my trust in whatever she said was best.

She smiled. "Get over here and hold your daughter, and you have to name her."

We had agreed that if we had a boy, she would name him, and if we had a girl, I would take the honor.

Pierre grabbed my hand. "I'll help you, Daddy."

I walked over, and my angel handed me an angel swaddled in white. Her round, perfect face was a beautiful, baby version of Dulce, with the prettiest brown eyes, nose, and perfect lips. Her head was covered with thick black strands of silk. She looked like a baby doll. My lips touched her virtuous skin, and I deeply inhaled her mixed fragrance of new baby, fresh powder, sugar cookies, and rose petals. Joyous tears dropped down my cheeks.

I was in awe. "She's gorgeous, just like you, doll."

"What are we going to call her, Daddy?"

"Baby Doll."

Pierre lovingly stroked her hair, and I saw a protector in his eyes. He kissed her forehead and said, "I love Baby Doll, Daddy."

"That's cute for a nickname, fellas, but she needs a government name."

I closed my eyes and kissed Baby Doll's face again. "Meet Paris Ella-Monroe."

A sunny smile beamed across Dulce's face. "I love it, Perry."

"Me too, Daddy."

We kissed all over Paris, and she slowly blinked.

Willie Kinsman clicked and rewound the dial on his camera one last time. "I'm going to split, family. I've got some great pictures."

I handed Willie a dollar bill. "Thank you, young man. Tell Bear to drive you home."

Dulce yawned. "I'm *so* sleepy."

It had been twenty hours of battled labor in the delivery room. So, I didn't doubt that she was exhausted.

Pierre snuggled next to her. "Me too, Mommy."

"You two get some shut-eye. Me and Baby Doll will look out the window."

Dulce kissed us. "I love you forever, my loves."

"There is no love greater than I possess for all of you, Forever Mine."

I walked to the window and soaked in the happiest moment of my life. I had everything I'd ever wanted. Everyone slept peacefully under my watch, and my gaze drifted to the view of the courtyard. I whispered in Paris's ear, detailing the wonders I witnessed outside: pink and white blooms on the apple trees, the freshly manicured lawn, and a tropical-colored flower garden. The wind coughed, and flower petals soared through the air like butterflies.

Suddenly, the warning hairs on the back of my neck stood at attention. My senses signaled the presence of an attack. My eyes held on to peace through the window while my third eye concentrated on an enemy infiltrating hollowed territory.

Mayor Dunstan tiptoed across the forbidden line like a grotesque gnome.

"Creed, it's business hours, and I was on my way to your office as *you* requested. But, when I strolled down Grant Street, I *knew* there were some fancy Negroes in this hospital by the Cadillacs and Mercedes parked outside. Since the Creeds are the fanciest Negroes in town, I saved myself a trip." He grinned like he had hit the lottery. "You and Empress have a precious family—precious jewels need *extra* protection. Congratulations on your newest gem. Boy or girl?"

My blood bubbled like lava. "None of your *fucking* business."

His face turned red as a rotten tomato. "In my city, your business is my fucking business, Creed. I'm done playing with you and Empress. The games end today."

I clenched my teeth. "Have a shred of decency and get out. I'll meet you outside."

"City Hall. Back parking lot. Fifteen minutes. *Alone.*"

He turned and walked away.

I kissed Pierre and whispered in Dulce's ear, "I have to go, doll." She opened her eyes, dazed. "*Why?*"

I kissed Paris and placed her in Dulce's arms. "Dunstan just left. I'm meeting him at City Hall."

Her eyes grew wild. *"That motherfucker came in here?"*

I grabbed her face and transmitted my strength to her. "A pistol is under your mattress."

In the corner, I unlocked my weapons briefcase. I slid my knife on my ankle and placed two guns around my waist. Under my vest, I stuck two pistols in the holster. I strapped the invisible armor over my shoulders—weight passed down from my forefathers to fight the hatred and pain lashed against them since they were stolen from Africa.

I got on my knees and thanked God for the vulnerable space and time to transmit and receive love from my family. Although brief, I cherished the gifted minutes of total tranquility, which was an unanswered prayer for Negro men—most of us couldn't fathom the freedom to love without worry. I prayed for protection.

Pierre touched my shoulder. "Daddy, are you getting ready for war?"

I kissed his hand. "Son, a soldier stays ready for combat."

"That white man called you Creed and Mommy, Empress."

"Remember, we only use our code names with strangers?"

"Is Mommy a soldier, too?"

"Mommy is the Queen of Queens, and I'm the King of all the Kings. You and your sister are our royal descendants. It's my duty to lead our knights and protect our empire."

"Is that why you carry so many guns?"

"Every man has the right to arm himself with guns. Guns allow us to protect the lives and freedom of our families and loved ones. Do you understand?"

"Yes, sir. Can you give me a code name and teach me?"

"I will teach you when I get back. *Do not ever* touch a gun until I teach you how to properly use it. It is not to be played with." I wrapped my Army tag around his neck. "Your code name is Knight Creed, and this is your shield."

"You need your shield for battle."

While removing my shoe, I whispered, "Army soldiers carry two tags. I always keep one in my shoe. You're my son, Knight Creed, protected by the shield. So, stay close to Mommy and Paris because your shield protects everyone around you."

He saluted. "I promise to protect our dolls while you're at war, Daddy Creed."

"At ease, soldier," I told my son, giving him a big hug. Then I carried Pierre to the bed and whispered in Dulce's ear, "Doll, when Bear comes back, tell him, *Ether.*"

Red, Tony, and I drove past a line of coppers parked in front of City Hall. The back parking lot was empty, except for Dunstan's Rolls Phantom, the sheriff's car, and Irishman's 1932 Thurmond, an Irish collector's car.

The Chief of Police, Blakely Wraith, stepped out first. I could see in the light that he was a younger, slimmer version of his older brother, the late sheriff, and wore a permanent scowl on his face. Behind him, a pit bull. Mayor Dunstan, Irishman, and two goons stepped out of their cars and stood in a straight line.

I grabbed Ready's trusty cane. "Let's shake a leg, gentlemen."

Tony, Red, and I got out of the car, and immediately, Chief Wraith's dog hounded us.

"Come to your master, Jigaboo," Wraith commanded.

The dog ran and sat next to him, and it took everything in me not to shoot Wraith.

Mayor Dunstan stood tiny between Wraith and Irishman. "Creed, I told you to come alone."

"I don't take orders from you or anyone."

Irishman laughed. "Everyone knows you're tied to your broad's apron."

"And I'm covered with her scent, trained to harm anyone wishing her harm."

Wraith smiled. "Sounds like my bitch, Jigaboo—she's trained to kill, especially the one who killed my brother. And she got a good whiff of your Brooks Brothers suit and any extra funk you carry, jiggs."

Red and Tony pulled out their pistols.

"I don't wear Brooks Brothers. My wife boss designs all my suits, whiggs."

Dunstan interrupted. "Creed, I want my money."

"We're not giving you a dime."

Irishman's goons pulled out their machine guns.

"I told you, *Creed*, that game is over."

"No one is playing, *Mayor*. Your police chief has organized a white group of racists, and they're terrorizing the colored people in your city."

"His job is to restore our order," Dunstan explained, "and my job is to restore our jobs."

"We're moving things back into their proper order," Wraith added. "It's a new day for you new Negroes."

Everyone drew their guns, and Tony, Red, and I retreated to Red's Cadillac.

Tony grabbed my arm and whispered, "Let me get in the backseat so I can stretch my legs, youngblood."

As soon as the car moved forward, Irishman's goons unloaded their Chicago Typewriters. Gunfire sprayed around us, sailing through the windows and sending glass shatters everywhere.

As a marksman, God would silence everything around me, and my targets—no matter how far away—always appeared crystal clear before my eyes. I had six bullets and five targets, and I never miss. In the parking lot were Dunstan, Irishman, Chief Wraith, and two goons. I had their chests locked, but my empowered finger was cramped on the trigger. I battled a divine force that prevented me from firing. My mind had moved rapidly into the future, and my soul wouldn't allow the inevitable repercussions to my wife and kids if I killed five white men at City Hall, even though my mind wanted to.

Red turned sharply left onto Broadway.

"Is anyone hit?" I asked in a panic.

"I got nicked in this aged leg," Tony answered.

Red passed Tony a whiskey flask. "Nigga, don't bleed out in my new Caddy."

"Man, what do you want me to do?"

"Stop bleeding until I can patch you up."

I stared at Tony's leg, oozing with blood. "Red, you are not a doctor, and this is not 1919."

Tony shook his head and chugged down the hooch. "Youngblood, we don't do doctors. You know how this goes, Captain. We've patched each other up on the battlefield with less."

"I understand that, clearly. But we're in the city, and the hospital has professional surgeons a few blocks up the street."

Red kept driving until he pulled into the back alley of The Palace. We helped Tony hobble to the basement.

Philly opened the door. "Oh shit! Are you okay, Tony?"

"It's just a scratch."

Red wrapped Tony's sock around his thigh and grabbed the tool kit. "Youngblood, he has two wounds. Go to Empress's office and grab her sewing case."

He poured more whisky over Tony's open flesh, and Tony yelled for sweet Jesus.

"Are y'all dizzy from that old-ass whiskey?" I asked.

Red set a match flame to a pair of pliers. "Hurry up, Captain, and get the damn sewing kit."

I took off running and fumbled with the keys to open Dulce's door. I grabbed her pink satin bag. When I returned, Tony was drinking more liquor. On the table were two bloodied bullets and pliers.

"Youngblood, burn that needle and thread it with a long piece of string," Red instructed. "Not too long, though."

I pulled out the first spool.

"Not pink, new Negro!" Tony yelled. "How would I look with pink thread laced through my leg and thigh?"

I burned the needle, threaded the brown like Dulce had taught me, and handed it to Red.

"You two are crazy."

Philly and I watched Red sew Tony's open flesh together like a torn piece of cloth. After all the hollering, cussing, drinking, and jokes, life seemed back to normal.

CHAPTER 27
ETHER

PERRY "SNIPES CREED" SAVAGE

May 1939 - Gary, Indiana

If envy were a woman, it would be hatred's twin—both emotions hump on the heart like diseased skanks. They climax poison into their prey's conscience, killing the kindness in the spirit and leaving the victimized in a panicked state of fear.

Fear, like hatred and envy, is not only heart-wrenching but crippling. Whether alone or in a pack, if these emotions fester unattended, the damage, like the claps, is life-threatening. My mind was trained to stop victimizing thoughts before they inflected demise into my spirit. But after a disturbing discussion with the fellas at Bobby's Barbershop, fear had penetrated beyond skin deep for the first time.

We don't want another Le Marais. We don't want another Black Wall Street. This was the headline screaming across Negro newspapers across America. Massacres initiated by white folks were not only murdering Negroes but killing Negroes' progress across the globe.

On Black Wall Street, Memorial Day 1921, thirty-five blocks of Negroes' legacy, prosperity, and human life in America were decimated in two days by white folks diseased with hatred, envy, and fear.

The entire town of Le Marais Isle, without the divinity of God's intervention, would have drowned. Their lives had been saved, but the progress of another thriving town—built for us and by us during the country's era of Reconstruction—had also been annihilated by the same culprits of Black Wall Street: hatred, envy, and fear.

Both massacres happened during a time Americans were supposed to be celebrating. Views like Dunstan's, who believed opposites can never be equal, looked at the world in terms of black inferiority versus white supremacy. *How can Negroes thrive in a society designed with lines of racial divide?*

Mayor Dunstan's "It's a New Day" had the fearful white folks of our city armed, dangerous, and criminally protected by the government. Fueled by his vendetta to avenge Wraith's brother, our police chief used his armed force, pit bull, and newly appointed deputies to terrorize the Negroes in our neighborhoods. Chief Wraith had kept the surface of his police department's hands clean by using his deputies to do all the dirty work. Whatever funds the mayor hadn't stolen were poured only into the white side of the tracks. So, the gleam that had once shined as the mirror of our white counterparts was becoming poorer and grimier by the day.

Whenever colored folks filed complaints, the mayor and chief threw up their hands, claiming no crimes had been committed. With no control over how city funds were dispersed and because deputies were not under police jurisdiction, there was no action or accountability for the multitude of damage done to our community.

Negro citizens had gotten sick from the racial tension, which had spread like the gas ether. And like ether, the city only needed one spark to spread a deadly fire, and unfortunately, doomsday was upon us. As a soldier who understood the rules of engagement, I took the liberty of arming the citizens on our side of the tracks with the knowledge and training to combat the flames.

Operation Ether was our weapon to fight against fear. My mission had become that every Negro civilian had access to a firearm and instruction to properly engage. My team of men— Bear, Geese, Red, and Tony—volunteered their time to assist me, and when word spread to all the other colored servicemen in our city, we worked together to prepare our town for battle because we knew, like Le Marais and Black Wall Street, a war was coming. I fantasized about a life for our kids like Matthieu LeBlanc's, who basked in colorless joy. For Negroes, life in a world ignorant to color was as fake as Peter Pan's Never-Never Land. I wouldn't have believed a person like Matthieu existed had I not met him in person. So, in America, the Colored were forced to confront the colored divide, and I wanted my city ready on the front lines.

We were in Bobby's Barbershop, getting haircuts. After a deep discussion about being a Negro in America, we started joking, smack-talking, and smoking like we always did to end our time on a high note. Suddenly, copper sirens rang loudly outside. Walking down Broadway were dozens of white protestors led by Chief Wraith and his unleashed pit, Jigaboo. In their hands were guns and signs that read: *Give Us Back Our Order. Give Us Back Our Jobs. It's a New Day.* My blood boiled.

The fellas and I stepped outside, armed at attention. Chief Wraith and a tall, white protestor with a needle-sharp nose walked over.

Wraith smiled upside down, deepening his scowl. "Good afternoon, Creed."

Jigaboo growled and barked. Wraith snapped his fingers.

"Sit, Jigaboo. My bitch listens to her master," he said with sick satisfaction.

"Your dog needs a leash. It's been attacking citizens and mauled a little boy."

"Jigaboo and I thought he was an armed robber."

"He was ten years old, playing with a toy in front of his house."

"He's gonna live, ain't he?" Wraith asked.

The needle-nosed protestor rolled his eyes. "Yeah, be grateful that nigger's alive."

I was beyond disgusted. "Get your ass away from here, and go back where you came from."

The protestor gripped his pistol. "Make me."

Red stepped forward.

"Chief Wraith, remove your people from our neighborhood," I demanded.

"All citizens have the right to peacefully protest," he said.

The needle-nosed man yelled, "Give us our jobs and order back!"

"Take your employment concerns to the crooked-ass mayor in City Hall," I answered. "And, Wraith, the Negroes expect the same courtesy when we decide to protest on the other side of the tracks."

"What?" he asked shockingly.

"We want armed police escorts, too."

He laughed with a frown. "Contact my secretary to check my schedule."

"Chief, I didn't know you had a secretary," Needle Nose chimed in.

Chief Wraith frowned harder. "I don't."

They walked away, amused at their grotesque humor. All the Gary business owners and citizens stood outside with their weapons in plain sight. The white protesters shouted while lingering, but once the police dispersed, so did they. The streets were suddenly quiet once again.

May 1939 - Chicago, Illinois

During May, I'd stayed at The Palace most nights. I'd spent my days helping citizens with firearms, securing The Palace, and keeping business afloat while Dulce healed with the baby and Pierre in Chicago. My family was tucked away in one of Countess LeRoux's old houses on Chicago's South Side.

Emotionally and physically drained from the day with Wraith, Pitbull, and Needle Nose, I changed my overnight plans and headed home. It was the Sunday of Memorial Day weekend, and I usually stayed on duty at The Palace during high traffic and holiday times. Instead, I drove to Chicago to stay with my family.

My family was my vacation; wherever we were together was my island resort. I left my tension outside the front door and snuck inside. I kissed Dulce and the kids while they were asleep and filled the tub with hot water. Then, I lit a couple of candles. The flamed wicks and steamy vapors soothed me. I shut my eyes. My thoughts floated nowhere while my body marinated in bubbles like hot gumbo. I got a strong whiff of roses and sugar cookies, followed by soft hands on my feet.

My body relaxed deeper. "Damn, doll, you always know when and how to touch me."

She smiled. "I feel the same way about you."

"Bring me some sugar."

Her lips melted over mine.

"Perry, I've missed you. I thought you were staying at The Palace tonight."

"I needed to hold my family."

"Crazy day?"

"I left the day outside so I can focus on you."

"Perry, we need to talk."

I pulled her close to me. "What's shaking, doll?"

"Why are you teaching our son how to shoot pistols?"

"Why are you teaching him how to read?" I asked.

"He can't survive without reading."

"He can't survive in fear."

"Perry, he's only a boy."

"To *us*, he's a boy. To *them*, he's a manly threat."

She didn't respond.

I touched her face. "In the world's eyes, Pierre is a strong, tall Negro-nigga and a threat to civilization. I'm raising him to know that only God is above, below, and before him."

Dulce frowned. "Fuck the world."

I smiled and kissed her forehead. "Focus on the books and let Daddy teach our son how to be a man."

"I need Daddy to teach *me* a lesson," she said, heading towards the door.

"Don't tease me, woman."

"The doctor said my body is healed." She threw her nightgown in my face. "Captain Perry Blair Savage, I'll be in the other bedroom waiting for my first assignment."

Before I knew it, I wrapped Dulce's legs around me like a lifesaver and gripped her ass on the bathroom sink.

Smiling, she grabbed my neck and asked, "What kind of hocus pocus made you move that quickly?"

My lips caressed her clavicle as my poetic words flowed from them.

> *"Hocus Pocus, De Leche magic,*
> *Laced love water, sugar sweet addict*
> *One snap of her fingers, I'm in-between*
> *Those hips, my fantasy, ice cream dream*

Comatose, don't wake me, I wanna play
Captain, May I…keep coming my way
Under my command, bodies soaked, sauna,
Flights heavenly, serene, Nirvana."

Our heated flesh connected and embraced. Dulce's honey skin was my aphrodisiac, and I eagerly drowned inside her flood waters.

"Perry, how I've missed you."

Her wet tongue wrapped around mine, and I gripped her closer. When her full breasts rubbed against me, my body stopped listening to me. My mind drifted above us, and every nerve in my body exploded. I kissed the love cries that streamed down her face and held her against my chest as we trembled in ecstasy. Afterwards, she fell asleep in my arms on the sink. I dressed us and carried her to the bed where Pierre and Paris rested like angels.

In the middle of the night, I awakened to Paris on my shoulder, Dulce on my chest, and Pierre wrapped around my legs. I was covered with love, draped in my sanctuary.

It was the break of dawn. The sky was purple with orange ribbons. Hidden behind the horizon was the sun, golden like a bagel. "If I Didn't Care" by The Ink Spots blasted through the lively house. Dulce had Paris in her arms, and Pierre sang and waltzed around them in the kitchen. Cinnamon brown sugar French toast and smoked bacon traveled through the house.

Pierre ran into my arms. "Good morning, Daddy! Will you play baseball with me?"

"Get your ball and glove. We'll play after breakfast."

I wrapped my arms around my Dulce and Paris and gave them kisses. "Good morning, dolls. You're up before the sun."

"Hey, good-looking. Paris wakes us up at five-thirty every morning, so our day starts early. You have a bunch of mail that Bear brought from the house. One is from Alexandre Dupont."

The phone rang, and it felt like a warning siren. Paris started screaming in an octave I hadn't heard before as I answered.

"Hello?"

"Snipes."

"What's shaking, Bear?"

Paris's screams and the music were drowning out Bear's words, making it impossible to hear what he was saying.

"Slow down, Bear. Doll, turn down the music."

"Paris loves this song. It calms her," she said.

"I can't hear, Bear. Speak up."

He was muffled. "Snipes, there's been fires and Philly..."

"Fires?" I asked.

"Fires?" Dulce repeated.

My heart dropped, and I was no longer listening to Bear.

I released the telephone receiver from my ear and looked around. "Where's Pierre?"

"What fires, Perry?" she asked again.

"Turn off the platter and quiet Paris. Where's Pierre?"

Dulce stuck her breast in Paris's mouth and turned down the music.

She yelled for him. *"Pierre?!"*

In a panic, I ran into our bedroom. *"Pierre?!"*

Dulce looked behind the curtain in the living room, his favorite hiding spot. *"We're not playing hide and go seek, Pierre. Where are you?"*

He didn't respond, and we got more desperate as we scampered around the house. The missing seconds felt like hours, and we met in the kitchen without him. The house screamed with silence.

From the basement, there was a loud pop like a firecracker on the Fourth of July. But I knew that sound too well. It was a bullet fired from inside a Smith and Wesson. The sound snatched my soul through my chest. My body moved faster than time, which didn't feel fast enough. I swooped my rifle from under the kitchen table. Without stopping, my feet flew down the hallway. I could see the basement door, and it was cracked open.

"*Pierre?!*" Dulce shrilled behind me.

I leaped for the handle and flung the door open.

Pierre was at the base of the steps holding a pistol. He looked up at me.

"I got him, Daddy."

I darted down the steps and secured him against my chest. My arms trembled as life returned to me. I inhaled gasoline. At our feet, the needle-nosed protestor rested stiff in a red puddle of blood.

My face was drenched, and I kissed Pierre's face.

"Hand me the gun, son. Are you okay?"

He pulled my Army tag from beneath his shirt and saluted. "Knight Creed protected by the shield, sir."

I squeezed as much of my love into him. "At ease, soldier. You are so brave, and I'm proud of you, son. I love you so much. Go with Mommy."

"Yes, sir. Can I have my glove and ball?"

I snatched his ball and baseball mitt before the perpetrator's oozing blood consumed them.

Standing at the top of the stairs, Dulce had Paris tucked in her bosom and held a pistol in her hand. Her eyes were wild.

"Come here, Pierre," she called to him.

As he ran up the stairs, I said, "Doll, go to the bathroom, lock the door, and lay in the tub."

CHAPTER 28
FREEDOM

EMPRESS CREED

May 1939 - Chicago, Illinois

I once believed money was the only key to unlock the Negros' cage of oppression. But I found the Harry Houdini to Uncle Sam's fortress, and it was freedom.

Freedom was the only foolproof escape from the enslavement of imprisonment, and as the innocence in my children's eyes seemed to enter my soul for the first time, my mind uncuffed itself from my body. I suddenly felt like the fearless wild child I had once been on Chicago's South Side. I was freed.

"Mommy!"

I snapped out of my renewed pathway of thought.

"Why are we soaking in a tub with no water?"

Pierre was rolling his ball between his legs. I was sitting behind him with a gun in my hand while Paris rested peacefully against my bosom.

"Pierre, are you sure you're okay, sweetie?" I asked.

"Yes, ma'am. I'm ready to play."

"Can you tell Mommy what happened in the basement?"

"I was getting my baseball and glove, and a robber climbed in the window. Daddy said if I ever see a robber to hide quietly in my secret place until he leaves."

"That sounds like a good plan. Why didn't you stay hidden?"

"Daddy also said if I had a clean shot from my hiding spot, take the robber out, and he'll take care of the rest."

"Where did you get the gun?"

"Daddy had put it in my hiding place. Did I do something wrong?"

"No, sweetie. You were very brave."

He pulled out his dog tag with virtuous pride. "I'm Knight, protected by my daddy's shield. So can we skip breakfast and play baseball?"

Perry unlocked the door, and a strong gust entered the bathroom. I exhaled.

Pierre jumped into his arms. "Daddy, can we play baseball now?"

"Eat your breakfast first. We'll play at Miss LeRoux's house later. Doll, I packed your bags."

"Where are we going?"

"The Palace caught on fire, and Philly got burned. I want to check out the damage and go see him in the hospital."

"*Fire?* I'm going with you."

"No, you're not," he said.

"Whoa! At ease, Captain. I'm the Empress of The Palace."

"And the perimeter falls under my jurisdiction. So, you aren't going anywhere until I say it's secured."

I pulled him to me. "I married a hoodlum."

He kissed me and smiled. "No, *I* married a hoodlum—*you* married a soldier. So, at ease, Empress Creed, and let me do my job."

Countess and I sat in her kitchen, surrounded by boxes.

"Are you redecorating your kitchen again?" I asked.

She shook her head no as she guzzled a glass of fruit and vegetable water. I refocused my attention on Perry and Pierre playing baseball in her backyard.

"Can you make me something to seduce a dog?" I asked Countess.

"What kind of dog? Man, woman, or canine?"

I laughed. "A pit bull."

As she rinsed out her glass, the rays reflecting from the diamond on her left ring finger blinded me.

I snatched her hand. "Did you and Major get hitched?"

"I haven't given him an answer."

"Why?"

"'That man drives me crazy.'"

"What did you say?"

"Nothing."

"Countess!"

"When he tried to take his ring back, I wouldn't let him."

"When did this happen?" I asked.

"Last week. And he hasn't written or called me."

"When are you going to talk to him?"

"I'll tell him when I move to Harlem and let him know I'm having his baby."

"Baby?"

"Yes, that man loved a baby into me. I felt him penetrate through my tonic, and my mama confirmed it."

I put my arms around her. "Trust me, marrying a Savage is a dream. Plus, Major told me he couldn't wait for you to have his redhead sons."

"No fooling?"

"No fooling. So, stop fooling around and let that man love you."

She rolled her eyes and fumbled around the kitchen. Then, she poured a few clear oils into a spray bottle.

"Use three squirts."

I took a whiff. "I don't smell anything."

"Dogs sense of smell is forty times ours. Our ancestors used this to charm bloodhounds when they ran for freedom."

"What's in it?"

"Lavender, vanilla, ginger, and trash."

"Trash?"

"*Oui, mon amour.* Trust me."

May 1939 - Gary, Indiana

That night, Perry and I attended the annual Memorial Day Mayor's Ball, the year's biggest event. After decorating the graves of soldiers who had died at war, the city would gather and party on their side of the tracks while watching the sky illuminate with fireworks from City Hall.

Perry and I had gotten ritzy and were parked in the lot across the street from the City Hall entrance. The doors had opened for the annual gala, and white folks dressed in black tie and American colors were filing in. The event was invitation only, and Negroes had never been in attendance unless put to work.

I was dressed in a red beaded evening gown that fit my motherly curves and flared at the knees, with hundreds of feathers flocking into a train along the ground. Perry wore a black tuxedo with a red tie and cummerbund.

Holding a briefcase full of money, he frowned. "I don't trust these folks, doll. A white nigga just tried to kill my family."

"We are fighting a white man's war, and as Queenie advised, we need a white ally if we want to win."

A limousine stretched and parked next to us. Perry exhaled and walked cautiously to my door. He held out his hand, and I got out. Before we got inside the limo, the driver met us at the door. We slid inside and faced Irishman and Shane Killian.

Shane Killian was a young, handsome man with vanilla skin, reddish blonde hair, and turquoise eyes. Next to him sat his new, pregnant wife. She and I discreetly winked when I sat across from her.

Shane introduced himself and smiled. "Hello, Mr. and Mrs. Creed. Please, meet my gorgeous wife, Orla Roisin Killian, and you know my uncle, Irishman Conan."

Perry shook the Killian's hands while he and Irishman glared.

"Congratulations, Mr. and Mrs. Killian," I said to break the tension. "When are you expecting?" I asked them.

She rubbed her belly. "November twenty-eighth."

"Mr. and Mrs. Creed," Shane said, "my uncle and I want to call a truce. I know I won't beat Mayor Dunstan without having the Negro vote, so if you help me get in office, I'll ensure fairness for all citizens in our city, no matter the side of the tracks."

"How can we trust you?" Perry asked.

"I am a man of my word. And I want our children to grow up in a different world."

"A mayor can't change the world," Perry said.

"But mayors change the city, and cities change the world."

"Does your uncle have the same worldview as you?"

Irishman responded in a tone more Irish than before. "My family comes before the world."

"My uncle understands that to hate Negroes is to hate my wife and his future kin."

Irishman cleared his throat. "But they are more Black Irish than Negro, Shane. Orla speaks Gaelic, for God's sake."

Orin was pale enough to pass for white, but she snapped, "My grandmother was a colored slave, *uncle.*"

"But your father and his descendants were born in Ireland. So, you're more like an octoroon, and your baby, *Irish*."

Killian interrupted. "The color in their blood doesn't matter. They are a part of me, which makes them part of you."

"Mr. Killian, you have our support," I assured.

Perry slid him the briefcase filled with five thousand dollars.

Killian shoved it back. "No, put that money into the fire-damaged businesses on Broadway. Uncle, shake Mr. Creed's hand to show good faith."

Irishman reluctantly stuck out his hand. "Stay on your side, and we'll stay on ours. For the record, my dislike for you has nothing to do with your color."

Perry looked through him as they shook hands. "For the record, I don't care enough about you to not like you."

Killian smiled. "Great progress, gentlemen."

Irishman split. Perry and I exited the limo with the newlyweds and walked to the door. Mr. Killian handed the doorman four tickets. We all walked in together, and the white crowd drew back like a massive tide. Before Dunstan could react, the *Gary Tribune* snapped pictures of the four of us.

Killian used that opportunity to announce his decision to run for mayor with the slogan, *Gary is one great city.*

Dunstan stood in the middle of the dance floor, red-faced and dumbfounded. Perry and I waltzed past him as the band played "Over the Rainbow" by Judy Garland.

He spun me around. "You look gorgeous, doll."

"You are quite debonair, good-looking."

"Tell me, how do you know Mrs. Killian."

"Orla Killian was born Orin Roisin Broudair, Countess's cousin," I whispered.

"No fooling?"

"No fooling." Before he lectured me about how he despised surprises, I said in a hurry, "I hired her before we got hitched, but she's madly in love with him now. So, she officially resigned to focus on her new life."

Perry dipped me and kissed my lips with a gratifying smile. "Let's go home and really cut a rug. This shindig is a snooze."

As we stood at the front door, I reached inside my pocketbook and removed the spray bottle Countess had given me. I sprayed us three times. As we walked to our car, Jigaboo charged our way.

"I will shoot that dog," Perry grumbled.

I gripped his hand. "At ease, Captain. Countess knows her herbs."

Jigaboo looked like she hadn't eaten in days. Her heavy drool dribbled down both sides of her mouth as she leaped in the air. Perry reached inside his holster, and instead of pulling out his pistol, he tossed her a piece of beef jerky.

She caught it in her mouth while getting a quick whiff of Countess's potion. Then, she began to feast at our feet.

I pet the top of her head. "Hey, Boo. Good girl."

"Sic 'em, Jigaboo!" Wraith yelled from a distance. *"Sic 'em!"*

After opening my car door, Perry kissed me.

Wraith caught up to us and hollered, "Sic his nigger ass, Jigaboo."

Perry and I got inside and laughed hysterically. Chief Wraith had lost his power. Boo was no longer listening to him, and neither were we.

CHAPTER 29
PART OF ME

DULCE ELLA-MONROE SAVAGE

August 1939 - Gary, Indiana

Despite his late entry into the race for Gary's city mayor, Killian won by a landslide, gaining Negro and white supporters who believed "Gary is One Great City." Dunstan's corruptive sins were exposed, making him "Gary's Most Hated." He was slammed with a slew of criminal charges that kept him hidden behind closed court doors, drowning in a pool of debt. Chief Wraith and his crooked coppers were disbanded from the Gary PD and disappeared underground.

The Depression was finally done putting a whooping on America's ass, but with the Nazis aggressively seeking world domination, Perry and I decided that for this fight, our family would get in the ring as *Parisian Nègres* instead of Negro Americans. We also decided we would rumble as Mr. and Mrs. Perry-Blair and Dulce Ella-Monroe Savage, leaving the illicit operation and legacy of Mr. and Mrs. Snipes and Empress Creed in the ashes with the burnt-down Palace.

We sat in our car, posted where the Palace had once sat, for the last time. Perry and I paid contractors to get Bobby's and Mae's businesses back new since the insurance claim had been denied from the fires.

Philly had almost died getting the last bundle of stash out of the basement, so we gave him and Treasure enough dough to last for the years ahead. Bear and Beloved got hitched and moved to Harlem. Her girls either retired or went to work for Butta. Red and Tony had split and went to the underground. Geese and Juno got engaged and expanded his BBQ restaurant in Robbins, Illinois. Everyone else scattered into new beginnings.

I remembered the magical memories I had at The Palace with Mama Lee, Ready, Perry, and everyone who was a part of my life. My heart was full, and I was ready for the next chapter.

Perry stroked my hand. "What's shaking, doll?"

"Do you know how much I paid for that building?"

"How much?" he asked.

"One checker."

"No fooling, doll?"

"No fooling. Matty sold it to me for one dollar."

He lifted his eyebrow. "Doll, it's time for you to let your little nickname for Matthieu burn with this building, don't you think?"

He waited for my reassurance. Then, there was a saving knock on my window. I rolled it down with a huge grin on my face. It was Mrs. Mary Lee. She always dressed like she was going to church and made the best lemon pound cake in the city.

"Empress, you did something great for our town—Mama Lee and Ready are smiling from heaven."

That warmed my heart like Mama's lemon tea.

"Thank you, Mrs. Mary."

"Mr. Creed, did you know that after all those years I played the numbers, I finally hit, and your business burned down with my winning slip. But that's alright, 'cause God saved all the souls in that building."

"How much did you win, Mrs. Mary?" Perry asked.

She shook her head. "Three hundred dollars, but God *is* good."

Perry reached inside his pocket and counted ten fifty-dollar bills.

"All the time, He is good," Perry said, handing her the money. She stuck the roll of cash into her brassiere. *"Amen."* Then, she pulled her gun out of her clutch. "Because of you, I keep my pistol on me at all times."

He laughed. "Be careful with it."

"Nobody bet not *fool* with me, or they're gonna get it where the good Lord split 'em. God bless y'all!"

We burst into laughter as she strolled off.

"Perry, you know she was lying."

"I know."

Pierre jumped in the front seat. "Mommy and Daddy, can we fly to France now?"

August 1939 - Chicago, Illinois

Perry, Pierre, Paris, and I were on Matthieu's private plane at Chicago's Midway Airport, and I couldn't stop fantasizing about our future. The seat hugged my body, and gratitude was melting my heart. Pierre skipped up and back down the aisle. Paris snuggled against my bosom, and I caught Perry's uneasy reflection as burden weighed down his eyes.

I got up and sat next to him. I caressed his hand.

"What's shaking, Captain?" When he didn't respond, I continued, "The flight will be fine, and there are enough sickness bowls on this flight to last you over forty hours."

I giggled, but he returned my lightheartedness with heavy silence—a stillness that covered the span of the plane. The engine rumbled, and the white flight stewardess appeared from the pilot's cockpit.

Perry stepped over me, took Pierre, and whispered something in his ear. They kissed as he positioned him into his seat. Then, he towered over me and stuck out his arms. I gave him Paris, and he began speaking softly into her ear. She smiled, and he placed her cheek against his.

I touched his face. It was soaked with tears.

"Perry, you are scaring me. What's shaking?"

His thumb traced my lips. "My doll, heart, and soul. I never thought God would bless me with my perfect completion."

"Why does it feel like you're leaving me?"

"I will never leave you."

"Perry, it's time to confess the truth. You are scared of heights, good-looking. But I promise to hold you the entire flight."

"The war here isn't over."

"At ease, Captain."

"I have to end this, or it won't end."

"Snipes and Empress Creed already ended it. The war *is* over."

"I need to finish Wraith. I promise you will see me in Paris, doll. Matthieu has my instructions."

"Perry Blair Savage, I love you more than my own life, and I'm not leaving without you, damnit."

Our tears kept our lips glued to each other as he whispered, "I'm so proud of you, doll. There was a time I had to beg you to love me. Now it's dripping from your pores. Being in love with you has been more than a dream come true. Thank you, Mrs. Savage."

I held the back of his neck and pleaded with the strength of my kiss—praying if I didn't let him go, the flight would have to depart with him on it. I prayed I would love him so hard that he would surrender to me and stay in his seat. I was breathless but didn't let up. Everything grew blurry, and I got weaker. Then, he held me in his arms and began to breathe into me. I opened my eyes. No matter how hard I tried, he out-loved me every time.

He stroked my hair and ended our embrace with a forehead kiss. "I love you, Forever Mine."

He headed for the exit door, turned, and tipped his hat with a smile.

Pierre waved. "Bye, Daddy."

"I love you, Knight. Take care of our dolls."

Pierre saluted.

As the distance between Perry and us grew, so did the intensity of my longing for him. The plane jetted past him on the runway, and his image became fainter and smaller until his presence shrank to a mustard seed and disappeared.

August 1939 - Paris, France

We arrived at Paris's Orly Airport, and I had morphed into a character—stuck in life's novel between the pages of fact and fiction. It was a muggy day with sun rays poking through the clouds. I had no idea of the date or time.

Matthieu was gleaming in a private terminal, waiting next to Charles. I marched blankly towards them, but without my oxygen, I was lifeless, led by an invisible puppeteer. Pierre introduced himself and his sister. Matthieu's words to me fell on deaf ears. He led us to the car, and I followed. In the backseat was a bouquet of red roses.

I struggled to speak. "You didn't have to do that."

"Those are from Perry."

There was a sealed letter with his handwriting on the envelope.

August 7, 1939

Bonjour and welcome home, Savages.

PBS

Matthieu played with Pierre in the backseat while I held Paris. Charles was driving as we moved along the photogenic road. When I looked into Paris's eyes, I saw Perry, and my yearning for him took my breath away. Slow streams fell from my eyes as I searched for air.

Charles stopped in Montmartre and parked at 52, rue Pigalle. Matthieu smiled as he handed me a set of keys. I was confused.

"Dulce, I'm simply the messenger," he said in his heavy French accent. "I was told to hand you these keys and wait with your children in the car until you return."

I stuck my key inside the lock, and Charles opened the door. I stepped onto the sparkling wooden floor and inhaled fresh lemon and lavender. A crystal chandelier hanging overhead reflected small rainbows on the walls. I passed the dressing rooms and a register counter and proceeded through the backdoor into a stockroom. My eyes grew large at the sight of four fancy Singer sewing machines. On the table was a bouquet of roses. Beside the roses was another sealed envelope with Perry's writing.

August 7, 1939

Surprise, doll! When we came to Paris for our honeymoon, I met Alexandre Dupont, Matthieu's trusted friend and business partner. I had given him dough to invest in guns, bullets, and steel on the Stock Exchange. I was a little dizzy from the scotch and cigars and had forgotten about it until I received his letter the day after The Palace burned down. Because of the war, that small transaction has made us extremely wealthy. Think of how many Negroes would prosper if we had access to this knowledge. Doll, I want you to read up on investing in the library and get with Alexandre Dupont. He is a genius Colored mathematician and told me he would teach you and Pierre how to invest in stocks. Enclosed is the deed to Dulce Paris, the first of your future boutiques. I believe the world will love you and your designs as much as I do, and I'm grateful God blessed me to be the man to make your lifetime dream come true.

Forever Yours, Forever Mine. PBS

My hands were trembling, and I refocused on my surroundings through my tears. The deed belonged to Dulce Ella-Monroe Savage. I dropped it on the table and screamed.

In the car, I was in shock and unable to speak. Matthieu entertained Paris and all Pierre's questions, giving him the city tour and historical explanations of all the monumental buildings we whizzed by. Charles drove from the city into the countryside, along mountainous green hills.

We stopped in front of a yellow and white house surrounded by freshly planted flowers. In the cobblestone driveway was a black and red Mercedes. We walked onto the front porch, and Pierre and I sat on a familiar white rocking bench. At our feet, another bouquet of roses and a sealed envelope.

August 7, 1939

Forever Mine, I picked this house because it sounds like the one that gave you great memories growing up with Mama Lee, and I wanted our family to feel her spirit. I know how you felt about the rocking chair, so I had it flown from home. There are things in the house that will ease your longing for her.

Like us, our kids are going to run shit, but they'll lead others through the sunshine, not underground. I wish I were there to see your face and carry you over the threshold.

You are emblazoned in my soul, so we are together forever. I
love you infinitely.

Forever yours, Captain Pierre Blair Savage

"Pierre, what did Daddy give you in Chicago?" I asked while
wiping the tears from my eyes.

From under his shirt, he pulled out Perry's father's ring
hanging from the necklace. Suddenly and unexpectedly, an icy
gush from Mother Nature's breath breezed over us, and the hairs
all over my body stood up. I became flushed.

I grabbed my chest, deeply inhaled, and stood up. "Matty, I
need a *huge* favor."

"Anything for you, Dulce, darling."

"I need your jet."

"Of course. When?"

"Now."

He looked deeply concerned. "Did you forget something
important?"

"Not something. Someone."

CHAPTER 30
JESUS WALKS

SNIPES CREED

August 1939 - Gary, Indiana

Strapped with the shield of God's protection, I crossed the forbidden tracks and passed green fields on both sides of the street. While driving, I saw families, children playing, Cadillacs, barbershops, churches, ice cream parlors, grocery stores, and boutiques. It was like I was observing Gary through a mirror. Everything looked identical except for the color of our skin. It showed that we were more alike than different, but fear, envy, and hatred prevented white folks from seeing it.

I parked in front of Irishman's pub, River Green. I got out holding Ready's cane in one hand and a leather briefcase in the other. I calmly walked through the door. It was early in the morning, but a group of men were already drinking at the bar. They turned in my direction but kept drinking.

"I need to talk to Irishman," I demanded.

"He ain't here," one of them responded.

"He's always here."

"*Let him in!*" Irishman yelled from the back.

I followed one of them around the bar. Through the bar door, Irishman was sitting at a wooden desk across from a white man in a painter's uniform.

"We agreed to stay on our own side of the tracks."

I slid the briefcase filled with all the dough he had given to me when he hired me for the patsy job to bring down Dulce.

"I'm here for business, but I need to speak with you alone."

"Everybody *go.*"

One goon stopped on the way out. "We don't trust this coon."

Irishman raised his voice. *"Go."*

After everyone left, I asked, "Where's Wraith?"

"You are one bold Negro, but I didn't think you had a death wish."

"What kind of statement is that?"

"You and anybody with your skin color shouldn't go anywhere near Wraith and his white supremacist group. They hate you and are up to no good."

"What do you care?"

"My nephew has me looking at things a little differently."

"If you and your nephew know Wraith is planning to harm the Negroes in this city, what's being done to keep Gary 'One Great City'?"

"I haven't told my nephew because I mind my own business, and so should you."

"Tell me where Wraith is, and you'll never see me again."

"I know I won't 'cause you'll be dead. Creed, save yourself. Take your family far away from here and never come back."

I slid him a roll of extra dough from my pocket.

He sighed and tossed it back. "Miller Beach, Third Avenue. At a dead end, there's a large cross in front of a small log cabin surrounded by woods. Get ready—it's going to be a war."

I gripped Ready's trusty cane. "I was born ready, and for your information, when I enlisted in the United States Army, I swore to defend all the citizens of this country. So, the people in this town are my business."

I was parked on Third Avenue in Miller, looking through my binoculars. Just as Irishman had described, tucked deep in the woods was a tiny, red log cabin that looked like it belonged in Minnesota. On the left was a large wooden cross. In front of the house, there were two trucks and two cars. As I drove slowly, I noticed railroad tracks suspended on a hill above the backyard. I circled around Fourth Avenue and headed down Grand Boulevard. Turning onto a dirt road, I rocked along the gravel. I kept going until I was surrounded by mountains of sand dunes and wooded hills. I backed my car between tulip trees.

Strapping two rifles across my chest and four smoke grenades, I was ready more than ever to rid the world of Wraith and his racist supremacists. I got out of the car. I was surrounded by a variety of trees, overgrown weeds, and wild stalks that towered over me. I snatched the machete strapped on my back and hacked through the weeds, creating a pathway to the rail tracks perched atop the hill.

It was August, and the humidity was thick. I was drenched in sweat, and the mosquitoes were biting. I heard a loud whistle as a train came chugging in my direction. I ran towards the locomotive. When it passed by, a gust of wind surged and cooled me.

I lay on my stomach with my rifle and waited for the railcars to clear. When they did, I saw five rows of ten white chairs facing a wooden cross in front of the woods. A loud ruckus and yelling came from inside the house. Then, four men dressed in white shirts, tan pants, and President Andrew Johnson masks bust through the back door carrying a young colored boy. His wrists were tied together, and he was kicking wildly as they struggled to detain him. Two men forced him still with a blow to his stomach. When he cried out, they placed masking tape across his mouth before stretching his body and flinging him across a table.

"You're dead for what you did, boy!" one of them screamed.

I had my eyes locked on four new targets; all I could think of was saving the young soul in their grasp. My heart raced, and without thinking, my finger pulled the trigger four times. I threw a grenade and ran through the smoke and down the hill. I made it quickly to the table and cut the rope tied around the boy's wrists. He was trembling, and I yanked him off. As we sprinted up the hill, shots were fired from behind and zoomed past us.

When we reached the top, I snatched the tape from his mouth. "Are you okay, son?"

"Yes, sir, Mr. Creed."

My vision cleared, and I couldn't believe it. "Willie Kinsman?"

"Yes, sir."

We quickly embraced, but I noticed men coming straight for us.

"Run to the west, son, along the rail tracks. Stay low, and I'll catch up to you." I handed him a pistol. "Run as fast as you can, and no matter what, don't look back."

He took off, and I threw another smoke grenade down the hill. Visible to me through the cloud were three more targets, and I executed three clean shots. A single file line of men dressed as Andrew Jackson snaked from the backdoor like a centipede. I threw my third grenade and sped off.

I caught up to Willie and grabbed his hand. He screamed.

"It's me, son. Keep running."

Shots were fired from behind us. I tossed my last grenade, took his hand, and turned into the wooded pathway I had created earlier.

Suddenly, he stopped and cried, "My feet, Mr. Creed!"

I looked down as he stood hunched over his swollen, bloodied feet and ankles that had been brutalized.

I wept for him and took his arm. He limped in agony beside me. Loud barking and distant yells were gaining momentum towards us. I spritz him three times with Countess's dog potion.

"Son, you are so brave. I know it hurts, but dig deep and picture your feet with wings. Take a deep breath and run with all your might. We're almost there."

He nodded. "Yes, sir."

Wraith's pit bull pounced towards us, but instead of attacking, she stopped and stood at attention.

"Good girl, boo," I whispered as she wagged her tail.

Willie and I didn't stop again until we made it to the car. I held my breath until we were back on Grand Boulevard. As I drove, I reached for Willie's hand, and he took it. Through his whimper, he began beautifully singing Billie Holiday's "Strange Fruit."

I'd seen horrific postcard images of lynchings boastfully sold as town souvenirs—Negroes murdered on display and surrounded by the smiling faces of white adults and children. I thanked God I was able to prevent another one from happening.

"When will it end?" I cried out loud.

Willie threw his arms around me and sobbed into my shoulder. "Mr. Creed, I thought I was dead. They said I was dead."

I placed my arm around him. "Remember, the devil is a lie."

After Willie Kinsman's frenzied emotions were calmed by his parents, he told us the men had snatched him while he was snapping photos of railcars parked near the tracks on Broadway Avenue. They had accused him of killing the late Chief Wraith and said they were going to lynch him like the boys in Marion, Indiana.

Willie's father was a photographer for the *Chicago Defender* and had connections to the NAACP. We were sickened with grief.

I split from their house, and my everything ached. I ached for all the innocent Negroes lynched and imprisoned. My heart was heavy, and I wanted all the hatred gone, but I didn't have that kind of power.

After a quick soak in the tub, I got dressed. Then, I closed my eyes and visualized my family. I pictured them happy in our home in Paris, away from all the chaos in America.

It was only before noon, but I knew the war had just begun, even if I had killed Wraith. I needed to see it through until I knew it was over. After dreaming of my family, I pulled up to the post office for a quick tick. I took out a piece of paper from the glove compartment and wrote a love letter to Dulce, Pierre, and Paris to ease my soul. I sealed the envelope and ran inside.

Lost in blissful seconds of daydream, I walked vicariously back to my car. I touched my car handle but went blind from a dark sack placed over my head. I didn't give my perpetrator the satisfaction of a yell and was punched in the gut.

"It's a new day, new nigger," someone huffed in my ear.

With a sharp blow to my head, my heart dropped, and I was transported into a living nightmare. I was beaten until I blacked out and then awakened, still surrounded by darkness. I fought to open my eyes, but I couldn't see a thing through the tiny slits that I had once used as windows to view the world. I took a breath and choked on the sour smell of my bloodied flesh.

Hung by my wrists with numb limbs, I wondered, *Am I a corpse?* If I hadn't died, I was ready to go. The ache in my bones had disappeared and moved into my soul. An animal of some sort groaned and began licking between my toes.

"Is he dead?" a man asked in a deep southern accent.

"I think so."

"Wraith, what should we do with him?"

"Burn him." He paused. "Actually, no more fire. Neighbors already complained about smoke and gunfire from all the ruckus he caused earlier."

"What if we bury him out back?" one of them suggested.

"Do you have something to put him in?"

"I have two troughs we can put together like a coffin."

"Alright, but make it quick. Our rally is in two hours."

After another blow to the back of my head, everything went black.

I awakened, cramped inside a hollow box, and gasped for air. My scent had left me. I had no tears. My body had suffered drought. When I wiggled the bones of my extremities, nothing moved. But I heard muffled voices growing more distant as dirt seeped through the cracks of the makeshift coffin. Dust blew over me, mixing with an unfamiliar wetness I suddenly felt dripping down my face, creating a multitude of mysterious balls on the surface of my skin. I was dead, I thought—alive only in thought, which tortured me. And I had failed my mission and family. My heart burst in agony. I tried to scream mad, but no fucking sound came out. Finally, my thoughts muted, and the thickness of my deceased departure engulfed me.

CHAPTER 31
DON'T LET ME BE MISUNDERSTOOD
EMPRESS CREED SAVAGE

August 7, 1939 - Paris, France

When Mama Lee died, I watched her take her last breath. The closer she had gotten to death, the stronger I had felt her spirit grow inside me. It was an eerie, unrestful feeling that swept over me like a chilled breeze, and I vowed I would never let another person I loved die without a fight. As I watched Matthieu sweet talk Henry Ford, the wealthiest man in the world, to allow me to use his pilot to fly me back to America, I knew for a fact luck was a devil's allusion, and God was indeed the light guiding my life.

When it was time to board, I threw my arms around Matthieu LeBlanc. "You are my angel."

"I'm merely a vessel, Dulce, darling. I wish you would tell me who you left in America that you need to bring back?"

"I left a part of me, but I won't be bringing it back to France."

"I don't understand."

I kissed his cheek and smiled. "It's best for both of us that I'm misunderstood. I love you, Matty."

The pilot was awaiting me, and I didn't have a minute to spare.

As I bolted onboard, he said, "Mrs. Savage, we're stopping in New York for gas before we reach Chicago."

I sat down. "We're getting more than gas, mister."

August 8, 1939 - Harlem, New York

I gained six hours when I landed in New York City, and every second was precious gold. Unlike most cities when it's close to midnight, Harlem didn't blink. It was bright-eyed and bushy-tailed twenty-four hours a day. I had been praying since I left France. I knew I needed God's protection and forgiveness for the sins Empress Creed was about to create. I had planned to leave her in America, but before I buried her for good, I needed to summon her one last time to save my man.

My taxi pulled up to Perry's brothers' place. Major, Bear, Geese, Slide, and Styles were dancing and joking on the stoop.

I lifted my head to God before I wreaked havoc. "Amen."

When I hopped out of the cab, they stopped dead in their tracks.

"Empress?" they asked in harmony.

"Hey, fellas."

"Where's Perry and the kids?" Major asked.

"Perry's in trouble. I came back for soldiers and a bunch of guns. Major, can you call in a favor?"

"Anything. What's shaking?"

"I need Bumpy."

Beloved and Juno sat next to me on the stoop. Beloved was four months pregnant, and Juno, who was visiting Harlem with Geese, was a month pregnant behind her. I was elated for them, but all

I could think about was Perry. My breath was shorter than it had been, and I felt my oxygen slipping away.

Beloved gripped my hand. "Don't worry. Snipes is the baddest soldier this damn world has ever seen."

Juno gripped the other. "And you're the baddest broad, so I know you'll bring him home, Empress."

It had been two hours since I arrived in Harlem, and Bumpy and two men finally rolled up to the stoop.

I kissed Juno and Beloved's hands. Irritated at time's relentlessness, I gave them a smooth five.

"Bumpy, thanks for coming on short notice and for bringing help," I expressed.

"I had to come straight away, Empress. Snipes saved my life, so every minute I get to breathe is borrowed from Father Time. And the extra hands are courtesy of Queenie, and for that glitzy gold and diamond dress you made for her birthday."

We ran into Major's basement. I looked at my watch.

"Everybody strap up," I told them. "We don't have time to waste. We have to get to Gary *now*. I want Perry in my arms by noon."

"*How?*" Bumpy interrupted. "It takes at least twelve hours to get to Indiana."

Major handed pistols to his brothers, and they placed them inside leather suitcases. "I was wondering the same thing."

"We're flying," I answered.

"*What?*" everyone asked.

"On what, Empress?" Major jived. "Magical *fucking* dragons?"

Slide chimed in, "No plane service is going to let a bunch of niggas with guns board their aircraft."

Bear attached knives to his ankles. "They'd love to throw a bunch of niggas in the slammer for life."

"*Hell yeah*," they recited in unison.

"Cool it." I strapped another .22 on my thigh. "Nobody is going to the slammer, and we ain't flying on fucking dragons. We're a bunch of niggas with a bunch of guns about to board a private jet flown by Henry Ford's pilot, fellas."

August 9, 1939 - Chicago, Illinois

It was the first time everyone except me had flown. We were all stricken with air sickness and threw up for three hours straight, filling up our sickness bowls. When we landed at a private hangar at Chicago Midway Municipal Airport, we bolted to the tarmac for fresh morning air. The sun gnawed at our eyes like fingers.

Countess was there, waiting with a group of men and four Cadillacs. Major walked past her, and she grabbed his hand.

"*S'il te plaît,* Major," she begged. "*Oui, mon amour. Je t'aime.*"

"Hell no, Camille. It's been weeks."

"I haven't taken off my ring because I love you, Major Savage. Sorry I took so long, but I've been transferring my operation to Tommy to be with you—for good. Time had gotten away from me, but I don't want to waste another minute without you. Forgive me." Countess kissed along his neck. "*S'il te plaît, Major, mon monsieur, mon amour.* Don't you still love me?"

"You know I'll always love you, but..."

"Say no more. *We'll* be waiting for you in Harlem."

"We *who?*"

She grabbed his hand and placed it on her belly. "Meet your strawberry seed."

He fell to his knees and kissed her stomach. "You truly drive me crazy, woman. When I find my brother, this will be a real celebration."

August 9, 1939 - Gary, Indiana

On the ride to Indiana, I closed my eyes and dreamt Perry was at the house, smoking a cigar, listening to platters, and reading *The Chicago Defender*. But when I awakened with shortness of breath, I knew my dream was just a fantasy.

We pulled up to our house on Washington Street with two hours left till noon. My heart sank. No car was outside. Inside was immaculate, like Perry had never been there, but that wasn't too odd because he was the neatest person I knew. Everyone pulled up chairs into the living room and awaited my command. Before I spoke, there was a loud knock at the door.

Bear removed his pistol. "I'll get it, Empress."

Mrs. Mary Lee was on our front porch, holding a lemon pound cake. "Good morning, Bear. I was dropping off a gift for Mr. Creed."

I walked to the door. "Come in, Mrs. Mary."

She stepped inside. "*Hallelujah*, there are some fine men in here."

"Have you seen my husband?"

"Not since he saved Willie Kinsmen from that lynching."

My heart hit the floor, and based on everyone else's jolted reactions, she could see we had no clue what she was talking about.

"It happened a couple of hours ago, but they're both safe."

"Where are they?" I asked.

"Mr. Creed dropped Willie off at home. That boy is a wreck. Poor thing. His parents drove him to Ohio about an hour ago."

"Dear God. What about my husband?"

"Somebody just told me they saw his car at the post office, so I came by to deliver this cake for our hero."

"I'm going to the post office straight away, but I want you to wait for me. If he comes by here, tell him I said to stay put."

In two shakes, our posse arrived at the post office. Perry's Cadillac was parked in front, and I exhaled with relief. He wasn't in the car, so we ran inside the postal office, but still no sign of him. Instead, we were greeted by the postman.

"Is everything okay, Empress?" the postman asked.

"Is my husband here?"

"No, but he mailed a letter to France not too long ago."

The pit of my stomach flipped upside down. I looked at his brothers, who looked just as devastated. We all sprinted back to Perry's car. All that was inside was a pen and a piece of paper on the passenger seat.

"Fuck!" I screamed before I gathered my senses.

Perry was definitely in trouble, and I had an idea who would know where he was.

"Let's split, fellas."

"Where to?" Major asked.

We raced down Broadway, over the railroad tracks, and turned onto Pennsylvania Street. Dominating the corner was a miniature replica of the presidential White House. After parking in the circular driveway, we gathered around the door, and I softly knocked.

Dan Dunstan peaked through the crack. When he saw my face, he tried to close the door, but Bear kicked it open. As we stormed inside, Dunstan immediately got in his boxer's stance. He quickly swung at Bear's face, barely missing his kisser.

Major put his barrel in Dunstan's face. "We don't have time to watch you get your ass beat."

Dunstan turned red. "Negroes aren't allowed in this neighborhood."

We stood nose to nose. "Lucky for us, no one cares about you in this city anymore."

"What do you want?" he asked.

"Where's my husband?"

"I don't know."

Bumpy smiled. "Empress, I'll take it from here. Getting niggas to talk is my specialty."

His guys grabbed Dunstan. Bumpy punched him in the face and wrapped his arms around his neck.

"Snipes taught me this move."

He held Dunstan until he slumped into his arms. Then, they dragged him down the hallway. Within minutes, they dragged him back to the foyer, soaked with water, bloodied face, and drooped eyes.

Dunstan coughed up a mouthful of water. "Wraith has him."

"Where?"

"I don't know."

Bumpy punched Dunstan in the stomach. "Do you remember now, chump? Or will another visit to the toilet help your memory?"

"I-I-I heard he's somewhere in a cabin in the woods at Miller Beach," Dunstan stuttered. "Look for a huge crucifix in the front of it. But I swear to you, that's all I know."

Bumpy's men tossed him to the ground. Dunstan stumbled to the couch.

"But you're too late to save him, Empress Creed."

I pulled out my .22. "You better pray we're not, or I'll kill your life…twice."

Dunstan removed a pistol from under the sofa. We quickly drew our weapons on him. To our surprise, he placed his barrel against his right temple and closed his eyes.

Before he fired, he whispered, "Forgive us, Father, for we have sinned."

It was noon, and every minute beyond my deadline felt like hours. We sped down Broadway. Before we crossed the tracks, Irishman and a large mob of armed white men stopped us.

Irishman came to my window and tipped his hat. "Good afternoon, Empress."

"What's shaking over here?"

"I heard folks from my side of the tracks were planning to do some damage on your side. My nephew gave this city his word— 'Gary is one great city'—and I'm making sure it stays that way."

His juxtaposition shocked me, but before I could comment, he continued, "Your husband came to see me this morning, challenging me to do my part for the people of this town. Wraith is planning a massacre, and Creed demanded to know where he was so he could stop him, but they got to him first."

Barely above a whisperer, I uttered, *"No."*

"I want you to know that your husband, Snipes Creed, went out with honor, a true American soldier, Empress. He killed seven trained men and saved a boy from a lynching."

"How do you know all this?"

"I own a 'special' cleaning business, and our services were rendered to clean up the mess."

"Do you know where my husband is?"

"Wraith and his men killed him."

Tears stormed down my face. "Where's Wraith?"

"Miller Beach. Third Avenue. Look for a little red cabin in the woods. A huge cross is out front. They're getting ready for 'The New Day.' So, as I told your husband, if you and your calvary decide to head up there, be ready for a war."

Unwilling to wave our white flag, our caravan pulled up to Mrs. Mary Lee sitting on our porch. She ran up to the car.

"Did you find Mr. Creed?"

"Mrs. Mary…" I paused, fighting back the tears. "…I need you to spread the word *Ether*. White folks are planning a massacre."

She pulled her pistol from her pocketbook and saluted. "They're gonna get it where the good Lord split 'em, Empress."

We parked in the back alley and marched into our basement. I unlocked all the safes and places where Perry kept our weapons. The room was quiet as everyone grabbed smoke grenades, pistols, shotguns, and rifles.

Major cleared his throat and wiped tears and sweat falling down his face.

"Perry was one year younger than me, but Daddy left him in charge because he always took care of us like he was the oldest. He's fought motherfuckers for everyone in this room and was willing to die for each one of us. And those white niggas, as he would say, are going to feel the wrath of the Savages today. Irishman said our brother died with honor, and we're gonna kill them with honor."

I wiped my face while nodding in agreement. "You don't have to tell us twice. Let's shake a leg, fellas."

As they walked past me, I spritzed them three times with the bottle Countess had given me.

"Wraith has a pit bull he calls Jiggaboo. That coward keeps that dog attached to his hip. This potion protects us. I want Wraith alive—we need to know where Perry's body is."

On the way to Miller Beach, I smoked nonstop. I needed oxygen, but it was gone. My hands trembled, and I started hyperventilating.

Major tightly gripped my hand, which eased me a little. He parked in front of the house, which matched the description

Irishman and Dunstan had given us. Everyone got out. My hands were locked around my rifle. The sun was hiding, and a storm was brewing over our heads. A light drizzle sprinkled from the sky.

Slide, Styles, and Geese slashed the tires of all the automobiles and trucks parked out front. Then, they scampered up a hill overlooking the house and ran alongside the railroad tracks behind it. At the same time, Bumpy and his men ran on each side of the house. I stayed out front, gripping my rifle. Perry had taught me to be a sharpshooter, so I waited for my targets with the scope pressed against my eye. Major and Bear bust through the front door. Smoke swelled from the backyard. After a series of deadly-sounding shots, I expected a melee, but Major ran out alone and grabbed my hand.

"Empress, we don't have much time. All of them had on damn masks, so we shot up Wraith. Bumpy and Bear are questioning him while he's still breathing."

We ran to the backyard, and it was a warzone covered with smoke and bodies that had blended into the tall grass. Face down, next to a podium, was a man being interrogated by Bumpy.

"Where is Snipes Creed?" Bumpy yelled while Bear crushed the man's bloodied leg with his foot.

The man laughed. My heart shattered when I got closer.

"Take off my husband's jacket, white nigga!" I hollered.

He laughed harder. "I bought this at Brooks Brothers."

Bear snatched the jacket from his back and handed it to me. I inhaled Perry's Pour Un Homme men's perfume, still fresh around the collar. Major kicked Wraith onto his back and stomped his chest.

Tears spilled from my eyes as I pointed my rifle in his face. "Where is my husband?"

"He's where Negro murderers and thieves belong. Don't you see? You'll never win 'cause niggers are cursed descendants of Ham."

Anger bubbled inside me and flowed through my pores like burning lava. My emotions exploded, and I crossed into the shadow of death. Lifting my rifle, I shot Wraith dead. I had to kill him twice, so I shot him again.

My body turned icy. I trembled to my knees. An eye for an eye left me feeling hollow inside. I had no tears left, so my soul cried. *Am I cursed?* I pondered.

The wind huffed coldness, and it began to rain harder. I covered my trembling body with Perry's jacket. Drained, I closed my eyes and rested on the wet grass.

Major whispered, "Empress, we have to go."

"We need to find Perry," I told him.

"He's not here."

"Major, I'm not leaving without his body."

"We'll have to come back. It won't be long before the coppers come."

I snuggled with Perry's jacket and deeply inhaled his scent again. "Go ahead and leave me."

"Empress, you know Perry wouldn't want that. We are getting you back to my niece and nephew safely and as quickly as possible."

The grass was a comforting mattress, and I began to whimper. My tears and the rain created a small puddle that seemed to baptize my pain. Boo began licking the salted water pond against my cheek.

Major raised his rifle. "I should kill that racist dog."

I pushed his gun barrel. "Her name is Boo, and she's been mentally victimized like the rest of us."

She locked her teeth on my dress material and ripped it, but I didn't care.

Major touched my shoulder. "We gotta fade, *now*."

Boo barked hysterically while circling me. Everyone surrounded us.

"Empress. Time to split."

Major helped me up. "That dog is going to get us thrown in the slammer for life."

I ached as I dragged behind them. Boo ran behind me and pressed her head against my thigh.

"I can't take you to Paris with me, Boo."

She sank her teeth into Perry's jacket and jerked me towards her.

"Let the jacket go, Boo."

She growled and locked her jaws. I tried to yank it away. Luckily, it didn't rip like my dress, and we fought like we were playing tug of war. We were both sliding in the mud.

"Let go!" I yelled. "I need this jacket, Boo."

Major put his rifle up to Boo's schnozzle. She let go and cowered with a whimper. We finally took off, but Boo came for me again, gripping the tail of Perry's jacket. This time, I aimed my rifle at her face.

"Boo, I'm not playing—I will kill you for this coat."

She whined and got behind my legs. I was exhausted but instantly noticed she was pushing me towards the woods.

"Empress!" Major called from the car.

I looked down and realized through my frustrated tears that Boo was pleading with me with her eyes. I kneeled before her, giving her my full attention.

"Do you know where Perry is, Boo?"

She barked with confirmation. I nodded.

"Take me to him."

She took off, and I booked after her. We cut across the mayhem in the backyard, through the clearing smoke, and into the backwoods. Tall stalks smacked against my face, which whipped me to move faster. Weeds and grass scratched against my skin, and the rain was coming down like hail drops. I hopped over sticks and trudged through muddy puddles, focused on Boo's trail.

My heart pumped like an African Djembe as my body surrendered to the spiritual power pulling me through the woods. Having long lost my shoes, I felt my ancestors carrying me on their backs. Boo stopped in the middle of the wilderness. I looked around for a clue.

"What now, girl?"

She started digging. I dropped to my knees next to her and scooped, using my hands like a plow. Major huffed from behind me, but I didn't look up. He started digging next to me with a large branch.

"Bear," he shouted, "get the others and find some fucking shovels."

Within minutes, our gang was digging like savages, searching under a storm for what we hoped was our buried treasure.

We were knee-deep in a huge hole, and Styles' shovel knocked. It boomed, and everyone stopped.

"Dear God," we uttered, then moved faster and faster, clearing the top of a large wooden trough.

Bear removed the top, and everyone gasped in horror. Perry was unrecognizable. I would've denied it was him if it weren't for his wedding ring.

He was a dark-skinned man, but the color had left his skin. His eyes were swollen shut, the size of golf balls. His bruised lips were pumped so fat that they had split. His face was puffed like a stuffed marshmallow, and I traced the lines of his jaw, which had been buried under the dried blood. Bear lifted his limp body, and he and his brothers placed him carefully on the ground next to the hole we'd dug. Major checked his pulse, and the deepening of the worry lines in his face marked the scorn of a mourning heart.

I kissed Perry's forehead, and it was still warm.

"No!" I screamed and placed my ear against his heart.

It wasn't beating, so I placed my lips over his mouth. His breath had left him, but I refused to accept the facts before me. I exhaled and started pumping my breath into him. He didn't move.

"Come on, Perry. Breathe damnit."

I pumped his chest several times and breathed into him again with every ounce in me.

"*Breathe*, Perry!" I screamed. "I'm not leaving you dead."

Major placed both hands over Perry's heart and began pumping after my every breath.

My lips were glued to his. "I'm your oxygen, Captain. Please, breathe."

Geese knelt next to us and placed his fingers over Perry's wrist.

"I feel something!" he yelled.

Major placed his ear on his chest. "*Hell yeah*! Let's get him to a hospital."

Bear placed his body inside the trough, and we shook a leg to our cars. Boo ran behind us, slid next to me in the backseat, and started licking Perry's face.

"Thank you, God," I cried.

CHAPTER 32
YOU MOVE, I MOVE

DULCE ELLA-MONROE SAVAGE

August 9, 1939 - Gary, Indiana

The loud, beeping sounds from the hospital machines were the most soothing sounds I had ever heard. My heart was officially grooving to the beat of life, and I had my oxygen back. I knew Perry was alive when the machines rang with a steady flow. His clean room was filled with wet, filthy, sweaty thugs. We looked like we had been entrenched in war, but the hospital staff ignored our stench and acted like we had on our Sunday's best.

A tall, colored doctor walked into the hospital room. "Mrs. Savage, I'm Dr. Lewis. Your husband is really banged up and has broken ribs. He suffered a concussion and has a lot of contusions. His oxygen levels and blood pressure are extremely low, but he's stabilizing. He's strong as an ox, so he'll be fine with rest and fluids."

I lay next to him. "Thank you, God."

"Can he hear us?" Major asked.

"He's sedated."

His brothers gathered around him. One by one, they each hugged and kissed him.

Major touched my shoulder. "Empress, Bumpy and his men split. We're heading out before the coppers come around."

"I'll see if I can get you a pilot."

"*Hell no.* We're driving back to Harlem."

A few hours passed, and Perry's color returned. I leaned over his face and brushed my lips over his sweet melons, not caring that they were swollen and busted.

Before I rose from his face, he whispered, "Don't stop, doll."

"*Perry.*" I cried and kissed all over his face. "You don't have to tell me twice."

He tried to open his eyes. "I better not be in heaven."

"You're at the hospital. Your brothers and Bumpy left a few hours ago."

Boo licked his toes and rested her head on his leg.

He cracked a smile. "I told you, I married a hoodlum."

"Yes, you did, Captain, and I'll take a life twice for my soldier."

He took my hand. The tiny slits of his eyes opened like the window shades to his soul.

> "*Forever yours, eternally, forever mine,*
> *One source, universe, 'til the end of time.*
> *Spiritual love spoken without diction,*
> *Souls mate, heavenly, benediction.*
> *My Empress, Your Captain, One Creed,*
> *Two Savages, Uncaged, Forever Freed.*
> *Happy Anniversary, Mrs. De Leche.*"

I leaned over to respond, but the medication had pulled him back to sleep. I snuggled against his shoulder and rested my eyes. Then, there was a knock on the door.

A woman's voice came from outside. "Mrs. Empress?"

"Mrs. Mary Lee?"

"I brought you and Mr. Creed clean clothes and food."

"Come in. Thank you so much. How is the city?"

"I never thought I would see the day coloreds, whites, our city mayor, and police come together to keep Gary 'One Great City.' We sent those crazy crackers running back south."

What if folks came together to protect the world? I wondered.

She exited the room, and a white man dressed as a house painter entered stiffly like a tin man. In his hand, a leather briefcase.

"Empress Creed?" he asked.

"Who's asking?"

"I have a special delivery, but I need confirmation."

"I'm she."

He handed me a sealed envelope with a note on the front.

For you, my cleaning services were free of charge. Cheers to a fresh start.

Irishman

I carefully removed the seal. Inside were two stacks of photos. The first stack was the house in Miller in mayhem, with bloody evidence of our crimes. The second stack was the same house, orderly, with all traces of chaos erased, including the wooden cross.

"I was told to discard this once you've seen it," he said.

I handed it back to him. "Tell Irishman thank you. We owe him a solid."

He pulled a shiny aluminum painter's pan from his briefcase and placed the envelope inside. Then, he poured liquid over it. The paper boiled and liquified. He added a few drops to the liquid, and it evaporated into smoke, leaving the metal pan shiny like new. He placed his chemicals into his briefcase, tipped his hat, and vanished.

With my heart full, sleepiness took over. I kissed Perry's face, and a sudden chill swept across my body. I stepped outside his room.

"Nurse, may I have a blanket, please?" I asked.

A light brown woman with long, kinky hair dressed in a white nurse uniform and hat turned. We stood and reflected each other's eyes. She had my face, nose, and ears. We were the same height with matching red lipstick. Our heads tilted to the right, then the left. Our bodies shifted side to side. We moved in a synchronized rhythm. She was my mirror.

A beautiful woman dressed in a blue suit grabbed the hand of a tall, light brown-skinned man with curly hair. He resembled W.E.B. Du Bois and wore a navy steel mill uniform. His mouth and eyes were stuck in shock.

"Dear God," we all said in unison.

Without my permission, tears fell down my face, and I lost the feeling in my legs.

The tall man caught me before I hit the ground. "I've got you."

In the sitting area outside Perry's room, we sat with bottles of Coca-Cola. Eva James shared a story about a handsome soldier named Perry Savage. She had met him in Chicago while she was a nursing student at Provident Hospital. They talked once, but she never saw him again.

When she graduated from nursing school, she worked as a nurse at Provident. She worked there for years until she pulled her medical records and saw conflicting reports of her birth. One doctor had reported two healthy baby girls after her mother gave birth, and another from a different shift reported one child. There were no birth certificates or proof of another baby, but they knew something was wrong.

She and her parents had raised hell in search of her mystery twin sister. The physician and one nurse had died. The other nurse was in a nursing home with Alzheimer's disease. But when Eva saw Perry Savage listed as her current patient at Methodist, she remembered his name.

Dr. Lewis mentioned how she and I could be twins, and when she saw me, she knew I was her sister and called her parents to confirm.

I told them about how I'd grown up on the South Side of Chicago. The woman who had raised me was a prostitute and left me a suicide letter confessing she'd stolen me from a happy couple from Provident Hospital. I recalled when I met Perry—he'd sworn I had a twin and had asked if I was related to any Jameses. I thought it was a pickup line.

Before I could finish talking, I was wrapped in a three-way hug. No more words escaped our mouths, just tears. We exchanged instant love, and I felt complete.

Weeks had passed, and Countess had mailed Perry a healing elixir from Harlem. With little pain left in his ribs, Dr. Lewis called his speedy recovery a miracle. We walked to the hospital's flower garden in the courtyard, where we sat on the bench.

Perry kissed my palm. "The last time I saw this place, I was holding Paris for the first time. It was so peaceful like it is now... until that motherfucker Dunstan showed up."

"We don't have to worry about that happening again."

We closed our eyes, and a warm breeze swirled around us, enclosing us in a small tornado.

My head jerked from a slight tug at my scalp. I turned, and it was Dan Dunstan, standing buck naked in an open robe and top hat.

"Dunstan?"

"Nurse James," he smiled in a stupor, "your hair is so divine."

Perry twisted Dunstan's wrist and whispered, "I should kill you right now, motherfucker Dunstan."

"Is motherfucker another one of my names?"

Eva ran outside. *"Perry."*

"Nurse James! I'm scared. This man is hurting me, and this woman stole your face!" Dunstan yelled.

"She's my sister, and the man will let you go."

Perry reluctantly released him, and Eva closed his robe.

"Dulce and Perry, Mr. Dunstan shot himself in the head and has suffered amnesia."

He removed his top hat, and his head was covered with bandages. He smiled again.

"Nurse James, why didn't you tell me that my name was also motherfucker? I like it better than Dan."

He began to twirl, and Eva clenched his hand. "Okay, Mr. Dunstan, you've had enough fun. Tell the nice people goodbye."

He tipped his hat. "Goodbye. It's been divine."

Perry waved and placed his arm around me. "Bye, motherfucker."

CHAPTER 33
I PUT A SPELL ON YOU

DULCE ELLA-MONROE SAVAGE

August 1939 - Paris, France

The ending to the tale of Empress Creed had proven America had the potential to become a Negro's kingdom, where colored dreams could come true, but Dulce Ella-Monroe Savage would no longer reign in Uncle Sam's empire. America was an unruly broad to me, and we're through—my country 'tis of thee. France is my new dame. *Je t'aime, mon nouvel amour.*

Perry and I finally descended to our new homeland at dusk. Mother Nature had painted the sky orange, red, and indigo. The airport was surrounded by green fields filled with purple irises and oak and maple trees. Perry, Boo, and I stepped off Matty's plane, and no, I hadn't burned my little nickname for him yet. It was gorgeous pink outside as we stood on the tarmac waiting for Charles, but a plum-colored Cadillac pulled up instead.

Surprisingly, Red and Tony exited the driver and passenger seats, and I was elated.

Red grabbed our luggage. "We couldn't take our eyes off you two for five seconds without you getting into trouble."

Tony rubbed Boo's head. "We're never leaving your side again, youngblood."

"No fooling?" Perry asked.

"No fooling."

Red drove us through the artistic city masterpiece until we were surrounded by endless green hills covered with lilies. I rolled down the window to smell the coolness and feel the breeze against my face. We drove up a small hill onto a cobblestone driveway. When we stepped outside, the sun dipped behind the sea of maple trees along the green mountains. Red and Tony smoked cigarettes while Boo ran freely in the front yard of our yellow, white, and terracotta brick cottage. I rocked on the rocking chair and inhaled Perry's sweet teakwood perfume.

"I love this rocking chair, Perry."

He kissed my forehead. "Doll, it's so peaceful, just like I prayed for. Where are the kids?"

"With Belle and Matthieu."

As I started towards the door, he stopped me, pulling me against his chest.

"I'm carrying you over the threshold."

"The doctor said to take it easy."

He picked me up and opened the door. "No way am I taking it easy on you."

I grabbed his face and kissed him. *"Oh la la, monsieur."*

He stepped inside and flicked on the light.

"Surprise!"

The whole family was there. Pierre jumped into our arms, and we attacked him with kisses.

Countess held Paris wrapped sweetly in a blanket. *"Bonjour,* brother and sister."

"Y'all finally got hitched."

Major threw his arms around us. "Damn, right. My Strawberry is permanently covered in my chocolate."

Geese lifted Juno's ring finger. "Your baby brother, too."

Perry's smile widened when he saw Juno's stomach. "The Savages have been busy."

Major pulled him close. "Damn right, and we're here to celebrate as one blood."

Major, Bear, Geese, Slide, and Styles wrapped around Perry in brotherly love.

Perry kissed all over Paris and Pierre. "My eyes are sweating from all this love."

The record player started, and "Mood Indigo" by Duke Ellington played through the speakers. I eased past the lively living room into the kitchen. On the table, a bowl of fresh lemons sat next to Mama Lee's lemonade pitcher. I felt her smile and heard her singing Bessie Smith's "Need a Little Sugar in My Bowl."

Perry's warm arms wrapped around my waist. His lips melted on my neck.

"*Mmm*, fresh sugar cookies and rose petals. Thank you for setting this up, doll."

"We have a lot to celebrate."

"Who do we thank?" he asked. "God or Lady Luck?"

"*God.*"

THE END

ACKNOWLEDGMENTS

"Girl, write the damn book."

—Mr. Lott, my heavenly African American History
teacher from William A. Wirt H.S.

Mr. Lott, thank you for believing in students like me and for instilling your invaluable knowledge of African American history and culture in us. Thank you for continuing to teach me life lessons in my dreams.

Grandpa and Grandma, Geese and Dolores, thank you for sharing your experiences with me, growing up as Negroes in Chicago's South Side and on the colored side of the tracks in Gary, Indiana.

To my great-grandfather, Tomas Gonzales, *The* Thomas Smith Sr., thank you and Mrs. Mary Lee for building the Smith family legacy.

The Smith Elders, thank you for your contribution to the family

Chicago's South Side, Harlem, Louisiana, and Montmartre, France, thank you for cultivating our ancestors' music and artistry.

Gary, Indiana, I can't thank you enough.

Blues, Jazz, R&B, and Hip Hop, thank you for your artistic influence on the world.

To my ancestors before me, thank you for paving the way, and to my descendants, thank you for inspiring me to leave a legacy for others to follow.

Thank you, God, for everything.

WWW.BLACKODYSSEY.NET

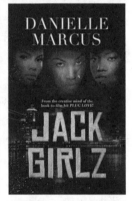